Alexandra C...
still has strong...
from being a...
radio and television. She is a Fellow of the Royal
Society of Arts.

ALEXANDRA CONNOR

Hunter's Moon

HarperCollins*Publishers*

This novel is a work of fiction. The names, characters and incidents portrayed in it are the work of the author's imagination. Any resemblance to actual persons, living or dead, is entirely coincidental.

HarperCollins*Publishers*
77–85 Fulham Palace Road,
Hammersmith, London W6 8JB

www.fireandwater.com

A Paperback Original 2001

3 5 7 9 8 6 4

A catalogue record for this book is
available from the British Library

ISBN 0 00 651352 2

Set in Sabon by
Rowland Phototypesetting Ltd,
Bury St Edmunds, Suffolk

Printed in Great Britain by
Clays Ltd, St Ives plc

This book is dedicated to my sister Diana Brierley-Jones. Love you, kiddo – but I still haven't forgotten the marshmallow . . .

Acknowledgements

Many many thanks must go to my editor, Susan Opie, whose advice is always sound, whose criticism is always fair and whose support has helped me immeasurably. The best person to have in your corner! Thanks also to Yvonne Holland, my copy editor, who really gets under the skin of the books. A round of applause also to the sales reps on the road who go out and sell the books for me. Thankyou ladies and gentlemen. And as for Martin Palmer – what can I say? You're a one-off.

Hunter's moon – the moon following the harvest moon.

Brewer's Dictionary of Phrase and Fable

Prologue

1911

It took a moment for him to realise what he had done. A second spent staring at the dead woman, then a quick glance upwards to the bedrooms. Outside the sky was coming into moonlight, a horse stamping its feet in the driveway and whinnying with impatience. He turned down the gaslights. Then he saw a figure silhouetted in the doorway.

Panic made him fling open the window next to him and climb out, then run down the lawn towards the drive without daring to look back. Breathing heavily, he headed towards the road leading down to Oldham. A couple of men passed him and nodded automatically. He was known, a man of importance. Their superior. They would remember seeing him ... He stopped, watched them pass. Then as soon as he heard their footsteps die away he started running again.

The moon – a hunter's moon – had now risen and he thought fleetingly how it would sneak under the blinds back at the house and fall across the carpet. It would glow, melancholic, on every surface, wiping its yellow feet on everything it touched.

He stopped; looked round. He would get away. But where? He had nowhere to go. *This* was his town, his home. This was where his family was ... Sweating, he leaned against the wall of an alleyway, limp with terror. Calm yourself, he thought, be calm. It was a mistake, a *mistake*. You can get over this, you can live with this.

Unexpectedly, an uncanny peace came over him. He could do it, he *would* blot it out, put it up on a shelf at the back of his memory and leave it there.

He began to walk again. Yes, he *could* live with it. All he had to do was to close down his conscience, find a way to stop the sickness welling up. He had thought fleetingly of giving himself up – but how could he explain what he had done? How he had lost control and hit out – and then kept hitting.

They would go to the house and see that it had been no accident, no random blow, but a concentrated violence of blows. A determined intent to kill.

At first, they wouldn't believe it of him. Not him.

You have to forget it, he willed himself. But the calm had gone and in its place was the knowledge that he could never forget it. Oh Jesus, he breathed, oh Jesus . . .

He could never go home. Never go back. He would run instead, and hide and hope they never caught him. But at night, every night, he knew he would replay what he had done. Over and over.

He kept running, but even now he could hear and see her on the flagstones and cobbles. Every lamp carried her eyes in its light; every bush and wall he passed, her figure.

And overhead the wide yellow hunter's moon tracked him and illuminated every step of the useless, hopeless way.

Part One

Chapter One

1915

Barely thirteen yards from the railway viaduct stood the sour corner building of the children's home. It had been built in the 1830s to house the abandoned or orphaned offspring of the industrial towns Oldham and Salford. The smaller, surrounding semirural villages like Dobcross, Diggle, Uppermill and Failsworth were poor, populated with mill and pit workers, but an illegitimate child there was usually assimilated into the extended family. Often, daughters caught out had their bastard offspring raised as their sibling. As for the incest, that was a brewing undercurrent in the worst slums, but those unlucky offspring were also soaked into the family, unsure of their parentage and belligerent with the outside world.

But in the larger towns, like Oldham and Salford, there was not the same tightly meshed community. It was not uncommon for an infant to be abandoned on the stone steps of the Netherlands Orphanage, without even a name to call its own. These were the forgotten children, often sickly, frequently little more than a day or so old.

It was no real secret where these children came from: most were the casualties of streets like Grimshaw Street, or the notorious area called The Bent. From the 1850s most of Oldham's Irish population lived here, a small webbing of streets occupied by low pubs, brothels and boarding houses where the hopeless ended up. If you found your way into The Bent, the chances were you wouldn't get out again.

For a child born there the future was bleak. If a girl had

a struggling, but respectable family, she might end up in one of the mills; a boy in the pit. But those were the fortunate ones. All too often the children of The Bent became ensnared in thievery or prostitution. Of these, the lucky ones – if you could call them lucky – were the ones abandoned at Netherlands Orphanage.

Their future was harsh, but secure – set to the rule of order and religion. If they survived a sickly start they would be fed and clothed, even taught a trade in time. Behind the soot-darkened, red-brick walls, a fierce little army of poorly paid staff sucked children with no name and no past into their regimented system. A few of the staff were tyrants, getting their revenge on the world by bullying their charges, but some – a few – were kindly.

The orphanage was run by Miss Clare Lees, a tall, prematurely stooped woman in her fifties, who had risen from being an orphan at the home, to its principal. Not that anyone would ever refer to her past to her face. To all intents and purposes, she behaved as though she despised the children under her care and had nothing in common with them. But it was a front. She was as much a slum child as the ones under her care.

Clare Lees had never married, never had children, and had seldom ventured far from the high walls of the home. This was her kingdom, here she was ruler. The terrified child who had been abandoned fifty years earlier had metamorphosed into an unfeeling martinet. It was not her nature to be cruel, but kindness eluded her. She could not feel – or show – what she had never experienced.

The kindness was left to others, who had come in from the outside. Like Ethel Cummings.

'Alice, come here!' she hissed under her breath.

A little girl obediently got to her feet and walked towards her. She was small for her age and dark-haired, her eyes black-fringed. She had a very mature face for a child, looking almost like a tiny, exotic woman.

'Alice, what's that in your hand?' Ethel asked kindly, leaning down, her bulk making the movement awkward.

'Nothing.'

The matron looked at her. 'Alice, show me.'

Reluctantly, the little girl opened her hand. There was a pebble in her palm.

'Why, it's just a stone –'

'It's a jewel!' Alice said defiantly, closing her fingers over it. 'And it's mine.'

Ethel sighed, then glanced over her shoulder as a bell rang. The sound echoed emptily down the corridor. One ring, two rings. Ethel breathed out and relaxed. Thank God it wasn't for her, she had had enough of Miss Lees for one day.

Hurriedly she moved Alice down the narrow corridor towards the nearest dormitory. It was empty, as most of the children were in the yard taking their daily exercise. More like prisoners than children, Ethel had said to her husband, the little things pushed out in all weathers, walking round and round in circles. They should be playing, running on grass and climbing trees . . .

'Give over, Ethel,' he had replied. 'You'll lose your job if you keep trying to change things.'

'But it's not good for them!' she had answered hotly. 'When I think how our boys were brought up –'

'They weren't orphans,' Gilbert had retorted, his tone sharp. 'Oh listen, luv,' he'd said more kindly, 'you do what you can for them. Don't make waves or that cow Lees will fire you and then what good will you be to any of them?'

Ethel had known he was right. So she bit her tongue repeatedly, and bent under the myriad tyrannies of Netherlands. It seemed to her that many of the children were cowed by the sheer size of the home, and the fact that they had nothing they could call their own. Nothing to cling on to for comfort. Every piece of clothing had been handed down many times over: when a child grew out of it, it was patched and passed on to another. Likewise with shoes. Even underwear, faded with use, was boiled and handed on.

Every child had short hair too, in order to make sure that there was no outbreak of nits – and to make it easier for the staff to comb and wash on Monday nights, when queues of little bodies waited silently for their turn at the tap. None of the children complained, in fact they spoke little and in whispers to avoid drawing attention to themselves. There was no individuality and any high spirits were soon dampened by the crushing indifference of the system.

Naturally the boys and girls were separated and housed in different wings. The doors spelled it out for them – 'BOYS' over the entrance to one side of the home, and 'GIRLS' over the entrance of the other. They exercised at different times too and could – for all they knew – have been in a single-sex institution. Clare Lees was very firm about there being no fraternising. After all, wasn't that how these children had come about? Boys and girls getting together . . . ? She shuddered at the thought. Oh no, she would have none of that behaviour.

Punishment was harsh if anyone ever broke her rules. Several years earlier one girl had somehow formed a friendship with one of the boys. Notes had been exchanged, secrets, longings, written in Poor Home script. It had been innocent and silly, but when it was discovered the girl was made an example of in front of the school. Her hair had been cut to her scalp, and round her neck was hung a board with the word 'WHORE' in red letters. She wore the board for a month.

Now Ethel looked down at the little girl in front of her and then impulsively gathered Alice into her arms. She knew she shouldn't – it was frowned upon to show affection – but this little one was so different from the others.

Immediately Alice responded and nestled against her, her eyes closing. If the truth be known, Ethel was afraid

6

for Alice Rimmer. She was too pretty, for a start, too full of spirit which even years in the orphanage hadn't dampened. Where her spirit came from, God only knew. Her background was a mystery, the only information sketchy. Apparently she had come to the home when she was nearly a year old. Some council man had delivered her early one November morning. Her parents were dead, he told the principal; Alice Rimmer was just another poor child of the parish, destined to live off charity.

Ethel remembered first seeing Alice when she came to work at Netherlands a few months later. She'd been more outspoken then, and had showed her surprise at Alice's appearance.

'Oh, what a beautiful child! This one will be adopted all right.'

Irritated, Clare Lees had shaken her head. 'No, she's to stay here. No one's to adopt her.'

Ethel's mouth had fallen open. 'But she'd find a home, no trouble.'

Miss Lees' tone was impatient. '*No one* is to adopt this child. Alice Rimmer is to stay here until she is old enough to leave and find her own way in the world.'

Still sitting on the edge of the dormitory bed, the matron stroked the top of Alice's head and frowned at the old memory. It wasn't right, she thought. Alice could easily have found a new family, new siblings . . . She looked down at the four-year-old sitting on her lap. Oh luv, where did you come from? She had the look of breeding, that was for sure. Such a stunning child wasn't from farm or factory workers. Ethel had seen the usual depressing run of poor children: the whey complexions, the undernourished limbs, the flat expression in the eyes.

But there was a gloss about Alice which she *had* to have inherited from money and position . . . Ethel rocked the child absent-mindedly. She was so distinctive that her looks would give her away anywhere. But although Ethel had asked the office secretary – very furtively – about Alice, there was nothing to discover. Only that her parents were dead. Apparently there were no grandparents, no brothers and sisters, no home. Alice Rimmer was just another foundling

She didn't look like the usual foundling, Ethel thought for the hundredth time. Maybe some society woman had been caught out, leaving the pregnancy too long to abort the unwanted child. It would certainly explain the exotic looks. Ethel put her plump arms tightly around the child. Maybe one day she would see a photograph in the paper and it would all click. Maybe Alice was the child of royalty or nobility, Ethel thought fancifully, her parents still alive somewhere. Of course! That was why she wasn't able to be adopted. Her own people meant to come back for Alice one day.

And then again, maybe they would leave her in Salford, and forget her. It happened all the time. Children no one wanted, no one gave a damn about . . .

Ethel took hold of Alice's hand, her fingers still clutching the pebble. One day you'll come into your own, my love, she thought. One day it will all come out. No one can hide the sun under a blanket for ever.

Chapter Two

The door banged closed behind Ethel. The overcast day made the room dim. Heavy furniture, old-fashioned and well polished, surrounded her, the floorboards shining like glass. The children did that. It was one of their duties – to keep the principal's office in immaculate condition. It was good practice for them, Clare Lees explained, for the time when the girls went into service.

Nervously Ethel glanced at the clock on the mantelpiece. It was hideous, she thought, with thick black hands and a bad-tempered tick. Her glance wandered to the window, but there was no view worth seeing, only the high wall about four yards away, mottled with chimney soot, with not even a weed to break up the lines of brick monotony.

A bell rang outside. Once, twice, three times – dinner, Ethel thought. In a minute the children would make their way to the dining room. But they would move quietly, not like normal children, and quietly they would stand for grace and then quietly sit down. Unnatural . . .

'Mrs Cummings.'

Ethel jumped at the sound of her name and got to her feet as Miss Lees walked in. Automatically Ethel smoothed her uniform over her prominent bosom and straightened her white matron's cap.

Clare Lees moved over to her desk, her stooped figure casting a shadow on the glossy floorboards. Her dress was dark, the hem brushing her ankles, her laced boots functional. Calmly she turned to look at Ethel, her eyes weary and suspicious at the same time.

'Sit down,' she said, taking a seat herself behind her

desk. Her voice, Ethel noted, had little trace of an Oldham accent. Odd, that. 'I want a word with you.'

'Yes, ma'am.'

'You're a good worker, but you spend too much time with the children.' Clare laced her fingers together. She wasn't cruel, just remote. 'We have a home to run here, we can't afford to waste time –'

'It's not wasting time, talking to the children,' Ethel replied warmly. 'They need a bit of affection, attention. It's only right.'

'I know what's right for Netherlands,' Clare Lees replied coolly. 'This isn't the first time I've had to talk to you. I thought you'd learned your lesson. But you can't seem to abide by my rules, Mrs Cummings. Why is that?'

Ethel bit her lip. She had done what she swore she wouldn't. Her bloody mouth! Why couldn't she hold her tongue, like Gilbert said?

'Miss Lees,' she replied quietly, 'you're right, I should do as you say.'

If she lost her place here she would lose a reasonable wage and God knew, she needed to bring money in. Her sons had been sent to fight in France, although Gilbert was too bad with his chest to be called up. But he did have a part share of a window-cleaning round and helped with the odd flitting when they were pushed. Yet although money was tight, there was more to it than that. Ethel needed to stay at Netherlands for other reasons. The children. She might be fooling herself, but she believed they needed her; needed someone they could talk to. The ones that *wanted* to talk, that was. Like Alice . . . Suddenly Ethel realised that if she lost her job she would probably never see Alice again.

'Miss Lees, I'm sorry,' she said, her tone placating. 'Truly I am.'

Ethel knew that grovelling would work, and it did. The principal smiled her snow smile . . .

You could have been quite a handsome woman, Ethel thought, someone's wife, someone's mother . . . Pity shifted inside her heart. It wasn't that difficult to see the lost child in the woman sitting in front of her.

But Clare Lees' next words shook Ethel to the core.

'In particular, it has been brought to my attention that you are paying too much attention to Alice Rimmer.'

Ethel flushed. 'Well, I –'

'We can't have favourites here,' Clare went on, seeing from Ethel's face that she had scored a direct hit.

So she *was* fond of the child. Well, well, well . . . Clare sighed to herself. She was ashamed of the fact, but she didn't like Alice Rimmer – and she wasn't sure why. Perhaps she was too pretty, too wilful, but something about the child rankled.

'Alice Rimmer could turn out to be a difficult girl,' Clare went on. 'She's very high-spirited, giddy.' She expected Ethel to interrupt, and was almost disappointed when the matron didn't. 'I think she's a child we have to control and watch carefully. I want her to leave Netherlands as a credit to us.'

'I think she will,' Ethel said carefully. 'In fact, I'm sure she will.'

Why was the principal so rattled about Alice? Did she know something about the child which no one else did? Or did she simply dislike her?

Clare sighed. 'Mrs Cummings, haven't you noticed that Alice Rimmer can be defiant?'

'Well, she does have a mind of her own.'

Clare's gaze hardened. 'That's what I'm afraid of. Alice Rimmer is an orphan. She has no *reason* to have a mind of her own. The girl has no family – and no chance in this world unless she knows her place. She has no cause to be proud – or to think that she's special.'

Oh, so that's it, Ethel thought, you can see something in Alice which you *envy*. She might be orphan, but she has the looks and spirit which could enable her to make something out of her life. Ethel glanced down at her hands. She would have to be very careful from now on.

She didn't believe that Clare Lees was vindictive, but she was certainly insecure – and that made her dangerous. Netherlands was her whole world. Outside there was only disorder. The country was at war, but within these walls there was little hint of the chaos beyond. Inside, Clare Lees could control everything. Or so she thought.

But Ethel also knew instinctively that, given time, Alice would escape the home and survive outside. Which was why Clare Lees was jealous of her. And jealousy, Ethel was aware, could destroy people.

'I'm glad we've had this talk. We needed to get matters sorted out. After all,' Clare said, rising to her feet to deliver the final blow, 'it would be a pity to lose you.'

Chapter Three

Winter came in fast and hard that year, Netherlands cold, the fire in the girls' dining room inadequate and only warming the nearest table – which was where the staff ate.

It was a bitter Sunday in November, Miss Lees toying with some tough lamb for lunch. On her left sat her assistant, Dolly Blake, and on her right the Reverend Grantley studied the gravy which had just been poured over his meat. He sniffed, his head bent down, intoning the grace automatically although he was still eyeing the gravy through half-opened lids.

No one was uncharitable enough to mention the vicar's strange hair, or the fact that it was patently dyed. He was, after all, the only cleric who attended Netherlands regularly and he was responsible for reporting back to his superiors to ensure further financial support. So he was flattered and indulged by Miss Lees and all the staff. They puffed up his vanity and fussed him into thinking he was important – something he needed to believe desperately. A petty man, he had long given up his dreams of advancement. Bullied outside, he liked to visit the home where he was superior, the foundlings in awe of him.

Dolly glanced at the top of Mr Grantley's head and winked at Ethel, sitting further down the table. Ethel smiled back, watching her. Dolly was a natural politician, with her sights set on running Netherlands after Clare Lees retired. 'Why not?' she had said to Ethel. 'It's a good job. Better than the mill or cleaning out some snotty cow's fire grate at five in the morning.'

The vicar finished grace and then prodded his meat to

check for signs of life. Satisfied that it was beyond resurrection, he cut off a piece and began to chew. Slowly.

'So, Mr Grantley,' Dolly said, in her best voice, the one she used for people she thought were her betters, 'how are you keeping? I heard you had had a cold.'

He swallowed manfully, his expression all holy tolerance.

'I . . .' A piece of gristle stuck in his throat and he coughed loudly, waving his napkin in front of him like a white flag. 'I've been better.'

You can say that again, Ethel thought, looking at Dolly, who was all mock sympathy. It'll do you no good; the vicar's not powerful, he's just the governors' poodle. Oh, Dolly, she mused, you think you're so clever.

'Perhaps a little whisky would help,' Dolly went on, adding hurriedly, 'for medicinal purposes, of course.'

'I believe in setting an example,' Mr Grantley replied, finding some gristle in a back tooth and sucking his teeth reflectively. 'I have to be careful. A man in my position knows that all eyes are on him.'

Nodding, Dolly watched him suck his teeth again and looked away. The man was a pig, but it didn't do to let her thoughts show . . . Like the children, she ate hurriedly, hungrily, her thoughts turning elsewhere. When she finished work that night, she would go to her room and write a letter to Andy. He had been posted to France to fight. Silly sod, he shouldn't have volunteered like that, Dolly thought. Why not wait until he was called up? It was all right being a hero, but what about *her*?

She missed him . . . Her eyes wandered round the rows of tables. The girls sat together in ages, the smallest ones nearest to the staff table. When Andy and she got married they could run this place, no problem. He'd be caretaker and she'd be principal. The thought warmed Dolly, almost made the food taste good in her mouth. Her eyes glanced over to the vicar, still picking at his lamb. He's lucky to get it in wartime, Dolly thought. They don't have lamb in the Army. Andy would be grateful for it, but not this old coot. I hope he chokes.

A child sneezed suddenly, Dolly frowned.

'Oh no, not a cold. That's all we need,' she said to Ethel, hurriedly reassuring the vicar, 'It's not your cold, of course,' as if there were a pecking order to chills, 'but we have to be so careful here, Mr Grantley. If one child gets a cold, they all do.' And that meant more work, she thought to herself. One snotty nose was all it took . . .

Ethel knew exactly what she was thinking. Dolly might think she could fool the vicar, but not Ethel, She looked back to her plate. Honest to God, she thought, this was never *lamb*! It tasted more like something that had been pulling a cart yesterday. She chewed on a piece of the hard meat and then looked down the table again.

'I find it so bracing, this cold weather,' Dolly went on, her voice ludicrously forced. 'So good for the lungs.'

'Not if you're recovering from a cold,' Mr Grantley said darkly, turning over a suspicious-looking piece of meat with the end of his knife. 'I've heard that chill weather can turn a cold into pneumonia. I had two parishioners who died last winter from colds. Never stood a chance. They were fine one Sunday and then,' he paused, flicking over the meat like a corpse on a slab, 'bang! Dropped down dead. From cold. Pure cold.'

More likely that they'd frozen their bloody arses off in your church, Ethel thought wryly.

'Well, you must take care of yourself, vicar. No one would want to miss one of your services,' Dolly ventured, watching, glassy-eyed, as the clergyman began to pick at a piece of gristle stuck in his front teeth.

'I am *always* available to my flock, cold or no cold. I have to be.' He sucked his teeth forcefully to release the wedge of gristle. 'People look up to me; they look to me to set an example.'

Ethel was certain that Dolly did not see the humour of the situation, and regarded her thoughtfully. Dolly's high spirits were a little too excessive for lunch with Mr Grantley. She must have heard from Andy, Ethel thought. Did she *really* believe that she had it all worked out? Most of Salford knew that Andy was writing to a number of lovesick girls. At the last count he had three fiancées, one putting on a lot of weight recently . . .

Dolly's blonde hair was bent towards the vicar's dyed pate. There was no chance she'd be running this place one day, Ethel thought. Dolly Blake might be pretty and clever, but she wasn't what the governors looked for in a principal. She was too flash. Too obviously on the make.

If anyone was going to take over from Clare Lees it would be the quiet man sitting at the head of the next table. Ethel studied Evan Thomas curiously – the narrow head, long nose, and large luminous eyes the blue of iris. A very delicate creature, too frail to be sent off to fight. Ethel smiled to herself. Oh, Dolly might think she was smart, but Evan was the one to watch.

Suddenly there was a commotion, a shriek of temper as a glass was thrown across the dining room. Miss Lees stared open-mouthed, Dolly wide-eyed, Mr Grantley poised with his fork halfway to his mouth.

It was Alice. Screaming, standing up on her seat as the girls around her shrank back. They knew there would be trouble, but she seemed immune to everyone. Her face was pink, her fists clenched, a steady wail coming from her open mouth. Ethel got to her feet, roughly caught hold of the child and physically removed her from the dining room.

Her hand fastened over Alice's mouth as Ethel paused outside the door and listened. At first there was a stunned silence, followed by the angry scrape of a chair being pushed back. As fast as her stocky legs would carry her, Ethel hurried away. Alice had relaxed in her arms and was heavy as Ethel hurried up the narrow back stairs and on into the pharmacy.

Out of breath, she deposited Alice in a chair and put her hands on her hips.

'What . . .' Ethel puffed, '. . . what . . . was . . .' She breathed in deeply. 'What was all that about?'

Alice was quiet, surprised by the anger coming from the only person who had ever shown her affection.

'Alice, talk to me!' Ethel snapped. 'Miss Lees will be here in a minute and she'll take a bad view of this. You're in trouble, my girl. You don't know how much. Alice, you have to help me to help you – now, what happened?'

'She took my jewel.'

'What?' Ethel said, baffled.

Alice looked up, tears on her black lashes. 'Annie Court took my jewel. I felt her hand go in my pocket and she stole it.'

'What jewel? Oh, you mean your stone.'

'It's a JEWEL!' Alice shrieked. Her voice was rising again.

She's going to have hysterics, Ethel thought frantically. Oh no, not *that*. Hurriedly, she bent down to the child. 'Alice, pull yourself together! Miss Lees will be here any minute –'

But it had no effect. Alice had lost all fear of anything. Her cheeks burned red, her fists clenching as she swung her feet against the chair. Ethel was shaken and remembered all too clearly what had happened a few years ago. There had been another child who had been troublesome – prone to tantrums, Miss Lees said. One day the child was transferred to another home. No one knew where. Ethel wasn't about to have that happen to Alice.

So she grabbed the hard green soap in the sink and worked at it frantically, lathering up some thick white foam. Then, she grabbed Alice by the scruff of the neck and smeared the foam around the child's mouth. She

17

screamed – just as the door opened and Clare Lees walked in.

Her glance took in Ethel and the red-faced child, who was apparently ill, foaming around the mouth. Anger left her at once. This wasn't a bad child, but a sick one.

Appalled, she glanced over to Ethel. 'God, what is it?'

'She's having a fit, ma'am,' Ethel said calmly. 'If you'll just let me deal with it ... Having people around only excites them more.'

Clare Lees nodded, and backed out. When Ethel finally heard her footsteps die away she got a cloth and wiped Alice's mouth. The child was silent, her huge dark eyes watching Ethel.

'Now look what you've made me do! Made me lie for you.' Ethel wiped the beautiful little face. 'They'll think you're ill now, not just a child having a tantrum. You'll get away with it this time, but not the next.'

Alice's tongue tasted of soap and her mouth hurt from where the towel had rubbed it. But she knew that Ethel had saved her. Had looked out for her. No one else had ever done anything like that before. The child put her arms around Ethel's waist and buried her head emotionally in her apron.

'Aye, luv, you'll have to learn to be good,' Ethel said gently, stroking her hair. 'It's a hard life, and it gets harder. Don't go looking for trouble.'

Alice was crying softly, the sound muffled. She was so highly strung, Ethel thought anxiously, and that was dangerous anywhere. In amongst a family, with supportive parents, it could be managed, but here ... Ethel shivered. She didn't want to see Alice's spirit knocked out of her. How sad that the child had inherited a volatile character along with her beauty. A mixed blessing, to put it mildly.

'You must *learn* to be good,' Ethel urged, her voice soothing. 'Be good. Be quiet, sweetheart. Don't make waves. Please.'

*   *   *

Evan Thomas was walking out of the front gates of Netherlands, completely unaware that he was being watched. His slight tall figure in his dark coat was huddled against the cold November rain, his hand over his mouth. He paused, coughing hoarsely, as he padlocked the gate behind him. The cough had kept him out of the war. Most of the other men in their twenties had been called up, but Evan's life had changed little. He coughed again, then moved on into the street and out of Clare Lees' gaze.

As he disappeared from sight, Clare found herself curious, wondering where he was going. Sundays dragged. Her hand idled along the side of her desk, her fingers tapping the wood. Mr Grantley was hard work, she thought; it was a nuisance to have to make him feel so important. But what could she do? She relied on his good feeling to make things smooth for her with the governors.

Clare stepped back to the window. The empty area of gravel drive was dull, unchanging. It had been like this when she was a child here, and it would be like this after she had gone . . . Her mood darkened with the dull day. Dolly was angling for her job, Clare thought, smiling coldly. What a fool the girl was. But Evan Thomas was another matter.

He wasn't orphanage fodder. He was educated, his parents both teachers in Wales. So why come to the North of England? Clare had asked him when he applied for the post. 'It's good to get away and see other places,' he had replied. 'Good to see as much of the world as possible . . .' Clare wasn't sure of that.

Her gaze moved back to the gates. She *had* been outside, of course. But infrequently. There seemed little reason to go out. The home provided everything she needed. It gave her accommodation and had its own chapel. She could work, eat, sleep and pray – what else was there? As for the shopping, that was done by the kitchen staff on Clare's orders, never by herself. Even the governors of Netherlands Orphanage came here to see her.

Clare leaned her head against the glass, wondering where Evan Thomas was now. Was he in the town, or visiting friends? Maybe he had a girlfriend. She blushed at the thought, mortified at the feelings it provoked in her. Why should she care? He was nothing to her, and besides, he was thirty years younger than she. He wouldn't be interested in some spinster with rounded shoulders and no charm.

But she hadn't always been like this. She had been young, once. The high black gates of the home suddenly looked different to Clare – terrifying and inviting all at once. She ran her tongue over her dry lips. It was raining hard. All the children would be in their dormitories now, learning the religious collect for the day, and most of the staff were relaxing. On an impulse, Clare hurriedly put on her coat and hat, then left her office by her own private exit.

The gates were huge, only yards away, the rain blowing into her face. Her heart speeded up as she hurried towards them, her hands shaking as she took out her key and unlocked the gates. In another instant Clare Lees was *outside*. Firmly she pulled the gates closed behind her and looked ahead.

The street was empty. The vast Victorian viaduct threw its massive shadow, its arches mouthing at her. *Go back, go back*. Nervously, Clare moved a couple of feet to her right and then felt her head begin to swim. Breathing rapidly, she unfastened the collar button of her coat and noticed that her palms were sticky.

She could remember the first time she'd come through these gates – wearing a dress which was too long for her and a coat which smelled of stale cooking fat. Only seven years old. Her mother had died and Clare had stayed beside her body for two days and two nights in their shabby rooms in The Bent. A neighbour had finally found them and before Clare knew what was happening she had been taken away and brought to Netherlands Orphanage.

'Little one, come and sit by me,' her mother had said when she was so ill, lying in a poor cot of a bed beside a damp wall, with a cheap print of a sailing boat on it. The sounds of the pub below came loudly up through the bare floorboards. Her mother's face was gaunt, the eyes flat. A stupid face in reality, but the hands had been kind. They had held on to Clare and pulled the thin blanket over both of them. 'Little one, one day we'll get out of here, and go away. Go off to somewhere sunny. We'll have a garden, and servants . . . I love you. I love you.'

Clare stopped, her mouth half open, the shocking memory a fist in her heart. The street was still empty, nothing familiar in it, nothing she remembered from over forty years ago. I could run away, she thought, then remembered that she was a grown woman. Besides, she had nowhere else to go. Her gaze lingered hopelessly on the street ahead of her. She studied the dark viaduct; watched the rain making the cobbles shine.

They had buried her mother in the same graveyard as her father and that was that. The end of her family. The end of her life outside. Slowly Clare tipped back her head and felt the rain on her face. Netherlands had become her prison, she knew that. She was serving a sentence which would only end at her retirement, and even then she would stay on. And die there.

The cold rain fell against her eyelids and ran over her cheeks. Memory and longing beat to the rhythm of her heart.

Then, slowly, she turned and walked back through the gates, locking them after her.

Chapter Four

Years passed and no one came for Alice Rimmer. No one sent letters or called, no one discovered a relative or remembered a friend of the Rimmer family. The foundling remained where she had been placed – behind the high walls of Netherlands. Forgotten.

Ethel never got over the fact that Alice could have been adopted. But it was more than her job was worth to say anything. Better to hold her tongue and keep an eye on the child and look out for her as best she could. But she never stopped wondering who Alice was, or where she had come from. And she never stopped hoping that she would find out one day.

'I've always said it and I'll say it again – that child is well bred,' Ethel told Gilbert firmly, 'and she's growing up fast. Ten this Friday.' She paused, then leaned on the pile of ironing in front of her. 'I was thinking, Gilbert . . .'

He glanced up at the wheedling tone, his broad face suspicious.

'Oh aye. Your thinking usually costs me money, or sleep.'

Ethel smiled winningly. 'I was wondering – would you mind if I brought Alice home for her birthday?'

'Here!'

'No, London Zoo,' Ethel replied archly. 'Of course here. She's hardly ever been out of that home – none of the children has. It's like a world of its own.' Ethel paused, wondering how to put it best. 'Alice needs to think she has some family.'

Gilbert's forehead creased into frown lines. He had

given up the removals now, and was making wooden toys in the shed to keep himself busy – and to make a bit of money. Tommy Field's market sold them – well, now and again.

'Look, luv, we have our own family. Alice Rimmer isn't our responsibility.'

'And that,' Ethel snapped back, 'is probably what her mother once said!'

He sighed, knowing that Ethel had already made her mind up.

'But what about Miss Lees?' he continued gamely. 'She doesn't like any of the kids to get out and about – and she's not one for favouritism, you've said so often enough. Besides, is she really likely to agree to a child – especially Alice Rimmer – coming here for a birthday treat?'

Ethel frowned. 'Who said she had to know it was a *birthday* treat? Look, Gilbert, that child needs a change, and I intend to give her one – and Clare Lees isn't going to stop me. Where there's a will, there's a way.'

Which there was. A little white lying on Ethel's part and she convinced Clare Lees that Alice needed a way to run off her 'excess energy'. She wouldn't mind taking her out and about, now and then. After all, Ethel said reasonably, it would stop Alice stirring up the other children, wouldn't it?

So the following Friday Gilbert found himself sitting opposite a little girl in a plain print dress, her black hair in plaits, her eyes huge and wary. Obviously nervous, Alice was sitting with her hands on her lap, terrified of the old man watching her. Gilbert was also terrified. What the hell was he supposed to say to a child?

Paralysed and silent they both looked up relieved when, a moment later, Ethel walked in with a cake.

'It's a birthday cake, for you, Alice.'

'For *me*?' The child replied, her voice low. No one had celebrated her birthday before. In fact, only Ethel had ever mentioned it. But now here she was, out of Netherlands, with a cake! It was too good to be true.

Beaming, Ethel put the cake in front of Alice, then lit the ten candles on the top. As soon as she saw the flames, Alice reared back in her seat, alarmed.

'No, luv, it's all right.' Ethel laughed. 'It's a candle for every year you've been born. Ten candles, ten years.'

Alice stared into the flames, each of them reproduced in the dark pupils of her eyes.

'Blow them out and wish,' Ethel urged her.

Gilbert was watching the little girl and then glanced at his wife. A *cake* of all things! I wonder how much that cost. They hardly ever had cake these days, what with money being so bloody tight.

Urged on by Ethel, Alice leaned towards the cake, took in a huge breath, and blew. The candles went out all together, thin trickles of smoke curling up from the spent wicks. She smiled, then clapped her hands together and giggled. The sound was so infectious that Gilbert found himself laughing too.

Excited, Alice leaped to her feet. 'Oh, thank you, thank you!' she said, hugging Ethel tightly. 'It's the best thing that *ever* happened to me.'

She chatted on and on after that, all shyness gone. Gilbert put down his paper. Fascinated, he listened to the stories of the home and tut-tutted where he thought it was appropriate. Knowing that she had an audience, Alice was vibrant, her voice rising and falling, her eyes brilliant, her hands waving in the air as she talked.

On the sidelines, Ethel watched, amused. Yet even she was surprised when Gilbert went out for a moment and then came back from the shed with some of the wooden toys he had made.

Diffidently, he showed them to Alice.

'I . . . I made these,' he said, pushing a toy horse and a camel across the table towards the little girl.

'You *made* them?' she asked, astonished.

Gilbert nodded, puffed up with pride. Carefully he lit his pipe and sat down in his battered easy chair.

'I learned to carve from my father. He could make anything.'

Alice's eyes were fixed on the toys.

'Go on, you can touch them,' Gilbert said.

Ethel raised her eyebrows. Well, she thought, this *was* a turn up. Her husband was normally so possessive of his carvings. Things were going better than she would have dared to hope.

Slowly Alice picked up the camel and turned it over in her hands. Then she laughed and picked up the horse. In another moment she was racing them along the table, Gilbert watching her, Alice hooting with laughter. She felt secure, happy in this little house, and was so giddy with excitement that she lost her grip on the horse and it fell over the edge of the table.

As it landed heavily at Gilbert's feet, its head snapped off.

Alice froze in her seat, watching as he bent down. Ethel too was holding her breath. Carefully Gilbert fingered the broken toy, then glanced over to the child. For an instant he was enraged, but when he saw tears running down Alice's face he faltered.

'It were badly carved,' he said, coughing. 'It weren't your fault, luv.'

But she knew it was. Knew he was lying to be kind to her. She had broken the toy and ruined everything. They wouldn't ask her to their house again. No one wanted a stupid clumsy girl around. No one ever wanted her around for long.

Brushing away her tears, Alice stammered, 'Sorry, I'm sorry –'

'Like I say, it weren't well made,' Gilbert persisted manfully.

Mortified, Alice got to her feet and turned to Ethel. 'I should go back now –'

'You don't have to,' Ethel said, her heart shifting. Oh, bugger the bloody toy! Why did that have to happen? 'Stay a while longer, Alice.'

She shook her head. 'No, I should really go back.' She turned to Gilbert. 'I'm so sorry about the horse, Mr Cummings ... really sorry.' Then she looked back at Ethel. 'Thank you for my cake. It was the best birthday I've ever had.'

Chapter Five

Alice cried herself to sleep that night, her head under the blankets so that the others girls wouldn't hear her. They would have gloated, she knew. They had all been so jealous that Alice had been allowed out. Why her? they'd asked. It must be because she was so pretty. Matron's favourite.

Some of them would have liked to bully Alice, but there was something about her which stopped them. She was so confident, not like the rest of them. It did no good telling her that she was an orphan like everyone else; Alice would simply shrug her shoulders and walk off. She was special, she told them; she was only at the home temporarily. Her family were coming back for her, she said. *Her rich family.*

They laughed at her, but there was something about Alice Rimmer which made them wonder. She didn't have the scarecrow looks of the rest of them and could stand up for herself – maybe her people *would* come back for her. After all, she had hinted at coming from an important family. Her mother, she said, was famous.

But the fantasy Alice had created over the years she had been at Netherlands felt sour that night. She kept her head under the pillow, tears exhausted. The matron had always cared about her, given her little treats and protected her – but she wouldn't any longer. She would hate her now, now she had broken the horse . . .

Alice turned over onto her back. The sounds of the other girls' breathing told her they were asleep as she crept over to the window and looked out through the wide bars. From where the dormitory was situated on the third floor, she could see the other wing of the home, the boys' wing.

Totally separated from the girls' wing, the school sandwiched between the two, it could have been in another county. The children never mixed, went to church at different times and ate at different times. Segregated, all contact forbidden. Two independent entities, within sight, but never in touch.

Alice sighed. Far away she could just make out some lights on the Heights. She wanted to be out there. Longingly Alice remembered what she had seen that day: the streets, the shops, the people. Ethel had walked her across town, buses passing by them intermittently. She had even called into a greengrocer's on the way home, holding tightly on to Alice's hand. Mesmerised, Alice had looked at the 'Epicure' tins on the shelves and the mean-looking bacon slicer on the counter.

Beside her, a middle-aged woman in a fur wrap had waited patiently, her hat topped with feathers. Alice had stared at the woman. She was beautiful. Like *her* mother would be. She'd studied the woman, observing the dark brown hair, the strong attractive features, and the confident voice. *Her* mother was definitely just like that, Alice had thought, looking longingly after the woman as she left. *Her* mother was out there, somewhere. In these streets. She was alive. In fact, they might have passed her. She might even have been *that* woman . . .

Sighing at the memory, Alice continued to stare out of the window. She had been out of the home and she had seen the world. But now she was back in disgrace. Mrs Cummings wouldn't invite her again. She would have to wait for years and years to escape. Until she was fourteen, when most of the Netherlands girls left to go out to work in service. Four whole years. Chilled, Alice shivered and slid back under the sheets, pulling her coat over her. Fighting tears, she tucked her cold hands into the pockets to warm them and then stiffened.

In the darkness her hand closed over a strange shape.

A smooth, wooden shape. Carved in the image of a camel.

Clare Lees was going to put a stop to all this nonsense before it got out of hand. It was Ethel Cummings's fault indirectly. You shouldn't favour one child above the others. She should never have allowed it, but it had seemed a good idea at the time. God knows, Alice Rimmer needed to work off some of her excess energy. Stiffly Clare Lees rose to her feet, her neck aching. As though the child wasn't enough of a handful already – and now this.

'Come in!' she barked, Alice walking into the gloomy office slowly. 'Sit down.'

She did so, her eyes fixed on the principal.

'Alice, I've been hearing some very silly things. Apparently you've been telling the other girls that your mother is coming back for you. She isn't.' It was better to be blunt, Clare Lees thought. No point letting the child live in a fool's paradise.

'She *is*,' Alice said defiantly.

Clare Lees was unnerved by the vehemence of the girl's retort.

'Now look here,' she said coldly, 'I'm in charge of Netherlands, and what I say goes. You have always been a handful, Alice Rimmer, but I had thought lately that you were settling down. It appears that I was wrong.'

Alice was listening, her breathing fast.

'You were abandoned here, and you have been cared for by Netherlands, due to the charity of others. You owe this home a debt of gratitude. Delusions of grandeur will not work here.' Her eyes fixed on the girl, who still looked defiant. Clare's dislike flared like a newly lit torch. 'You are a nobody, Alice, a foundling. You have no family. No one's coming back for you. *They left you.* They didn't want you.'

Alice took in her breath, but said nothing.

'When you leave here you'll have to work and make

your own way in this world. It is better,' Clare Lees paused for effect, 'to learn your place now. Life can be very hard, Alice. No one likes an upstart.'

Alice didn't know what an upstart was, but she knew it was bad.

'Remember – I can make your life here very difficult, if I choose to,' Clare went on. 'Extra duties, extra work – they could soon break your spirit and make you toe the line. But I'm giving you a chance. Mend your ways – and your manner – and you and I could still get on.'

Alice looked down. A triumphant Clare Lees read the action as submission and thought she had the upper hand.

'Stop these fantasies. Stop talking to the other girls about your dream world. Stop pretending you're better than everyone else.' She walked over to Alice and looked down at her. 'I expect you to change. *Now*. I want a calm, quiet, obedient girl. A girl who knows her place. Do I make myself clear? Well, *do I*?'

That night, Alice Rimmer ran away.

Chapter Six

Alice had no idea where she was going, only that she had to get out of the home. She crept downstairs after everyone was in bed, stole out of the back entrance, crossed the yard, and climbed over the locked gates. No one saw her. When she jumped down on the other side she felt a rush of excitement. There was no one about, but then a late bus passed by, its wheels throwing up rain from the gutter.

If she was caught there would be hell to pay. She knew that. But somehow Alice didn't care. What right had old Ma Lees to tell her that she was a no one? How did she know? *You are a nobody. No one's coming back for you* ... The words drummed into her head. *A nobody.* No one's child ... It wasn't true! Alice thought helplessly, walking along the dark pavement and keeping to the shadow of the wall. She had had a mother and a father, everyone did. They must be alive somewhere. Somewhere outside. Where she now was.

But where could she begin looking? She imagined old Ma Lees' face when she presented her parents to her; when she said, 'Look, this is my father and this is my mother.' Oh, she wouldn't be so spiteful then, Alice thought. Not when she was a *somebody*, someone's child, not a foundling to be pushed around.

The rain came down chill with the wind and made Alice shudder. The road which had looked so inviting was suddenly menacing, unfamiliar. A stout woman passed, looked at her curiously and then moved on. Alice paused momentarily outside a pub. The lights were on, the sound of raucous laughter drifting out into the dismal street. A song twanged haphazardly from an out-of-tune piano. Alice pressed her face to the etched glass. Inside she could just make out the backs of the customers, and smell the beer and cheap cigarette smoke. Then someone coughed, and a man staggered out of the door, pushing into her as he made his unsteady way home.

Her parents wouldn't go to a place like this, Alice thought. They wouldn't be smoking and drinking in some Salford backstreet pub.

'Oi, you!'

She turned, startled by the man who had doubled back and was watching her, weaving unsteadily on his feet.

'Wot you staring at?'

'Nothing,' Alice said sullenly, her fear making her belligerent. 'What are you staring at?'

He leaned towards her, sour-breathed. 'You nowt but a kid, wot you doing out so late? Waiting for yer father?'

'My father isn't in there!' Alice said heatedly. 'He's . . . rich. He doesn't come to places like this.'

Unexpectedly the man laughed. 'Oh, rich, is he? So why are you hanging about Salford at this time of night? You some little princess in disguise, come slumming?'

Biting her lip to control her fear and indignation, Alice stood up to him. 'It's nothing to do with you –'

'I bet he's just another drunk, propping up the bar in there,' the man said, his voice slurred. 'Yer mam sent you to call him home before he spends the rent money?'

'He's not like that!' Alice said heatedly, walking away and then turning. 'My father's important and my mother's well known. A beauty.'

'Yeah, and I'm Rudolph Valentino,' the drunk sneered, pulling a half-bottle out of his greasy coat and taking a swig. 'And the more I drink, the more I believe it.'

Alice hurried off, moving under the viaduct and beginning to mount the steep street. If she was honest, she wanted to double back, but was afraid to meet up with the man again, so she kept walking ahead. Soon she was drenched, her hair dripping down her back, her skin chalk white. Wrapping her arms around herself she hurried on. She then realised that she was lost. The streets meant nothing to her, she had no idea of where she was, and there was nothing familiar in sight. The outings she had had with Ethel had been in daytime and Salford hadn't seemed so grim then, but under the dim gaslamps the streets looked sour, the alleys gloomy. Disembodied voices and shouts came from behind doors and drawn blinds, the rain drumming on the cheap tin roofs of outside lavatories. Alice was afraid suddenly, stopping and looking round. Where was she going? Did she really think she was going to find her parents this way? When she didn't know who they were, where they were, or what they looked like?

She had acted like a fool, Alice thought. Here she was out in the cold, lost, and there was no one to help her. No one was even looking for her. Scared, she dug her nails into her palms to stop herself crying and turned, trying to see the viaduct, the only landmark she remembered. But all she could see was a man, the drunk, a way off, walking towards her and, startled, Alice began to run.

It *was* him! she thought. He would catch her and then what? Her feet pounded on the pavement and then she saw a cobbled ginnel and dived in, catching her breath.

At once, a hand descended on her shoulder.

She screamed.

'Hey, miss, it's all right,' the policeman said pleasantly. 'What are you doing out and about this time of night?'

Relief was quickly followed by a sense of failure. Her big adventure was a sham. She was just a stupid, lost kid.

'I . . . was walking.'

'Where?'

'Around.'

'Around where?' he repeated, leaning down towards

her, his moustached face kind. 'I think I should get you home, don't you?'

'I don't have a home.'

He blinked. 'Come on now, there's no argument that bad that can't be settled over a pot of tea. Your parents will be worried about you, lass.'

No they won't, Alice thought hopelessly. 'I don't have a real home. I'm at Netherlands.'

'Ah,' he said simply, taking her hand. 'Well, I think perhaps it's time you were back, little one.'

She wanted to be grown up, but instead Alice held gratefully onto his hand and walked back to Netherlands with him in silence.

Ethel would say afterwards that it was the turning point. When Alice was brought back to the home that night she was cowed and defeated. You could see that all the fight had gone out of her, Ethel told Gilbert. It was hardly worth while Clare Lees punishing her; she didn't seem to care any more. The petty duties Alice was given she completed without complaint, without resistance. She wouldn't even talk about where she had gone that night. Or why.

'Are you all right, sweetheart?' Ethel asked her a few days later.

Alice nodded. 'I'm fine.'

Compliance was more worrying than an outburst, thought Ethel.

'No more running away now, Alice, promise me. It did no good, no good at all.' She paused to see what effect her words were having, but the girl's face was bland. What is she thinking? Ethel wondered. Or is she plotting something?

The truth was that Clare Lees' words had cut Alice to the bone and forced a change in her. It was one thing to be put in a home, quite another for someone to spell out what you already knew. That *you weren't wanted*. Alice's hatred for the principal was absolute, although she wouldn't admit it to anyone. She would keep her own counsel, that was the only way to survive at Netherlands. But her loathing for Clare Lees burned with such force that she wondered if it shimmered around her like a heat haze.

Clare Lees had crushed her dream. The one thing which Alice had clung to – the hope that her parents, in particular her mother, might come back for her – had been snatched away. Some humpbacked spinster had told her she was a no one and that she never would be.

Well, she would show her! Alice thought. She would show Clare Lees what she was made of. One day she would get out of the home and really find her family. They would explain that it had all been a mistake and welcome her back. They would be rich and she would come back in furs and riding in a new motorcar. She would gloat over Clare Lees and pay her back for every single cruel word.

That was the night that Alice Rimmer grew up.

Chapter Seven

Evan Thomas paused under the viaduct and lit a cigarette, inhaling the smoke and then tossing the match into the gutter. The sun was shining, which pleased him, and he hummed under his breath as he walked along. Oh yes, Evan thought, life was really quite good.

He had a new girlfriend and unless he was very much mistaken, he was impressing Clare Lees even more than usual. Evan sniffed the air and pretended that he was back in Wales. The daydream lasted for as long as it took a rag-and-bone man to ride by, his horse depositing a heap of foul-smelling dung on the roadside.

Pulling an expression of disgust, Evan moved off. Oh yes, Clare Lees was getting to need him more and more. If he played his cards right she might consider early retirement. After all, the woman must be over sixty. He would be kind to her, let her retire and teach a little now and then. There was no reason to be unpleasant; after all, she had made it all possible for him.

He liked to imagine how popular he would be. Liked to think of how everyone would love him after the old bag had gone . . . Evan sighed. He would have to make changes, bring the place into the present, get himself noticed. The governors seemed to like him well enough – better than that ridiculous Dolly Blake.

Evan thought about pretty, ambitious Dolly and her bullish boyfriend, Andy. Not many brains in poor Andy. Just brawn. He smiled. Dolly was such a fool; it had all been so easy. She had fallen for his line as soon as he had spun it her way. And she had *kept* falling.

She was waiting by the park gates now, her blonde head shining in the sunlight, her face a mixture of pouting prettiness and hard-nosed guile.

'Evan,' she said softly, her lips pressing briefly against his.

'Hey now, we have to be careful in public –'

She pinched his arm. It hurt. 'Why's that, Evan?'

'You're the one with the fiancé,' he replied smoothly, leading her into the park and away from prying eyes. Andy might be dumb, but he was big enough to flatten Evan.

'Oh, Evan,' she said, stopping and pulling him towards some bushes, 'I've been thinking about you since Thursday. Do you really love me?'

He cupped her breasts in his hands and nuzzled against her neck 'Now that's a silly question, girl. You know how I feel about you.'

Dolly wasn't totally satisfied with the answer and pulled herself – and her breasts – away from him.

'Don't get all clever with me, Evan!' she snapped. 'I want a proper answer.'

Well what was the proper answer? Evan thought. *I'm using you, my dear. Just to get you off the scent whilst I make sure I get the upper hand at Netherlands*. He knew the type Dolly Blake was: so clever she would cut herself. She *thought* that she was stringing Evan along, whilst he *knew* that he was manipulating her. Evan touched her cheek, trying to cheer her up at he looked at her. Dolly thought that by being Evan Thomas's girlfriend she could protect her own interests. He would either help her to get where she wanted, or she would get it by default. And bugger poor Andy. If Evan Thomas was going to the top – she was going with him.

Or so she thought.

'Oh, come on, sweetheart,' Evan said, pulling her to him. 'There's no one like you.'

'I dare say there isn't,' she retorted, her face flushed. 'If you're playing fast and loose with me, Evan, you'll live to regret it.'

He stood back from her, his expression injured.

At once, she was contrite. 'Oh, Evan, I'm sorry, I just care about you so much.' She took his hand and kissed it. 'I don't mean to say the things I do; I just want us to be together.'

'What about Andy?' Evan said, as though he thought of the other man as a rival.

'*What* about him?' Dolly replied. 'I'd drop him like that,' she clicked her fingers, 'if you asked me to marry you.'

Jesus, Evan thought, no bloody way! He wanted Dolly safe with her dollop of a fiancé. In fact, it would suit him best if she married Andy. That way he could never get caught. Marry Dolly Blake! Was she crazy?

'You know how I feel about you,' Evan replied, pressing her hand to his cheek, 'but I can't marry until I've proved myself, got my career on track.' He looked into her eyes wistfully. 'You do see that, don't you? I'm an ambitious man. Dolly. It wouldn't be fair.'

Her brain took the words and sifted them like lump flour. In the end the meaning was unpalatable. Not that she would let Evan see it. So he thought he was taking her for a ride, did he? Well, time would tell.

Gently she laid her head on his shoulder and sighed.

'I understand, luv,' she said, letting her hand move inside his jacket and touch his chest. 'Honestly I do.'

When Dolly came back to Netherlands that evening she was preoccupied, ready for a fight with anyone who crossed her path. Using the side door, she let herself into the home and paused in the corridor. It smelled of chalk and a less pleasant urine odour coming from the toilets nearby.

Sniffing, she walked into the back room beyond and snapped at an old bald man sitting smoking a pipe.

'Mr Baldwin!'

He looked up, eyes rheumy. 'Aye?'

'The toilet smells.'

'What d'you expect? It's a toilet, not a bleeding perfume factory,' he replied, sucking on his pipe and turning away.

Irritated, Dolly stood in front of him. 'They need some more disinfectant –'

'Aye, stop yer bleating! There's many houses round 'ere that don't have a lavvie – like yers, I'll be bound.'

'Now, you just –'

Irritated, Mr Baldwin stood up and waved his pipe at her. 'I do what I can 'ere. The wages are bloody awful for what I have to deal with. As for the lavvies – they'll be swilled out again in the morning.'

'But –'

Impatiently he flicked his hand to shoo her away. Will Baldwin had been at Netherlands longer than anyone. He could remember being the caretaker when Clare Lees was a child, he didn't need some cheap tart like Dolly Blake telling him what to do.

'I've told you, Miss Blake, it'll be done again in morning.'

'I have –'

'Oh, go off and pick a fight with someone else!' Will replied, adding slyly, 'You want to stay away from Welshmen and stick with yer own sort. You'd be better-tempered if you did.'

Dolly's face flushed as she stood, tongue-tied, for a moment and then flounced out.

As she made her way back down the corridor she was listening for any sound, any child on whom she could vent her spleen. The boys' section was silent, behind the locked doors, and in front of her there stretched the long gloomy corridor which led to the girls' part of the home. It was empty, dimly lit by spluttering gaslight.

Her shoes tapped on the shiny floor as Dolly hurried along. She thought at one point that she heard something, but when she paused there was only silence. On she paced,

39

seething, and then rounded the bend to find Alice walking towards her.

'What are you doing here at this time of night?' Dolly snapped.

Alice paused. She was carrying a tray with a cover over it.

'I've come from the sanatorium,' she said quietly, looking into Dolly's flushed face.

'At this time? I doubt it.' Dolly pulled the cover off the tray Alice was carrying. 'What's this?'

'Matron asked me to take it back to the kitchen –'

'I didn't ask what you were told to do with it, I asked what it was.'

'Hilly Barker's supper.'

Dolly paused to consider. Hilly Barker had been ill for some time, coughing and periodically feverish. She had been in and out of the sanatorium for the four years she had been at Netherlands. And she was getting worse. Not to worry, the doctor had assured Clare Lees, it's not contagious. It was just that Hilly was getting weaker by the day.

'Hilly Barker?'

Alice nodded, keeping her head down.

Dolly stared at her, taking in the dark good looks that had intensified since Alice had turned ten. She would be stunning one day, Dolly realised, her temper increasing at the thought.

'It's a waste of good food,' Dolly went on, staring at the unappetising meal. 'She should have eaten it. There are children starving abroad.'

'Hilly tried, but she's no appetite –'

'Since when have you been a doctor?' Dolly bellowed. 'You're altogether too big for your boots, Alice Rimmer. We had trouble with you before, didn't we? I thought you'd learned your lesson.'

Alice said nothing, just waited. The tirade would pass

in time. Dolly Blake was peevish, but her viciousness was always short-lived.

'Sorry, Miss Blake.'

'You *should* be sorry,' Dolly went on, the corridor echoing her words. 'Miss Lees doesn't want any more trouble from you, Alice Rimmer, or you'll be sent away.'

Staying silent, Alice stood with her head bowed. She knew that Dolly had no power to send her away, but she was going to be careful, just in case. The only people she cared about were at Netherlands – Ethel and Hilly. She didn't want to lose what little she had. So she bit her tongue, as she had learned to do.

Obviously getting bored with her attack, Dolly sighed. 'How is Hilly?' she asked, toying with the cuffs of her dress.

'Poorly.'

She glanced back at Alice. God, the girl was getting tall. 'Why you?'

'Pardon, Miss Blake?'

'Why are *you* looking after Hilly Barker?'

'Matron asked me to,' Alice replied, her voice low.

'Aren't you worried that Hilly might have something contagious?' Dolly asked meanly.

'No.'

Dolly snorted and tossed her blonde head. 'She could have smallpox for all we know.' She leaned towards Alice and looked into the spectacular dark eyes. 'If Hilly Barker *did* have smallpox you could catch it. It blinds you and leave pockmarks all over your face. Makes you ugly. Really ugly.' She studied the girl's perfect skin and felt a sudden urge to slap her. Then, just as soon at the feeling had come, it passed.

Dolly waved Alice aside. 'Go on, get on with whatever to have to do,' she said, capriciously. 'Go on!'

As Alice hurried away, Dolly stood for a long time looking after her. But she didn't even see the girl any more; she was thinking about Evan Thomas and Clare Lees, and wondering how she could make her future secure. Deep in thought, Dolly stared at the linoleum, the colour of treacle. She shivered suddenly and rubbed her arms with her hands. What she had to do was to get closer to Clare Lees. She had to become the principal's confidante. Her ally.

She looked around. The walls were bare, without paintings or colour. Netherlands was a lot better than some of the other homes, Dolly knew, but it was hardly a place to choose to grow up in. No fires here, no little touches of home. No soft beds . . . Dolly thought of Evan again, and then of Andy.

Smiling, she touched her lips with the tips of her fingers. Oh, she would sort it out. Andy was a handsome man, not too bright, but good in bed. She smiled slyly. As for Evan Thomas, well, he would have to be taught a lesson, wouldn't he? A little demonstration to show him that he wasn't dealing with a common tart.

Calmer now, Dolly walked on. Ahead of her she could see the heavy door of the principal's room, 'Miss Clare Lees' inscribed in gold lettering. Dolly stopped, glanced round, and then touched the letters, imagining it reading 'Miss Dora Blake'. Or 'Mrs Andrew Fellows'. Or 'Mrs Evan Thomas' . . . Sighing, Dolly let her fingers fall away from the wood.

Then she turned away and retraced her steps – never realising that she was watched by a silent Alice Rimmer at the turn of the stairs.

Chapter Eight

'Hilly?' Alice whispered.

The girl turned over in her bed and then sat up, surprised.

'Alice, what are you doing here?'

'I came back,' Alice said, pulling the edge of the blanket around her shoulders.

'Where have you been?'

'Just walking round the streets.'

'But if they catch you –'

'They won't,' Alice said certainly. 'It's four in the morning. No one's about. How are you feeling?'

'Not too bad,' Hilly replied, leaning back against the pillow, her voice low so as not to waken the girl in the next bed. 'I felt stronger today.'

'You look better,' Alice lied, touching her friend's forehead. 'Matron said you might go out for a walk tomorrow.'

'Alice, you shouldn't be here,' Hilly replied, her fine, ash-blonde hair lank against her pale face. 'You'll get into trouble.'

'No, I won't,' Alice reassured her. Smiling she held up a key. 'See this? It's the sanatorium key.'

'Where did you get that?' Hilly asked, horror-struck. She knew Alice only too well, knew how the placid exterior hid a wilful streak. They had been friends for years, both of them now fourteen. Only Alice looked fourteen – and Hilly looked like a sick child.

Without Alice, Hilly would have given up a long time ago. The home was dispiriting, gloomy. She had no family and nothing to look forward to – until the day that Alice had arrived at her bedside with her dinner. From then on, things had changed. Soon Hilly was eager to see her and hear the gossip. Alice Rimmer might seem quiet to everyone else, but she was a wicked talker and missed nothing.

It was through Alice that the sickly girl lived vicariously. And it was through Alice that Hilly heard about Evan Thomas and Dolly Blake and Clare Lees. Without her, Hilly would have known little of the tiny world of the home, but Alice told her everything – a spy, reporting back all her trivial espionage.

At first Hilly had spent a third of her time in the home, but as she grew weaker she became more tied to the sanatorium. Ethel had always been kind, but it was Alice who provided the entertainment. Before long, Hilly came to know Alice as no one else did.

It was in Hilly that Alice had confided about Gilbert Cummings's broken horse and what Clare Lees had said about no one wanting her. It was also Hilly who'd heard about Alice's ambitions – and fantasies. It seemed a small price to pay, Hilly had thought, as she'd listened to Alice talking about her phantom mother. She knew that it was a fantasy, but what did that matter? Alice was the only person who had chosen to spend time with her. Everyone else kept away, forgot her.

And as the years passed, and Hilly took up permanent residence in the sanatorium, Alice remained constant. She fussed her and petted her as though she was her child, Hilly thought, moved by the frequent kindnesses. Yet there was also a hidden recklessness about Alice which terrified her. Alice might pretend to others that she was quiet and subdued, but Hilly wasn't fooled. Alice had sneaked out of the home several times, just to walk around the town. Or so she said.

But one night she had told Hilly the real reason.

'I think I'll see her.'

'Who?' Hilly had asked, bemused.

'My mother,' Alice had answered, surprised that she hadn't already guessed. 'One day I'll bump into her, you'll see.'

Hilly had felt pity well up in her. Neither of them had parents, or even just mothers. That was reality. She could accept it so why couldn't Alice?

'Your mother might be dead, you know.'

Alice had looked at her and shook her head firmly. 'No, she's alive.'

'How do you know?'

'Because I do!' Alice had snapped angrily. 'I know she's alive, Hilly. I feel it.'

'Did anyone ever tell you that?'

'No.'

Hilly's voice had been quiet. 'So you don't know for sure?'

'I know,' Alice had repeated. 'I think Miss Lees knows something too.'

'Why d'you think that?'

'A hunch.'

'What kind of hunch?'

'I don't know, Hilly! It's just something I've always believed. And I'll prove it in the end.'

Sighing, Hilly had tapped the back of Alice's hand. 'Don't go out again, please. If they find out –'

'No one will find out,' Alice had replied patiently. 'I know what I'm doing.'

And she seemed to, because she was never caught. Alice's nocturnal wanderings didn't uncover her mother, but they bred in her some wildness of spirit. Another child would have been terrified, but Alice was past that. She was quick, kept to the shadows, watching people, events, soaking up the outside world the only way she could. Then, as she grew older, Alice stopped fantasising and began to talk about other ways of finding out about her past.

Now Alice dropped her voice to a whisper as she leaned towards Hilly. 'They have personal files in the office.'

'What!' Hilly said, startled.

Alice motioned her to be quiet. 'I said, they have files on all of us here. On each child. They're in the principal's office. And I want to see mine.'

Hilly sat up in bed, alarmed. 'Don't do it, Alice! Please, if you're caught, they'll send you away.' Hilly looked close to tears. 'I couldn't go on if you weren't here.'

Alice shook her head, her voice barely more than a whisper. 'No one will find out. I've got hold of the key.'

'Oh God!'

'All I have to do is to look in the files. Then I'll lock them up again and that's it. Trust me, Hilly, no one will find out.'

'No!'

'*Yes!*' Alice said emphatically. 'I have to know who I am, and where I come from. And I *will*.' She slid a key out of her pocket and showed it to Hilly. 'This is it. This is what will get me in. Then when I look at the files, I'll know.'

Rising wearily to her feet, Ethel yawned and stretched her arms over her head. God, she was tired. The work didn't get any easier. And as for working nights, that was a lark and no mistake. Still, with Gilbert unemployed she had to take what opportunities there were. She walked to the mirror and rearranged her white cap. It had seen better days, but then so had she.

They were all getting on – Clare Lees ageing rapidly, and as for that toe rag Evan Thomas ... Ethel snorted under her breath. He was still sniffing around Miss Lees, still sucking up to her, although by now he must be wondering when she was going to retire. Dolly Blake was hanging on too. Ethel laughed to herself. Some time back, Dolly had got exasperated with Evan and issued an ultimatum: marry me, or it's over and I'll marry Andy. Good luck, he had replied, I hope you'll both be very happy. It wasn't what Dolly had expected and so she was forced to do some nifty back-pedalling. She hadn't really meant it, she explained, she just wanted him to tell her where she stood.

Up to her knees in horse muck, Ethel thought when she heard about it. But whatever she said, it did no good. Dolly might have started off thinking that she would use Evan to further her ambitions, but now she was in love with him. The more he refused to make a commitment, the more she clung on, the eternal fiancé, Andy, always in the background – with his other girlfriends to keep him company. What the hell Dolly was playing at Ethel couldn't imagine, but Dolly Blake was not going to let go of Evan Thomas. Ever. God makes them and the Devil pairs them, and that's a fact, Ethel thought.

If her guess was right, though, the ambitions of both Dolly and Evan were no nearer to being fulfilled. Still active, Clare Lees wasn't going anywhere just yet . . .

Ethel yawned again and walked over to the door, looking down the corridor.

All was quiet, but then what did she expect? Old Baldwin was flaked out in his bunk in the basement and who else would be walking about at this time? It seemed daft to have her on night duty; the boys were all in bed in the other wing and she had looked in on the girls only half an hour ago. Only Alice had been awake.

But then Alice was always watchful. Ethel sighed. The little girl who had come to the home had certainly grown up. She was fourteen now and comely, very comely. Before long she would have to find work – all the girls did. But what kind of work would Alice find? Not factory work, or service. No, Ethel thought, there were plans for Alice.

Not that the girl knew about them. But Clare Lees had confided in Ethel not so long since; said she had hoped that Alice would teach at the home. She was bright, she said, very quick. It would be a waste to send her out to do menial work. Miss Lees had gone on to say that she wanted to train her, even hinted that she might like to see Alice Rimmer take over as principal in due course. That would be a turn-up, Ethel thought. Alice, of all people. Didn't Miss Lees know how much the girl hated Netherlands? Didn't she realise how much Alice hated *her*?

Apparently not, Ethel thought, opening a window and breathing in the cool summer air. It had been an unseasonably stuffy day and now the temperature was chill. Her eyes regarded the bare courtyard. Someone should have planted trees and bushes there long enough since. It would have made the place more cosy, more welcoming.

A sudden noise made her pause. Ethel turned and looked upwards at the ceiling above her. It sounded like soft footsteps overhead. Was Clare Lees up and working at this hour? It wasn't likely; she kept to regular hours. So who was it?

Picking up a full bottle of linctus as a make-do weapon, Ethel moved into the corridor. The dull gaslight threw long shadows, the far end in darkness. Slowly she moved towards the stairs and walked up them, one by one. It couldn't be a burglar – there was nothing to steal.

At the door of the principal's office Ethel paused and looked in. At first she could only made out the shape of a person and then, as her eyes adjusted to the lack of light, she recognised her.

'*Alice!*'

The girl spun round, startled.

'Alice, what *are* you doing?'

She faltered. 'I . . . I . . . heard a noise.'

'At this time of night? You should be in bed,' Ethel replied, walking in and staring at the girl. Her concern turned to suspicion suddenly. 'What *are* you doing in here?'

'Nothing.'

Ethel's glance moved to the open drawer. 'Alice! How

could you?' she snapped, genuinely shocked. 'What are you looking for?'

'My file,' Alice said defiantly. 'I want to see it.'

'You want to see the back of my hand, my girl,' Ethel replied, grabbing hold of Alice's arm and leading her to the door.

She struggled. 'I want –'

'If Miss Lees finds you here you'll have cooked your goose once and for all, and no mistake,' Ethel said hotly, then dropped her voice. 'Good God, Alice, do you want to ruin your chances? She thinks well of you – you could jeopardise everything by doing this. She would never trust you again.'

'I don't care!' Alice said hotly. 'I want to see my file.'

Annoyed, Ethel pulled the girl to the door, closed it and held out her hand.

'Give me the key.'

'I don't have it.'

'Don't lie to me!' she replied. 'Give me the key.'

Defeated, Alice handed it to her and Ethel locked the door. Then she put the key into her own pocket and marched Alice downstairs in silence. When they got back to her room, Ethel let go of the girl's arm and looked at her.

'You have no idea how disappointed I am in you. I thought you'd stopped doing stupid things, Alice. I thought you'd settled down.'

Alice hung her head. She was crushed by the obvious contempt in Ethel's voice.

'Why did you do it?'

'I wanted to see my file. No one would have shown it to me – so I thought I would find it for myself.'

Wearily Ethel sat down and then gestured for Alice to take the seat next to her.

'Alice, no one knows anything about your family or your past.'

'There must be something written down,' Alice replied. 'There must be some record.' She looked hard into Ethel's plump face. 'I have to know. It's driving me crazy.'

'You're driving yourself crazy,' Ethel retorted.

'I bet if it was you, you'd want to know.'

Ethel looked at the girl curiously. She was right: if their situations had been reversed, she would have wanted to know. Besides, she had always been curious about Alice Rimmer herself. Maybe there *was* something written down, something to tell them where she had come from.

'I have to know . . .' Alice said pleadingly. 'I'm sorry if I've disappointed you. You've always been kind to me, but . . .' She paused and her face became defiant again, '. . . I *have to know*. Can't you see that? Ethel, you can understand that, can't you?'

Ethel glanced away. She had always been too lenient with Alice, had always been too fond of her. In fact she had grown closer to her over the years, Alice coming to visit – although always uneasy after the incident with the toy horse. Birthdays had been remembered, at Christmas there had been presents sneaked in, and Ethel's pride on seeing Alice grow up had been almost as great as seeing her own sons mature.

But now Ethel was angry with her. The stubborn wilful streak hadn't gone, after all. It was just hidden, concealed.

'How did you get hold of the key?'

There was a moment's pause before Alice answered.

'Miss Lees sometimes uses her side door. She locks the main door – but she leaves the key in. I slid a piece of paper under the door, then pushed out the key from the outside. It fell onto the paper and I then pulled the paper under the door with the key on it.'

'Very clever,' Ethel said coldly. 'Where did you find out about that?'

Alice's voice was low. 'I read it in a book.'

Sighing, Ethel looked down. 'Go back to bed.'

'But –'

'Go back to bed, Alice!' she repeated, and watched as the girl left the room.

For a long time Ethel sat in her chair and listened to the clock ticking, and the water pipes clanking as someone flushed a cistern upstairs. She thought about Alice and worried. The girl was too reckless. It was madness to think of breaking in to look at her records!

Then suddenly Ethel remembered that the bottle of cough linctus that she'd taken to use as a cosh was still up in the principal's office. Startled, she sat bold upright. If Clare Lees found it she would know that Ethel had been there. She wouldn't know about Alice, because Ethel would never tell her, but she would have to explain what she had been doing in the principal's office in the middle of the night.

Ethel felt faint with anxiety. She would be sacked, the money finished, and no references. Her reputation would be ruined . . . There was only one thing for it, she had to get the bottle back. Hurriedly she got to her feet, went back up the dim stairs and moved towards the principal's office. Once there, she felt into her pocket and took out the key, unlocked the door and let herself in.

Moonlight shafted over the desk and along the floor. Ethel strained her eyes to see the bottle in the semidark. Finally she spotted it and grabbed it, moving quickly back to the door . . . Then she turned back. She paused, tempted. She looked at the desk. Her mouth dried, the moonlight falling over the wooden surface.

Get out, she told herself, get out now, before it's too late. But she couldn't. Suddenly she had to know what was in Alice's file. Putting down the bottle again, Ethel ran her tongue over her dry lips and opened the drawer. Hurriedly she sifted through the A – Z listing, stopping on R. With shaking hands she lifted out the file on ALICE RIMMER.

She would be fired if she was caught. Out on her ear

. . . Just put the file back, Ethel, she urged herself. Just put it back . . . But she couldn't, and slowly opened the file. The moon shifted a little, throwing its helpful light over the paper as Ethel read the lines written on the first page. She reread them, and reeled, momentarily giddy. Then she slammed the file shut and turned.

On unsteady legs she walked to the door, clutching the bottle of linctus. Clumsily she relocked the door and then pushed the key underneath it as though it had fallen out of the lock. Holding tightly on to the banister rail she then moved down the stairs and back into her room. Once there Ethel Cummings fell into her chair and stared ahead of her.

Finally, she knew where Alice Rimmer came from. Knew who her parents were . . . A darkness settled over the room and over her heart. What she had read she wished she had never seen.

What she had read she would never forget.

Chapter Nine

Late the following afternoon Ethel came back to Netherlands for her next shift. She had not slept during the day and every enquiry of Gilbert's was met with preoccupied distance. Each time she closed her eyes, Ethel saw the damning lines written in Alice's file. Each time she opened her eyes, she saw the same words printed in headlines and snapping from newspaper stands.

Unusually quiet, she went back to work and then, finally, she sent for Alice. It took a while for the girl to arrive and during that time Ethel washed and rewashed several bandages which had never been used, just to keep herself busy.

Finally there was a soft rap at the door.

'Come in, Alice.'

She walked in nervously and stood before Ethel, certain that she was about to be told that her nocturnal adventure had been reported to Clare Lees. A long moment passed, and then another. Alice finally looked at Ethel, concerned.

'Are you all right?'

'There's nothing wrong with me,' Ethel replied more sharply than she meant. 'I wanted to have a word with you.'

How would she say it? How could she phrase the next lines? She paused, studied Alice and felt all the old affection well up in her. Dear God, what good would be served by telling her? What purpose? *She* had been shattered by the news; what would it do to a wilful, excitable girl?

It would ruin her, Ethel realised. And in that moment she made her decision.

'Alice, I thought about what you said last night.' Ethel paused, considering her next words. 'I realised that it was only natural that you wanted to know about your past and your parents. Well, I went back to the office last night –'

Alice's eyes had widened. 'What?'

'Ssssh!' Ethel cautioned her. 'This is between us. No one else must ever know. Listen to me, Alice, I have something to tell you.'

The girl stared at her, hardly breathing.

'I went back and I looked for your file,' Ethel paused again. 'I looked once and then again. *There was no file.* I'm sorry, but there was nothing to see.'

She could feel the hope leave Alice's body, see her eyes dulling, her lips pale. *There was nothing to see. Nothing.*

Gently, Ethel put her arms around her. 'There, there, luv, I had to tell you. I couldn't leave you wondering, could I? Couldn't leave you imagining all sorts.' She held on to the fourteen-year-old, and lied. 'I'm afraid no one can tell you anything, luv. Because there's nothing to know.'

Chapter Ten

1927

The world had changed radically in the aftermath of the Great War. Outside the grim Netherlands Orphanage there were posters of women with their hair shingled, their hemlines raised. Some even wore make-up, and at the cinemas in Salford Mae West and Greta Garbo heralded in a new age of glamour. As did Charlie Chaplin, the little man taking on the big boys. Everything was changing, speeding up. In March the land speed record of over 200 miles per hour had been set and in May Lindbergh flew the Atlantic solo.

But at Netherlands Orphanage little had changed. The old regime was still intact, Clare Lees still the principal. She was badly stooped now, her dowager's hump making her irritable, her voice shrill with the onset of old age and lost hopes. Evan Thomas had hung on too. He had thought his ship would have come in by now, but it appeared to have hit some unexpected rocks. Having been made deputy head several years earlier he was surprised to find himself *still* the deputy head, but he reckoned that he had come so far, it would be folly to give up now. After all, he was only thirty-six, and life still held promise.

Dolly Blake had also remained at Netherlands, but she had aged less phlegmatically, and now had a bitter expression about the mouth. Her ambitions had faltered and when time passed and she had looked close to being left on the shelf, she had decided that Andy was her best option. After all, nothing stopped her from seeing Evan Thomas *after* she was married.

Except Andy wasn't quite the fool she'd taken him for. He had given up his other women, but had never trusted that Dolly would be so honourable. Two years after their wedding he'd come to pick her up from work one night unexpectedly – to find Evan Thomas with his hand down his wife's blouse. All Dolly's explaining, begging and cajoling had had no effect. Andy had left her.

The shock had rendered Dolly temporarily insensible, and Evan – sporting a spectacular set of bruises inflicted by an enraged Andy – had backed off fast. He didn't want to have Dolly hanging round his neck, emotionally or professionally. After all, there had been a scandal and muck stuck.

Being a man, he had escaped the worst of the fallout, but the unfortunate Dolly had a 'name' now. It was obvious to everyone that the governors would never approve her promotion. Evan knew it. And Dolly knew it.

Rejected by her lover and deserted by her husband, Dolly had become a public laughing stock. The only place she could escape the gossips was Netherlands Orphanage, and to there she had retreated. The last person in the world to assume Clare Lees' example, overnight it appeared that Dolly Blake became a prude.

'You should see her,' Ethel told Gilbert one Sunday as she folded the washing. 'All buttoned up and tight-lipped, like some outraged virgin. If she sees one of the boys even looking at the girls she goes mad. Not that they can help it – the lads all hang around the railings when it's time for church, ogling the lasses. Natural, I call it, but Dolly and Miss Lees think it's something smutty.'

Gilbert laughed, paused in the carving of one of his wooden animals. It was just a hobby now, each one taking months to complete as he grew older and slower.

'There's nothing like poacher turned gamekeeper,' he said. 'I always said that the boys and girls should mix; having them separate like that makes them all the keener.'

He stared at the figure he was carving. 'What about Evan Thomas? Still thinks he's king of the midden?'

Ethel's expression hardened. 'He's going to stay until Miss Lees retires or pops her clogs. That one's hard-faced, all right. Too cocky by a half.' She leaned against a pile of washed sheets. 'You should see him, strutting about, bossing everyone behind Miss Lees' back. A right toerag. Thing is, he thinks the job's all but his – now that Dolly's out of the running. He has no idea that Miss Lees has other plans.'

Gilbert smiled conspiratorially at his wife. 'Our girl?'

She nodded, beaming with pride. She had never told Gilbert what she had discovered that night so long ago, and she never would. Instead she had watched over Alice with even more care and was rewarded by seeing her grow up well, gradually calming down. For Alice Rimmer had changed radically, both in appearance and temperament. It was not that she was any less emotional, simply that she had learned how to suppress her feelings, to control her outbursts. Her hotly exotic looks had cooled too. Beautiful she was, but quietly so.

The sensual strangeness had now been replaced by a true allure. The pale oval face, the dark eyes, the glossy hair were remarkable, and as Alice matured into a young woman she gave off an almost electrical charge. No one failed to recognise it, and many of her peers at Netherlands were jealous of her.

Only Hilly Barker bore Alice no resentment. Grown into a frail, elfin figure, she was as close to Alice as she had always been and was devoted to her. And so she should be, thought Ethel. After all, hadn't Alice looked after and confided in Hilly when no one else wanted to know the sick girl in the sanatorium? Oh yes, Ethel thought, Alice was nothing if not loyal to her friends.

Another type of girl would have taken advantage of Hilly's devotion and some of the younger girls' slavish admiration – but Alice didn't. Her thoughts were concentrated on one thing, and one thing only – to get away from Netherlands. Out into the world.

'I *have* to get away,' she had said months earlier. 'I'll go mad if I don't.'

Ethel had soothed her, as ever. 'In time, you will. But you've got the chance to get an education, Alice, so you should take the opportunity. Teachers get well paid and they're respected. You could do a lot worse.'

Alice knew Ethel was right. Knowledge was the only way to gain respect. So she set to and she studied. Temperament and spirit were controlled. Outbursts only led to punishment and isolation. With a massive effort of will Alice learned to control her natural ebullience. Inside, she might be raging, but outside she seemed almost content with her lot.

The only one who was never fooled was Ethel. She had an instinct that Alice was plotting something, but had to admit that she was impressed by the girl's application. Especially lately – now that Alice had confounded everyone by becoming Clare Lees' favourite.

She didn't ingratiate herself with the principal, but she was a quick learner and more than willing to take on some of the rudimentary teaching of the smallest children. The school inside Netherlands was makeshift, the education basic – but who was prepared to spend money educating foundlings? The future mill workers, pit boys and domestic servants? The books they had were out of date, the maps hopelessly old-fashioned, but Alice didn't seem to mind. She could see an opportunity for herself – and she was going to take it.

The shift in power had been noticed by everyone. Evan Thomas was caught off guard and Dolly was white hot with envy.

Not for the first time, Ethel had taken it on herself to send out a warning to Alice.

'I thought you hated Clare Lees,' she had said a month earlier. 'What are you up to now?'

Alice had turned her dark eyes on the matron ingenuously. 'Why should I be up to anything?'

'Because I know you,' Ethel had replied. 'I've known you since you were a child, and I can tell that you're up to something.'

Alice had slid her arm through Ethel's, the matron's skin warm and soft to her touch. 'I'm fine. I'm doing well now. I thought you'd be pleased.'

Ethel had studied her carefully. 'I have to say that you're the last person I ever expected to see teaching here.'

'I love teaching,' Alice had replied, 'and the pupils seem to like me.'

Ethel had continued to study the remarkable face. But she didn't accept the story – Alice was too beautiful to stay hidden away at Netherlands for ever. It might be all right for poor Miss Lees, but Alice was born for better things – and she had the beauty and the wit to achieve them.

'Well, you be careful,' Ethel had replied warningly. 'I still say that you're up to something. Watch out that you don't tie a knot with your tongue that you can't undo with your teeth. Evan Thomas thought he was the favourite – he won't like being the loser.'

'Don't worry,' Alice had reassured her, 'I'm doing fine. Honestly, Ethel, I'm doing fine.'

Sighing, Ethel returned her thoughts to the present as she picked up the laundry. Then she looked at Gilbert. He had grown to love Alice over the years and she had seen in him a surrogate father. Something she desperately wanted. Something she had craved since she was a child. The trouble was, Ethel thought, that she already *had* a father – a man who might still be alive.

'I think Alice might make a career of teaching,' Ethel said. 'I hope so. I want her to settle down and marry some nice lad –'

'Hey, she's only seventeen!' Gilbert said sharply. 'Give her a chance.'

'Marriage *would* settle her down,' Ethel responded. 'A good solid home life would be the making of her.' She thought back to the damning facts that only she knew. 'The right man would give Alice stability.'

'She's got stability,' Gilbert retorted. 'She's much less excitable than she used to be.'

Ethel shook her head. 'Not really. That's just what she *wants* you to think. That's what she wants *all* of us to think.'

Clare Lees prided herself on the good job she had made of Alice Rimmer's upbringing. The hysterical little girl who had arrived at Netherlands had been moulded into a clever young woman. She had calmed down, was reliable, and the children loved her. Oh yes, Clare thought, she had really achieved something with that girl.

Awkwardly she rose to her feet, her shoulders rounded and aching. The cold always made the pain worse, but what could you do about it in the middle of a Salford winter? Slowly she moved over to the fire and poked at the cheap coal. The room smelled damp to her, but maybe she was imagining it. Soon she would be in too much pain to keep going, but she had to hold on a bit longer, until Alice was twenty-one. Then she would be ready.

Clare gazed into the half-hearted flames. She had managed to raise more money from the governors, but she was well aware that Netherlands was hopelessly out of date and would require far more to be spent on it. They needed better plumbing, electrification throughout, updated furniture, desks, even coat pegs. And books. Lots of books to replace the dog-eared volumes which had passed through the hands of countless orphans.

The governors saw her as a dinosaur; Clare knew that all too well. She was a joke to them, but they couldn't dislodge her because she had been loyal and given good service; dedicated her life to Netherlands . . . Clare nudged the coal with the tip of her boot. It shifted in the grate and sent up a little puff of smoke.

Alice would bring a breath of fresh air, a young outlook. That would impress the money men. They would look at Netherlands in a new light then, not as some outdated Victorian anachronism. Clare stretched her hands out to the fire to warm them. Thank God that no one knew the truth about Alice Rimmer, she thought. If they had, all her careful plans would fold. But how could anyone find out? The solicitor who had sent the child to her so long ago had died, and the single evidence of Alice's past was in a locked-up file to which only Clare herself had access.

Settling herself down on a chair in front of the fire, Clare thought of Alice's secret and how it had weighed on her mind. A year ago something had suddenly prompted her to remove Alice Rimmer's file from her office. It had always been in safekeeping there, but its very existence had been beginning to nag at her. At first she had decided to destroy it, but that had seemed too extreme, so in the end she had put it in the bank with other confidential papers. There no one would find it. Clare knew only too well that people like Evan Thomas and Dolly Blake would be dangerous with such knowledge.

It would not have mattered had Alice Rimmer been just another foundling. If she had been a plain, dull child she would have sunk into the background; gone to work in a mill or as an undermaid for some well-off family. A different child would not have had the wit or the spirit to spark interest – but Alice had never been an ordinary child and she had all the making of an extraordinary woman.

Clare Lees' envy of Alice had faded as the years bent her shoulders and took away all ambition or curiosity about the world. Now she merely admired Alice. The skittish child had grown up and become a responsible person, a young woman she could trust. And there were precious few people Clare Lees could trust.

She knew she was – and always had been – surrounded by opportunists. The Welshman was always waiting for his chance and was proving a jealous rival to Alice. As for Dolly Blake, she was washed up, a bitter woman consumed with righteousness. If she was getting no affection in her own life, no one else would. Every woman – simply by nature of being female – was now suspect to Dolly.

But Alice . . . Clare relaxed and then rubbed her shoulders. If she carried on the way she was, Alice Rimmer could be a person of some status. Memory came back quick and sharp – Alice Rimmer had been *born* to privilege but life and circumstance had take it away from her. If she knew the truth Alice would want far more than Netherlands had to offer. She would want her birthright – the birthright Clare Lees had so vigorously denied.

But it had been for the best, she reassured herself. It had been hard to shatter a child's hopes, but it had cured Alice. In fact, she had no curiosity about her past any more. She never referred to her family or asked questions. The spirited, overconfident little girl had been reined in: Alice Rimmer would be content to live the life organised for her. She would serve, as Clare Lees had always done. She would do her duty.

It was the least she could do.

Chapter Eleven

'Sssh, keep your voice down,' Victor said, leaning towards the gate which separated the boys' quarters from the girls' at Netherlands. His fingers reached through the railings timidly and touched the back of Alice's hand. The feel of her skin warmed him, touched him to the heart.

'Victor, can't you sneak out?' she asked, her eyes searching his shadowed face.

'It's not safe, tomorrow maybe.'

She nodded, disappointed but resigned. A sound behind her made Alice turn, but it was only a night bird in the bushes. To her right she could see the light burning in Clare Lees' office.

'We have to be careful.'

'We're always careful,' Alice replied, not a little impatiently. How could he be so patient? She knew he cared for her.

Memory came in a tidal wave.

It had been a hot August day last summer, sun beating down the yard, dusty outside. Drowsy children had hung about listlessly in their dormitories, the staff idling in the corridors. Clare Lees had had visitors, the governors, the murmur of their voices coming low and lulling on the warm air. Alice, walking in the yard outside the main doors, had glanced over to the boys' quarters – to see a tall, blond youth watching her.

Startled, she had looked away. Then turned back. He'd stared at her and then smiled slowly, as though it was something he was unused to doing. Nervous, Alice had looked away again, and when she had finally glanced back he had gone.

Yet later, still on that drowsy day which had hung its head to evening, when she walked back out into the yard he was there again, watching her.

'Who are you?' Alice had asked, walking over.

She had seen him on and off for years, but had never dared speak to him before. Well aware of the trouble she would be in if she was caught talking to one of the boys, Alice had glanced round to check that no one was watching her. She'd felt excited, her old spirit flaring.

He'd pressed his cheek to the bars. 'I'm Victor, Victor Coates.'

'How old are you?'

'Eighteen. And you?'

'Sixteen.' She'd moved closer to him.

His eyes were steel grey, the lashes brown. It was a strong, open face, not at all alarming. After all that she had heard about boys and how they were not to be trusted, Alice had been disinclined to believe Clare Lees. What did she know, a spinster, a woman who had never had a man of her own?

'We shouldn't be talking . . .'

'I know,' Alice had agreed, her voice dropping further. 'How long have you been here?'

'Since I was seven.'

'What happened?'

He'd frowned. 'Huh?'

'Why did you come here?'

'My parents died.' He had paused. 'How about you?'

Alice had stared down at her feet. 'My parents are dead too. I came here when I was only a year old.' She'd looked back to him, fascinated. 'Don't you go out to work?'

He'd nodded. 'I'm an apprentice at the cabinet-maker's, Mr Dedlington's.'

Alice had digested the information. An apprentice. That

meant that Victor got out of Netherlands every day, went into Salford. A free man, almost.

'Do you have to stay here?'

'Until I'm qualified, yes,' he'd replied, glancing over his shoulder. 'I give my wages over every week to Miss Lees – I just get to keep enough for tobacco and a few bits and pieces.'

'Why do you have to give up your money?' she'd asked indignantly. 'You earned it.'

'It's just the way things are here. When you start working, you'll have to do the same.'

He had looked round again, knowing what he risked by being discovered. No more pocket money then, and in all likelihood they would take away his apprenticeship and give it to another boy. But he couldn't tear himself away from Alice.

'I'm not giving my money to them!' she had replied hotly.

He had seen the flicker in her dark eyes and had been awed by her. 'Are you working already?'

'I'm learning how to be a teacher –'

He had whistled under his breath. *A teacher*, now that *was* really something.

'You must be smart.'

'Smart enough to want to get out of here,' Alice had replied, leaning against the railings.

She had realised in that moment that this was the first conversation she had ever had as an equal. Ethel and Gilbert loved her, but she was a surrogate daughter to them. As for Hilly, she was grateful and looked up to Alice as her role model. But Victor was different; they had talked easily, from the heart.

'You'll get out in time.'

'Not if Miss Lees has her way,' Alice had replied quietly.

His curiosity had been stirred. 'How d'you mean?'

'She wants to train me up to be her assistant.' Alice had

replied. 'I think she wants me to stay and eventually take over from her.'

Victor had been goggle-eyed with amazement.

'God . . .' Then he suddenly turned and moved away, leaving Alice standing alone by the gate.

But not for long; she too had heard the footsteps and had already been making her way back to the entrance when Evan Thomas moved in front of her.

'Hello, Alice,' he'd said pleasantly, his Welsh accent strong.

'Hello, sir,' she'd replied, moving past him.

Immediately he had stepped into her way.

'You look pretty this afternoon, Alice.' She had said nothing. 'Pretty as a picture. Almost flushed about the cheeks. What's that with, then?'

'The heat, sir,' she had replied coolly.

He couldn't have seen her talking to Victor or he would have reported her to Miss Lees already. No, Alice had realised, he was just fishing, scenting something in the air.

'You want to watch overheating yourself, Alice. You should stay indoors and not excite yourself.'

She had looked him square in the eyes. I know you don't like me, Alice had thought. But I'm not going to be stupid enough to let you catch me out.

'You're right, sir,' she'd said at last, walking past him. 'Thank you for your concern.'

That day was almost a year ago, and since that time Alice and Victor had become more than friends. As Clare Lees relied more and more on her protégée, she little realised that Alice was sneaking off to meet Victor Coates whenever she could. Although she had bored of her evening wanderings, Alice now found a new reason to escape Netherlands. Victor might protest, insist that they were heading for trouble, but he always gave in.

They would usually meet under the viaduct, Alice waiting impatiently, or running to Victor if he arrived first.

What began as an innocent prank soon altered, though; their friendship was immediate – and so was their attraction. Aware of her age and wary of her exuberance, Victor tried to resist. But they were children who had had little affection in their lives and now took it, greedily, from one another.

It was dangerous in more ways than one. If Clare Lees found out, Alice's rise would be over and the hated Welshman would become the favourite again. And with him would go Dolly Blake, clinging to his coat-tails like an angry beggar. Then what would there be left for Alice? Going into service, or a factory. But there was something else to consider. If they were caught Victor would be sent away. Alice shivered. If Victor was sent away, her life would be empty. And she couldn't follow him, because she would never know where he had gone. They would never tell her.

She couldn't bear that; couldn't stomach the thought of losing him. They had tried to resist each other, only touching hands at first and whispering to each other, but after a year passed every touch of the hand became more powerful than the last. Her voice he heard above everyone else's; his face she saw amongst the scores of children at the home. They had found love in each other and were holding on to it against all the odds. And the very danger of their situation made their feelings stronger daily.

So the months passed. With Clare Lees, Alice was dutiful and patient. She would made a fine teacher, Clare said, it was good to know that the future would be in a steady pair of hands. Ethel was proud of her too. As was Gilbert. But at night Alice forgot every duty heaped on her head and crept out to the town. Or, as this evening, to the partition railings where she rested her cheek against the bars, only an inch away from Victor's.

'Do you love me?' she asked, looking up at the huge summer moon.

'You know I do,' he whispered.

She moved towards him, her hands pressed against the bars. 'Then why don't we run away?'

'They'd catch us!'

'They wouldn't!' Alice replied firmly. 'Don't you want us to be together?'

'More than anything,' Victor replied, 'but it would be wrong. We have to wait, Alice. I'm nineteen now; when I reach twenty-one I'll have finished my apprenticeship and we can get married –'

'That's two years from now!' Alice replied, her face half lit by the yellow moon. 'How can you ask me to wait two years? You don't have to work with Clare Lees. You don't want to get away from here as much as I do.'

He caught hold of her hand. She could get so excited, he thought, so fired up.

'Ssssh!' he warned her. 'Two years isn't long, Alice. I love you, you know that. If we wait we can do it right –'

She pulled her hand away from his. 'I don't want to *do it right*! I want to live now, not in two years' time. Anything could happen in two years!' Her voice rose suddenly and she got to her feet to move away.

Hurriedly Victor caught at the hem of her summer dress. 'Hey! Don't run away, let's talk, Alice, please.'

But she was past talking that night. Angrily she pulled away her skirt and moved off, Victor watching her as she turned and walked through the heavy double doors of the entrance hall.

He waited for her at the viaduct the following night, and the night afterwards. But she didn't come. On the third night he waited in the rain and then, after midnight, turned to leave. Only then did he hear her footsteps and moved back to the railings, just as Alice – wet hair sticking to her head – ran to him and brushed her lips hotly against his neck.

Victor's hand grasped hers. 'Oh, thank God, thank God. I thought you'd never come again.'

68

'I had to,' Alice replied. She had tried to keep away, but couldn't resist any longer. 'I missed you, I missed you so much.'

'Then you agree that we'll wait?' Victor asked her, holding her face in his hands.

'Yes, yes!' she said, tossing her wet hair away from her face. 'If I can . . . I'll try, Victor. But I hate it at Netherlands. I hate it more and more every day. I'm lying to everyone, even Ethel. As for Clare Lees, I'm betraying her and it makes me feel so guilty.'

'But she was never kind to you.'

'I know,' Alice agreed, 'I know! But all this creeping about's not funny any more. I care about you, Victor. It was a joke at first, but now, if anyone found out and they sent you away . . .' She took in a quick breath and he clung on to her.

'No one will, we just have to be careful, that's all.' He could sense her panic, her alarm. 'Calm down, Alice, please. We have to be very careful and wait.'

She nodded, the rain falling down from the dark sky.

'We have to meet less often –'

'No!' she shouted, her arms wrapping around him, her body pressing against his. He was aware of her scent and passion, aware that he wanted her more than anything.

'Sweetheart, you know as well as I do that we can't hide our feelings,' he said quietly, his hands moving into her hair and turning her face up to his.

Slowly he kissed her cheeks, her closed eyelids, her mouth, his excitement rising, their bodies moulded into each other. He thought, for a drowsy instant, that he was drowning.

Suddenly he drew away. 'Alice, we have to be more careful. We'll give ourselves away. Someone will see us if we don't hold back a bit.'

'I can't live without you.'

'We'll meet up every Sunday night. *Every Sunday*, here

at the viaduct. If one of us can't get away, we'll meet at the railings at Netherlands after lights out.' He kissed the tips of her fingers. 'Alice, we have to be clever and get through this. We have to be cunning for another two years. Then we're free. You understand, don't you? You can do what I ask, can't you, sweetheart? Can't you?'

Her heart was pumping fast, her head spinning. How many Sundays were there in two years? Could she live through them? But what was the choice? If she was careless she lost Victor. And if she lost Victor, she lost everything.

Her hand went up to his face and cupped his cheek.

'I love you,' she said earnestly. 'The time will pass quickly, Victor, won't it? It will, won't it?'

In the courtyard of Netherland Evan Thomas lit a cigarette and then carefully blew out the match. He sniffed the air and then brushed some nonexistent fluff off his shoulder. Summer nights – he usually hated them. Too hot to sleep, too hot to work. But not too hot to walk . . . His full lips curled into a satisfied smile and he inhaled deeply.

Women were all the same. They could never keep their heads. He slipped back into the shadows and watched as Alice ran noiselessly back into the home. Now where had she been? he wondered. She had obviously sneaked out, but to where? And why?

The Welshman smiled again, truly happy. Alice Rimmer had caused him some grief, but perhaps he would soon be able to repay the compliment. All he had to do was to watch her and find out what she was up to, then he could expose her . . . She had been so smug, so certain of her standing with Clare Lees. She had usurped him good and proper. But that was all about to change. When their beloved principal learned that her protégée was not quite as perfect as she seemed . . . Oh yes, Evan could imagine the fracas which would follow. Clare would feel betrayed and would be sure to punish Alice. Off the pedestal the girl would go, and back on would go Evan.

How sad. But there you were, Evan told himself, he had a duty to do. Alice Rimmer had defied the home's rules of conduct; shown her true cólours. She was deceitful; certainly not the kind of woman to look after children.

He whistled between his teeth. He was tempted to tell Clare immediately, but thought it better to bide his time. After all, what *had* he to tell her? Only that Alice Rimmer sneaked out at night. If he went now, it was simply his word against the girl's. And Clare liked Alice Rimmer. God forbid, Clare might even take her side. But if he waited and could find out *why* Alice went out – and if he could give Clare Lees *proof* . . .

Yes, that was what was needed. Proof . . . Evan sighed. The rain had stopped and the night was placid again. Like himself. Slowly he unlocked the wrought-iron gates and passed through them onto the street outside. It looked commonplace to him.

He was thankful that it looked so tempting to Alice Rimmer.

Chapter Twelve

The governors of Netherlands were exasperated with Clare Lees – and not for the first time. She was too much of an authoritarian, they said. Times had changed, there was no need for Victorian values any more. They had to hand it her, though; she had done sterling work at Netherlands, but her regime was outdated.

They told her so. She told them that she was preparing someone – one of the orphans – to take over from her in a few years' time. This was news.

The Reverend Mr Grantley helped himself to three more biscuits and leaned his head towards Mrs Tomkinson, wife of Albert Tomkinson, wealthiest man in Salford. She moved away from the dyed head looming towards her and smiled stiffly.

'A new brush always sweeps clean,' she said.

Mr Grantley nodded and swallowed his second custard cream. Beside him sat the local MP, Sir Henry Hollis, irritable as a cornered wolf. The vicar addressed him.

'I think –'

'What's that?' Sir Henry said, leaning towards Mr Grantley, his thin face pinched with irritation.

'Mrs Tomkinson was talking about Alice Rimmer, the young lady who might take over from Miss Lees.'

'When?'

The clergyman sighed. 'In a few years. Miss Lees has just been telling us about it.'

'I didn't hear anything about some foreigner.'

The vicar paused in his chewing and looked at the old man. 'Which foreigner?'

'This one you're bloody talking about, Grantley!' he snapped. 'Don't horse me about, I'm not a man to mess with.'

Mrs Tomkinson leaned across the vicar, the feather on her hat brushing crumbs off his biscuit.

'We weren't talking about a *foreigner*, Henry. We were talking about the young lady who is going to take over from Miss Lees.'

'I don't like foreigners!' Sir Henry went on. 'You can never understand a thing they say.'

Mr Grantley smiled obsequiously. 'I don't think –'

'You're right there,' Sir Henry replied, 'You never did think much. I could never see why you were made a governor here anyway.'

Mrs Tomkinson leaned further towards the old man, the vicar forced back into his seat.

'I think it's a good idea to train someone new for the position. We need new blood. Besides, the girl is an orphan; has been here since she was a child. From what I've heard, she seems admirably suited.'

The girl was at that moment waiting outside. Clare Lees had primed Alice carefully and was determined that her charge would impress the governors. It would reflect well on her, and besides, if Alice Rimmer succeeded to her job, Clare would never have to relinquish her status at Netherlands entirely.

Nervously, she went out to bring Alice before her inquisitors.

'You know what to say, don't you?'

Alice nodded. She was dressed in a navy suit, her full dark hair pulled back. The remarkable face was composed. Thank God, Clare thought, that its beauty had toned down – now that the wildness was gone.

'I know what to say,' Alice replied evenly.

'I'm relying on you,' Clare responded. 'This is the chance of a lifetime, Alice. Do us both proud.'

Breathing in deeply, Clare ushered Alice before the governors. It was another sweltering day, Mrs Tomkinson looking like a broiled chicken under her feathered hat, Mr Grantley still chewing on his last biscuit. As for the old man beside him, Sir Henry seemed as dry and hard as a rock bun.

'Sit down, young lady,' he said, watching as Alice did so. 'We've heard a lot about you. A great deal. You seem to have impressed Miss Lees. So you want to be principal here in due course?'

Alice nodded, then wondered how she had been cajoled into this position. No, she wanted to say. I don't want to be principal of this dismal place. I don't want to be another Clare Lees. I want to run away with Victor and get as much distance between myself and these grim walls as I can.

But she didn't say it.

'Miss Lees believes I can do the job –'

'Speak up!' Sir Henry snapped. 'I can't stand a woman who whispers.'

'I said I believe I can do the job,' Alice repeated, turning to look at Mrs Tomkinson.

The woman was watching her with an expression of interest and envy. She had been taken aback when Alice walked in; this was not the obedient little mouse she had been expecting. This was a beauty, a young woman who looked like she could turn heads and hearts. Hardly someone who would be satisfied with Netherlands.

'Are you *sure* this is what you want?' she asked Alice coolly. 'I mean, Netherlands is not the most exciting place on earth. My husband was saying only the other day that he couldn't for the life of him see why anyone would want to work here.' She turned her head, the feathers on her hat wiping the underneath of the vicar's nose. 'It would be hard work.'

'Indeed, indeed,' Mr Grantley replied, nodding violently.

'But you would be repaying the debt you owe,' Mrs Tomkinson continued. 'I mean, Netherlands has been a home to you since you were a baby.'

A *home*, Alice thought angrily. What kind of home was always damp, cold, overcrowded, comfortless? What kind of home, Mrs Tomkinson, Alice wanted to ask, never held its children? Or picked them up when they cried? I don't owe you a thing. Not a bloody thing.

But she said nothing of what she was feeling, her eyes unfathomable. 'I think I could do the job –'

'That's not what I'm asking, is it?' Mrs Tomkinson replied. 'I need to know – we all need to know – if you are *suitable*.'

Alice studied her dispassionately. She knew who Leonora Tomkinson was and wondered how a woman as ridiculous and plump as she was could have landed a rich husband. Rumour had it that her Albert wasn't faithful, but Alice doubted if his wife minded. After all, she had the power and the money, why should she worry about her husband's flings?

'I've been at Netherlands nearly all my life,' Alice went on calmly. 'I know how the home runs.'

'But would you be prepared –'

'What?' Sir Henry interrupted, 'what about *affairs*?'

'No one said anything about *affairs*!' Mrs Tomkinson snapped, her head whipping round and catching Mr Grantley in the eye with a feather. 'I was about to ask Alice Rimmer if she would be *prepared* to dedicate her life to Netherlands.'

'I didn't hear that –'

Mrs Tomkinson rolled her eyes. 'Because I hadn't got around to saying it.'

'Then how could the girl answer?' Sir Henry asked blithely.

At this point Clare Lees interrupted. 'I took the liberty to write out some notes for all of you about Alice,' she said, gesturing to the papers in front of them. 'They explain why I think she is qualified and what her qualities are that make her the best candidate for the post.'

'I thought you were keen on your Welsh deputy head?' Mr Grantley said, ducking to dodge the pheasant feathers.

Clare was not about to be sidetracked. 'Mr Evans has many good points, but I feel that Alice – although so young – would make the better principal.'

'Well,' Mrs Tomkinson said, looking over to Alice. 'She certainly seems very . . . composed.'

'I was thinking the very same thing,' the Vicar chimed in.

Ignoring him, Mrs Tomkinson asked Clare Lees, 'Do you think that this girl could really be your successor?'

Alice could feel her temper flare. They were talking about her as though she wasn't there. And what could she do about it? She was a nobody, some orphan who had to be grateful for any consideration. She was beholden to them – these powerful people who had given her a home, who were now considering her for a position as lifelong dogsbody. It made her sick, Alice thought. She wanted to knock off Leonora Tomkinson's ludicrous hat and push the Vicar's dyed head into the plate of biscuits.

Clare Lees was aware that there was a friction in the air and did her best to soothe it.

'Mrs Tomkinson, Alice has the makings of a very good teacher, and she is very reliable. She works hard and explains her lessons clearly.'

'I dare say . . . but are you willing to make running Netherlands your life's work?'

Alice smiled, almost surprised to be addressed directly.

'Yes,' she lied, the sarcasm tingling her tongue. 'it would be an honour.'

They were selling her into slavery, Alice thought, the dull drone of Leonora Tomkinson's voice continuing, Sir Henry peering at her through his thick glasses. Her attention wandered to the courtyard outside. It was Friday; soon it would be Sunday and she would see Victor again. Her eyes fixed on the wall outside, sunlight making it temporarily golden.

She should tell them that she wasn't interested in being the principal – but what would that do? Result in her being sent off to a menial job outside. But so what? Alice wondered. Outside it would be easier to meet up with Victor . . . Oh Victor, she wondered, why don't I tell them that I don't give a damn about any of this?

Then she remembered what he had told her so many times. *You have a chance to be someone, take it. I'll be a qualified tradesman and you'll be a teacher. When we leave then we can make some real money. Think about it*, he'd urged her. *You're too clever to be a nobody.*

So she went along with it.

'Alice?'

She turned to Mrs Tomkinson. 'Yes, ma'am?'

'I have to tell you that I'm not wholly convinced –'

'Well, I like the girl,' Sir Henry interjected.

Mrs Tomkinson gave him a look that should have turned him into a pile of ash there and then.

'I like her and I think it's a good idea. I'm not a man to mess with and I approve,' the old man went on, Clare Lees beaming. 'You have my permission to train her up. We need a good-looking young woman to bring this place into the present.'

Clare Lees wasn't sure why Alice's good looks made her the right candidate, but she didn't complain. If she got her way, that was all that was important. So she happily ushered Alice back out into the corridor and briefly tapped the girl's shoulder.

'You did well.'

For a moment Alice felt a real guilt. She wanted to confess that she was a fraud, that she didn't want the job. Then she thought of the odious Welshman and smiled.

'Thank you, Miss Lees.'

'Mrs Tomkinson needs to be won over, but Sir Henry has the real clout, so what he says, goes,' Clare went on. 'This is an important day, Alice. This is a day which marks out the rest of your life.'

The words wedged firmly into Alice's chest like an arrow tipped with poison.

Chapter Thirteen

It was a wicked late summer that year. Temperatures were high, the mills belching out their fetid smoke into the muggy overhang of sky. Salford steamed under the sun, the doors of the terraced houses thrown open to let in some air, the streets greasy with the light evening showers which did nothing to cool, only increased the humidity. The warmth – unexpected and oppressive – fell like a smothering mattress. The town was choked with hot people, flea-bitten dogs and food going rancid before its time.

But inside the thick walls of Netherlands it was cool, untouched by the heat. Untouched by anything.

'Good Lord,' Ethel said to Hilly, mopping her forehead. The girl was sick again, back in the sanatorium. 'I've just got back from town and it's smouldering. I can't take this heat, and as for Gilbert, he's a martyr to the summer.'

Hilly smiled her long-distance smile.

'They said there would be thunderstorms.' Her voice was weak, as insubstantial as she was.

'Good God, I hope so. Something has to break,' Ethel replied, folding some sheets and peering at a hole in the cotton. 'I've never known it so hot.'

Later that night Ethel was lying next to Gilbert, a single sheet over them both. Then thrown off. Then pulled back again.

Sticky and overtired, Gilbert grumbled, turning constantly.

'Aye, Ethel, it's like sleeping next to a fire, luv. Get over your own side of the bed, you're burning me up.'

His wife, hair damp against her neck, was not in the mood to be patient.

'It's as hot for me as it is for you, Gilbert Cummings! You want to stop grumbling. I've hardly had any bloody sleep and I've a job to go to in the morning.' She rolled her bulk over and lay on her back, Gilbert muttering beside her.

She couldn't sleep so she might as well think. Her thoughts turned to Alice immediately and Ethel smiled to herself. It had been a real worry for a long time, wondering how the girl would turn out, but things were going to be OK. The governors had been impressed by her, Sir Henry Hollis especially. As for Clare Lees, she had been beaming when she told Ethel – for once confiding, even happy.

Oh yes, Alice was set up nicely. She would take over from Miss Lees and, Ethel hoped, meet some nice young man and marry him. She should have children too. After all, the principal of the home didn't have to be single, did she?

Ethel frowned as Gilbert nudged her. 'You're leaning against me, luv, move over.'

'There was a time when you'd have done anything to have me lean against you,' she teased him, feeling Gilbert take her hand.

Again, her thoughts wandered. How *would* Alice meet a man at the home? The place was full of children and the few teachers there were hardly eligible. Ethel thought suddenly of Evan Thomas and grimaced. Now there was a man who could tell a lie and prove it . . . No, Alice would have to get out and about more to find a suitor.

It was silly the way the home was run; the children kept apart. They should be mixing with the local children long before they left – learning to act and behave naturally. As if the sigma of being an orphan wasn't enough, Ethel thought. She had heard what the townspeople said; how they kept their distance from the Netherlands offspring and advised their children to do the same. *Don't go staring at the orphans. They have to rely on charity. If you're bad, you'll be sent to that big ugly building and left there . . .*

Local gossip had long since sentenced Netherlands to be an island in the midst of the town. Many of the people outside might be poor, but they had families, which was more than a Netherlands child did. The shabby hand-me-down clothes didn't help either. Ethel had heard of many of the girls going out to work in service and being teased. As for the boys, there had been a number of fights caused by people mocking the institution head-shaving and wooden clogs.

Some of the children bolted when they came of age and left the town. Tommy Cotterall had done just that and ended up – two years later – in Strangeways for theft, a fact which only compounded people's suspicions of the orphans. Others automatically slipped into the role of sub-servient dogsbodies and lived their lives in the shadows. They should be grateful that they had been given a home, a job, a chance, the mantra went.

Hardly any of them made anything of their lives. But how *could* they? Ethel wondered. The education was rudimentary and they had no social graces. They were orphans, the stigma running through them like a place name in a stick of rock.

But Alice . . . she was going to be the one to show them all. She was going to make them proud. People would look at her and be impressed, and in time she would become a marvellous figurehead for Netherlands. And no one, but *no one*, would ever know who she really was. Least of all herself.

Uncomfortable again, Ethel moved.

'Oh, stay still!' Gilbert moaned. 'You're like fly on an elephant's arse.'

She jabbed him in the ribs and turned over.

What would Alice have done if she'd discovered her

past? The thought made Ethel sweat. It would have been a disaster and, knowing Alice as she did, Ethel realised she would not have been able to cope with the knowledge and the damnation it would surely bring. No one would have given her a chance if they had discovered who her father was; and if Alice had known, highly strung as she was, she would have been crushed under such a burden.

Thank God, Ethel thought, that there was no need to worry any more. The past was just that, the *past*. A secret no one knew, and no one could uncover. Alice Rimmer was safe from the gossips.

And from herself.

Chapter Fourteen

The heat built up over the next three days and by Sunday evening the town was smouldering. In the park the trees hung listlessly, the gravel outside the entrance door of Netherlands dusty and whitened. Buses droned past the gates and when Mr Grantley read the sermon at evensong the air was drowsy, eyelids drooping closed amongst the congregation.

Everyone agreed that the heat couldn't last, but the promised rainstorms hadn't come. Slowed by the temperature and her arthritis, Clare Lees took a while to reach the lectern and when she read the lesson her voice snuffled amongst the pews like an animal looking for shade to hide. The day had seemed to pass like a dream, nothing substantial, and when the service was over the congregation walked out into the humid air and winced.

As always, Alice had sat next to Clare Lees and stolen a few glances at Dolly Blake, stiff in a paisley dress, her round face shiny. Behind her had sat Evan Thomas, as glossy as an apple, catching Alice's eye and smiling. She had not smiled back.

Standing on the hot gravel outside, Alice paused and glanced at her watch. In three hours' time she would see Victor. The thought soothed and excited her at the same time. Victor, who was so sensible; Victor, who was planning their future; Victor, who loved her, controlled her impulses and made her think of their future.

She wondered how she could possibly have lived without him. How *could* she have endured the grind at the home? The persistent lecturings of Clare Lees? The yawning future which would have loped before her so unappetisingly? Without him, Alice knew she would never have gone on. She would have run away, done something reckless.

But there was no need to be reckless now. She had found her rock, her man. All she had to do was to follow his lead and they would be together ... She glanced at her watch again. Hurry up, she urged, hurry up. I want to see him, to touch his hand, to hear his voice. Loving Victor was easy. The easiest thing that she'd ever done.

'Expecting someone?'

Alice turned at the sound of Evan's voice. His brown eyes were hard as nuts.

'No, should I?'

'I just wondered. You keep looking at your watch.'

She shrugged, but her heart was thumping. This was a man who hated her and would do anything to ruin her. Be careful, Alice told herself, be very careful.

'It was a good sermon.'

Unexpectedly, Evan laughed. 'Oh really, how can you say such a thing?' He leaned towards her. 'You're a good liar, aren't you, Alice?'

A vein was throbbing in her neck. 'No better than you, sir,' she answered back.

He was nettled by the remark. 'I doubt if I'm in your league,' he replied peevishly. 'You've had so much practice.'

'I don't know what you're talking about –'

'Secrets . . .' he said distantly. Then his tone brightened. 'I'm off now. Going out tonight. I bet you wish you could go out, Alice, don't you? A pretty girl like you could go dancing, have the lads all of a – flutter.'

The sun had gone down, but the air was moist, hot, and clung to her like a demanding child.

'I'm happy where I am.'

'There you go,' Evan said, smiling, 'lying again.'

Alice watched him walk towards the gates and stayed

watching him until he passed through them and locked them behind him. He paused to look through the bars at her and she shuddered. There was something about his look, some smugness, that made her stomach churn.

'Are you OK?' Hilly asked, walking over and looking at Alice anxiously.

'I'm fine,' Alice replied, her voice strained. Eager to shake off the feeling of unease, she slipped her arm through Hilly's. 'Glad you're out of the sanatorium.'

'Me too. I don't suppose I'll be out for long, though.'

Alice squeezed her arm. 'You're getting stronger every day.'

Laughing, Hilly teased her. 'Oh, Alice, that's a lie and you know it.'

The word tingled in the air and, spooked, Alice turned back towards the gate. But there was no man looking in. And all she could see was the quick flash of a bicycle wheel as it passed on its way to God knows where.

Clare Lees was slumped in her easy chair in the office. Her back hurt her and it was painful even to move. So she had wedged herself against the seat and waited for the spasm to pass. Which it would, in time. Her eyes fixed on the print on the opposite wall. It was of a man on horseback, wielding a banner ... Above her head she could hear the sound of footsteps running and then a door banged closed. She winced. How many times had she told the children not to run? Dolly should stop it, or Evan ... Then she remembered that Evan was off that night. Clumsily, Clare shifted in her seat again and looked out of the window. Her throat tightened. She hated the view, loathed the dull block of gravel and the closed mouth of the gates. Hated the sign in wrought iron – 'NETHERLANDS HOME FOR CHILDREN' – and the chained padlock glinting in the dying light.

It was just because she was in pain, she told herself.

Before long she would feel better, more like her old self . . . But although the spasm lifted after a while, her mood stayed sombre. The darkness was coming down and the Sunday night town was falling quiet. Only muffled noises from hidden lives crept intermittently over the closed gates.

Shivering, Clare felt herself grow cold in the humid air, and lowered her head. Something pressed against her heart and hung around her chair.

The world was wicked that night.

'I love you so much,' Victor said, holding Alice's hand tightly. His skin seemed to burn into hers. 'I could see you in the chapel. You looked so beautiful.'

They had arranged to meet at the viaduct, but that morning Victor had signalled their private sign in church to say that they should meet at the Netherlands railings after lights out instead.

Alice nuzzled against the bars, the metal for once warm to the touch. 'I've been thinking about you all day. I could hardly wait to see you.'

He put his hand in his pocket and brought out a brown paper bag, passing it to Alice through the railings.

'What's this?' she asked, surprised.

'Open it,' he said simply, watching her face as she did so.

'It's perfume!' Alice said excitedly. 'Oh, my God! I've never had perfume before.' Carefully she dabbed a little on her wrists and drank in the scent, her eyes closed. 'Thank you, Victor, thank you.'

He thought in that moment that if he died there and then he would never be happier.

'It must have cost so much,' she whispered. 'How did you afford it?'

'I saved up,' he said proudly. 'Only the best is good enough for you, Alice. In time we'll only have the best. You wait and see, one day we'll have a fine house and money. You'll have enough perfume to bathe in.'

She laughed, the sound throaty, mesmeric.

'I love it . . .' Alice said, 'and I love *you*.'

The heat curled around them as she put her arms through the bars. He did the same and for an instant it seemed that there was nothing between them. Nothing holding them apart. The night, soft and heavy, closed over them. High above a huge late summer moon – a hunter's moon – came out from behind a cloud. Its vast yellow face hung overhead and threw its light down on the two embracing figures.

Then another light came on. A sudden light. Torchlight. Alice turned, blinded, Victor holding on to her.

'Who is it? Who's there?'

There were two people, but Alice couldn't make out who they were until they were almost upon them. Then the torchlight was lowered slightly and she saw Evan Thomas – and Clare Lees. Alice's voice dried in her throat, her head falling forward.

Victor clambered to his feet. 'It's all my fault!' he blustered. 'If you want to punish anyone, punish me. It wasn't her fault. I convinced Alice to come here.'

'A nice try,' Evan replied, delighted, 'but this isn't the first time, is it?'

He had watched Alice for the past ten days. She hadn't sneaked out of Netherlands again, but his patience had finally paid off when she met up with Victor that night. It was perfect, Evan thought; nothing could look so incriminating. And from the way they had been clinging on to each other it was obvious to him – and to Clare Lees – that their relationship was not platonic.

Rigid with shock, Alice did not move, her hands still clinging to the place on the railings where Victor had been. She could sense Clare Lees looking at her.

'Is this true, Alice? *Have* you met up with this boy before?'

She nodded, too sick to speak.

'You've been going behind my back all this time?' Clare Lees went on. She seemed more stooped, older. The Welshman was grinning like a jackal at her side. 'How *could* you? How *could* you repay me like this? I trusted you –'

'Leave her alone!' Victor shouted back, frantically climbing over the railings and jumping down on the other side. Without thinking, he caught hold of Evan and shook the older man's shoulders, shouting at the top of his voice. 'We've done nothing wrong! We love each other, that's all. *We've done nothing wrong!*'

Incensed, the Welshman pushed Victor away.

Clare Lees walked over to Alice and stared down at her. Hatred seeped out of every pore.

'You should be in the dirt,' she said finally. 'That's where you came from – and where you belong.'

Chapter Fifteen

Worse was to follow. After Clare Lees told Alice to leave Netherlands immediately, Victor was similarly banished. As Clare Lees and the odious Evan walked off together, Victor turned back to an ashen-faced Alice.

'We'll marry, sweetheart, we'll get through this.'

Her expression was a blank. 'Did you hear what she said? She knows something about me, about where I came from.'

Victor snatched at her arm as Alice started to move towards the retreating figures.

'Leave it be, leave it –'

Angrily she shook him off and called after Clare Lees: 'What do you mean – *I should be in the dirt*? Where did I come from? Who am I?'

The hunter's moon shone eerily down on Clare Lees' face as she turned to her former protégée. Disappointment and rage made her ugly. But even then, even after she had seen Alice betray her and realised that her dream of the future was over, even then she wasn't cruel enough to strike the final blow.

'Get out of here. Just get out, Alice.'

'NO!' Alice's voice rose shrilly. Victor tried to pull her away but she would have none of it. She had nothing to lose any more and wanted the truth.

'Tell me! Tell me who I am!'

'I don't have to tell you anything,' Clare Lees replied, her voice hard with rage. 'I owe you nothing –'

'You owe me the truth!' Alice snapped. 'Please, for the love of God, tell me and I'll go away. Please.'

Sensing real anguish, Clare hesitated. What better way to punish Alice Rimmer once and for all? She would never know the truth from her. She could sweat and beg and cry – but she would never tell her. The truth was ghastly, but how much worse was never knowing.

By her side, Evan Thomas watched Alice writhe and saw his chance to strike. Had he been less willing to injure her he would have noticed Clare Lees' reticence; but he had hated Alice too long and wanted her gone too much to hold back. His spying had extended further than merely watching Alice. He had – on a recent errand for the principal – taken the opportunity of rifling through the old papers in the bank when he had been asked to deposit something. His surprise at coming across Alice Rimmer's file in amongst so much dull paperwork had been acute, but what he had read there was dynamite. He had wanted to shout what he knew from the rooftops, but had kept the secret, and – as was his way – decided to bide his time. Until the perfect moment arose.

'Your father was David Lewes,' he said, walking closer to Alice and looking into her face. 'If the name doesn't mean anything to you, he was the man who killed his wife. Your mother. You want to know who you are, Alice? You're the daughter of a murderer. How does that feel, to know what you are?'

Staggered, Clare Lees felt her legs weaken and then saw the look on Alice's face. The girl was staring at Evan Thomas, Victor beside her. She said nothing. Moments passed. The smug look on Evan's face disappeared. Then, finally, Alice turned and walked to the gate.

'Open it,' she said over her shoulder.

Stunned, Evan did as he was told. Victor ran to Alice's side but she shook off his hand. 'Don't! You don't want me. Stay away. No one should come near me.'

Then she moved through the heavy iron gates and before Victor could do anything she pulled them closed with a metallic clang; leaving herself on the outside and him on the inside.

Gently she reached through the bars and touched Victor's face.

'There was always something between us, wasn't there? Always something which kept us apart. You should be glad of that now.'

Chapter Sixteen

It was well known that the stupidest family in Salford were the Booths. Rumour had it that Mr Terence Booth – who worked at the UCP tripe shop – volunteered for the German army when he was called up. As for his wife, Lettie Booth, she made dresses – cheap ones for the mill girls and the women in the surroundings streets who couldn't afford 11/9d for a summer frock from the Co-op. So Lettie codged up some pretty nifty designs with end of rolls from Tommy Field's market. But she sold them too cheaply, hardly making a profit and working like a dray horse constantly to make ends meet.

Lettie was a master on the sewing machine, but otherwise semiliterate. Small, with a short-sighted stare, only she could see something fanciable in her husband, a redhead with jug ears. It was inevitable that they married, and before five years were out, they had had three little Booths, all red-headed, all jug-eared and all impressively stupid.

The Booths lived in Trafalgar Street, just a few rows from the town centre. Two doors away from their poky terrace house lived the Hopes, fierce as Huguenot martyrs, and in between lived a solitary single woman, called Alice Rimmer. She had moved into the rented accommodation a week or so before and was apparently ill.

'I've not seen hide nor hair of her,' Lettie said to her husband, who was holding a sheet of newspaper up to the fire to set it going. The summer heat had gone, Northern chill in its place. 'D'you suppose she's all right?'

The fire took suddenly and lit the bottom of Terence's newspaper. He jumped back, Lettie beating down the flames with her apron. He was left holding half of a sheet of smouldering paper, the fire roaring in the grate.

'Good blaze.'

Lettie nodded. The fact that it had nearly taken the house with it didn't seem to occur to her.

'Well, what d'you think?'

'I think it's a good blaze –'

'About the girl next door?'

Terence frowned. 'Maybe she's shy.'

'Oh yes, maybe that's it,' Lettie replied thoughtfully. Trust Terence, he could always get to the nub of the problem. 'Perhaps I should call round on her.'

'Best leave it at the moment,' the oracle replied, puffed up with his own wisdom. 'What's for tea?'

Anna Hope was looking at her husband, Mr Hope. She never called him by his first name – no one did. It was Mr Hope to everyone, even to her, and that was fine. He was brushing down his old-fashioned suit and about to return to work, his stern expression never lifting as he then turned and examined the papers in his cheap briefcase. Church work. Or was it work for the Oldham MP? Anna wasn't bothered, as long as it got her husband out of the house

In silence she waited until he had finished reading, cleared his throat and checked his image in the mirror. A dark moustache, neatly trimmed, gave him a faintly rakish look, quite at odds with his serious demeanour. The moustache had been the thing which had first attracted Anna to him, and the thing that had made her mother suspicious.

'Never trust a man with a moustache,' she had said warningly. 'They chase the girls.'

Well, Anna didn't like to contradict her mother, but Mr Hope wasn't the type to chase girls; didn't like them as a race, thought them flighty, empty-headed. Which was why he liked his wife. Anna was stern, unbending, a lady down to her corsets.

'I'll be home after seven,' he pronounced, extending his cheek to his wife to be dutifully pecked. 'Thank you for dinner, my dear.'

His accent was Northern, but affected in the vowels by many years of sucking up to richer, more powerful people. At thirty, Mr Hope had thought he would be someone; at forty he had started to get nervous; and at fifty he was now certain that he was doomed to the life of a gofer. *Mr No Hope*, Anna called him. But never to his face.

'I saw the girl who moved into next door,' Anna said suddenly. 'Looks flighty.'

Mr Hope was pleased to hear it. After all, what would a decent girl be doing living alone?

'I think you should stay away from her,' he said warningly. 'No point mixing with the wrong sort.'

Anna nodded, turned her wheelchair to the front door and let her husband out. She stood watching him until his stiff little figure had busied itself off round the corner and then moved back indoors, resting her ear against the adjoining wall to see if she could hear any signs of life from her neighbour.

At that moment Alice was sitting staring at an empty fire grate. She had sat there on and off for days, only moving to do the necessary functions of living. Otherwise she remained immobile and didn't care what happened to her. The house had been rented by Victor, who was still working out his apprenticeship at Mr Dedlington's. He had asked for an advance on his wage and was granted it – along with a warning that it was the first and last time.

The night that Alice had left Netherlands, Victor had followed, catching up with her in Dudley Street.

'Wait for me!' he had called after her, running to her side. 'Alice, where are you going?'

'Does it matter?'

Her face had been devoid of expression and his heart had shifted. The appalling truth – coming so cruelly – had shaken him, but it had not affected the way he felt about Alice. They *would* marry, he decided. It was sooner rather than later, but they could manage somehow. They would have to.

'Alice, don't run away from me. This changes nothing –'

'It changes everything,' she'd replied dully. 'You don't want me, not now.'

'I love you.'

She had hung her head, weary with shock. 'David Lewes. My father . . .' She'd turned to Victor. 'I have to find out more –'

'Why!' he had snapped, unusually impatient. 'It'll do you no good.'

'So what do I do? Forget it? Forget what he said –'

'It could have been a lie.'

Alice had shaken her head. 'Oh no, that was no lie. Didn't you see Clare Lees' face? She's known all along.' Her voice had dropped. 'I don't know what to do.'

'Marry me.'

'What! No, I have to work things out. I can't let you carry me. You have to think about it, Victor, think about what I am. What this means.'

He'd caught hold of her and pulled her to him. 'It means nothing. *Nothing.*'

So she had allowed Victor to lead her to Mr Dedlington's house, where he'd knocked his employer – and his wife – up. They had been surprised to see the two young people on their doorstep, but too kindly to turn them away. Instead, the Dedlingtons had listened to Victor's story and Mrs Dedlington had tut-tutted, put a blanket around Alice's shoulders, and made tea. Mr Dedlington, who had been touched by the tale, had given Victor the address of a friend of his and by midnight the small house on Trafalgar Street had been opened up for them.

'No funny business, mind you,' Mr Dedlington had warned Victor as he'd been handed the key. 'I won't have my kindness thrown in my face. Your young lady can stay here – but you can bunk up on our couch until you're wed.'

Victor had shaken Mr Dedlington's hand. 'You won't regret this. I'll make up for it.'

'Well, see that you do,' the older man had replied, not unkindly. 'I'll have Miss Lees down my back in the morning and if I'm to help you, you have to help yourself. It's a messy business, lad.'

He nodded, but his voice was steady. 'I'm going to marry Alice. Everything will work out, honestly it will.'

Mr Dedlington had looked into the young face and sighed. 'Do you know about the Lewes case?'

Victor had shaken his head.

'Well, lad, just so you're aware what you're getting yourself into . . . It were a long time ago, up at Werneth Heights. The Arnold family were very rich – big landowners – and the father had his fingers in more than one pie. He had two daughters, Dorothy and Catherine. David Lewes married Catherine. She was highly strung, very handsome, and they had two children –'

'Alice,' Victor had whispered.

Mr Dedlington had nodded. 'Aye, Alice and a boy. I never knew his name. They were only little when the tragedy happened.'

Victor had been watching his face carefully. 'What happened?'

'David Lewes killed his wife one night and ran off. The girl was sent away –'

'Why?'

Mr Dedlington had shrugged. 'Gossip said that she were too like her father to look at, and the old man wanted her out of the way. No reminders, like. Until now no one knew where she went.'

Victor had frowned, trying to take it all in. 'What about Alice's brother?'

'He stayed with his grandparents. They brought him up at first, then his aunt – Dorothy – married and brought up the kid as her own.'

'But how could they give away one child and not the other?'

Mr Dedlington had shaken his head. 'Who knows? Maybe she *were* too like David Lewes. Anyway, the old man, Judge Arnold –'

'He was a judge!'

'Nah, it were just a name for him. He were on the bench, a magistrate, a right hard bugger. More clout than he should have had, but money bought him that. No one could touch the Arnolds, so after the tragedy the family closed ranks and moved away. Went abroad for a few years. Maybe old man Arnold thought that the girl was tarnished with the same brush as her father, so best palm her off. Get her out of the family once and for all.'

Staggered, Victor had looked at the older man. 'But someone was bound to find out sooner or later?'

'And do what? I've told you, the Arnolds had – still have – money and power. There's no law that stops you giving away your granddaughter.'

'But what about David Lewes?'

Mr Dedlington had shrugged his shoulders. 'There were rumours flying round – he was mad, he was dead. Some said that the family had him sent out of the country. But no one knew for sure. No one ever knew. The case was scandalous, headline news – but only for a short while. Judge Arnold must have pulled some big strings, because it were hushed up fast. It was gossip all over town, all over the county one day. The next, silence. Whatever happened to David Lewes no one knows for sure. And if I know anything about old man Arnold no one ever will.' Mr Dedlington's wrinkled face had softened.

'You know what you've got yourself into, lad, don't you?'

Victor had nodded, his face set. 'I think so.'

'Well, my advice would be to let the past rest. Marry the lass and have your own children. Forget David Lewes and the Arnolds. Forget the past. There's only misery there. Nothing else.'

When Victor told Alice what his employer had said he left two things out – that she had a brother and that no one really knew what had happened to her father. Better to let her presume that David Lewes was dead and that there had been no siblings. Otherwise he knew that she would never settle until she had found them.

But Alice was in no state to find anyone. And now she was staring ahead, remembering what Victor had told her and wondering when she would find the energy to live again. The terror and humiliation of her last night at Netherlands had shattered her, Clare Lees' words stamping into her brain so deeply that Alice thought she would never stop hearing them – *You should be in the dirt. That's where you came from – and where you belong.*

Victor was being so kind, Alice thought. He had put his head on the line and was certain that he had the future all mapped out. But she wasn't so certain. Alice shifted in her seat, looking ahead. She had to get out and find a job, make money. It wasn't fair that Victor was doing all the hard work. She was going to be his wife soon; it was her duty to help him.

Her duty . . . Alice rose to her feet and paced the tiny kitchen. The house was cramped, and damp from not having been used for months. What furniture there was had been second- or third-hand, culled from skips and house clearances. The surfaces, once polished, were dull, the only mirror fly-spotted and cracked over the blackened kitchen range.

The place chilled Alice to the soul. She would have to

get out, go for a walk – do anything, but stop staring at the same bare floor and faded distempered walls. When Victor was there it was different; she could hold on to him and forget reality. But alone, the place swamped her.

Hurriedly Alice pulled on her coat and walked out into Trafalgar Street, scurrying past as she heard her neighbour open the door.

But she was too slow. Lettie Booth shouted out a greeting.

Reluctantly, Alice turned. 'Hello.'

'Oh, hello, luv,' Lettie replied, the thick lenses of her glasses magnifying pale, weak eyes. 'I were coming round to see you later. See you were all right.'

'I'm fine,' Alice said quietly.

'Going for a walk?'

She nodded, tried to move off. But Lettie stopped her, too stupid to see that she didn't want to talk.

'I know what trouble's like, been in plenty myself. Oh, not that I'm saying you're in trouble. But if you were, there's always a willing ear next door for you. You're so young and so pretty . . .' Lettie dropped her voice to a whisper. 'You needn't worry about clothes.'

Alice frowned. 'What?'

'Clothes,' Lettie repeated dumbly. 'I've still got my three's baby things. In good condition – well, give or take a darn or two.'

Aghast, Alice was rooted to the spot. So *that* was what everyone thought. That she was pregnant.

Her voice hardened. 'I'm not in trouble –'

'Your secret's safe with me,' Lettie went on blithely, oblivious to the effect her words were having. 'The baby can't help its start, can it? I'm sure you'll make a good mother.'

'I'm not having a baby!' Alice snapped, walking away. Then she turned back. Her voice was hostile. 'And I'd appreciate it if you would tell everyone that. Tell everyone Alice Rimmer isn't that kind of girl.'

Her anger was so intense that Alice didn't realise what she was doing, or where she was going. Absent-mindedly, she boarded a bus and paid her fare, not even hearing what the conductor said to her. Instead her eyes fixed on the view outside. Then after a moment they moved to her reflection in the window looking back at her.

She was lost. Not on the bus, but everywhere. Her whole world had been shaken, like a pocket turned inside out. It was true that she loved Victor and wanted to be with him, but the cost had been so great. Humiliation burned inside her. How many people knew about her past? If Evan Thomas had found out, had he kept it a secret? Unlikely, Alice thought. He would have wanted to spread the dirt. 'Gossip sticks like shit to a blanket,' Alice had overheard Mr Dedlington say. And he was on *their* side. Others would be less charitable.

But then again, maybe there would be no need for Evan Thomas to tell anyone else. He had used the knowledge to damning effect and got what he wanted – Alice's banishment and fall from grace. Why should he give her another thought? Carefully Alice studied her reflection in the bus window. Her face was a white oval, the dark eyes huge and sad.

The bus stopped suddenly, the conductor calling out, 'End of the line, all off here.'

Surprised, Alice rose to her feet. 'Where am I?'

'Union Street.'

'Where's that?'

The man looked at her suspiciously. 'Now don't take the mickey, there's a good girl.'

'Honestly, I mean it. Where is Union Street?'

'You're in Oldham, miss. In the town centre.'

She had come all the way from Salford to Oldham in a daze.

Slowly Alice got off the bus and looked around. She felt nervous, unused to the world outside and the people hurrying past her. How could she get back to Salford? Trafalgar Street? What bus should she catch? What tram? And besides, did she have enough money for the return fare?

Nervously she looked round, then noticed the large building a little way off. It looked official, important, and so Alice walked towards it, thinking to get directions there. It was only when she reached it that she saw written over the door 'OLDHAM MUNICIPAL LIBRARY'.

She was about to turn away when a thought struck her. *The library would hold all the local records for the area.* Her feet moved quickly up the steps, her throat dry as she walked to the reception desk.

Two women – one extremely tall – were deep in conversation and ignored her.

'. . . Well, I said – "You're neither use nor ornament."'

'Nah!'

'I did! And when he –'

Alice coughed. 'Excuse me.'

Both women turned and gave her blank looks. 'Yes?' the tall one intoned.

'I was wondering where the records were kept.'

'We don't have music here, luv,' she said, laughing at her own joke. 'Try the High Street.'

Alice could feel herself flushing, but held her ground. 'I meant newspapers. Old newspapers.'

The shorter woman shrugged. 'What d'you want them for?'

'I want to look at them. Please.'

The tall woman sucked in her cheeks, her companion smiling.

'What you looking *for*?'

Alice thought quickly and remembered a game she had played with the small children back at Netherlands.

'We're doing a project about how life was around here fifteen to twenty years ago.'

'My mother could tell you that,' the tall woman sneered. 'And tell you the scandals too.'

'So can I see the records?' Alice persisted.

The woman looked her up and down. The girl was shabby, and no more than twenty. But for all of that she was a stunner. She would have liked to refuse Alice, but couldn't think of any reason to do so. Instead, she reluctantly moved out from behind the desk and showed her to a cluttered back room off the main library.

One bony hand swept along a line of heavy-bound volumes.

'This here's all the newspapers since 1900. Well, in this area, that is. You know, like the *Oldham Chronicle*, the *Manchester Guardian* and the *Manchester Evening News*.' She studied Alice carefully. 'You a teacher?'

Alice kept her head down. 'Training to be.'

'What school?'

What could she say? Alice wondered. She could hardly say Netherlands. She was no longer working there, and besides, everyone looked down on the home.

So she lied. 'I'm learning to be a private tutor.'

'*Private tutor*, hey?' the woman repeated, suddenly at a loss for what to say. 'Well, there you are. Have a good look, I'll be back later. Oh, and don't get fingermarks on the pages.'

Alice waited until the door had closed before she took down the first volume. It was heavy and dusty, beginning at 1900 and ending at 1910. Alice thought for a moment. She had been sent to the home when she was one year old, in 1911. So was 1911 the year that her mother had been killed?

Eagerly she pulled down the next book and flicked through the yellowing clippings. A woman with a dog was on the front page. The dog had saved her life ... Alice flicked over. There was news of European countries, a long hot summer and heavy rainfalls in the East, but nothing other than trivia. She turned another page. An advertisement for Spencer corsetry and Pond's Vanishing Cream leaped up from the page, but nothing more revealing.

Frowning, Alice took off her coat and pulled up a chair. Looking down she was suddenly aware of a hole in her thick stocking and hurriedly pulled it under her left foot. Then she went back to the book. She turned the page. She saw a face. Two faces. She stared.

The dimmest memory crept into her brain. *A long dark stairwell, looking down on to a black and white floor, someone carrying her. And the smell of gardenia* . . . Alice swallowed, staring at the man's face and then looking to the caption underneath.

DAVID LEWES – murderer

The room heated up in an instant, as her eyes focused then blurred on the grainy newsprint image. Shaking, Alice held up the clipping and looked into her father's face. There was no striking resemblance, but she could see some hints to her parentage in the dark eyes. He had been a handsome man, her father . . . Slowly Alice turned her eyes on the photograph next to his. Underneath it, read:

CATHERINE LEWES, daughter of 'Judge'
Arnold, savagely murdered by her husband at the
family home, The Dower House, Werneth Heights,
12 November.

Her hands trembling as she held the paper, Alice read on. Her mother had been butchered with a knife, her father was missing. She read the sentence twice. Then again. *Her father had butchered her mother and run away* . . . Alice could feel her pulse quicken and stood up, pushing the book from her. Her heart was banging in her chest. Faint, she leaned against the wall, then she walked over to the window and leaned out, gulping air. A man was walking with his small daughter, holding her hand and smiling.

Her hands went up to her forehead and massaged her temples fiercely. She had grandparents, so why had she been sent to the home? Why . . . ? She wanted to know but at the same time was afraid of the truth.

After several minutes she turned and walked back to the newspaper cutting. She sat down, pulled the book towards her again, read on. Her grandparents had gone abroad after the tragedy, her grandmother suffering a stroke which left her a semi invalid. Her aunt, Dorothy, had been treated for shock, as she had been the one who had found her sister's body. Alice scanned the next paragraph, looking for any mention of her. Finally there was a brief line – '*David and Catherine Lewes had two children, who have been taken on by relatives.*'

Taken on by relatives . . . Two children . . . Alice felt her heart pumping again. She was reading it wrong, she thought wildly. She must be. Everyone had told her that she had no relatives when she had been dumped in a home. And all along she had belonged to the Arnold clan. Finding it difficult to gather her thoughts, Alice remembered the titbits she had overheard over the years about the Arnolds. Ethel had talked about them occasionally, and Mr Grantley had often referred to them in obsequious tones. They were probably the richest family in Lancashire.

And all that money and power had succeeded in what? In wiping Alice off the family tree. She had been abandoned and forgotten. Given away. It was a bitter blow. Alice tried to swallow the anger she felt. Why would they cast her off? And not just her. She had a sibling. So where was he or she? All the time she had believed that she was alone, they could have been together. It was cruel enough to cut off the children, but to separate them too – that was unforgivable. Hurriedly Alice read through the remainder of the report and then moved over to an article in the *Manchester Evening News*.

This report went further into the background of the Arnolds. Their power and influence, the old man's ruthlessness in business. Apparently Judge Arnold had had few friends, but many enemies ... His photograph repelled Alice: Judge Arnold had squat features, almost coarse, with unruly grey hair and flat, unreadable eyes.

Coldly she stared at the photograph and then looked at the picture of the murder house. It was huge and impressive, but sombre. In the photograph it looked as welcoming as Netherlands, with only the gardens to soften its stern walls. God, she thought, they had real money. And they had given her away. Let her live meanly whilst they lived in luxury.

But *why* did they give her up? Alice wondered again, shattered by another rejection coming so soon upon the last. Why couldn't they just keep her at a distance? Let her keep her name at least? But no, Alice thought, looking with hatred at old man Arnold – no, he had taken everything away from her, given her a commonplace name, and no history. He had blamed her for her mother's death as surely as though she had committed the murder herself.

Alice jumped as the door opened behind her.

'You finished?' the tall woman said, trying to see what Alice had been reading.

Nodding, Alice closed the book and stood up. 'Thank you very much.'

'Did you find what you were looking for?'

Alice glanced down, afraid that her face might give her away. 'I found a lot of things I didn't know before,' she answered honestly.

The woman walked past her, then slammed the books back on the shelf, sighing noisily. 'That's the thing about history. Always full of surprises.'

Chapter Seventeen

The family had returned to the house at Werneth Heights, Oldham two months earlier, but before long Mrs Arnold and her daughter, Dorothy, would be off again to winter in the sun. Somewhere in France, although no one outside the family knew exactly where. Old man Arnold liked to keep his life, and that of his family, private. He also liked to have time to himself, so he encouraged Alwyn and Dorothy to go away each year. After all, he wasn't left alone.

There was Dorothy's husband, for a start. Poor stammering Leonard, left with the old man of whom he was terrified. Ten years earlier Leonard Tripps had been introduced to Dorothy Arnold by mutual acquaintances. He had been smitten at once. She was handsome, easy to fall in love with. Her father had been another matter . . .

Leonard watched the old man unfasten his jacket and sit down at his desk in the den. He liked to think that he had won Judge Arnold over by his personality, but he knew he was fooling himself. His family's fortune was what had cemented the alliance between the Trippses and the Arnolds, an impressive rubber business being far more appealing that any of his personal virtues.

Their marriage was a great – though private – event in Oldham, and Leonard never once complained about taking on the upbringing of his wife's nephew, Charlie. He never complained because it would have done him no good; Dorothy had taken over the care of her nephew since her sister's death and thought of him as her child. What could Leonard say in the face of such commitment?

The tragedy which had left Charlie homeless was seldom referred to, but Leonard was well aware of the background. He knew that Catherine and David Lewes had had a daughter too – a baby, very much her father's pet. So much so, that when he killed the child's mother Dorothy could no longer stand the sight of her niece and had her sent away.

Years earlier, whilst the event was still fresh in some people's mind, Leonard wondered if anyone realised how great a part Dorothy had played in the banishing of her dead sister's child. He supposed that they did not, instead jumping to the conclusion that it had been Judge Arnold's decision. After all, people would never believe that the gentle Dorothy would do anything so callous. But Judge Arnold didn't give a damn what people thought – '*If they want to make me out to be even more of a monster, let them. I should worry.*'

'Leonard.'

Startled out of his reverie, he looked over to his father-in-law. 'Y-y-yes, sir?'

'I'm wondering where Charlie is.'

Leonard smiled weakly. Charlie would be up in his room, writing. Charlie was convinced that he was borderline genius, and his grandparents and Dorothy had encouraged the delusion. Yet Charlie's historical plays – so interminably long and so frequent – were, to Leonard, a subtle, innovative form of torture. He believed with all his heart that if the Army had had the use of Charlie's literary ramblings in the war, the Germans would have surrendered at the second paragraph.

'I t-t-think he's upstairs, writing.'

'Good boy,' Judge Arnold said approvingly. 'I always wonder where he got his talent.'

Leonard thought it came naturally, like belching, but simply smiled. What could you say about the favourite which wouldn't sound like sour grapes? In fact, despite himself, Leonard had grown quite fond of Charlie over the years. He was spoiled, at times idiotic, but harmless. Fun, if you caught him in the right mood. Short, swarthy and even-featured, at twenty Charlie was good-looking without any sensuality – not like his father or his mother, more like a collage of all the Arnolds.

Leonard stretched out his legs before him, relaxing. Then he saw Judge Arnold look over and sat upright again. He wondered, for the thousandth time what his father-in-law's Christian name really was. Then he smiled to himself. Maybe the old tyrant was called Cecil, or Hector.

'What's so funny?'

Leonard shook his head. 'I w-w-was just r-r-remembering a joke,' he said deftly.

'So let's hear it then.'

Leonard hadn't been in the Arnold family, under the same roof, without having learned to be quick on his feet. His speech might judder like semaphore, but his brain was nimble enough.

'The joke g-g-goes like this,' he began. 'What is the difference b-b-between a duck and a solicitor?'

Judge Arnold thought for a moment, then waved his hand impatiently. 'I don't know – what *is* the difference between a duck and a solicitor?'

'You can't tell a s-s-solicitor to stick his b-b-bill up his arse,' Leonard said triumphantly.

He had the satisfaction of seeing the old man's face slacken and then burst into laughter.

'Bloody funny, Leonard! Bloody funny!' Judge Arnold said approvingly. 'I'll tell them that at the club tonight.'

Turning back to his desk, Judge Arnold was soon immersed in work. Watching him, Leonard thought about Charlie, and then his own son, Robin. He missed him, always did when he was with Dorothy, but she would insist on taking him away with her for the summer.

'The heat is good for him,' she'd say. 'Honestly, darling, I know what's best for our baby.'

Leonard didn't like to tell her that what was best for their baby was spending equal amounts of time with both parents. To another woman he could have said, 'No, you stay at home with me and we'll go away together when I have free time,' but how could he say that to Dorothy?

The old man had made it clear from the first. Dorothy had suffered profoundly. She had found her murdered sister's body – what greater shock could any woman ever have? To find Catherine hacked to death was enough to turn a person's mind. It was to her credit, Judge Arnold had said, that Dorothy was strong enough to recover. From now onwards, they would have to see that her life was lived on an even keel. God knows, the old man had gone on, things had been terrible for a while. Straight after the murder the whole family had gone abroad, and only gradually could they face the house again – and the memory of Catherine's death.

So Dorothy was treated gingerly, her life kept as sweet as possible. If she ever thought of the murder – and Leonard had suspected many times over the years that she had – it was not to him that she turned. It was to the old man.

Three generations were under one roof, all ruled by him. And yet, Leonard thought, each of them, even the four-year-old Robin, lived separate lives. They might share some of the same rooms, and occupy the same address, but there was a distance between them which was eerie. Perhaps, Leonard mused, there was so much horror in the past, everyone had suppressed his or her feelings so much, that there was no elasticity of spirit any longer. Too many dark comers and hidden memories had culminated in a family living together, but emotionally apart.

Leonard could endure it, but he didn't want the same for his son. Dorothy would spoil the child too much, Robin would end up like the friendly and foolish Charlie, and Leonard didn't want that. He knew he was a weak man himself, but he didn't want his son to be the same. Money and power were Robin's birthright, but he needed something else – judgement and compassion.

Dorothy had suffered, yes, but she had acted ruthlessly with regard to her niece. Leonard would never forget that, nor condone it. Besides, her parents should have forbidden the action. The child was not to blame for its birth, nor for not being the favourite.

Leonard had always suspected that there was more to it, and knew from something Alwyn had once said – in a rare unguarded moment – that the baby had rejected Dorothy and cried incessantly for her father. Charlie had taken to Dorothy at once, but not the infant girl. How like his wife, Leonard thought, to punish the child for disliking her.

As he sat there musing, a sudden and strange sensation came over Leonard. He realised with astonishment that if he never saw his wife again he would hardly miss her. But he would miss his son. He would definitely miss his son . . .

Sighing, he rose to his feet and walked out. And his father-in-law watched him go – just as he watched everyone.

Mr Dedlington was uneasy, hanging around Victor as he finished off planing a bookcase. Aware of his scrutiny, Victor was unexpectedly clumsy, scratching the mahogany surface and hearing a sharp intake of breath behind him.

'Sorry, Mr Dedlington. I can fix it.'

'Lad, I wanted a word with you.'

As Victor turned round, his employer glanced away. Victor knew the look – bad news was coming.

'What is it?'

'I've had a visit, lad, from Miss Lees.' A pause, long enough to let the name do its damage. 'Look, I have a business to run, and I rely on Netherlands to supply me with apprentices. I always have done. My father did before me. It's an arrangement I've had with the home for years now.'

'Isn't my work good enough?' Victor asked, knowing that it had nothing to do with his skill. No, he thought to himself, don't you turn against me. Please.

'It's not that, Victor. It's just that the arrangement with your young lady is not respectable –'

'We're getting married, and you know there's nothing wrong in it. I sleep here, on your couch every night.'

Mr Dedlington waved aside the objection. He didn't like the situation he had been forced into, but he had no choice. He had a business to run, a wife and family to support. Victor Coates wasn't his responsibility. He had given the lad a chance, what more could he be expected to do?

'It's like this, Victor. You have to leave my employ – unless you part company with your young lady, and then you're welcome to stay and finish your apprenticeship.'

Victor blinked, stung. 'What?'

'It might be for the best.'

Laying down the plane, Victor stared at the older man. '*How* could it be for the best?'

'I'm not sacking you, lad; my argument's not with you.'

'But with Alice?' Victor countered shortly. 'What's she ever done to hurt you?'

'Nothing,' Mr Dedlington snapped, rubbing his forehead with his stubby hands. 'The world's not fair, lad. Things don't work out the way we want.' His voice dropped. 'They've got me over a barrel, Victor. If you don't break it off with Alice, you can look for work elsewhere.'

Victor stared at Mr Dedlington and saw him colour. He had thought it was such a kindness for his employer to help him, to find them the house to rent on Trafalgar Street. Mr Dedlington had loaned him money – a debt which had yet to be repaid – but having supported the couple so willingly it was a bitter blow that he was now turning on them.

'I can't give her up.' Sickened, Victor heard his voice harden.

'Then you lose your job,' Mr Dedlington replied, 'and you owe me money, Victor. Don't forget that. A debt's a debt.'

'I'll pay it back!'

'If you leave, I want the money on the *day* you leave.'

Victor stared at him, stupefied. 'You know I can't do that! I don't have any money.'

'So keep your job.'

It was blackmail, Victor realised. Neither he nor Alice had really escaped Netherlands. Clare Lees was still pulling the strings, still determined to get even with the protégée who had betrayed her.

'I can't give Alice up,' Victor repeated. 'What would happen to her without me? I love her, I can't abandon her.'

'She could get a job, she'd cope. Other woman do it all the time,' Mr Dedlington said sharply. He was in the wrong, and knew it. His guilt made him defensive. 'There are enough jobs going in this town. She'll not starve.'

'What possible good would it do you for me to break up with her?'

The older man stared Victor in the face. 'I've told you. I've a business to run. I'm not your father; I don't have to mollycoddle you, or your girl. Life's hard, Victor –'

Furiously, Victor threw down his plane and snatched up his coat. At the door he turned and looked back to his employer.

'I know life's hard! It always has been for me – and for Alice. Nothing came easy to either of us, but I would never have let down someone in trouble.'

Mr Dedlington was stung by the remark and turned away from the accusing look in Victor's eyes.

'You either report for work tomorrow and tell me that it's over, or you don't come back at all. And you've a debt outstanding, don't forget that. The choice is yours. But remember, Victor, there are many lads who would like your job. That girl's trouble. She came from trouble and she's already caused you plenty. Think on that you're not taking on too much to handle.'

Twenty minutes later Victor let himself into the house in Trafalgar Street. The cool damp air hit him as he entered and, looking round, he saw for the first time how really gloomy the place was. He hadn't noticed when they first came; had been too caught up in the excitement. But now he saw it as others did – as Alice must.

He missed her with sudden, hard longing. Life without Alice, without coming to see her, without dreaming of their future together – that wouldn't *be* a life. He would starve, die for her, die *with* her. But leave her? Never.

Calling out for Alice, Victor walked into the kitchen. The room was tidy. Lately she had spruced up the tired little house, bringing in flowers and lighting a small fire in the grate. She had even propped up some cheap postcards on the mantel, trying to make it look as though it was their home, as though they had had a history together.

His heart shifting, Victor then noticed a plate, covered by a cloth, laid out for him. Beside it was a note.

Dearest Victor,
    I have gone out for a while, but will be back soon. Your supper's ready for you.
    Loving you, always, always, always,
    Your Alice

Touched, he lifted the cloth. She had made him sandwiches, cut into delicate shapes, a bar of cheap toffee lying next to them. His favourite. The sight moved him so much that he sat down, staring at her note. He *couldn't* live without her, he *wouldn't* live without her. They would survive. He would find another job, it would work out.

The sound of the door opening brought him back to his senses. Walking in, Alice smiled at him.

'Hello, love. Have you just got in?'

How could he live without hearing that voice, seeing those eyes? It was absurd. Let her out of his life? She *was* his life.

'Just now.'

She touched his cheek. 'You look worried, what is it?'

'Nothing.'

But she knew him too well to be fooled. Two orphan children, they had bonded to each other so completely that their thoughts and emotions were read as easily by each other as someone else would read a newspaper.

'Come on, Victor, tell me.'

He settled her on his lap. 'There's a problem at work . . .'

'No!' she said anxiously. 'You love it there.'

'It's nothing I can't handle.'

She wasn't fooled; felt the lie. 'Victor, what is it?'

'Nothing. Honestly nothing.'

'What is it?' she repeated.

'Mr Dedlington's been . . . He's seen Clare Lees.' Alice's eyes fixed on Victor anxiously. 'She came to see him – and said that it would be better for his business if we broke up.'

Alice said nothing. She had hoped to come home and be able to talk about what she had discovered. About the fact that she had a sibling. She had wanted to tell Victor that it was all true. She *had* come from a fortune, from a great family – just as she had always imagined. She had wanted to tell him that Judge Arnold had seen his grand-daughter put away. In fact, she had wanted to cry about it and let Victor tell her that it was all right, because they had each other. She wanted to know that she wasn't alone.

But now she looked at Victor and realised that his life and career were about to penalised because of her. He would lose his job if he stayed with her, and all the future prosperity he looked forward to. His talent would be wasted. And why? Because he loved her. Victor Coates, honest, hard-working Victor loved Alice Rimmer, the off-spring of a murderer. The carrier of bad blood.

It was not going to end, or be forgotten, Alice realised. She had suspected as much when she first heard the truth from Evan Thomas's lips. Indeed, her first instinct had been to run out of Victor's life, but he had stopped her. And now what had happened? His job was at stake because of her. And how many other jobs, other opportunities, would be lost because of her? Would Victor spend his life forever held back by the woman he loved?

And would any love last under such pressure? Alice felt her eyes fill but bit her lip hard to stop herself crying.

'I'm not going to leave you,' Victor said firmly. 'I would never do that.'

'You need your job. You've been Mr Dedlington's apprentice for years. You're going to finish your apprenticeship before long, Victor – be able to make some real money. If you lose that, what else is there for you? A job in the mill? Gasworks?' She shook her head. 'No, you deserve that job. It was the first good thing that happened to you.'

'And you were the second,' he replied, lifting her hand and kissing the tip of each finger. 'How could I give you up, Alice? How could I work and sleep and think without you?' His grip tightened on her hand. 'You and I are a pair. We only have each other.'

'It's because of who I am,' Alice said quietly, her voice dull. 'Mr Dedlington's old enough to remember what happened nearly twenty years ago – how many others are?'

'It's old news. People forget. No one else knows –'

'Clare Lees and Evan Thomas know,' she replied evenly, then dropped her head. 'I'm not lucky for you, Victor. Nothing's gone right since you met me.'

Helplessly he buried his face in her neck. 'Don't say that! You're everything to me, Alice. We only have each other. I don't care about the job, it's not important. I just want you.'

Tenderly she kissed the top of his head, her eyes wandering to the corner of the room and resting on an old table. It was rickety, badly made, crude. Victor would never make anything like that, she thought. He created beautiful things, objects which rich people would buy. His hands could earn him money, raise him in the world. She could only hold him back.

Her gaze stayed on the chair, her heart closing down. She could see the images in the old newspaper clippings – her mother, her father, Judge Arnold. She could have been someone – not an orphan, patronised into submission. But it was worse than that: she wasn't just a foundling, she was damned, marked out by her father's actions. And how much of him was in her? She knew how excitable, how fired up she could get; knew how anger burned inside her, how she raged inwardly. It had even frightened her sometimes. When she was growing up she had thought that others must feel the same, but they didn't. Ethel and Gilbert didn't. Victor didn't. Only she.

And why was that? *Because she was like her father?* She didn't know, but she was afraid that she might be. Did she really want Victor to suffer for her? To lose out? Worse, did she ever want to look at him and see that he had become wary of her? Or, God forbid, frightened? And even if that never happened, would he grow to resent her for hindering him? No, Alice thought desperately, no, Victor. I love you too much to risk that.

Infinitely gentle, she nuzzled his hair and drank in the scent of him. She committed it to memory, so that she would never forget it. Love was not going to save her; it was not going to be that simple. Her life was not going to follow a calm route. At Netherlands, they had been separated by iron railings. Outside, in the real world, it was the iron will of one woman who was separating them again.

Clare Lees. Alice shuddered, her chest hollow, empty. Silent, Victor held on to her, their bodies fitting together so perfectly, so tenderly, as they had always done. *Clare Lees*. And Judge Arnold. *Clare Lees, Judge Arnold...* Alice repeated the names in her head and stared blankly at the chair in the corner whilst deciding on the course of action which would change her life for ever.

Chapter Eighteen

The weather abroad had proved too hot for Alwyn so the family had returned to The Dower House, Werneth Heights, earlier than usual. Leonard was delighted, throwing his son into the air and greeting his mother-in-law politely.

'You look well.'

'I'm in a wheelchair!' Alwyn snapped back. 'No one looks well in a wheelchair.'

Turning away from Leonard, she beckoned for her husband to come over. He did so at once, bowing mockingly to her, Alwyn's smile making a woman out of her, instead of some handicapped martinet.

'Miss me, Judge?'

He pinched her cheek and then pushed her chair over to the window. The garden was cool, coming into its winter mood, the bushes darkly sombre.

'I thought of putting a Christmas tree in the middle of the lawn.'

'It's only October,' Alwyn replied, but she was glad that her husband was trying to please her.

God knew how long it would last. Soon he would get bored with her, and turn to the grandchildren for amusement. She would then long for the balmy foreign nights away from the Northern cold. She would grow bored and homesick – and then settle again, after November had passed.

Thoughtfully Alwyn watched as her husband moved away and picked Robin up. He could take anything in his stride, she thought. He had had to. People admired a man who was tough, a man who didn't crumble under pressure. Not like some. Any other man would have folded, but not him. He had kept the family together. And he always would.

Suddenly aware of her scrutiny, Judge Arnold turned round to his wife. He had to admit that she was a strong woman – he liked that about her – but she was deep. Oh yes, she was deep all right. Not one to show her feelings, not one to let you know what she was thinking. But affectionate. In the right place and at the right time. He couldn't have done with some clinging, whining woman hanging on his arm. Mind you, no one like that could have coped with what had happened to their family.

It was a shame that she had had that stroke, but the doctors had been baffled by her incomplete recovery. She should have been back to normal long ago, they said, certainly out of the wheelchair. But Judge knew that the chair was his wife's support. She had mentally withstood a tremendous amount, but something had to take the strain. With Alwyn, it was never going to be her brain, but her legs.

'Why *did* you come back early, Alwyn? What was the real reason?'

'It was hot.'

'You're a lizard; it has nothing to do with the heat.'

She glanced up at him coolly with her deep blue eyes. 'I missed the shops.'

'They have shops in France,' he said calmly.

He never begrudged her spending. After all, they had money enough to buy anything Alwyn fancied. Besides, he was a generous man, when all was said and done. Liked his family to have the best. It looked good to his competitors, showed them that the business was doing well.

'*What* brought you back?' he asked again.

This time, she answered him honestly. 'I want to talk to you about Dorothy –'

He cut her off. 'No!'

Breathing in deeply, Alwyn stared at her husband. She saw a man with heavy brows and a deeply lined face topped by a shock of wiry hair, now greying. She saw hardness in his face and resilience – the things she admired. But not now. Now she was worried about their daughter and she wanted to talk to him about it. It would do him no good to pretend that everything was all right. Dorothy was restless again.

'We have to talk –'

'I said no!'

'Oh, save that tone for your workforce!' Alwyn snapped back. 'You can't intimidate me.' Her hands smoothed her hair as though she was soothing her own temper. 'Dorothy is upset. She's been distant, uncommunicative. I wanted her home for November.'

Judge Arnold flinched.

'You know what it means,' Alwyn replied calmly. 'Memories don't fade for some people. I thought she was over it, but now I'm not so sure. Oh, come on, we have to talk about it.'

But Judge Arnold had snatched up his paper and was pretending to read. His daughter was skittish . . . Jesus, just what he feared. But then Dorothy was always was a bit preoccupied when the year wound round to 12 November . . . His attention moved to the window. Bloody awful weather, he thought, seeing the rain outside. Unwelcomed, his thoughts slid back relentlessly to the past.

It had been raining that night too . . . His eyes closed against the memory, but it came anyway. David Lewes, his son-in-law. So good-looking it hurt your eyes, he used to joke. Came from a fine family in Huddersfield, a good match everyone agreed. His daughter fell in love with David almost as soon as she saw him. And he returned the compliment. Who would have worried to have David Lewes courting their daughter? He was attentive, kind, always loving. They had married one year after they met and ten months later they had Charlie. Two years after that ... Judge Arnold closed his mind to the thought of the second child.

He could sense his wife's unease, next to him, but didn't open his eyes. The babies had been born in this house, at Werneth Heights. Away from prying eyes, from gossip. Two perfect children, born to two perfect parents. The house had been so big it had presented no problem for all of them to live under one roof. Catherine and her family had had one wing, he and Alwyn had had the other; shared it with Dorothy, their other daughter.

The rain slapped against the window, Arnold's spirits dipping into melancholia as the memory took its toll ... David had been under strain, overworking – nothing serious, but Catherine had been demanding, highly strung at times, and petulant with him. She had wanted all her husband's attention, *all* the time. Had put him before their children, always.

It had been a bad winter that year too. Rain had come on rain, the streets greasy, the town flat with grey water. In the factories and workshops the winter had dragged on cold, the workers grumbling, David taking on more and more of the workload ... Arnold shifted in his seat. Damn it, his son-in-law had asked for more responsibility! It hadn't been foisted upon him. David had wanted it.

But wanting it and being able to cope with it were two different things, and before long David's good looks had been mottled with lines and shadows. At times, even his natural kindness had been replaced with bouts of irritation. He'd become snappy, restless.

And Catherine had been so demanding. She had pleaded with him for more time, more money, more attention. Could he go away with her and the children? Could they buy a house of their own? She would be happy. No, he had told her, wisely, you would be lonely. So we'll stay here, Catherine had countered. All right, all right ... A day later she had been off again: I want to move. No, I want to stay. It would be better for the children if we lived elsewhere. No, it's better for them here.

Make up your mind, David had told her, exasperated. Arnold had agreed with him. If you want to leave Werneth Heights, wait for a while until I get the new mill up and running and then I'll have more time. We'll move then ...

Catherine had kissed him fiercely, moist eyes on his, a supple body pressed against his own, her own father embarrassed, turning away at the show of passion.

'I love you David,' she had whispered. 'Love me, always love me, won't you?'

Judge Arnold had beat a hasty retreat back to his own wing, but not before he had heard the uncomfortable sounds of lovemaking begin. Catherine's urgency obviously irritated and excited David at the same time. Heat, passion and annoyance all pooling together on the other side of The Dower House.

Closing the connecting door, Judge Arnold had leaned against it. He could still hear his daughter's hurried words. *Love me always, David. Love me always. I couldn't live without you. If you left me I would kill myself ...*

At dinner that night Catherine had been subdued, sated. David had talked business with his father-in-law. The storm had passed. Again. But Judge had felt the air pulse with tension and had glanced repeatedly towards his child.

'What is it?'

Catherine had been luminously beautiful. 'I'm so happy. So happy with my life.'

A shudder had fallen over his heart at the sound of the words ...

'Are you listening?' Alwyn said heatedly, snapping the remembrance. 'You looked miles away. The business with Dorothy is manageable, don't worry. We can cope with it.

We always do.' Slowly she moved the wheelchair over to his seat and rested her hand beside his. Not touching, just lying side by side.

But the memory had unsteadied him. 'Why did you bring Dorothy home? Why bring her *here* for the anniversary? I thought we'd agreed that this was the worst place for her to be then.'

Alwyn shrugged. 'She asked me to bring her home.'

'You didn't have to agree to it!'

'I couldn't stop her.'

He shook his head. 'It's not right. It's asking for trouble.'

Alwyn smiled at him as they exchanged glances. 'We can handle trouble, my dear. We've had enough practice, after all.'

It was a cool evening as Alice caught the late bus from Trafalgar Street to the centre of Salford. Victor had fallen asleep in the chair and she had crept out, closing the door silently behind her. Pulling the collar of her coat up around her neck, she had gone to the end of the street, where she'd jumped on a bus. It had taken ten minutes to get to her destination, but now she was here, she was suddenly fearful.

Finally she knocked on the door. There was no response. She knocked again and waited. On the third knocking, she was rewarded by a light going on overhead and a woman in curling rags poking her head out of an upstairs window.

'Who's there?'

'It's Alice, Alice Rimmer.'

'Oh, hello, luv,' Mrs Dedlington replied. 'I'll come down.'

A moment later she was ushering Alice into the kitchen. From above came the sound of heavy snoring.

'That's our Gordon,' Mrs Dedlington said smiling, 'driving 'em home.'

'I wanted to have a word with him,' Alice said softly, 'but if he's asleep . . .'

Mrs Dedlington could see the distress on the girl's face and led her to a seat. 'What's up?'

'Victor has been told that he has to choose between me and his job.'

'He *what*?' Obviously Mrs Dedlington knew nothing about it.

Alice rushed on. 'Miss Lees is putting pressure on him. Apparently Netherlands and your husband have had an understanding for years. She's forcing his hand. I don't want Victor to lose his job with your husband, Mrs Dedlington, I want him to stay – and he won't if he's forced to choose. So I'm going to prevent him having to make that choice.'

Mrs Dedlington was listening sympathetically, a comical figure in her hair rags. 'What you going to do?'

'Go away.'

The older woman sighed. 'No, love, surely not. Wherever would you go?'

'Somewhere a way off. Out of Salford. I'm no good for him. I don't bring him luck.' Alice paused, fully realising that Mrs Dedlington knew her story and knew whose child she was. 'Victor can do better for himself.'

'I doubt he'd agree –'

Alice cut her off. 'Of course he wouldn't! He loves me.' Her voice wavered. It was tough having to be strong when you were about to leave the person in the world you loved most. 'When I go, I don't want Victor to find me. That's why I'm here. I was going to ask your husband to reconsider, but that's not right –'

'If you give me a minute, I'll make him think twice about it!'

Alice shook her head. 'No, it would be wrong. Victor and me . . . Oh, it was never going to work out, Mrs Dedlington. I should have known that, but I needed him so much and I love him so much.' She struggled to keep her voice steady. 'I want to ask you a favour.'

'Anything,' the older woman replied, touched.

'Will you tell Victor that I've gone to London?'

'*London!*'

Alice nodded. 'He has to think I'm a long way away or he'll look for me. Tell him that I had to take some of his money – it's only very little. I'll repay him when I've got a job. I'll send the money to you to pass on to him.' She reached out and touched the older woman's hand timidly. 'Will you look out for Victor, Mrs Dedlington? Make sure he forgets me and concentrates on his work. He's so much talent, don't let him waste it.' She bit her lip. 'Later . . . in a while, will you make him see other girls, encourage him to find someone else? Don't let him be lonely.'

Mrs Dedlington gripped Alice's hand tightly, unable to speak.

'. . . Will you promise me this?'

Mrs Dedlington nodded. 'I promise. But where will you go, Alice?'

For a long moment Alice looked into the older woman's eyes and then answered her: 'I'm going somewhere I should have gone a long time ago. I've something to do. Another debt to repay, if you like.'

The tone of her voice made the older woman anxious. 'Come on now, girl, don't do anything stupid.'

'It's not stupid, it's fate,' Alice replied coldly. 'Something was set in motion at long time ago, and it's got to run its course. A normal life wasn't meant for me. I always knew I was different, but not *how*.' Sighing, Alice got to her feet. 'Thank you for your kindness to me, and for the kindness I know you'll show Victor.'

Mrs Dedlington jumped to her feet. 'Don't go, luv. We can work something out –'

'No, we can't,' Alice replied, moving to the door as the older woman tried to stop her. 'I have to go.'

'No, stay, please. Alice, come on, I'll wake Gordon up.'

Reluctantly, Alice pulled away her arm and opened the door. 'Let your husband sleep, Mrs Dedlington. Let him and Victor sleep on. Tomorrow will come soon enough.'

Chapter Nineteen

Leonard was walking with Robin, talking animatedly about birds.

'The one with the red breast has the same name as you,' he told the child. 'It's a robin.'

The little boy stared at the bird and then at his father, smiling. He liked being with him; it was better than being with his grandmother in her wheelchair, and his mother, who fussed him all the time.

For his part, Leonard was almost singing. His son was home for the winter. He laughed to himself, giddy with happiness. No more solemn evenings with Judge, talking about business; no more drawn-out dinners – his child was home and Leonard felt as though he was on holiday.

He felt so good, in fact, that he could almost ignore Dorothy's mood swings. She had her mother for company, after all. He had Robin ... But Leonard was sufficiently astute to know that he was not enough for the boy. The child needed someone else, someone from outside the family. It would teach him to mix – something the Arnolds did precious little of. It was all well and good to give the boy everything materially, but Leonard had seen how Charlie how turned out, and he didn't want a repeat performance.

Robin was old enough for a governess now. He should be beginning his schooling. Certainly he should be talking to someone other than his immediate family. Leonard had to do something about it, because it was certain that Robin Tripps was not going to be allowed to mix with other children, or go to a local school. That was not the Arnold way.

They lived at home and were educated at home. The Dower House was the nub of each and every one of their lives.

Just *how* Leonard was going to convince the old man, or his wife was another matter. He could hardly cite Charlie as an example of how *not* to turn out. Besides, November was coming and this would be the first time Dorothy had been at The Dower House when the anniversary of the murder came around.

How would she act? Leonard wondered. It was obvious that Robin had to be protected from any distress, but how? Abroad, it was simple, but how would Dorothy behave on the twelfth when she came into the very room where she had found her dead sister?

He only had a few weeks to sort the matter out, Leonard realised, but sort it out he would. Smiling, he looked down at his son and made a promise: Robin would not suffer for the past.

It was time to move on. Once and for all.

Miss Youngman, of the domestic agency Youngman and Fleet in Oldham, was flicking through her post and sorting it before she opened for the day. The demand for staff was pressing, the wealthier enclaves always looking for maids and nannies. It was difficult getting the right people, though. The girls were too often flighty and didn't know how to treat their betters. Most of the ones who came through her doors were little better than mill girls or sales assistants, not at all the type she could send for a post in a prestigious private house.

Alerted by a figure moving outside the door, Miss Youngman looked up. The young woman had been hovering for nearly half an hour now, waiting for the agency to open, obviously keen.

Carefully the domestic agent studied Alice's dark, well-worn clothes. She was very clean, pressed and neat, but poor. Patently so.

Finally Miss Youngman opened the door, and let Alice in.

'Good morning, can I help you?'

'I was looking for a job.'

Slowly she studied Alice's clothes and the handsome face. Her voice was well modulated, quiet.

'What kind of job?'

'As a maid.'

'We have some positions,' Miss Youngman said efficiently, moving back to her desk and flicking through a stack of cards. Now, this was more like it. This girl had poise, class even. 'What kind of establishment were you looking for?'

'Somewhere large. I want to work in one of the grand houses.'

Miss Youngman couldn't blame her. 'Have you any training?'

Only as a teacher Alice nearly replied, but checked herself. She couldn't mention where she had come from. She had to be careful now. More careful than she had ever been. The old discipline was back.

'No, I have no training. But I can work hard and learn fast.'

Miss Youngman didn't doubt it, but she needed more than the girl's word. 'Where do you live?'

'I was looking for a living-in post,' Alice replied, not immune to the glimmer of suspicion in the woman's eyes. Sighing, she leaned towards Miss Youngman. 'I have no family and my parents are dead. I need a job and I need somewhere to live. I know that beggars can't be choosers, but I would like to work in a house with children.'

Miss Youngman studied her for a long moment. She admired Alice's honesty and was suddenly prepared to give her a chance. Riffling through her buff-coloured cards, she brought out one and read it aloud.

'Dr Greenwood is a widower, who lives on Queen's

Road. He needs a scullery maid for a month while his present maid is nursing sick relatives. It's hard work and not very high wages, but it would do as a start.' She paused. 'He's on his own, no family. But he's a fair employer. He has a housekeeper and a cook. Both of them I know and they'll teach you the ropes. If you do well there, perhaps we could find something a little more to your liking for your second post.'

Running down Trafalgar Street, Victor was out of breath and panicking. He had arrived home after work to find Alice missing, her few belongings gone from the gloomy house. After calling for her repeatedly, he'd rushed round to his employer's home to find Mrs Dedlington taking in the washing from the alley at the side of the house.

'Where's Alice?'

She took a wooden peg out of her mouth. 'Aye, lad, she's gone –'

'Where?' He was wide-eyed, almost hysterical. 'Where has she gone?'

'London.'

'*London*! She knows no one there – why would she go to London?'

Aware that several of her neighbours had come out to see what the rumpus was about, Mrs Dedlington ushered Victor into the kitchen and closed the door.

'She's gone and she doesn't want following, Victor,' the woman said, touching his shoulder kindly, 'She said she'd send back the money she'd borrowed, just as soon as she got a job.'

'I don't want the money!' Victor snapped, getting to his feet at Mr Dedlington walked in. 'This is all your fault! You made her leave, it's your fault.'

Shamefaced, the carpenter looked from Victor to his wife. But there was no comfort there; Mrs Dedlington took Victor's arm.

'Settle down, lad', she said resignedly. 'What's done is done. Alice has gone and she told me to tell you that she won't be back.' She could see his eyes register the words and then watched, distressed, as Victor stumbled to the door.

'I have to find her –'

At once, Mr Dedlington stood between Victor and the door. 'You can't. It were my fault, you're right, but Alice left of her own free will.'

'She left because she was pushed to leave!' Victor responded. 'You told me that I had to choose between my job and her. She knew I would choose her, so she left before I could make the choice.' He moved towards his employer, and Mr Dedlington stepped aside so that Victor could open the door. 'I don't want your bloody job. I want *her*.'

'Victor,' Mrs Dedlington said quietly, 'it's no good. She's upped and gone. She told me to tell you that she wanted you to stay here, she wanted you to get your apprenticeship and make something of yourself.'

Victor turned on the woman. '*Make something of myself?* How can I, without her? There *is* nothing without her.'

'You think that now,' Mrs Dedlington went on, 'but you won't in time. Victor, the girl doesn't want to be found. By leaving, she gave you a chance. Don't throw her kindness in her face. Don't make the sacrifice worthless.'

'But I need her!' Victor said despairingly, throwing himself down in a chair. Immediately Mrs Dedlington came over to him and put her arm round his shoulder.

'Alice has gone off for a purpose, lad. This isn't just about you and her.'

Victor stared up at her. 'What purpose? Alice has no one, nothing. I'm all she has in the world. What else *is* there in her life?'

'I don't know, but she's set on something.'

Slowly Mr Dedlington came over to Victor. He felt such shame that it burned in his mouth.

'I wouldn't blame you if you left. I was a bastard to do what I did. But if you stay, Victor, I'll make it up to you.'

'How could you? Alice is out there on her own. She's never been alone before. How do you think she'll cope? Nothing you could ever do could make up for this.'

'I never thought –'

'No, you didn't!' Victor snapped, no longer caring about his job or how he spoke to his employer. 'You were scared off, Mr Dedlington – bullied by the likes of Clare Lees. After all, who was Alice Rimmer in comparison to your bloody business? You always looked down on her, but you know something? Alice was worth two of you.'

'Hey, now, you watch your mouth!'

But Victor was past pacifying. 'You should have watched yours! Well, I hope you can live with what you've done. It's easy to dismiss someone of no account, isn't it? But whatever Alice was, she was never a coward. You *were*, and you have to live with that.'

Mr Dedlington was reeling from the onslaught, but his guilt prevented him from retaliating. Instead, he looked away.

'You can say what you like, it's true enough. But nothing's going to change what's happened. I'm sorry for what I did, but sorry's not going to alter anything.' He looked at his apprentice and felt the full force of Victor's hatred. 'Let me make amends. Please. I want you to stay, Victor. Please stay.'

Chapter Twenty

After two weeks in her new job, Alice sent Mrs Dedlington enough money to pay off the amount she had borrowed from Victor. There was no address on the note, only the repeated hope that Mrs Dedlington would keep an eye on Victor. That she would *look out for him*. She wrote,

> I have a job, nothing fancy, but I can manage. Is
> Victor all right? I want to know about him, but I
> shouldn't ask. You see, I don't want him to be
> upset for too long. I couldn't cope with that.
> Instead, I console myself with the thought that he'll
> settle down in time. He <u>will</u>. He was always the
> sensible one. Give him the money, please. And tell
> him I loved him – no, tell him <u>thank you</u>.
>   Alice

For twenty-four hours Mrs Dedlington wondered what to do; should she show Victor the note, or not? Should she simply give him the money? The decision was a hard one to make. The lad had been beside himself for days after Alice left, and had been nowhere near the shop. Or the house on Trafalgar Street. No one knew where Victor Coates was, but she presumed that he was living rough somewhere.

When Mrs Dedlington saw Victor again she knew without asking that he had been looking for Alice. He was jittery, had lost weight, his patience was short. Her husband – with whom Mrs Dedlington had had a fierce argument – found himself caught between his warring wife and his resentful apprentice. But he hadn't the nerve to fire Victor after what he had done.

Instead he asked Victor to return. And he refused. He went to the house on Trafalgar Street but couldn't stay. The postcards on the mantelpiece, the tea tray Alice used to set out for him, mocked him. Mrs Hope next door had more than an earful that day, as Victor smashed the crockery and then slumped on the floor, sobbing, his back to the unlit fire.

He missed Alice internally and externally, like someone waking without a sense. Their passion had, he realised, been a motivating force for him. Loving Alice had enlivened him, made him feel optimistic, hopeful. With her gone, Victor felt as he had as a child in Netherlands – cowed, bleak, without hope.

At first he believed he would find her, but as the days passed Victor came to realise that Alice was truly gone. Reality was indeed bleak. It was no longer *our* life, but *his*. The orphan was alone again. And he couldn't blame her for it, because she had done it to help him.

So it was a subdued Victor who had finally returned to Mr Dedlington's shop. He had been surly, unlike himself. As he had come through the door Mr Dedlington had glanced up, then gone back to his work. Victor had looked round at the tables and chairs, the vice, the tools hung up along the wall. He had missed working, missed the familiarity of it all. In the end, a carpentry workshop was the only place he could call home.

'How do, Victor?' Mr Dedlington had said as though his apprentice had never been away. 'Finish that chair leg for me, will you? There's a good lad.'

Victor had hesitated, looked at the old man and taken in the scent of the workshop. The smells of wood, paint and varnish had come back poignantly, almost evocatively. He would work hard to try to forget Alice. Or maybe he would make enough money to buy a shop of his own. Then she would come back . . .

Victor had swallowed; picked up the dun-coloured apron hanging on the back of the door. Slowly he had pulled it over his head and tied it behind his back. If he stayed here Alice would always know where to find him . . . Absent-mindedly, Victor had then picked up the chair leg and let his fingers run over the wood. Routine, safe and predictable, had called him back home.

So was it worth upsetting him now, Mrs Dedlington thought. Showing him the letter might just set him off again. Her fingers tingled against the paper and then finally she pushed it behind a biscuit barrel on the mantelpiece. She would put away the money in safekeeping for Victor, and later on, she would tell him what had happened. Later on, when the wound wasn't so raw. When he could hear Alice's name without flinching.

She would do the best she could for him. Just as she had promised.

Alice knew little about Oldham and it took her a while to get her bearings. Before long, however, she realised that Queen's Road was one of the best addresses in the town. The cook told her that she was lucky to be working there in her first position, and the housekeeper was emphatic that Queen's Road was the zenith of domestic achievement.

And all the time Alice was well aware that she was being watched. She knew it from the moment she was woken and set to work, the old, three-storeyed house cold and dark as she lit the gaslamps and began to prepare the food. Not to make it – that was the cook's job – Alice's was more menial. Out in the side kitchen where the wind blew under the door, she peeled the potatoes for later and collected the milk in the enamel container, freezing to the touch, from the delivery man.

Emptiness was just as cold inside her; homesickness a hard knot in her stomach. She dreamed of Trafalgar Street, and worse, she dreamed of Victor's arms around her. Her longing for him did not diminish. In fact, several times she was tempted to return, hide, and wait for a glimpse of him. But she never went back. That part of her life was over. She had made her decision and would stick to it.

But it hardened her, made her bitter inside. Other people's actions had forced her to Netherlands, other people's actions had now forced her into service. She was haunted – not by her own behaviour, but by the injustice of others. Love, companionship and a future had been ripped away from her, and unwelcome as the feeling was, Alice began to hate.

Yet she kept her feelings to herself and kept herself removed, working hard, but withdrawn from her companions.

From the first, the cook and the housekeeper treated Alice with obvious interest. They asked her where she came from, and she told them what she wanted them to know. Then they wondered behind Alice's back just how long it would be before a girl so good-looking would be courting.

But Alice had no interest in courting anyone. Instead she settled into a routine which had been followed for decades by numerous servants. At five in the morning, she was woken by the knocker-upper and rose to wash and dress. In the dim light she pulled on her black uniform and white cap. Then silently she went downstairs and laid the fires, dusted, and finally took Dr Greenwood's breakfast into the morning room at eight.

She saw little of her employer as she was never there when he came down to eat. Glimpses caught through the high windows told her that he was an unremarkable man, always in a hurry. He had no family and few friends. As a doctor, he was called out at all hours, and many times Alice would get up and look out to catch a glimpse of him getting into his car – a large, sombre car, one of the first in Oldham.

The housekeeper told her that Dr Greenwood had been widowed ten years.

'No lady friends, though,' she sighed, one day during Alice's third week there then changed the subject, anxious not to be caught gossiping. 'You can have your half-day today, Alice. Be back at eight o'clock.'

What was she supposed to do with an afternoon to spare, she wondered. Where did she want to go? Who did she want to see? But to stay in would excite more interest. So a sombre Alice left Queen's Road and caught a bus at the park gates. Idly, she gazed out of the window as it went round the town centre. The shops were full of clothes she had never seen before, make-up in chemists' windows, and Carole Lombard's face on the placards outside the cinema. Women walked past chatting to each other and pushing babies in prams. The world seemed so relaxed to her, so foreign. How could she – a foundling – ever fit in?

The town seemed a life away from Netherlands, or even Trafalgar Street. In fact, it was alien and terrifying. Getting off the bus, Alice walked uncertainly down Union Street and then paused outside the Pelican Tearooms. She was hungry and needed to eat. Digging into her purse, she brought out her money and then, satisfied that she had enough, went inside and ordered tea and a scone.

The waitress was dressed in a uniform not unlike the one Alice wore at Dr Greenwood's and took her order with something bordering on amusement. When her tea arrived, Alice sipped at it cautiously and looked around. Her hand shook a little as she lifted the cup and once or twice she wiped her damp palms on the coarse wool of her skirt.

She missed Victor so acutely that it felt as though a thorn had been pulled across her heart. The hurried leaving, the urgency to find a job, the settling into Queen's Road – all had occupied her and kept her busy. But now, settled into the harsh monotony of routine, Alice felt only loneliness.

Maybe Victor would come to find her. No, she thought, how could he? He thought she was in London ... She sipped the hot tea. Maybe she *would* go round and take a look at him in the workshop. He wouldn't have to see her, she would just look ... No, no, she wouldn't. She had gone, best never to go back ... Loneliness left a dull pain in the pit of her stomach, the scone untouched.

It was no good thinking about Victor, or the past. She had to look ahead, Alice told herself. Stoically she picked up the scone and took a bite, forcing herself to eat. She had to be strong, look after herself. No one else would. No one would ever look out for her now; she was alone. As alone as she had been the day she was left at Netherlands by the Arnolds. *The Arnolds*.

The scone balling up in her dry mouth, Alice pushed aside her plate. For the hundredth time she thought of the photographs in the newspapers, the pictures which had crept up to her cold room at night, the ones which followed her into the scullery in the dark hours of the early morning. Images of Judge Arnold had leaped up from every surface, and each window had contained the words she had remembered – and burned over.

How could they abandon her? Alice had raged inwardly. How could they have thrown her away? How could her father have done what he did, so that years later his daughter would be hounded for it? There was no escape for her. She was branded by her birth, by their sins – and she suffered for it. Over and over again.

It wasn't fair, she had thought that morning, slamming down the plate she was washing and pushing her hands into the cold water, up to the elbows. Fury consumed her, the chilled water having no effect on her white-hot anger. The Arnolds had done so much to hurt her and *escaped*. They had never been punished. All the punishment had been hers. *She* had been the orphan, *she* had been the outcast, *she* had lost her home, her name, her man.

Taking in a deep breath to calm herself, Alice stared at the hard scone in front of her. She couldn't live like this, she thought, she *couldn't*. She would go mad . . . Revenge came in suddenly. It was bitter, yet comforting, regulating her breathing. The Arnolds should be punished for what they had done. And who better to punish them than *her*?

The thought soothed her. She would get her own back. Who could blame her, after all? No one could say they didn't deserve it. And besides, who would stick up her for now, but herself? But how could she get her revenge? Alice sipped her tea, her eyes dark. She had committed to memory their address – The Dower House, Werneth Heights. The time had come to go there. Excitement and fear mingled inside her, but she was determined. It was time to settle old scores.

The waitress came over to the table to clear away.

'How do I get to Werneth Heights?' Alice asked, her voice low.

The woman looked at her in open amazement. 'What d'you want there?'

'I just want . . . I want to go there, that's all.'

The waitress blew out her cheeks. 'Well, you won't get a bus into Werneth Heights. You have to get the number 19, which stops a way off, and then walk the rest.' She collected together Alice's cup and saucer. 'There are only a few houses there. Big ones. It's the nob area. D'you know someone up in Werneth?'

Dodging the question, Alice rose to her feet. Carefully she sorted out her bill and then, awkwardly, offered the waitress a tip.

'Cheers,' the woman said, surprised at her generosity.

But as Alice moved to the door, the waitress wondered what such a woebegone figure wanted up in Werneth Heights and felt suddenly sorry for her. Putting down the plates she was carrying, she hurried back to Alice.

'Look, this tip's too much. Take it back,' she said,

handing Alice the money. 'You look like you need it more than I do.'

It was six fifteen. Werneth Heights was quiet, and dark. Only a few lamps lit the surrounding trees, and from behind high walls illuminated windows threw their light on to opulent lawns. Timidly Alice walked past the first of the impressively big houses and felt herself horribly out of place. Tugging at her sleeves to make them longer, and smoothing her hair, she knew only too well that she looked like a servant. And why would a servant be idling along, gawping at the houses?

Her feet sounded on the gravel and made every step obvious as Alice hurried on. Perhaps it had been a bad idea, she thought; maybe it would be better to come back another time. In daylight. But as she turned at the next bend Alice came face to face with the house she had committed to memory, the house she had seen in all the old newspaper cuttings. The Arnold house. The house where she had been born.

Her first sensation was one of awe. God, she could never even walk in there, she thought – and then realised that this was the very house where she should have been raised. *This was her home.* This was her inheritance, her right. These riches should have been hers ... Too far away on the other side of the wall to see detail, Alice could, however, make out the shapes of stone statues at the entrance doors and hear the faint sounds of a car engine purring in the garage.

It looked more like a institution than a house, she thought – not that dissimilar to Netherlands in its oppressive bulk. Slowly she moved along the garden wall, catching snatches of the house between the hedges and trees. Her mother had died here. Her father had killed her mother here. And afterwards she had been spirited out of there and forgotten ... Alice's eyes fixed on the windows, her brain running and rerunning the newspaper reports. Her mother had been battered, stabbed. Her father had run away. She was the offspring of a murderer.

The implication hit her forcibly. She shared her father's blood, her father's characteristics. They were similar in appearance, but what likeness was there *inside*? Imagination had been bad enough, but to see the bleak building in front of her the true horror of what had happened seemed to hit her like a body blow. She stared at the house. Which window, which room, had seen the murder? From which door had her father run away? Who had found her mother? And how had she looked that night after her father had killed her? Alice stopped suddenly and leaned against the wall for support. Nausea welled up in her and she opened her mouth, gulping in air to steady herself.

She was marked out. She could never have a normal life – how was it possible? Even if no one ever found out about her past, *she* would know. Her father was a murderer, but what had made him kill? What was in him which had made him a killer? And was it in her?

Her legs buckled suddenly, her knees hitting the gravel path before she had time to throw out her hands and break her fall.

'Hey there!' a voice said hurriedly, 'D-d-d'you want some h-h-help?' A man was helping her to her feet, a slightly built man with prominent blue eyes.

'I'm fine. I'm fine.'

'You d-d-don't look fine,' Leonard replied. 'Come on, you need to sit down for a minute and get your bearings.' He guided her towards the gates and, startled, she suddenly stopped.

'No! I can't go in there.'

'And you c-c-can't stay out here,' he countered. 'It's getting dark and you're n-n-not well. Come on, I won't take no f-f-for an answer.'

So Leonard Tripps, son-in-law of Judge Arnold, husband of Dorothy, guided Alice towards The Dower House. It had been sixteen years, ten months and eleven days since she had last been inside those walls.

Chapter Twenty-One

'What the hell has he brought in now? Another of his strays?' Judge Arnold said, watching Leonard through the window, making for the servants' entrance. Abruptly he rapped on the glass. Leonard looked over. With an impatient gesture, Judge beckoned for his son-in-law to come in, pointing to the slight girl beside him.

Moments later Alice was standing in front of Judge Arnold, Alwyn watching her from her wheelchair.

'So what have we here?' Judge Arnold said, studying Alice from head to toe. She was poorly dressed, in obvious hand-me-down clothes, her shoes shabby but well polished. 'Who are you?'

Alice had been looking down at her feet, but when she caught Judge's eye he felt a sudden jolt of surprise. Well, she looked like a down-and-out, but she was a feisty one, all right.

She, for her part, hated him on sight.

'My name's Alice Rimmer,' she said simply, wondering for a moment if the name would score a direct hit. But obviously the home had given her that name, and it meant nothing to the Arnolds.

'And what – *Alice Rimmer* – are you doing prowling about outside at this time of night?'

Leonard stepped forward. 'She f-f-felt faint –'

'I'm not surprised,' Judge Arnold replied. 'I would be faint, creeping about in the dark.'

'I wasn't creeping about,' Alice replied, her voice a shock to him. A well-modulated voice, not at all working class.

Judge Arnold had no truck with cheek. He had been

in charge of too many men for too long to take insolence.

'So what *were* you doing?'

'I was . . . lost.'

It was Alwyn's turn to intervene. Slowly she wheeled her chair closer to Alice and, picking up her glasses, scrutinised her. Finally she put her glasses down and looked over to her husband.

'Don't be such a bully. The girl looks exhausted.'

Surprised by the unexpected show of support, Alice smiled faintly at her. Alwyn did not respond, but she liked the look of the girl, liked the spirit which was obviously just below the surface. Besides, it was exciting to find some little wanderer out in the cold. It broke up the monotony of the evening.

'Would you like something to eat?'

'Alwyn!' her husband blustered. 'I don't think we have to treat her as a guest until we find out exactly why she's here.'

But Alwyn waved his objection aside with a flick of her hand. 'She's told you what she was doing – she was lost.'

'Huh!'

'And I believe her,' Alwyn concluded, turning back to Alice. 'Where do you come from?'

'I have a job in Oldham at the moment. I work as a maid for a doctor on Queen's Road. I finish there in a week's time. Today was my first day off,' Alice hurried on, well aware that Judge Arnold didn't believe a word she was saying. 'So I went out to explore the town. You see, I don't come from Oldham.'

Perhaps if she threw down enough clues, something would trigger off a remembrance, Alice thought. There would be a showdown then. And God, how she wanted that. How she *longed* for that. She would reveal who she was and tell the Arnolds just what she thought of them. But the clues so far had effected no response. They either didn't remember anything about their granddaughter, or her removal from the family had been arranged by a third party.

Somehow such a possibility made the situation even worse and Alice found herself willing one of them to confront her.

'Where do you come from?' Judge Arnold asked.

'Salford.'

'Oh,' he said simply, losing interest. Salford was a poor town, much of it slums. The likes of the Arnold family had no interest there. Either now, or in the past.

Infuriated, Alice felt her face colour.

Alwyn saw the change and found herself intrigued.

'So where will you go after you finish working for the doctor?'

'I don't know yet,' Alice replied honestly.

'W-w-would he give you a r-r-reference?' Leonard asked suddenly.

Raising her eyebrows, Alwyn turned to look at her son-in-law. 'Why ask that?'

'Because we m-n-need a new maid. You said so yourself only this morning. Dorothy needs a r-r-replacement for Betty w-w-when she leaves in a fortnight.'

Judge Arnold had been growing bored, but now his attention was galvanised. 'We don't hire wastrels off the streets,' he said coldly. 'Give the girl some food and send her on her way.'

Colouring with embarrassment, Leonard was unable to look Alice in the face. But she never flinched. Instead she stared at the old man and loathed him. You're my grandfather, she thought, this is my home. Yet you want to feed me and send me off like a stray dog, doing just enough to absolve your conscience. Oh no, she thought, her spirit flaring, you won't get off that lightly.

She turned to Alwyn. 'I *would* like to be considered for a job here. I'm a good worker and very careful.'

'I dare say you are,' Alwyn replied, amused, 'but there's more to being a lady's maid than being careful.'

Lady's maid to her own relation, Alice thought. It was almost laughable. What a perfect way to infiltrate this family and get back to where she belonged. Nervousness gone, Alice summoned up all of her charm.

'Please, give me a chance,' she asked Alwyn. 'Please. I can do it, I know I can. I've always been quick to learn.'

Leonard stepped forward, moved by Alice's plea. He raised his eyebrows quizzically at his mother-in-law.

'What's the h-h-harm? Dorothy needs a maid and we can check out this young l-l-lady with her employer.' He could see his mother-in-law waver and pushed his advantage. 'Alice is young, she c-c-could be trained to our ways.'

Alice was watching him and wondering just how easy it would be for them to train her to their ways.

'Well, the final decision lies with Dorothy,' Alwyn replied at last. Tugging the bell rope she asked for her daughter to be sent down to the drawing room. Whilst they waited, she turned back to Alice. 'What about your family?'

There was only a moment's pause. 'I have no family. They're dead.'

'I'm sorry,' Alwyn replied automatically.

Then the door opened and Alice turned to see a tall woman walk in. The first impression Alice had of her aunt was confused. Dorothy was slender to the point of gauntness. Her hair was pale auburn, her face tranquil, and yet there was an unease about her which seemed to resonate on the very air. Gliding in, she smiled at Alwyn and kissed Leonard on the cheek, avoiding her father as she sat down in front of the fire.

Finally she glanced over to Alice . . . There was no recognition in the eyes. Why should there be? It had been so long ago and Alice had been only a year old when this woman – and this family – had banished her. Besides, there was no family resemblance to give her away. Obviously Alice took after her father's side more than the Arnolds.

'What did you want to see me about?' Dorothy asked her husband quietly. Her voice was uneven, like someone who had just been woken from sleep.

'D-d-darling,' Leonard said, moving over to his wife, 'something incredible h-h-has just happened.'

'Huh!' snorted Judge Arnold again.

Dorothy gave her father a look which Alice found hard to read. 'What has happened, Leonard?'

'This young l-l-lady is called Alice Rimmer.' Again, no reaction. 'She was l-l-lost and ended up here, where I f-f-found her about to faint.' Dorothy watched him, but her expression was unfathomable. She was either very stupid, or very sly, Alice thought. 'Well, Alice is a m-m-maid for a doctor in Oldham, but her position f-f-finishes in a week and then she'll need a n-n-new situation.'

Dorothy was listening to her husband, but looking at Alice. 'So?'

'You need a new maid after Betty leaves.'

'So?'

Leonard sighed. 'Darling, Alice w-w-would be perfect.'

'Fine.'

'Is that it?' bellowed Judge Arnold. 'Just fine?'

Dorothy turned her languid gaze on her father. Is she drugged? Alice wondered.

'I agree to her being my maid. What do you want me to say?' Dorothy's voice had risen, then dropped again as she turned back to Alice. 'You're very pretty,' she said at last. 'Very pretty indeed. That's not always a good thing. To be too pretty.' Sighing, she then turned away.

Leonard glanced back to Alice happily. 'Well, it seems you've g-g-got a new job. S-s-s-subject to references, of course.'

'Who would have thought,' Judge Arnold said, staring at Alice with barely disguised suspicion, 'that getting lost would prove so fortuitous?'

Chapter Twenty-Two

Picking his teeth with the nib of his pen, Charlie watched Alice in the garden. She was playing with Robin, her dark hair coming loose from her cap. God, he thought, she was incredible. He had told his aunt the same, and Dorothy had said something bland about not getting involved with the servants. But Charlie – stupid to a fault – had still tried his luck. And had his face slapped for it.

His passion had cooled only slightly. She'd been at The Dower House a week now and he found Alice mesmeric. So he wrote about her at length in his poems and dedicated his sentimental offering – about the Trojan Horse – to her. Only the previous evening the whole family had been subjected to this romantic saga – written by Charlie, recited by Charlie and stage-managed by Charlie. It was, Leonard said later, like being crushed by an avalanche of fudge.

Judge Arnold, however, was suspicious of Alice. Usually servants *wanted* the attention of their masters, especially foolish young masters who would come into money. But she had made it clear from the start that she wasn't interested in Charlie. Amazing, Judge Arnold thought. After all, his rich grandson wasn't handsome, but when had that stopped a woman on the make?

So perhaps Alice Rimmer *wasn't* on the make . . . Judge Arnold sniffed and turned from the window, back to the letter on his desk, which he had reread several times over the last days. The reference had been sent before they'd agreed to hire Alice, and it had been excellent. She was a good and willing worker, it said, always tidy and polite. She was, Dr Greenwood had assured him, unobtrusive about the house.

The Judge would have liked to write back to the good doctor and tell him that Alice Rimmer was about as unobtrusive as a whale in a teacup. Apart from the smitten Charlie, it had not escaped his attention that little Robin was spending more and more time with the new maid. Oh yes, Judge Arnold thought, Alice Rimmer was certainly making her presence felt.

Filing away the reference, he then thought about his daughter. He wished with all his heart that Dorothy and her mother had decided to stay away from The Dower House. The 12 November was tomorrow ... Unable to settle, he paced the room.

It was a bad move to have Dorothy here. It couldn't be good for her. He had already seen a change in the few weeks since she had been home. Her control was slipping, restlessness increasing daily.

A knock at the door interrupted his thoughts. 'Come in.'

At once Alice walked in, carrying a tray.

'Why isn't the housekeeper doing that?' he asked, more harshly than he meant. But there was something about Alice which provoked him.

'She's very busy and asked me to bring it to you, sir.'

Was it his imagination, or did she make the word *sir* sound as though she was mocking him? 'Whatever ... You can go.'

Nodding, Alice turned to leave, but was immediately called back.

'You seem to be getting on with my grandson very well.'

She smiled coolly. 'Robin is a lovely child, sir.'

'I know.' He paused. 'How do you get on with my daughter?'

The question caught Alice off guard, but she kept her composure. I can be just as crafty as you, she thought. After all, I *am* one of you.

'It's a pleasure to work for Mrs Tripps.'

'I didn't ask that!' he snapped, walking closer to Alice. 'There's something about you, girl. You're not servant fodder. I deal with rubbing rags every day – can spot them a mile off. And you're not of that ilk.' His eyes were hard. 'Where did you come from really?'

'I told you. Salford, sir.'

'What did your people do?'

'They're dead, sir.' Her heart thumped and she struggled to hold her composure.

A showdown was not what Alice wanted now. She had something else in mind, something altogether more damaging. Her plan was to gain by stealth what should have been hers by right. To damage from within. She was going to wheedle her way into the very core of the family, make herself indispensable, needed – and then she would have her own power to use as she saw fit. *When* she saw fit.

'Before your parents died, who were they?'

'They died when I was a child,' Alice answered, hurrying into the lie. 'My grandmother brought me up. After she died, I went into service with Dr Greenwood. Will that be all, sir?'

He wanted suddenly to slap her face, to knock the barely disguised insolence out of her. But he knew he couldn't and felt humiliated at being so easily provoked. Breathing in deeply, Judge Arnold turned away.

'That will be all.'

Once outside the door, Alice sighed and then leaned against it for support. Her face was ashen. Slowly she ran over Judge Arnold's words and her answers in her mind and then touched her heart with her left hand. It had been difficult, but she was all right. She hadn't given herself away. He was suspicious of her, but he knew nothing.

Consoled, Alice walked back to the servants' quarters. She never realised that she had been watched, that Dorothy had stood at the head of the staircase and looked down on her. Her aunt's face, as ever, betrayed little. Only her eyes, watchful and wary, gave her away.

'You have to come and read to me,' Charlie begged Alice as she walked through the kitchen and out into the yard beyond. This she didn't need; her own brother acting like a giddy fool around her.

'Charlie, grow up. You're too old to have someone read to you.'

'You read to Robin –'

'Robin is four,' Alice replied, pushing back Charlie as she walked into the outer shed and collected the potatoes the gardener had left there that morning. 'Besides, I'm too busy to fool around wasting time.'

'Then let me help you,' Charlie offered pathetically. 'I could help. I could.'

Alice paused and turned to look at her brother. Charlie was standing in the weak sunlight, dust motes floating on the warm autumn air. The smell of the hay from the stables was soporific, soothing. Soon the cold would come and batter the house for winter, but for the moment there was this brief, fleeting memory of summer. Which couldn't last.

Alice looked at the gangling youth in front of her. How could she have ever been jealous of him? Oh, if he had been spoiled, vicious, she could have hated him. But Charlie was so gentle, so eager to please. She didn't even mind the fact that he had had everything, whilst she had had so little. Because Alice knew that if the positions had been reversed, Charlie would never have survived.

'Take these back into the house, will you?' she asked at last, watching as he picked the basket up gratefully. The next question was out of her mouth before she had time to check it. 'Did I understand what someone said? That Mrs Tripps isn't your real mother?'

Charlie shook his head. 'No, she's my aunt.'

Keeping her voice steady, Alice continued, 'So where's your mother?'

'I can't say ... Well, I can say she's dead,' Charlie replied hesitantly. 'She was killed.'

'I'm so sorry,' Alice replied, walking into the laundry and knowing that Charlie would follow. 'But Mr Tripps is your real father, isn't he?'

'Oh no, my real father's dead too. Leonard and Dorothy took me on when ... Well, they took me on.'

Alice looked into her brother's face. It was so easy to interrogate Charlie.

Guiltily, she pressed on: 'Both of your parents are dead? That's terrible, I'm so sorry.' She reached for a bundle of sheets and began to fold them. 'How did they die?'

Hovering on one foot and then the other, Charlie looked at the young woman in front of him. Alice was folding the sheets, her hands busy, her eyes lowered. He liked her so much, there was something so comfortable about her. He could talk to Alice as he had never been able to talk to anyone else, not even Leonard. But he still couldn't tell her about the past. He could tell no one about that.

'I can't tell you about my parents.'

'Oh,' Alice said simply, but managed to put a rebuke in the word which cut through the muscle of his heart.

'I would, Alice! But I can't. My grandfather forbids it.'

'Then you must do what your grandfather says,' Alice replied, picking up the wicker laundry basket and heading back to the kitchen.

'It's a secret, you see,' Charlie went on, following after her. 'One we have to keep.'

'It's all right, Charlie. I had no right to ask.'

'Oh, you did. You did,' he reassured her. 'You can ask anything. It's just that it's the one thing we *can't* talk about. About my parents.' He held open the kitchen door to allow Alice to pass through, then followed her in. 'I would tell you if I could.'

She was all calm detachment. 'I've told you, it's all right. I'm a servant here, I should know my place.'

'But –'

Alice smiled at him distantly. 'Charlie, please. I have to get on with my work.'

'She was murdered.'

Feigning shock, Alice dropped the linen she was folding and stared at her brother. 'What?'

'My father killed my mother –'

'Charlie!' a voice called out suddenly from the head of the basement steps.

'Oh God, Judge!' Charlie replied, hurrying up the stairs. 'Coming, coming.'

Alice leaned against the kitchen table and bit her lip. She had been so close, so close to hearing the whole story from a family member. But she had been thwarted – and by Judge Arnold. The one who trusted her the least. How much he had heard of their conversation Alice didn't know, but it was too much of a coincidence that he should intervene just as Charlie was about to confide everything.

She would just have to wait a bit longer, Alice decided, snatching up another sheet and folding it roughly. After all, she had waited for nearly seventeen years already. What difference would a few more weeks make?

Chapter Twenty-Three

The weather turned suddenly and the morning of 12 November came in cold and blustery. Winds rocked the windows and blew down the chimneys. Alwyn pulled a silk shawl around her shoulders in the morning room as her husband read the paper. She watched him for a while over the rim of her teacup and waited for the inevitable conversation which was sure to come.

Which it did, ten minutes later.

'Perhaps I shouldn't go into work today,' he said at last. 'I might stay home for a change.'

'And get bored and under everyone's feet?' his wife countered. 'Get to the office, my dear, and terrorise the minions.'

He smiled wryly at the jibe. 'But it might be better if I was around.'

'We can cope,' Alwyn countered. 'Leonard is working from home and I'm here.'

'It's the twelfth –'

'Don't you think I know that?' Alwyn replied, draining her cup and signalling for the maid to leave the room. 'We'll get through it, we always do.'

'When Dorothy is abroad you get through it.'

'When Dorothy is *here* we'll get through it,' Alwyn countered, her tone determined.

Judge Arnold glanced towards the door. 'Where is she, anyway?'

'In bed. If she gets upset, I have a remedy. The doctor gave me some sedative – if it is needed.'

'You should never have brought her home.'

Alwyn sighed. 'She lives here, she can't spend the rest of her life hiding away on the twelfth of November. Besides, it was Dorothy's idea to come home, not mine.'

Judge Arnold leaned towards his wife. 'But is it wise? For God's sake, you know what I mean.'

Gripping his hand, Alwyn looked her husband in the eyes. 'If anything happens, it *will* happen and there's nothing we can do to avoid it now. Chances are it will be tonight anyway, when you're home. It won't happen in daylight.'

He shuddered suddenly, unexpectedly. 'Do you remember?'

She nodded briskly. 'Every day.'

'But how much does *she* think about it?'

'I don't know,' Alwyn said firmly, 'I'm not privy to my daughter's mind. I can just support her, that's all.'

'You could take her out today, get her away from the house.'

'She wants to be here.'

'What for?' he snapped, suddenly irritated.

'She has her own reasons,' Alwyn replied, exasperated. 'What do you want me to do? Drag her away? If she can face being here today – then so can we.'

Upstairs, in Dorothy's bedroom, Alice, having drawn her mistress a bath, was putting out her clothes for the day. She too knew exactly what day it was and had been surprised by Dorothy's choice the previous night. 'I want to wear white,' she had said. White – was that the colour she wore the night she found her sister dead? Alice wondered, tiptoeing over to the bed and looking down at the sleeping woman.

Dorothy's remote quality was obvious even as she rested. She was contained, controlled in her sleep, and yet her hands moved, her fingers working convulsively, as though they, and only they, were allowed to release the tension she carried.

Alice glanced at the clock and then – as instructed – opened the curtains. Her mistress did not stir. Outside the trees were blowing vigorously in the stiff wind, the pond rippled, the weathervane on the stables twisting and turning. It was cold, Alice thought, too cold to wear white.

'Alice, is that you?'

She turned, to see her mistress sitting up in bed.

'What time is it?'

'Nine thirty, madam.'

Idly, Dorothy rubbed her eyes with her hands. Her movements were slow. 'Did you set out my clothes?'

Alice gestured to the dressing gown. 'Everything you asked for, madam. It's cold, though; perhaps you might be warmer in something else.'

In reply, Dorothy swung back the bed covers and got to her feet. Padding across the floor, she paused only briefly to look out of the window and then moved past Alice and continued into the bathroom. Hearing her mistress sinking into the bath, Alice left the room.

Alice had discovered that neither the housekeeper, general maid nor butler had been in the employ of the Arnolds when the tragedy occurred. Alice had overheard the housekeeper say that her predecessor had been dismissed soon after the murder, and that the family had not used the house for the three years which followed. Apparently Dorothy had been taken abroad with her parents and Charlie. When the three years had passed they returned and new staff were hired. No one from the past remained.

Deep in thought, Alice jumped when Charlie came round the bottom of the stairs.

'Morning,' he said bashfully, dropping his voice. 'Sorry I had to run off like that yesterday. The old man, you know.'

She nodded, tried to walk on, but he stood in her way.

'My grandfather was asking about you.'

Alice's face remained impassive.

'He wanted to know what we talked about.'

'Did you tell him?'

'Not about what I said yesterday,' Charlie's voice dropped further. 'I hope you'll forget it too.'

'I already have,' Alice said evenly. 'Let me pass, Charlie, I have to get on with my work.'

'Is my aunt up?' he asked, looking towards the first floor.

'She's bathing.'

'I know they worry about her,' Charlie said, shivering suddenly. 'God, it's cold.'

'Then go into the morning room and get your breakfast,' Alice said good-naturedly, walking off.

Eventually Dorothy came down and toyed with some toast, whilst her father kept stealing glances at her – and Alwyn sipped her Darjeeling. If Dorothy was aware of their scrutiny, she did not show it. Finally, after she had finished eating, she stood up and called for Robin to be brought to her.

'Where are you going?' Alwyn asked.

'For a walk.'

'Where?'

'Around the garden,' Dorothy replied, looking from her mother to her father. 'What's the matter?'

'Nothing.'

She smiled suddenly, wrong-footing them. 'I'm fine. Just leave me alone, will you?'

Minutes later Dorothy was walking with Robin down to the pond. At the morning-room window Judge Arnold pushed his hands deep into his pockets and refused to take a phone call from one of the factory managers.

'You're making her nervous,' Alwyn said, eminently calm. 'Leave us alone.'

'But –'

'No! This time I want you to listen to me,' she said bluntly. 'Go to work. We'll see you later.'

When Alwyn was sure her husband had finally left, she wheeled herself around the morning room, going from window to window so that she could keep her daughter and grandson in view. The wind was tugging at their clothes, clouds on the horizon.

She watched them for several minutes, then moved over to the bell rope and jerked it violently, twice.

Moments later, Alice entered. 'Morning, madam.'

'I want to ask you to do something for me, Alice.'

'Anything, madam.'

'I want you to stay with my daughter today. Stay close by her. Don't let her out of your sight. Can you do that?'

'Of course, madam.'

'Someone else will see to your other duties,' Alwyn went on. Then she signalled for Alice to come closer to her. 'There's something about you, something I like. Would you say you were strong? I mean mentally strong, Alice?'

She nodded. 'Yes, madam. I would say I was strong.'

'Not given to panicking?'

'No, madam.'

Alwyn looked her up and down. She had been watching Alice since she came to The Dower House and was impressed by what she saw. The girl was composed, but there was spirit there. Alice Rimmer was no pushover, that much was obvious. Alwyn knew only too well that her husband disliked Alice, but was not sure why. Because he couldn't cow her? Or because he didn't trust her? Alwyn didn't know for sure, but *she* trusted Alice.

'My daughter might be upset today,' she said at last. 'She might be reminded of something unpleasant. I can't watch her all the time in this blasted wheelchair, so I need you to help me out. I don't want my daughter left alone for a moment. Not for a moment, do you hear?'

'Yes, madam.'

'This evening will probably be . . . difficult. If anything happens, I imagine it will happen then.' Alwyn paused, considering how much of her anxiety to reveal. 'Serve me well in this, and I'll make sure you're rewarded. Dorothy is my daughter and I love her.'

And she is my aunt, Alice wanted to reply. What would you think if you knew who was standing in front of you? Would you ask your *granddaughter* to do this for you? *Could* you ask so much of the very child you all sent away?

'Look after my daughter for me.'

Why should I, Alice thought, when none of you looked after me?

'I'll take care of her, madam,' Alice replied. The perfect servant. Born to serve.

Judge Arnold came home for lunch to a quiet house. No, nothing untoward had happened, go back to work, his wife said. We can cope here without you ... Two o'clock slid into three, yawned past four, and then the day began to fade into night. In The Dower House lights were turned on. Somewhere, probably in Charlie's rooms upstairs, a radio played.

Downstairs, Dorothy sewed. Her fingers were nimble, her eyes lowered. From her wheelchair, Alwyn watched her daughter, Robin sitting by his mother's feet. Dressed in her black uniform, Alice read to the little boy, her voice soothing. Now and then she glanced over to Dorothy, then continued.

At seven o'clock, Robin was put to bed. Judge Arnold and Leonard were away until late, visiting a new site. Taking her cue from Alwyn, Alice settled the child for the night whilst her employer sat with Dorothy, who was wearing her pristine white dress.

Shortly afterwards, Alice returned to the drawing room.

Surprised, Dorothy looked up from her sewing. 'What are you doing here, Alice? You normally go to your own room after you've put Robin to bed.'

Alwyn intervened immediately. 'I like to hear her read. Read some more, Alice, will you?'

Obediently Alice sat down on the chair between the two women and began to read again. But her thoughts soon drifted off the page and wandered back to the old newspaper cuttings she had seen. None of them had said *where* her mother was murdered. Where had it been? In the dining room? The hall? The bedroom? . . . Alice felt a shudder run over her and looked back to the book.

Was it this room? Here? She glanced at the carpet furtively. And what *time* was it when her mother was murdered? How soon afterwards had Dorothy found her?

Alice took in a breath and kept her head down. She could sense Alwyn's eyes on her, but did not look over to her employer.

'. . . *There was little anyone could do about it. There was nowhere else the boy could go* . . .' On and on Alice read, her lips moving, following the story, whilst her mind was drifting. God, the tension was almost unbearable. She had never thought that her plan would work so well, that she would be assimilated so firmly into the family, trusted so much that she was now sitting – marking down the hours – with the family she was deceiving. Calm down, she thought, calm down. Control yourself. You can't give yourself away now. Not now . . .

Turning over the page, Alice read on. All she had to do was to sit it out. Soon it would be getting late and Dorothy always retired early. Alice could settle her mistress and then go to her room and think her own thoughts. My mother was killed on this date seventeen years ago . . . My mother . . .

'What is it?' Alwyn asked suddenly as Dorothy stood up.

'I heard a noise.'

'No, my dear, no noise.'

'I think . . . I think there was.'

'There was no noise, Dorothy. Sit down and listen to the story.'

Frowning, Alwyn nodded for Alice to continue. But she had read only ten lines when Dorothy got up again.

'I want to go to bed now. I want to sleep.' Her voice was patchy, the words snatched. 'I need to sleep.'

'Very well, my dear,' Alwyn said evenly, then glanced over to Alice. 'Would you see my daughter to her room?'

Together they left the room and mounted the stairs. At the head of the steps Dorothy suddenly turned and looked down. A moon shone through the window and made white puddles in the hall below, the shadows blackened by comparison. For an instant Dorothy seemed about to descend again – and abruptly she turned away, almost running to her own room.

As she had been requested, Alice did not leave Dorothy that night. She waited until her mistress was settled in bed and then turned out the lights, leaving the dressing lamp on to throw a little illumination into the darkened bedroom. When she had done that, Alice settled herself into an easy chair by the window, pulled a rug over her knees, and waited.

The house went to bed. She heard the Arnolds retire, and the sinister creak of the wrought-iron lift which carried Alwyn up from below. Slowly silence fell. Dorothy slept peacefully. Outside a fox barked and the moonlight fell across the silk bedspread like a knife blade.

She imagined the murder. It was easy, in that quiet house, amongst the corridors and high walls. She imagined her mother's pain, her father's panic. It was so real to her that she could almost hear the screams and the noise of a door slamming. At one point, Alice even rose and looked out of the window, certain she would see some ghost of a running man . . . Then, finally at one in the morning, she fell into a deep, exhausted sleep.

Awakened by the sound of a voice, Alice sat up. It was soft, whispered. A dream voice – or was it? Hurriedly she threw off the rug and ran out into the corridor. The house was in darkness, but there was one chink of illumination coming from below. Hurriedly Alice ran down the stairs.

The light was coming from the drawing room, the room no one had entered that day. No fire had been burning and the air was cold as Alice stood in the doorway. The room was empty. Full only of ghosts. Shivering, she rubbed her arms to warm them and walked in further. She could see the outlines of furniture and the moonlight falling through the high windows.

Then Alice heard a noise. She froze, unable to move. Another noise followed. Then the hall door swung closed behind her. Gasping with fright, Alice moved forward and stumbled over a chair, struggling to her feet as she strained to see in the darkness.

'Who's there?'

Nothing.

'Who's there?'

There was a sudden mewling noise from low down. Alice turned, panicked, then walked towards the sound. At the window, she stopped dead in her tracks. In the moonlight she could just make out the figure of a woman on all fours, dressed in white.

'Madam?'

Dorothy looked up. Her eyes were darkly shadowed in the moonlight, and in her hand was a cloth.

'I have to clean up!' she said urgently. 'I have to clean up. Clean it all up.'

Alice stood transfixed. 'No. Let me, let me clean it up, madam –'

'I have to!' Dorothy snapped.

'Let me help you then,' Alice offered, bending down. But just as she so, Dorothy stood up. Her senses overwrought, Alice threw up her arms to protect herself as the woman towered over her.

'You won't tell, will you?' Dorothy asked hoarsely.

Alice stared upwards, terrified. 'Tell *what*?'

Dorothy's eyes were unfocused, the cloth in her hand.

'There's blood here. Lots of it. I can't tell anyone,' she went on, Alice getting to her feet and backing away. 'Sssh!' Dorothy said suddenly. 'We have to keep it a secret.' She moved again and Alice jumped aside. But Dorothy wasn't about to strike out at her and instead fell back onto her knees, working at the carpet again, rubbing it repeatedly with the cloth. 'I have to clean up.'

Alice could feel her throat tighten.

'It's clean now, madam,' she said, bending down and taking the cloth from her aunt's hand. 'All clean. You did well. There's no blood left.'

'None?' Dorothy asked wistfully.

'No,' Alice replied, 'none at all. And no one knows. No one knows anything.' She brushed the hair away from Dorothy's eyes, her heart shifting with pity. 'No one knows anything.'

Slowly she guided Dorothy to the door and up the dim staircase. Her aunt looked back a couple of times, but allowed herself to be urged on. Soon Alice had settled her back in bed and then she closed the door, locking it behind her and pocketing the key.

Only then did Alice walk downstairs and back into the drawing room. She stood for a long time looking at the carpet where her aunt had scrubbed at the pile. There was no stain, no old reminder of blood. But she knew that here, at this very spot, a woman had been killed. *Here* her mother had been murdered by her father.

Kneeling, Alice touched the pile. It was 12 November, the anniversary of her mother's death. It was a time for the family to grieve – it was expected of them – but no one would expect her, a servant, to mourn. And she should be the one to grieve the most. After all, she had lost the most. With her mother's death, a part of Alice's life had ended. She stared at the carpet, but there was nothing to mark out the place where Catherine fell. Only a damp patch.

Of the mother she had never known, the mother who – had she lived – would have loved and kept her child with her, there was no trace. The Arnolds would comfort Dorothy and each other, but no one would enter that room to find Alice – now lying on the carpet, her eyes closed to the hard light coming in cold from the high white moon.

Chapter Twenty-Four

Four years later

Leonard had to admit that old man Arnold was never going to retire. He had hoped, now that Judge was in his late sixties, that he might stop, but it was wishful thinking. Pushing fifty, Leonard would have liked to retire early himself and glide into a comfy old age – but there was no chance of that. Whilst Judge Arnold worked, so did he.

Judge was now sitting in the back seat of his Rolls, Leonard beside him, each with a pile of documents on his lap. What the hell is the point of working yourself to death? Leonard thought. They didn't need any more money, or power. He had his own fortune now, but instead of moving away with Dorothy she had insisted that they stay at The Dower House with her parents.

And Charlie – who had turned from a terminally stupid boy into an adorable moron. Leonard thought about his nephew. He couldn't dislike Charlie – after all, he had been trying to for years. But there was something so guileless, so damned innocent about the lad that it defied dislike. Of course it was patently obvious both to Judge and to Leonard that Charlie could never take over the business. He would never be able to control the workers, strike deals, or handle awkward suppliers. Goofy Charlie, with his manic hair and bow legs, would ruin the business within a year.

So what exactly is Judge Arnold planning? Leonard thought. To work until he drops? Then what? Pass the businesses over to me? Leonard didn't know, and he didn't ask. He might have married into the Arnold family over ten years earlier, but he was still thought of as an outsider.

If the truth be known, he liked it that way. Furtively, he stole a glance at his father-in-law and suddenly pictured Judge Arnold with a ring through his nose, snorting at the ground like a Highland bull. Leonard blinked and looked away. He didn't know which was worse – working with Judge all day or being subjected to Charlie's plays at night.

'I want a word with you.'

Leonard turned, smiling guilelessly. 'About w-w-what?'

'Business.'

What else?

Judge Arnold pulled on his glasses and scrutinised the papers on his lap. 'We need to make a bigger profit at the Goring mill. We were down last quarter.'

'But we made up for it at the Eden mill.'

'That's not the point! I want to see profits at *all* the mills. You need to work them harder. I rely on you to see to it that next quarter we're into a tidy profit.'

Leonard thought about arguing with him and then decided against it. Instead he nodded. 'D-d-did you think any more about opening a shop?'

Judge Arnold had been musing with the idea of a chain of shops around Oldham, Salford and Manchester, selling the cotton goods they made in the mills.

'I've thought about it,' he replied, then lapsed into silence. Obviously he wasn't going to tell Leonard *what* he'd thought. Instead, he dropped a bombshell. 'We're going off for a while, on holiday.'

Leonard felt his spirits rise. 'Really?'

'You needn't look so bloody pleased about it!' Judge Arnold retorted. 'I wouldn't be doing it, but Alwyn's insisting that we go away for the winter.'

His in-laws away! Leonard thought. How lucky could he get? 'W-w-where are you going?'

'France. From early November to February.'

This was getting better by the minute. 'We'll m-miss you.'

'Liar! You can hardly wait to see us go,' Judge Arnold barked, then paused, his expression serious. 'Dorothy needs a break.'

'*Dorothy's* going w-w-with you?' Leonard asked, aghast.

'Like I said, she needs a break. A bit of sun will do her good.'

'B-b-but –'

'She wants to spend some time with Robin.'

'But n-n-not me?' Leonard countered, regretting the words as they left his lips.

'Oh, grow up!' Judge responded. 'It's normal for a mother to want to spend time with her son.'

'B-b-but she's with Robin all the t-t-time.'

'Not on her own. Dorothy feels . . .' Judge Arnold wavered for a moment. 'She feels . . . Well, like he's growing up too fast.'

A bit late to think about that now, Leonard mused. His wife had been more than willing to pass over much of the care of their son to Alice, whose duties had gradually extended far beyond the original role of lady's maid-cum-housemaid. In fact, yearly Dorothy had seemed to grow more distant from Robin. There had even been talk of sending him away to school – something Leonard had vetoed instantly, for once standing up to the assembled ranks of Arnolds and fighting his corner. No child of his was going to be banished to boarding school. It had happened to him; it wasn't going to happen to Robin.

So why was Dorothy suddenly so attached to their son? Leonard thought he knew the answer only too well. *She was threatened by Alice's bond with Robin.* And no wonder. It had been a gradual progress, but for the last year or so Robin had thought of Alice as his surrogate mother. From what Leonard could make out, Alice hadn't particularly encouraged the boy, but her obvious affection for him had won the child over. And Dorothy was jealous.

'I c-c-could come with you.'

Judge Arnold gave Leonard an incredulous look. 'And who would look after the business?'

'B- b-but –'

'Oh, *do* stop stammering!' the old man snapped. 'It's like talking to a bloody woodpecker.'

Leonard breathed in and tried again. 'Y-y-you never go away,' he persisted, suddenly reckless. 'Why n-n-now?'

'I don't have to answer to you. You stay here and look after the business. There's many a man in Oldham who would love to be in the position you're in. Many a man. Remember, I'm trusting you to run things for me. Don't let me down.'

Leonard was unimpressed. He had inherited, and managed to keep, his own fortune. He was hardly incompetent.

'What about Ch-Ch-Charlie?'

'*What* about Charlie?'

Leonard felt his stammering increase. 'Is h-h-he going with y-y-you?'

'No. Charlie can stay with you,' the old man replied, adding with mock kindness, 'I can't take away all of your company, can I?'

Three months of Charlie, Leonard thought. Three months of a bitter Northern winter with only Charlie for company. He had a sudden image of being found – in February – stiff in a chair in the drawing room, having been prosed to death. Suddenly Leonard wanted to stop the car and get out. He was tired of going to mills and the rubber works, tired of trailing after Judge Arnold like a bloody sheep. He was nearly fifty, he thought, his wife and family should do what he said, not obey his father-in-law.

But he knew it would never change. Not for him, anyway. Robin, however, was another matter.

'Do you th-th-think Dorothy can c-c-cope with Robin alone?'

'She won't be alone, she'll be with us.'

Some comfort, Leonard thought wryly. 'B-b-but she's not used to doing everything f-f-for him. Sh-sh-she gets tired easily.'

Judge Arnold shifted in his seat, rapping the glass partition between them and the driver. The man slid back the glass.

'Yes, sir?'

'Don't drive so bloody slowly! I'm not in my hearse yet.'

The glass partition slid closed again; the old man turned back to his son-in-law. 'Dorothy has never been better in her life. She doesn't get tired so easily, and she doesn't get those funny moods.'

Leonard was surprised to hear him refer to his daughter's temperament. It hadn't been mentioned for years. In fact, Leonard had married Dorothy without realising that she had *moods*. It was only later, when she showed some instability, that it was explained to him why.

He had been sympathetic, of course. He loved her then. But he always glad if his wife was away in November. Yet a few years ago Dorothy seemed to recover, be more able to cope – around the time that Alice Rimmer came to work at The Dower House.

It appeared for a while that his wife had found a confidante, and a helpmate for Robin. Certainly Dorothy was calm and happy for a time. Then the tide turned. The confidante suddenly became the enemy. It didn't seem to be anything Alice had said, just the way Dorothy suddenly saw her help as interference. Leonard frowned. It was understandable, in a way. They had all – with the exception of Judge Arnold – relied more and more on Alice over the years. To Charlie, she had been all common sense; to Alwyn, she had been a companion; and to his beloved Robin, a friend.

In fact Alice had slowly and insidiously crept into the very workings of The Dower House. She had almost grown up amongst them, her good looks and poise marking her out from the other servants. Always educating herself, she was no fool and could hold a conversation with most, and so, before long, Alwyn had found her a better companion that Dorothy. Just as Robin did.

It would have made any woman jealous, thought Leonard, but how could Dorothy really blame Alice? She had never been that close to Robin, so how could she complain when her son bonded with another woman – the woman with whom he spent so much time? Leonard chewed the edge of his pen, staring ahead. Alice Rimmer had never seemed to want power, and yet it had come to her as though by right. Alwyn defended her to Judge Arnold and he had even found himself looking to her for advice.

Perhaps if she had been less handsome it would have been easier. But she never made a play for him, or for Charlie – Dorothy should be grateful for that. Many a women with half Alice's looks could have caused havoc. But then maybe Alice was causing havoc in another way . . .

He shook off the thought and returned to his father-in-law's previous comments.

'W-w-was Dorothy m-m-moody *before* the tragedy?'

Leonard was staggered to hear the words come out of his own mouth! You didn't question Judge Arnold – even if you were married to his daughter.

The old man stiffened at the question and then breathed in audibly, turning to Leonard. 'She wasn't as bad.'

Leonard pushed his luck. He was suddenly curious and anxious to pursue his advantage. 'W-w-what was Catherine like?'

The name sliced down on the car seat between them like a steel blade. Dorothy would never talk about her sister to him.

'Catherine?' Judge Arnold echoed.

They were passing Gladstone Street and heading out to the edge of town, towards the Goring mill. Row after row of terraced houses slipped by the car window, lines of washing fluttering in alleyways, the cobbles slick with earlier rain.

'Well, w-what was Catherine like?' Having found the nerve to ask, Leonard wasn't able to stop.

Judge Arnold's eyes fixed on his. They were fierce, an arcus around the pupils. Bloody hell, Leonard thought, he's not going to have a heart attack, is he?

'She was very highly strung,' he said at last, his voice curt. 'She was beautiful. The two girls were alike, but Catherine was troubled . . .' He gazed off, not realising that the car had stopped inside the mill gates. Surprised, Leonard let him talk. 'Catherine was very nervous, always jealous of her sister. She thought Dorothy was prettier, smarter. She copied her in everything she did, but she thought that she could never be as good as her sister.' Leonard could see the driver looking into his rear mirror and watching them curiously, wondering why they didn't get out of the car. 'When Catherine was married to David Lewes she knew that he was in love with Dorothy . . .'

Leonard was staring open-mouthed at his father-in-law. Judge Arnold seemed entranced, talking as though there was no one else there.

'Catherine couldn't bear the thought that her husband loved her sister. Then that man – that *bastard* – killed my child. He killed Catherine . . .'

'Because of Dorothy?' Leonard asked, his voice hushed.

A sudden knock on the window broke the spell. Startled, Judge Arnold came to his senses to see the mill manager bending down to open the car door. Breathing heavily, Judge fumbled with the lock, then staggered out into the rainy yard. Leonard followed. Then abruptly Judge Arnold turned back to his son-in-law and gripped his hand forcefully.

'What I said just then – forget it.' His voice was threatening. 'Forget every word. Let the past lie. Let it be, Leonard, or God knows, you'll regret it.'

Mrs Hope was looking out of her window on Trafalgar Street, tut-tutting under her breath. The comings and goings in that house, she thought. It was terrible. She would have to tell Mr Hope about it when he came home from the council meeting. Her eyes followed the girl to the door of number 18 and watched as she knocked.

She was a slip of a thing, Mrs Hope thought, not without a twinge of envy. Hardly seven stone to look at her. And blonde, like an angel. But she didn't look strong, Mrs Hope thought happily, not one to make old bones. The faint tapping on Victor's door echoed again, then suddenly the door opened and the woman walked in, out of Mrs Hope's sight.

Irritated, she wheeled herself from the window to the wall. Picking up the glass – which was always close to hand – she put it to the wall and listened. There was a faint mumble of voices, but nothing clear. She frowned and wedged her head against the glass, but the conversation was still elusive. She had seen the woman before, quite often, but didn't know yet if she was Victor Coates's new girlfriend.

Of course, Lettie Booth would know. But she couldn't ask her. It would be too galling to think of that stupid seamstress knowing more than she did. Better to just keep watch and see how things developed. Whatever anyone said, it was scandalous. A young woman with any morals wouldn't go visiting a man alone in his own house, sneaking around like that.

Oh no, Mrs Hope thought, no one with any moral fibre would behave like that.

On the other side of the wall Hilly Barker was sitting on one of Victor's kitchen chairs. The house had changed greatly since Alice had been there over four years earlier. The smell of damp was gone, the furniture repaired or replaced – most of it Victor's handiwork. Mr Dedlington had taught him some things well.

'So, Hilly, how are you?' Victor asked, sitting down opposite her and passing her a mug of tea.

She smiled her long-distance smile, the one he remembered from the home when he used to see her pass by with Alice. Hilly had been frail then, often ill, but somehow – against all the odds – she had survived and was now working in a family bakery in Royton. Nothing too strenuous. He could, Victor thought, even smell the fresh bread and cake on her. She smelled sweet and simple.

'I'm well,' Hilly told him shyly. 'I've even put on some weight. They tease me at the shop about it.'

They had met by accident a year earlier. Victor had been called in to the bakery to mend a table and Hilly had seen and recognised him. She had been wary at first, too shy to approach him, but when he had said hello to her, she had responded. They had shared history, and had chatted briefly about Netherlands. But then he had had to leave.

She had thought that she might never see him again, but the following week Victor had come back around closing time and delivered the table. Then he had waited for her coming off work and they had walked to Alexandra Park. Sitting by the boating lake, Victor had talked about the weather and the films at the cinema, and about a new book he had read called *Brave New World*.

He had seemed comfortable with her and yet Hilly had sensed that there was something else on his mind. Some questions that he wanted to ask, but couldn't quite bring himself to do so.

Finally, she had opened up the topic. 'I thought you were with Alice.'

He had flinched as though she had struck him. 'No, we broke up a long time ago. Alice went to London.'

Hilly had nodded, blushing. She had hurt him and that had been the last thing she had wanted to do.

'We were good friends, you know. Alice was very kind to me. So was Mrs Cummings, the matron. We were both so upset when Alice went . . .' Hilly's voice had trailed off for a moment. 'I knew all about what happened at Netherlands – how you two were thrown out.' She had paused then, waiting for him to speak. When he didn't, she had continued, 'Miss Lees is dead.'

'I heard,' Victor had replied. He had wished her dead so many times that when the event had finally happened it had been almost an anticlimax.

'Evan Thomas is the principal at Netherlands now,' Hilly had gone on. 'D'you remember Miss Blake? Dolly Blake?'

He had smiled dimly. 'Every boy at Netherlands would remember her.'

'She ran off with someone,' Hilly had said shyly, laughing. 'No one knows where.'

There had been a long pause between them. Victor had stared at the water of the boating lake and Hilly had wondered if he would want to see her again. After all, perhaps she had upset him talking about the past. About Alice . . . Yet Victor *did* ask Hilly out again, and for the last year they had been seeing each other regularly.

But not courting. Not really.

'Pretty dress,' he said, pulling Hilly's thoughts back to the present.

'I made it,' she replied, 'well – with some help.'

He smiled at her and she smiled back. There was suddenly the sound of someone moving about next door, Lettie Booth running her sewing machine, the whirring coming low through the brick partition wall.

'Mrs Booth . . .' Victor said, by way of explanation. 'She keeps that thing going all night sometimes. Her husband's laid off now. She says that he was too smart for the job and that they were jealous of him at work.' Victor laughed. 'Trouble is, she believes it!'

While he laughed, Hilly took the opportunity to study Victor, taking in the face which was now lined around the eyes although he was only in his early twenties. The thick fair hair was sprinkled with wood dust, his hands calloused, but clean. She wanted suddenly to reach out and touch his arm, feel the muscle under the skin, but was too shy.

Instead she walked over to the basket she had brought with her. 'I've got some cake.'

'You won't be the only one putting weight on,' he teased her.

'And a meat pie.'

Victor took the hint. 'I hope you're staying to share it with me. Hilly?'

Almost giddy with pleasure, she turned away and busied herself with plates and cutlery. As she did so, Victor watched her and remembered another woman busying herself in that same kitchen, a taller, darker woman who made him ache with longing. Alice, his Alice, always *his* Alice. A memory came back sharply: how she had cooked him a piece of fish, cutting fresh parsley and dropping the little green leaves into the white sauce. Wonderful, he had thought at the time.

Victor blinked, seeing Hilly again. Four years had passed since Alice left and he wondered why it was that he couldn't love Hilly. Maybe it would just take time, he thought, maybe just more time. She was pretty and sweet; she was caring and would make a good wife; they were both alone in the world – what better match could there be? He didn't want to love her as he had loved Alice, didn't want to *make* love to her with the same desperate need. That much feeling was dangerous, something he could never, *would* never, allow himself to feel again. Hilly was safe in that she did not provoke passion. She needed protection – and he was willing to protect.

And yet . . .

'Ready?' Hilly asked, turning round with the serving spoon in her hand.

Not quite, Victor thought, not quite.

Chapter Twenty-Five

Maisie Grey was feeling pretty smug. Things were turning out better for her than she could ever have imagined. After all, she had only been working for the Arnolds for six months and now she had been invited to go away with them to France for the winter.

Judge Arnold had just told her, and the smile was still on her face as she came out of the library and crossed Alice on the stairs. Her round, plain face was sly with triumph.

'I'm going away.'

Alice paused, a few of Robin's books under her arm. She had looked after him in increasing measure for four years, during which time she had grown to love the child that only she knew was her cousin. A tutor had been called in after Leonard had dismissed the boarding school idea, and Alice had soon shown her own learning ability. Mr Matthews was not slow to see promise and encouraged Alice, teaching her what he knew. She had sat in on Robin's lessons, and when the child went to bed she read his school books and taught herself everything she could. Having already had a reasonable education at Netherlands, she had made progress rapidly, Mr Matthews taking almost as much interest in her education as in Robin's. The secret and unspoken agreement had suited them both: Mr Matthews had had help, and Alice received an unconventional teacher's training.

At the time Alice realised that it was one further step up the ladder she had set herself to climb. It was true that she had become indispensable to the Arnolds, but how much more power she would have if they made her Robin's nanny. Only Judge Arnold was still suspicious of her. She knew why. Much as Alice tried to hide it, her hatred was – although unnoticed by the others – palpable to him. He had guessed from the first that she was up to something and as her influence grew, so did his distrust.

Revenge was Alice's one and only motivation. Everything she touched, passed or admired at The Dower House, she saw as hers. Each ornament, each book, each piece of china had been stolen from her. Why should she eat off earthenware from the market when they dined on Royal Worcester? Why should she shiver in a cold bedroom when they slept in heated rooms? Each day brought a new grievance into her heart: each servant's duty became a slight to her, a reminder of how far she had fallen. And who had pushed her.

Bitter inside, she concentrated all her thoughts on her plan. She grew handsome, but took little pleasure in it. She had no interest in a suitor; she had lost the one man she had ever loved, indirectly because of the Arnolds. Everything she had ever suffered was because of the Arnolds.

So she hung on, growing inside their family like a parasite in the belly of a house cat. Over time she learned their weaknesses, their strengths, their confidences. With an impassive face she commanded trust and no one suspected that they harboured a revengeful spirit in amongst them. Judge Arnold might wonder, but he knew nothing. How could he possibly have discovered who she was? Alice was secure. Safe, to plot and wait for the right time to strike.

Because that was what she would do: strike at the family and bring them down. She didn't know how yet, only that she would. One day she would have The Dower House, she would own the china, the antiques, the paintings. She would make *them* feel the bitter taste of rejection and humiliation.

But after everything had been going so smoothly for a

while, Dorothy's attitude had changed towards Alice, and she had found herself suddenly ostracised by her. All attempts by Alice to repair the situation had been rejected. It was bad enough to know that Judge Arnold mistrusted her, but to feel the cold blast of rejection from Dorothy hardened Alice's soul. But she never thought of leaving, no matter how difficult things became. The need for revenge was too strong inside her.

Besides, Alice had grown to love Robin, who had become her surrogate child, and to pity her aunt. It was not Robin's fault that he had been born into the Arnold clan. It was chance, fate. So Alice's anger against the family had softened as her love for Robin had grown. She might have wanted to punish the family and see herself in The Dower House, but her obsession had begun to wane.

But when Dorothy turned against Alice all the old feelings welled up and the bitterness intensified. She had been dismissed again, thrown to the bottom of the pecking order. Her brief ascent to grace now over, she was plummeted back to the servants' quarters without so much as an explanation. It was one humiliation too many.

Instead of being weakened, Alice stood her ground. However rough things became, she would not be forced to leave Robin, or be pushed out of The Dower House again. She would recover her status, however long it took, ignoring Judge Arnold's patent dislike and Dorothy's rejection. Even Alwyn – once her ally – was no longer to be counted upon. She was getting on, wicked-tempered with pain and uninterested in anything outside her own ill health.

It was down to the housekeeper to manage The Dower House, and when Alice was removed from the position of Dorothy's lady's maid she found herself suddenly shunted over to take care of Robin full time. It was the one move Alice did not resent and saw as a triumph. From then onwards she kept to herself, her move from the main servants' quarters to a small bedroom off Robin's nursery making distance easy. She might see little of the family, but she saw much of her cousin and that was fine by her.

Slowly, determinedly, she built up her power again in the family by being reliable, and there. Always there. Leonard was soon complimenting her on Robin's progress and even Alwyn had renewed Alice's reading duties, which, after that first 12 November had become the pastime of many evenings.

But when Maisie Grey arrived to be Dorothy's maid, the status quo shifted again. At every opportunity she lorded over Alice. She feigned astonishment at her rival's treatment, her envy fed her spite. Alice might be beautiful, but it didn't really matter, did it? It was she, Maisie, who was the lady's maid now. And it was she who was going to France with the family.

'I said I was going away,' Maisie repeated now.

Alice shifted Robin's books from one arm to the other. 'I heard you. Where?'

'To France.' The girl was luminous with spite. 'With the family.'

Unease settled on Alice as she fought to keep her voice calm. 'All the family?'

'Yes,' Maisie said cheerfully, 'apart from Mr Tripps, that is.'

'You mean *Master* Tripps –'

'No, I don't,' Maisie countered. 'Robin is coming to France with us. It's Mr Leonard Tripps and Master Charlie who are staying behind.'

Alice could feel her mouth dry. They couldn't take Robin away without her! Take him away with this petty, peevish girl? How would he do his lessons, his work? How would he manage without her? She had looked after Robin for years; he would be lost without her.

'I have to pack. Excuse me,' Maisie said, with a smirk on her face.

Knowing that it was probably useless, Alice looked for help from the only source open to her. It took ten minutes to find Leonard. He was sitting in the semidark at the back of one of the greenhouses, smoking. He leaped to his feet when he saw her.

'God! I th-th-thought you w-w-were the old m-m-man.'

Alice smiled. She had always liked Leonard, thought him the kindest member of the family, although she knew he was weak. But not *that* weak – Leonard had stood his ground a few times, even though he was patently terrified of his father-in-law.

'I didn't mean to startle you, Mr Tripps.'

Relieved, Leonard breathed in the smoke from his Havana, his expression blissful. 'N-n-nothing like a g-g-good smoke.'

Alice watched him for a moment and then dived in.

'I hear that the family's going away . . . and that Robin's going with them.'

Without appearing to notice anything, Leonard had caught the expression of bewilderment on Alice's face. It was a lovely face, he thought, one whose beauty he had noticed on and off for years. Just as he had noticed that Alice never had any friends calling, nor any young men come courting. Why was that? She never asked for holidays either, and on her day off never gave any hint to where she was going.

It seemed such a long time since he had rescued her outside the walls of The Dower House. It had been a lucky chance, Leonard thought. He liked Alice and admired the way she was bringing up his son. He also strongly disapproved of Dorothy's treatment of her, although he was powerless to stop it. It was cruel – but then jealousy did strange things to people.

'That's r-r-right, they're all off. J-j-just Charlie and me left.'

'Am I not to go with them, sir?'

Bugger it, Leonard thought, why does it have to be left to me to explain? 'No, n-n-not this time, Alice.'

She nodded, then turned to go.

'Y-y-you've done a g-g-good job with my son, thank you.'

She didn't move. Just stood there, and then Leonard realised that she was close to tears. The greenhouse was growing darker by the moment, the smell of late jasmine making the night dance. Alice's face was shaded, her eyes deep. He thought for one blinding moment that he had never seen such a beautiful woman.

'I'm s-s-sorry,' he said, moving over to her and putting an arm around her shoulder. 'S-s-so sorry.'

It had happened before he realised it. One instant she was standing there, the next he had kissed her.

The slap came unexpectedly and made his face burn, his hand going automatically to his cheek.

'I n-n-never meant –'

But Alice didn't stay to listen to his excuses. She turned on her heel and left him to the scent of flowers and the acrid taste of humiliation stinging the evening air.

Chapter Twenty-Six

All that winter Alice kept her distance. She imagined at first that she might be sacked, but Leonard was not as vindictive as his wife. Instead she stayed at The Dower House and did little, the housekeeper taking on the care of Leonard and Charlie. Parted from the one person she loved, Alice missed Robin constantly and used the time to learn what she could, begging extra books off Mr Matthews. Dorothy had found a temporary tutor abroad, and Mr Matthews was still smarting. Underoccupied, he was glad to help the enthusiastically studious Alice.

Yet the tutor found her serious and remote, almost aloof. Wondering what had happened, he put it down to her disappointment at being left behind. But he was startled by the change in her. All kindness seemed gone; the young woman who had been so consistently caring with her charge was now abrasive – of few words and fewer smiles.

A spinster in the making, Mr Matthews thought. He had seen it all before: nannies who started out young and hopeful seeing their chances fade as the years passed. Not that he had expected it to happen to Alice Rimmer – she had seemed to have more spirit. Yet now that very spirit was souring her, making her old before her time.

Throughout a long bitter winter The Dower House sulked under a carpeting of snow. Christmas came and went, New Year followed. There were celebrations, but Alice excluded herself. Although quietly besotted by her, Charlie's attention was beginning to drift. He had met a young woman who thought his plays were tremendous. Emily could sit for hours listening and, having no sense of humour whatsoever, never had the least desire to laugh.

Revenge kept Alice occupied better than any work. She now had every reason to get her own back on each member of the family. And she would, in time. Only one person was to be immune from her attack – her cousin, Robin. Much as she dreaded the others' return, she longed for his. He was, to all intents and purposes, the only family Alice had ever had.

So she bided her time and she waited. She turned the pages over in her diary and circled the day she would see Robin again. Her revenge had only been tempered by her love for him, but now she had discovered a way to punish the Arnolds *without* injuring Robin. She was going to take him over completely. She would love Robin, teach him, and spend all her time with him. In return he would grow to see her as his mother, his teacher, his friend, *his whole world*. When he was older and she was completely sure of his love, she would tell the Arnolds who she really was. They couldn't dismiss her then – and she would have Robin, because the boy would want to be with her, whatever happened.

All she had to do was to keep Dorothy and Leonard away from Robin as much as she could. It wouldn't be that difficult: the child had little love for his mother, and his father was always so busy. Oh yes, Alice thought, what better revenge could there be – to expose what the Arnolds had done to her, and then take their heir? It wouldn't be cruel. The child loved her better than them. It was obvious he would choose her . . . And when he learned the truth about her he would find she was his cousin, his own flesh and blood.

It was a dangerous plan, but it swallowed Alice whole and kept her awake at night. Her room was small – a servant's room, nothing like Dorothy's or Charlie's, a room without richness or status. But it wasn't going to be like this for much longer, Alice told herself. She had her plan, now she had to make sure it went exactly the way she wanted it.

She would have to be more ruthless. She would have to show the Arnolds that she was one of them. Their cruelty was in her blood too. Only this time, she wouldn't be the one to suffer for it.

Victor had agreed to meet Hilly after work that February evening, and they were going to the cinema to see Marlene Dietrich. He thought fondly of Hilly. She had made a big effort the last time they'd met, wearing a short wool coat and having had her hair bobbed. He teased her that she looked like one of the flappers who used to be all the rage.

Whistling under his breath, Victor locked the door of the workroom and set off for home. He would go to Trafalgar Street and get ready for his evening out. He continued to whistle to himself cheerfully, a Gershwin tune, and nodded to a couple he knew. It was cold, his hands deep in his pockets as he walked the Salford streets.

Then suddenly Victor remembered the letter Mr Dedlington had asked him to post. Damn it, he thought irritably, he had missed the last post. There was nothing for it, he would have to deliver it by hand. He looked at the address. In Oldham. If he caught a bus now, delivered the letter and then came straight back he could just make it in time to meet Hilly at the Roxy.

Annoyed by his own carelessness, Victor caught the next bus to Oldham and sat jiggling his foot as it crept along the snowy streets. Several times he glanced at his watch and hurriedly jumped off at his stop on Union Street. Checking the address once again, he asked a passer-by where Williams Row was and followed the instructions. Finally he posted the letter and, relieved, retraced his steps back to the centre of town.

But he took a wrong turning and, instead of making it back to Union Street, Victor found himself in unfamiliar streets leading away from the town centre. Cursing, he stopped and tried to get his bearings. Then he checked his watch. God, he had been walking for nearly twenty minutes. He was way off his route. Looking round, he saw a man strolling with his dog and asked for directions.

'You're in Werneth, lad,' the man replied. 'You've gone miles out of your way. You're heading away from town.'

Victor memorised the directions the man gave him and hurried off.

He would have to be quick, he thought as he half walked, half ran. He didn't want Hilly standing outside the cinema on her own. She would get cold and that was bad for her ... Victor paused at the end of the road. The man had said that one way led back to town, and that the other led to Werneth Heights. Only Victor couldn't remember which one to take ... By now exasperated, he took the left turning and walked on quickly, waiting to see the lights of the town shops. But there was no sign of town life. He paused, turned to look about him. And then froze.

There was a figure on the street a long way ahead of him. It was the figure of a woman. She was quite tall and very erect, the angle of her head achingly familiar ... Five years dropped away in that instant. He could feel as though it was only yesterday her hands touching his through the railings. He could see her face, the line of her cheek as she had listened to him. He remembered the excitement in her voice.

He was looking at Alice. At his woman, the woman he had loved so much, and still loved. Calling out, Victor ran down the street. But she didn't turn, didn't look back. He called again, but there was no response. And yet he knew it was her. Longing and loss welled up in him as he ran. But she merely walked faster and he finally lost sight of her after she rounded a corner.

Panting, he finally reached the corner himself – but there

was no one there. Snow began falling again, thick white flakes adding to the covering of snow already dressing the pavement. They fell quickly, but not quickly enough to cover the footsteps which she had left.

So he had not seen a ghost, after all. The woman had been real, she had left human footprints. *The woman had been Alice.*

Three days after the family returned to The Dower House Robin was brought down with a cold. A travel cold, the doctor said, nothing to worry about. Her charge given back to her care, Alice stayed with the boy that night, reading to him and giving him hot drinks. Dorothy enquired about her son, but was reassured by the doctor. Nothing to worry about, Dr Priestly repeated. It will blow over.

It seemed that it did. Two days later Robin was up and about. He had sniffles, but nothing serious. Happy to be re-employed, Mr Matthews resumed Robin's lessons but was surprised by the difference in Alice. The woman was soft again, her tenderness restored. My God, Mr Matthews said to his wife later, if that child was her own flesh and blood she couldn't love him more.

For his part, Robin was delighted to be back with Alice. His mother was dull, he said, his grandparents strict, and as for Maisie, she was hideous.

'You shouldn't say that,' Alice chastised him gently.

'But she is! She looks like a pig.'

'Oh no. Not a pig . . . A horse maybe.' Alice laughed, made a neighing sound and nudged Robin with her elbow.

She felt happy again for the first time in months, full of hope. Even Dorothy couldn't spoil her mood. Ignore me all you want, Alice thought, your son loves me. Loves me more than he loves you . . .

As for Dorothy, she saw how Robin loved Alice and felt as though someone had thrown acid on her heart. The distance she had put between them hadn't made any difference, after all. Her father had been wrong. Robin had not forgotten Alice, merely missed his companion more. In fact, if anything, Alice's grip was tighter now that it ever had been. Yet Dorothy knew she couldn't dismiss her, Robin would pine too much. So she was stuck with Alice, the woman who had once helped her and whom she now saw as a rival.

Meanwhile, Leonard was doing his level best to appear glad to see them all back. In truth he was relieved they had returned. The tension between himself and Alice had become unbearable.

'If y-y-you ask me –'

'No one did,' Judge Arnold barked at his son-in-law. His weight had increased, as had his temper. He hadn't enjoyed the trip, and loathed the food. Garlic, he concluded darkly, made you piss blood.

'I want to see the mill figures tomorrow,' the old man went on, eyeing up Leonard. 'And I want to see results.'

'N-n-no problem.'

'Waste of bloody time. I never could stand France,' Judge Arnold went on. 'Waste of bloody time and money.'

It was Alice who asked for Dr Priestly to be called again. She wasn't pleased with the way Robin was recovering. He wasn't eating enough, she said, and he was listless. Always ready to criticise, Dorothy accused her of making a fuss, of trying to prove how caring she was.

'I d-d-don't think that's fair, darling,' Leonard said evenly. 'A-A-Alice is paid to look after Robin.'

'She is paid to look after him, not take him over,' Dorothy replied, her voice low but steely. 'I'm his mother. I should know if my child is ill or not.'

So the two women watched over Robin and vied for supremacy. When Robin's cold developed again, it was Dorothy who insisted that she sit up with him, but it was Alice was came in during the early hours to find her mistress asleep. And it was Alice who wiped the sweat off the child and soothed him.

By the third morning of Robin's renewed illness there was so much tension in the boy's room that even the doctor commented on it.

'It doesn't help having bad feeling about –'

Dorothy was all muted fury as she looked at the heavy-set, bearded man. 'There *is* no bad feeling, Dr Priestly. I want to look after my son, that's all.'

'So why don't you agree on a division of labour? Alice can sit with him during the day and you can stay with him at night.'

Dorothy argued. She wanted to stay with her son during the day and let Alice look after him at night. So it was arranged. But on the fourth day Robin complained of a headache to Alice – further infuriating his mother, who was looking after him at the time and had briefly gone out.

'He should have told *me!*'

Alice looked down. 'It was just that I was there –'

'When I should have been!' Dorothy replied sharply.

'Does it matter, madam? The boy has a headache, what does it matter who he told?' Her impatience was obvious and rankled on Dorothy.

'Don't speak to me like that! I've had enough of you, Alice Rimmer. You should know your place.'

Alice was about to respond when she bit her tongue. What good would it do now? The most important thing at the moment was Robin.

'I think we should get the doctor again, madam.'

'I'll be the judge of that!' Dorothy snapped, walking back into the sickroom and closing the door.

She stayed with her son until nine o'clock, finally calling Alice to take over the night shift. Obediently she did so, and settled herself by Robin's bed. The boy was still, trying to smile, and asked her to read to him.

'I think you should sleep, sweetheart.'

'My head hurts.'

'Then sleep,' Alice repeated, touching his forehead. He was burning up. Why hadn't the doctor done something? 'Ssshh, sleep, Robin. Sleep, my love.'

Reluctantly he closed his eyes. Alice studied his face. The pale lashes were long, the mouth well formed. He would make a handsome man, she thought. And what would he do when he was older? He would meet some woman and marry and have children. She imagined seeing them in the decades ahead, when it was just Robin and her, the Arnolds far away. Robin would visit and tell her about his wife, his family, his work. It would be a grand future, Alice thought, something to make up for the past ... Tenderly, she stroked his cheek and then leaned her head on the edge of his pillow. A closeness fell over them. This is my child, she thought, and no one – *no one* – is going to separate us.

In his sleep, Robin stirred and then cried out once. Anxious, Alice leaned over and listened. But he was quiet again, breathing evenly. Relaxing, she rested her head back on the pillow, so close to him that she could hear his heart beating. A peace Alice had never known before came over her. This child loved her, had picked *her* to love.

At four Alice woke. Robin was soundly asleep. She rose and banked up the fire in the grate, her figure casting a giant shadow on the wall behind. The house was quiet around her. Slowly she moved over to the window and looked out. There was a huge moon – a hunter's moon – looking down on the garden. Its face was waxen, bland. No eyes, no heart to the moon.

Disturbed, Alice walked away from the window and back to the bed. She touched Robin's hand and hesitated. Then she did something she had never done before. She bent down and kissed him gently on the forehead. Yet the kiss seemed to take her strength away, seemed to pull all the warmth away from her. Confused, Alice straightened up – then touched Robin's cheek.

She felt the cold; the room moved round her. She felt the cold; the night closed in. She felt the cold and then screamed and felt nothing but the memory of cold lips, cold hands and cold heart.

Robin was dead.

Part Two

We love but once. Love walks with death and birth
(The saddest, the unkindest of the three);
And only once whilst we sojourn on earth
Can that strange trio come to you or me.

Ella Wheeler Wilcox,
'The Trio'

Chapter Twenty-Seven

Ethel was fast asleep when she heard the frantic knocking on the door. Alarmed, she jabbed Gilbert in the ribs.

He turned over impatiently. 'What is it?'

'Can you hear someone knocking?'

'No I can't! I'm bloody asleep.'

Snorting under her breath, Ethel threw the blankets off and slid out of bed. As quietly as she could, she opened the window and looked down into the street. There was a figure standing huddled against the doorway.

'My God, it's Alice!' she said, pulling on a dressing gown and hurrying downstairs.

Alice came in white-faced, her hair drenched with rain. She was shaking, hardly able to talk. It had been years since Ethel had last seen her, although Alice had sent Christmas cards and frequent notes, always thanking Ethel for what she had done in the past, though none had ever come with a return address.

'What's up?' Ethel asked. 'God, luv, what is it?'

'You can throw me out if you want, I wouldn't blame you,' Alice replied, her voice so low Ethel had to bend down to hear her. 'But I had nowhere else to go. I *had* to come here.' She looked into Ethel's face. 'Robin's dead.'

The name meant nothing to Ethel. 'Who's Robin?'

'Judge Arnold's grandson.'

The name Arnold struck out viciously. It was the name Ethel had seen on Alice's file. The name of the family who had abandoned her.

Oh Christ, Ethel thought, what has she done?

'What happened, Alice?'

'He died –'

'I don't understand! *Who* died? And why are you involved?' Ethel asked urgently, hearing Gilbert's footsteps coming down the stairs.

He walked in, sleepy-eyed, his hair dishevelled. Seeing Alice, he smiled warmly – and then stopped when he looked at Ethel's face.

'Make some tea, Gilbert,' she said firmly, then turned back to Alice. 'You have to tell me what's gone on.'

'He was ill –'

'From the beginning, Alice!' she snapped, then lowered her voice when she noticed the wet clothes. 'Dear God, girl, you'll catch your death of cold. Take that coat off.' She helped Alice out of her sodden coat and passed her a towel to dry her hair. 'Now, tell me what happened from the start – from the night you and Victor left Netherlands. I've heard all the rumours, but I want to hear your version.'

'I didn't want it to happen the way it did!' Alice said helplessly. 'We weren't doing anything wrong.'

'It's history, luv,' Ethel said, trying to calm her. 'What's past is past.'

'We were going to get married –'

'But you didn't marry Victor, did you?' Ethel pushed her. 'I saw him not so long ago; he said little, but he did say you'd gone off and left him.'

Alice let the towel drop onto her lap, her hair still so wet it was dripping onto the back of her hands. 'I had to. Clare Lees threatened his boss – Victor was asked to choose between me or his job.'

'And he chose his *job*?' Ethel asked incredulously.

'No, no!' Alice replied, shaking her head. 'I left him, so that he wouldn't have to make the choice. I left Salford and went to work in service in Oldham. Then I . . .'

'Go on.'

'. . . I went to look for the Arnolds.'

Ethel sat down heavily. So Alice had found out, after all. Jesus, what a mess.

Without speaking, Gilbert passed two mugs of tea over to them, then took a seat by the window.

'What happened when you found them, Alice?'

'It was a fluke –'

Ethel could hear the old frantic note in Alice's voice. Whatever had happened had terrified her. '*What* was a fluke?'

'It happened all so quickly. I got a job working for them – as a lady's maid to Dorothy Tripps. My aunt.'

Gilbert took in a deep breath behind them. 'Your *aunt*?'

Nodding, Alice glanced over to Ethel and registered the lack of surprise on her face.

'Did you know? Did you know I was related to the Arnolds?'

Ethel hesitated for a moment. Then she turned to Gilbert. 'I know what you're thinking! Why didn't I tell you? But I *couldn't* tell you. You like to have a drink sometimes, luv, and then you talk. It was better you didn't have anything to spill other than your beer.' She turned back to Alice. 'I knew about it a long time ago, since that night you looked for your file. Well, I lied. I *did* find it and I read it. But then I told you there was nothing in it. I thought that if you knew you might do something stupid. You had so much going for you then, Alice, you were going to be a teacher, to take over from Miss Lees –'

'You *knew*?'

Her eyes lowered, Ethel rubbed her face with her plump hands. 'I was trying to protect you. The Arnolds gave you up once – I didn't want you to stir up old memories, memories which would damage you more than they would damage them. You were always so highly strung as a child, but then you seemed to settle down. I thought it was for the best. I didn't want you doing something reckless and ruining your life.' Ethel paused, reading the look on Alice's face. 'You have, haven't you? Oh God, luv, what have you done?'

'Nothing.'

'*Alice, what have you done?*'

'Nothing . . .'

Frightened, Ethel leaned over and shook Alice by the shoulders. 'Tell me what you've done!'

'IT WAS AN ACCIDENT!'

'What? *What?*'

Alice felt her face drain of colour. Ethel's fingers were biting hard into her flesh.

'I wanted to get my revenge on them. I wanted to punish them –'

'*Punish them?*'

Alice hurried on. 'I thought that I could somehow break up the family. I wanted what they had, their name, power, money. It was mine by rights. I wasn't trying to take something that wasn't mine.' She felt Ethel's grip tighten. 'I wanted them to suffer and when their family was ruined, I wanted to tell them who had done it. Their own flesh and blood. I loved Robin, I would have taken care of him. He was like a child to me, my own child. He never loved them as much as he loved me.'

'No,' Ethel said simply, 'no.'

'I had no one,' Alice said shrilly, 'no family, and even Victor had been taken away from me. I was so alone. I wanted to strike back.'

'By trying to take over another woman's child?' Ethel was aghast. 'By breaking up a family?'

'They hurt me first. I didn't start it. The family was broken up when they sent me away.' Alice blustered. 'Why should they have so much, when I had so little?'

Ethel was staring at her as though she hardly knew her. 'Revenge only ever hurts the people who go out trying to get it,' she replied, her voice thick with disapproval. 'So, did you get this revenge?'

'Some of it,' Alice admitted, her head bowed. 'At first I was just a maid, but after I'd been there a while I was asked to look after Robin, Dorothy's son, my cousin, though no one knew he was related to me. But I got to love him so much –'

'That you wanted to take him over.'

'All right! All right! I *did* come between him and his mother. I encouraged him to love me more than her.'

'Oh, Alice . . .'

'I know it was wrong!' she snapped. 'Don't you think I don't realise? But they were all so patronising to me; they were so smug. I was a servant, nothing else, the lowest of the low. I lived there for four years, all the time seeing Charlie, my brother, have everything I should have had.'

'What happened to Robin?' Ethel's face was waxen, fear in her voice.

'I did nothing to him! I couldn't have hurt him. He was so easy to love and I took such good care of him. His mother said she loved him, but she didn't, not as much as I did.'

Shaking her head, Ethel picked up the damp towel, folding it over and over again. She didn't want to hear the next part. She was afraid that by hearing it she would be told something unbearable, and never be the same again.

'This child, this Robin – you said he died?'

'Last night.'

'What did you do, Alice?'

'I did nothing!' she said helplessly. 'I was looking after him and he had a cold, but he seemed to get better. Then he was poorly again. I told his mother to get the doctor, but she said I was fussing.'

Ethel leaned forward. 'So it isn't your fault? It can't be your responsibility if you told his mother to get help and she didn't.'

'She lied. She denied that I ever said it . . .' Alice paused, a chill running over her. 'She told her parents and her husband that I was lying. She was screaming, telling everyone that it was my fault, that I was negligent. That I had killed her son. Jesus, oh Jesus! I told them that I had asked for the doctor, but she said I was lying to protect myself.'

'*Were* you lying?'

'No!' Alice replied, her tone emphatic. 'I loved that child. I would have given my own life for him. I would never, never, have done anything to hurt him. *I asked for a doctor*. It was his mother's fault that Dr Priestly wasn't called and her son died. It wasn't *my* fault.'

'Are you sure?'

Alice stared into Ethel's eyes. Her expression did not waver. 'I did *not* harm that child. I did *not* neglect him. I swear it.'

'Christ,' Gilbert said softly behind them.

'Blaspheming won't help anyone!' Ethel retorted. 'Build up the fire, Gilbert, we need some warmth in here. And get the bread and jam out.' She rose to her feet and made sandwiches, passing a couple over to Alice. 'Eat.'

'I can't.'

'You have to. You need to get your strength back.' Ethel thought for a moment. 'They threw you out this morning?'

Alice nodded. 'They told me to pack and go. Told me that I was lucky they weren't calling in the police –'

'Jesus.'

'Gilbert, that will do!' Ethel snapped, her hands busy, nervously cutting slice after slice of bread. 'What did they say the boy died of?'

Alice shook her head. 'I don't know. Like I said, he had had a cold for nearly a week. He couldn't seem to shake it . . .' He *couldn't* be dead, he couldn't. Not her Robin.

'So why did they mention bringing in the police?' Ethel asked.

'Dorothy Tripps has wanted to get rid of me for a while. She took her chance. She was to blame – but if she blamed me she could clear herself and banish me at the same time.

After all, who would take a servant's word against hers?'

'And you never thought to tell them who you were, all the time you were in that house, working for them?' Ethel's voice hardened. 'Four years, Alice, you kept that secret. Four long years you worked for them and plotted revenge – and look what happened. You lost again, Alice, only this time you lost something you can never get back.'

'But I want him back, I want Robin back . . .' Her voice was hardly audible. 'I would give my life to get him back.'

'He's not coming back,' Ethel replied. 'But the Arnolds can't blame you because you're not to blame. It was a tragedy, but you have to learn to live with it. If I were you, I would forget the Arnolds and everything that's happened over the last four years.' Ethel saw then that Alice was crying silently. 'Tragedies happen, Alice. You know that more than most.'

'But he was only a boy. He'd had no life, no chance.' She took in a breath, her eyes dull. 'It *is* my fault. It's a punishment – because I wanted to hurt the Arnolds so much.' She banged her clenched fists on her knees and began to rock. 'I wanted them to know what it was like to be no one, I wanted that house for myself. I even dreamed of living there alone with Robin. I was mad, I couldn't see what I was doing any more.' Her voice spluttered, her nose running. 'It was my fault, it *was*.'

'No!' Ethel said emphatically.

'If Judge Arnold knew who I really was . . .' Alice said suddenly, rigid with fear. 'God, if he knew I was his grand-daughter, that I was David Lewes's child – David Lewes, who killed his daughter – he would never believe I was innocent, he would think I had done something to Robin to get back at the family.' She fought to breathe. 'Maybe I *did* mean to harm him without realising. My father was a murderer – maybe it's in my blood too.'

Ethel would hear no more. She pulled Alice towards her and held her in her arms. She had known from the beginning that Alice Rimmer was special, that she was somehow set apart. She knew that Alice could be remarkable – but she knew that she had the potential to destroy herself.

'Alice, listen to me!' Ethel said firmly. 'You are no killer. Wanting revenge was wicked, but it didn't result in a child's death.'

'I don't want anything now! I don't care about money, power, anything,' Alice cried against Ethel's sturdy shoulder. 'I just want him back.'

'It won't happen.'

'If only I had never gone to that house . . .'

Ethel sighed. 'I don't understand why you did. Dear God, Alice, the Arnolds never did anything for you. How could you possibly think there was anything other than tragedy there?' She paused. 'Mind you, whatever that family's done, they've been punished for it. The Arnolds have already lost a daughter, a son-in-law, and one grandchild. Now they've lost another . . . Stay away from them, Alice. Please, I beg of you, *stay away*.'

'Robin was my cousin –'

'Robin was the past,' Ethel replied ruthlessly.

'No!'

'Yes! *He was the past*. Remember Robin, but keep away from his family. Forget you share their blood, forget what they owe you, forget what they did to you. Forget them and you still have a chance. But if you go back, Alice, then you're as good as done for.'

Chapter Twenty-Eight

The news of Robin's death had spread long before the formal notice appeared in the paper. With it, had spread the rumour that his nanny had been negligent. Dorothy had made sure that Alice Rimmer would be punished. She knew only too well that *she* had been the one who had refused to call out Dr Priestly. Indirectly, the blame was hers. But there was no way she would admit it.

After having told her parents and Leonard the lie, it became easier and easier. Her hated rival was now driven out; what could a servant say to defend herself against the word of an Arnold? Dorothy genuinely grieved for her son, but her bitterness found some balm in torture. And she was not going to torture herself.

So she saw Alice driven out of The Dower House and she sat by her dead son's bed. And all the time her guilt was so intense that all Dorothy could focus upon was hatred. Before long, she forgot that Alice had asked for the doctor, and believing her own lie, told anyone who would listen that Robin had died from negligence. If the nanny had called for medical help sooner, her son might well have survived.

It was the doctor who finally scotched the rumour. Calling round to see the family at The Dower House, Guy Priestly told them that Robin's death had been due to a heart defect – which was only discovered post mortem. The cold had aggravated his condition and tragically killed him. No one, said the doctor, was to blame.

But the damage had been done. No other rumour followed the first, to say that Alice Rimmer had not been in any way responsible. Instead her name was tarnished and, deep in grief, she had no spirit to fight back.

The Cummingses insisted that she stay with them, Ethel to keep an eye on her and Gilbert to offer moral support, the only kind of help he could. But it wasn't enough. Bravely Alice tried to slip back into normal life, but she was pointed at and stared at in the street. Women whispered behind their hands in the grocer's and once Alice came home to find the Cummingses' door splattered with red paint: 'A CHILD KILLER LIVES HERE'. She knew she had to leave for the sake of Ethel and Gilbert as well as herself – but go where? To do what? Who would have her? She had no reference, only a reputation.

One morning, after she'd been at the Cummingses' house a few days, she dressed and was just about to leave the house, when Ethel came in.

'Where are you going?' she asked, taking in the black suit and hat.

'It's Robin's funeral –'

'You can't go!' Ethel said, astonished that Alice should even think of it.

'I have to. I *want* to,' she countered. 'I have nothing to be afraid of.'

'If you go to that cemetery you'll be crucified.'

'And if I don't go, I'll look as though I have something to hide,' Alice replied. 'And I don't have anything to hide.'

She moved to the door, but Ethel caught her sleeve. 'Don't go.'

'I have to –'

'Don't!' she repeated. 'If you loved that child, think of him. Think of how it will look. Don't go making his funeral into a carnival.'

Stung, Alice blinked as she took in the words. Then she turned from the door and, taking off her coat and gloves, walked back up the stairs to her bedroom.

*   *   *

Mr Dedlington was talking to his wife when Victor came into work. When he saw him, he blushed and smiled uneasily. For her part, Mrs Dedlington seemed sympathetic, but embarrassed.

'What's up?'

Mr Dedlington finally plucked up enough courage to look Victor in the eye.

'The missus and I were just saying that you'd had a lucky escape.'

'What?'

'That Alice Rimmer – she's let some poor lad die. Not looking out for him. Only a boy.' He rushed on. 'Good thing you've got Hilly now. She's a good sort, not like that Rimmer girl.'

That Rimmer girl . . . The girl that Victor had loved to distraction, the girl who had tried to save him over four years earlier, running off to London. Only it wasn't London, was it? Victor had been shaken when he'd first heard the news. The negligent nanny who was being gossiped about was not some anonymous servant, it was his Alice. She had left him and gone away, but only to Werneth Heights, to work for the Arnolds. God, Victor had thought when he'd heard, did anyone know she was related to the family? Apparently not; she had been working there as a nanny.

Victor knew Alice too well to suspect her. He had a hunch that she had gone to the Arnolds to exact some revenge – but he knew she would never hurt anyone, least of all a child. Hadn't she looked out for Hilly all those years ago? And the younger children at Netherlands? Knowledge and instinct told him she was innocent.

Others thought differently, and told him so. They were keen to damn Alice and when further news came out that Robin Tripps' death had been due to a heart defect many ignored the evidence. Like Mr Dedlington.

Throwing down his coat, Victor moved over to his employer, his voice dark.

'Robin Tripps had a bad heart. There was nothing any-one could have done to save that child.'

'Well, be that as it may, Victor, but that's not what we heard. His poor mother holds Alice Rimmer to blame –' he stopped talking as Victor caught hold of his shirt and lifted him bodily up onto his toes. 'Go on, talk about her! Everyone always does. But I knew Alice, and she would never, never, have hurt a child. And if I ever hear you say another bad word about her I'll kill you! God help me, I will.'

As Victor let go of his employer, Mr Dedlington fell back against the worktable, his wife running to his side.

'You're fired, Victor Coates!' he croaked. 'I've put up with enough shit from you! You might be a good worker, but there're plenty more where you came from. Get out of here!'

'With pleasure,' Victor replied, walking past both of them to the door.

'Go on, get out of here!' Mr Dedlington repeated, even louder. 'That Hilly Barker's too good for you. Get back with your own sort, Coates. I imagine Alice Rimmer will be glad to get anyone now.'

After having had a long talk with Ethel, Hilly decided on her course of action. It seemed the least she could do – to offer support. After all, Alice had looked out for her when they were little more than children. Finishing work at the bakery, Hilly took some of the surplus cakes, left out for the staff to take home, and put them in her basket, then took off her starched white apron and cap and hung them on her peg behind the back door of the bakery. Having pulled a plaid coat over her plain skirt, Hilly set off. The rain had stopped and a little bashful sunshine was trying to lighten the February gloom. She wouldn't try to walk all the way – it was too far – she would catch a bus for the last three stops to the Cummingses house in Salford.

It was all so unfair, Hilly thought. If anyone had asked her, she could tell them all about Alice. No one kinder, she could say, no one more protective. But no one *did* ask a sickly girl from a bakery shop, even though Hilly knew better than any of them what her old friend was like.

She wondered, as the bus passed the main fire station on Cleaver Street, whether Alice would be glad to see her. Perhaps she would think Hilly was being patronising. Was that the word? Hilly thought. She would ask Victor later, he would know. Victor knew everything.

And Victor, she thought suddenly, had loved Alice. The basket seemed a little heavier suddenly, the cake odour cloying. People thought of Victor and her as a couple now. They went out together regularly and had done for a while. But he had never asked her to marry him. The engagement rings the other girls flashed at the bakery had never materialised on Hilly's hand. Give him time, she told herself, it's just a matter of time.

The bus pulled up and let off some passengers, one man lighting his pipe before walking on. Hilly looked at him wistfully. That was all she really wanted, a man of her own. All she had *ever* wanted. To cook, clean and buy tobacco for her own husband. For Victor . . . But now she was going to see Alice, who was in trouble. Alice, who was Victor's old love.

The bus jerked to a halt: 'Andrew Street,' the conductor called out. Suddenly wrenched from her daydream, Hilly hurried off and then turned the corner into Cullen Street. At number 109, she knocked. Ethel came to the door immediately.

'Hello, luv. Come in.' She stood back to let Hilly pass, then bent over and whispered, 'Alice is upstairs, out of sorts. You want to go up?'

'Would she mind?'

'No,' Ethel said warmly, 'she would never mind seeing you.'

Well, Ethel thought as she watched Hilly's delicate shape move up the cramped staircase, this is a turn up and no mistake. She wondered then if she would have done the same in Hilly's shoes. Oh, Ethel knew that she and Alice had been friends as children, but Alice had fallen in the love with Victor. And Victor was Hilly's man now.

Deep in thought, Ethel walked back to the kitchen. Gilbert was trying to carve one of his toys, but his hands were clumsy now and the carving was crude. Ethel looked at him fondly, his head bent. I should never take for granted the fact that I have you, she thought. So many other people never have anyone to call their own. Uncharacteristically sentimental, she gently tweaked his neck, pulling a mocking face as he tried to slap her hand away. For an instant he was the old Gilbert – at the age Hilly and Alice were now – full of vim and quick with all the snappy comebacks.

Another knock at the door broke into her thoughts. 'Busy today. I wonder who this is?'

Pulling the door open, she raised her eyebrows.

'Hello, Mrs Cummings. I hope you don't mind my calling round. I came to see Alice.'

Oh brother, Ethel thought, letting Victor in. Did he know that his girlfriend was already upstairs? Had they agreed to meet here? Or had he come of his own accord, without telling Hilly?

'So,' Ethel said awkwardly as she ushered him into the kitchen, 'how are you?'

'Fine, and you?'

'I'm well. Hilly said the other day that you were busy at work. No rest for the wicked. I suppose you'd like a cuppa?' Ethel asked, straining to hear any movement from upstairs. Or better, the welcome sound of Hilly leaving.

'I wasn't going to stay long –'

'It doesn't take long to drink a cup a tea,' Ethel replied crisply, putting the water on to boil. She could sense Victor's tension. Not surprising.

'Hilly told me that Alice had come to stay with you for a while. Is she all right?'

It was there, Ethel thought, the look. The one and only look which you could never hide. He loved Alice. Still. He might go out with another girl, even marry another girl, but he belonged to Alice. Always would.

'Things are hard for her at the moment,' Ethel said honestly.

'People can be bloody cruel.' Gilbert chimed up, pushing his glasses on the top of his head. 'She doesn't want any more hurt, she's had enough.'

Ethel wondered fleetingly if her husband was trying to give Victor the gypsy's warning.

'I just wanted to call and say hello,' Victor replied, looking at Gilbert evenly. 'She meant a good deal to me, once.'

A quick flurry of movement overhead made Ethel jump, but before she could get to the door it was opened and Hilly walked in. She was smiling at first – and then she saw Victor. Baffled astonishment passed over her face, followed by the look Ethel expected – anxiety.

'Hilly,' Victor said.

She smiled stiffly. 'Victor.'

Well, at least they got the names right, Ethel thought, walking over to the grate and setting the kettle to boil. 'Hilly, d'you want some tea?'

'I should be going . . .' she said, looking over to Victor. Her expression was willing him to join her, or at least to explain what he was doing. But he didn't.

Instead he said simply: 'See you later?'

'Yes,' she said, her voice forced. 'That would be nice.'

Ethel had had a hunch that Victor would call, and had prepared the ground by telling Alice that he was courting Hilly. It would do Alice no good to be kept in the dark. Victor had been her man, once. But not now.

While Victor was upstairs talking to Alice, Ethel was

irritated to hear a tapping on the front door, followed by the unwelcome entrance of Alma Tudge.

Seeing her, Gilbert disappeared behind his newspaper.

'Hello there, Gilbert,' Alma said, bustling into the kitchen and sitting down, uninvited. 'I just thought I'd call by after I'd been up the doctor's.'

Reluctantly, Ethel pushed a cup of tea over to her neighbour. Alma Tudge was a widow, with no children, who owned the full three volumes of *The Family Doctor*. When her husband died, her health became her hobby. There was nothing Alma hadn't had, although she had no interest whatsoever in anyone else's health – or lives.

Wincing, she tapped her knee. 'The doctor said he'd never seen anything like it.'

'I bet,' Gilbert said, behind the *Oldham Chronicle*.

'He said, "With a swelling like that, it's a miracle you can walk." Oh, thank you, Ethel, a cup of tea's always welcome, although they do say that too much is bad for the nerves.'

Ethel shot Gilbert a warning glance. 'I thought your back was bad?'

'Oh, it were, Ethel!' Alma said, shifting in her seat. 'The doctor said that if I had more meat on my bones the pain would be more bearable. If I were more like you –'

'If you were fat, you mean.'

'Nay, Ethel!' Alma replied, her long narrow face penitent. 'Would I say a thing like that? A little padding is a godsend. It says in *The Family Doctor* that you have a much better chance in an illness if you have a stone you can readily lose.'

Ethel could see the paper shaking as Gilbert laughed behind it.

'I personally think,' Alma continued, 'that a hot mustard poultice would help.'

Ethel frowned, bemused. 'To lose a stone?'

'No! For my knee,' Alma went on, sipping the tea and

pulling a face. 'You want to get that Co-op tea, the one with the woman juggling on the label.'

Fascinated, Gilbert looked up. '*Juggling?* Why would they put a picture of a woman juggling on a pack of tea?'

'I really wouldn't know –'

'She's not juggling, Alma,' Ethel replied shortly, 'she's dancing.'

Alma frowned. 'Why would she be dancing on a pack of tea?'

'Why would she be bloody juggling if it comes to that?' Gilbert replied, exasperated.

'Well, be that as it may, it's good tea,' Alma replied, turning to the door as Victor and Alice walked in.

From the expression on Victor's face, he looked like man who had been starving and then given a plateful of poison. He was bewildered, unsettled – and longing to be with Alice again. Which was exactly what she was not going to allow.

'Hello there, Alice,' Alma said, the only person in Salford who was uninterested in the scandal.

'Hello, Mrs Tudge.'

Victor looked from Alma, rubbing her knee, to Ethel and then back to Alice.

'We could go for a walk if you like?'

'Oh, you don't want to go out, it's freezing!' Alma chimed in. '*The Family Doctor* says that chills should be avoided in February.'

'Are you still working for Mr Dedlington?' Alice asked, turning back to Victor and avoiding Ethel's glare.

'No,' he replied stiffly.

'So how long have you been on your own?'

Victor glanced at his watch. 'Two hours and six minutes.'

Ethel could see Gilbert frown, even though he was pretending to be reading.

'You left *today*, Victor?'

'Yes, Alice, I left today.'

'Why?'

'I had my reasons.'

'Which were?'

'Personal,' he replied, his voice tight.

Oops, Ethel sighed. Victor Coates would have some explaining to do now. Hilly would be upset, and as for him, he looked stricken. The love that had cost both of them so much was still asking a price.

'I don't think she is dancing or juggling . . .'

Everyone looked at Alma.

'. . . I think she's celebrating.'

'Celebrating making a cup of tea?' Gilbert answered. 'Do me a favour!'

Smiling, Ethel's gaze moved over to Alice, sitting with her head down, her eyes lowered. God, Alice, I love you, Ethel thought. Enough to push you out into the world again. This is no place for you, Alice – and this is not your man.

'Tea,' she said suddenly, slamming the pot down between Alice and Victor. 'And it's hot. Be careful you don't burn yourselves.'

Chapter Twenty-Nine

At nine o'clock that night Hilly was waiting for Victor in his kitchen. Anna Hope had spotted her going in and for once Hilly had been rude and turned her back on the old eavesdropper. With the door safely closed inside, Hilly found herself fighting tears, stunned by the depth of her feelings.

Victor had been to see Alice, without telling her. Well, they were old friends, weren't they? Yes, and old lovers, she thought despairingly. Her eyes moved over to the fireplace where she had propped up a photograph of herself and Victor. It had been taken last summer on the park boating lake. He had his arm round her – proof to any onlooker that he cared.

But how much? Hilly wondered. He had dragged his heels for years, when there was no reason for them not to be together. But now there *was* a reason – and her name was Alice.

Half an hour later. Hilly heard Victor's key in the lock. For a moment she wanted to run, but waited instead. It was obvious that she was about to humiliate herself, but she couldn't help it. Love propelled her towards the enviable and she felt powerless to stop it.

'Victor, talk to me,' she said as he walked in, smiling wanly at her.

He looked away.

'You still care about Alice, don't you?'

'I would have told you that I'd been to see her,' he replied, dodging the question. 'Everyone's talking about her. She has few friends at the moment and she needs support. I would have told you I'd been there.'

The overhead light was shining down on Hilly's face, making a little statue out of her.

'I don't mind; I understand,' she assured him. 'But I just have to know if you still care about her.'

'Hilly –'

'Oh, don't lie, Victor! I have to know the answer. I have to. I've loved you for so long, I *have* to know if you'll ever love me the same. I know that you and Alice were going to get married. I know it was a shock when she went off and you thought you'd never see her again. But she's back now –'

'It's over.'

'Is it?' Hilly asked him gently.

'I don't deserve you!' Victor replied, his tone bewildered. 'You should find someone who loves you, not hang around me. It's not fair.'

'It's my choice.' Her pale eyes were fixed on his, her voice soft.

'But doesn't it hurt?' he queried. 'Hilly, don't martyr yourself on my account. I can't say honestly if I love you enough. I don't know if we'll ever marry.'

She could feel her legs weaken, but pressed on. 'It depends on Alice, doesn't it?'

He nodded, aware of the injury he was causing and hating himself, but unable to lie.

'But she won't stay, Victor!' Hilly said quickly. 'I knew Alice long before you did. I knew how ambitious she was, how she wanted so much. She's determined to prove herself one way or another – she always was. Alice won't settle here, not now. She can't. People are gossiping; they'll make her life hell –'

His face coloured at the words. 'It's all lies!'

'I know!' Hilly replied, for once angry. 'I know it's lies. I know that you want to protect her, I know all of that. It's killing me to know it. I want you, Victor. I don't want to lose you to her – but I can't seem to do anything to stop it. I'm not as nice as you think; I can fight too. I want Alice away from here. I want her out of our lives so that things can go back to normal.'

He shook his head. 'If she had never come back it would be the same. I still wouldn't know if I wanted to settle down with you.' Timidly he put out his hand towards her.

Hilly wanted to knock it away, but she couldn't and grasped it instead. 'Listen to me, Victor. Alice will move on, I know she will. The question is – do you want to move on with her?'

'Oh, Hilly –'

'Don't pity me!' she cried hopelessly. 'Just tell me and put me out of my misery.'

'I don't think she'll have me back,' Victor said slowly.

Hilly's voice was hardly audible. 'But if she *did*?'

'I don't know . . .' He paused. 'Yes, I do. I would go with her, Hilly. God knows, I'm so sorry, but I would go with her.'

Throwing the last of the peeled potatoes into a bowl of cold water, Ethel wiped her hands and then turned to look at Gilbert. He was already half asleep. That was age, she thought. He spent so much of his time dozing now.

'Go up to bed, luv. I'll be along soon.'

He smiled drowsily and then yawned. Pecking her cheek, he climbed up the stairs. Ethel could hear him calling good night to Alice, who had already retired, and then heard her muted reply. As usual, she was keeping to her room. Ethel could hardly blame her, but sympathy was the last thing Alice needed. If she was mollycoddled now, she would never make it out into the world again.

Not that it would be so bad to have Alice around for ever. It would be company for her and Gilbert, like having a second family . . . Slowly Ethel piled the supper plates into the sink and ran some water over them. She could imagine all too easily how life would go on if she let Alice stay. In time the gossip would die down and Alice would find a job. She might eventually start courting someone who was safe, with a lowly job and little prospects. Her life would centre around a knot of Salford streets, fear making a hostage out of her.

Oh no, Ethel thought, not my girl! Not Alice. She had to fight back. She had done nothing wrong, and she had her whole life ahead of her – something no vindictive woman or interfering gossips could take away. Unless she let them. Unless she gave in.

Rinsing a plate under the water, Ethel thought back to the previous night. She had woken to hear muffled crying and knew that it was Alice. Robin's death would have been bad enough, but the recriminations which had been piled on Alice's head had brought her to her knees.

But she was not going to stay there.

Opening the kitchen door, Ethel called up the narrow staircase, 'Alice, come down here, luv, will you?'

Moments later the girl walked in shivering, an old cardigan of Ethel's, about four sizes too big, wrapped around her.

'Sit down, luv. I want to talk to you,' Ethel said, pulling out the chair next to hers at the kitchen table. 'Are you cold?'

Alice nodded, and as Ethel went to bank up the fire said: 'Let me do it.'

'No, luv, I can do it easily enough myself,' Ethel replied, resuming her seat. Her plump face was unlined and cheated her age, but the back of her large hands were mottled with liver spots. 'Alice, I've heard of a job for you.'

She looked up, frowning. Her eyes seemed to have sunk deeper into her head these past few days, her cheeks hollow. 'What?'

'A job, Alice,' Ethel repeated.

'But I can't –'

'Oh, yes you can!' Ethel chimed in. 'You have to get

back to work, luv. Not that I don't want you around – far from it. In fact, I'd even considering keeping you here, with me and Gilbert –'

'But I *want* to stay,' Alice said eagerly.

'I know you do – and that's why you can't.' Ethel leaned forward and tapped Alice's knee. 'You can't because – number one, you're beautiful. Number two, you're clever. Number three, you're brave. In short, Alice Rimmer, you are going to be someone in this world. And I am going to make sure of it.'

'I don't *want* to be someone –'

'Oh, you say that now,' Ethel replied impatiently, 'but now you're twenty-two. You think life lasts for ever. Go on twenty or thirty years, luv. When you're forty-two or fifty-two you'll hate this house and these streets. You'll hate being here and you'll hate being alone. Because neither Gilbert nor me will be here then. You'll be alone, the one thing that frightens you so much.' Ethel paused. 'You think I don't understand – how could I with a husband and children? But I do, Alice, believe me I do. I've been working at Netherlands for longer than I care to think. I've seen hundreds of children come and go from there, all of them as scared as you are. But they didn't have your looks or your brain. They didn't have a chance. You have.'

'I don't want the chance,' Alice said, gripping Ethel's hand. 'I want to stay here. Please, please let me stay here.'

'No,' Ethel said simply. 'I love you too much. There's a door on this house, Alice, and it's never been closed to you. It never will be. But I want you to get this job. You can come and stay with Gilbert and me weekends.'

'But –'

'No, you have to do this!' Ethel sounded harsh and yet her heart was burning with pity. 'The job's up at the TB sanatorium in Greenfields –'

'That's miles away!' Alice cried. 'And it's a terrible place.'

'It's bleak, that's true, but the people are all right. I know them, and although you're not a qualified teacher, they want to give you a chance to train.'

'I bet they do!' Alice snapped. 'No one wants to work there.'

'It'll be hard, luv, but it'll take your mind off what's happened. You can make a new start there.'

Alice stared at the woman who was the nearest she had to a mother. How could Ethel send her away, and to such a place? She remembered the little she had heard of Greenfields Sanatorium – a couple of the children at the home had been sent there. It was run on a strict routine, rest, nutritious food, exercise – and above all, fresh air. That was why the sanatorium was high on the moors, away from the towns – because it was healthier – and because some of the patients were contagious.

'They'll look after you well, Alice. No members of staff have caught TB off the patients. Your education is needed up there. You can do good, become someone.'

'Do they know about me?' Alice's voice was low.

'What? Where you came from? About Robin Tripps' death?' Ethel shook her head. 'No, it's a world of its own at Greenfields. It's a daily struggle to teach and look after the kids. No one has time for gossip, and besides, they're a long way from Salford, or the likes of Werneth Heights. Unless you tell them about your past, Alice, no one will ever find out.'

Chapter Thirty

Ray Berry was talking on the phone, his thick black hair dishevelled as he ran his hand through it for the third time. Cold to the bone, he could feel little heat from the fire in the grate, the draught from the window keeping the temperature low. One of his sponsors was withdrawing his support. Ray knew why – the man had recently opened a factory in Macclesfield and needed funds elsewhere. It was no time to be philanthropic, and no one made money from good works.

'I understand, but it's not a matter of –'

There was a mumble down the other end of the line. Ray held onto his temper.

'Yes, I see, but we need your help. We rely on it. When you promised us –'

Another mumble, this time the voice raised.

'All right! Maybe you didn't *promise*, but you implied –'

The caller was getting irate. Ray closed his eyes and took a deep breath.

'I see. Well, if there's nothing I can say to change your mind ... Right, goodbye then.' He put down the phone then banged his hand on the desk. 'Bastard!' he said fiercely, standing up and walking over to the window.

Lighting a cigarette, he looked at his watch. His brother would have told him that he was wasting his time, but that was Tommy's opinion, not his.

It was ten years since Ray Berry had taken over the Greenfields Sanatorium. It had been run by the council before and then, in 1920, they had threatened it with closure. Ray had heard all about it, but wasn't interested. He'd been involved in travel then, and collecting. His inherited money had made all things possible – especially selfishness. Ray had led a charmed life, a womanising life. He'd had girlfriends, cars, a flat abroad and the air of man who could either buy, or manipulate, anyone.

He'd been happy too; hadn't thought for a moment that his life was frivolous. After all, he'd been only thirty then – attractive in a muscular, heavy-featured way, and confident. Above all, confident. If anyone had said that Ray Berry would end up running a sanatorium on the moors outside Oldham, they would have been laughed out of court.

He was tough, quick-witted, born to be a leader of the pack. And Ray's pack had been the one which gambled, ran fast cars, and drank. He was, his peers would have said, a born hedonist.

Then one night Ray Berry had been driving a girl home and his car had skidded on a bend. He had fought to control it, but the vehicle had gone off the road into a ravine. Toni Palmer had lived in a wheelchair from that night on. Driven by guilt, Ray had spent fortunes taking her around the world – to specialists and cranks, anyone who might get her back on her feet. But nothing had worked.

She was still beautiful to Ray, but not to their set. To them, Toni Palmer had been a freak. An embarrassment. As if her suffering wasn't enough, she'd been excluded from her normal life. Becoming more and more intolerant of his friends' behaviour, Ray had tried to include Toni in everything he did. But he hadn't loved her, and she'd known that. He was just being kind. Eventually, Toni had taken an overdose. The accident hadn't killed her. Her lifestyle had.

Ray had never been the same after her death. From then onwards he hadn't been able to stand the sight of his peers. His parents had been bemused by the change, his younger brother telling him that he was just going through a phase. It's grief, Tommy had said, you'll get over it. Ray hadn't. He had caused the accident, but worse, he had not managed to save her afterwards. And he should have done . . .

Ray stubbed out the cigarette and glanced at his hands. A workman's hands now – from repairing the fence last week, which blew down every spring and autumn, when the winds came from over the moors. It was all right being a hermit, Tommy said, but he had to stop punishing himself. Ray smiled. His brother just didn't understand. Ray wasn't depriving himself of anything, he was just trying to put something back.

'Mr Berry?'

He turned. His secretary, the stick-thin Gladys, was ushering in a young woman.

'This is Miss Rimmer. She has an appointment.'

Ray studied his visitor. She was dark and dressed very sombrely for someone so young; sensible from the dark suit to her utilitarian black shoes. Sensible, but out of place. This was not a woman to be sombre. She was beautiful, no matter how much she tried to hide it.

'Please, sit down, Miss Rimmer,' he said, offering her a seat and sitting down himself. 'I believe you're interested in coming to work here?'

She nodded.

'I need a job.'

'So you're not interested in the children? Or the work we do here?'

She was sullen, didn't care any more. They needed help at Greenfields, so why wasn't he snatching her hand off? She had expected to be welcomed, not made to feel uncomfortable.

'I like teaching . . . I mean, I'm not qualified, but I want to be a teacher.'

'Have you any experience?' The same loaded question she'd be asked anywhere.

'No.' The same lie.

He frowned, stared at her. Intimidated, Alice looked down. It was freezing cold in his office and it smelled of cigarette smoke. On his desk were two telephones, a cup of cold tea and a stack of files. He was wearing his overcoat, trying to cheat the temperature.

'What can you do for us here?' he asked.

'I can look after children –'

'How do you know?'

'I looked after them at Netherlands,' Alice replied stiffly. They were a long way away from Salford; it was safe to talk about the home.

'You were at Netherlands?'

'I was an orphan there, from the time I was a year old,' she said calmly. 'Then I started to train as a teacher –'

'But you didn't continue?' he queried. 'Why not?'

'I was due to get married.'

His eyebrows rose. 'But you didn't?'

'No.'

Alice knew she should explain, but she couldn't, because she didn't really know what to say. Seeing Victor had been worse than she could possibly have imagined. There was no going back, even though she knew he still loved her. And she still loved him. It had been unbearable not to reach out to him, to touch him. He had belonged to her once, but all those little intimacies, all the looks and touches between lovers were forbidden. He belonged to Hilly now.

She would have to make sure that they were never alone again; never put temptation in their way. They had loved each other so much – did she *really* believe that feeling could have burned out? Away from him, she had thought so, but seeing Victor had brought it all back. Too late.

Not knowing what was going through Alice's mind, Ray was simply finding her difficult to talk to. How on earth could she respond to sick children if she was so awkward?

The interview was going to turn out to be a waste of time, Ray thought. Alice Rimmer wasn't the kind of person to work in a sanatorium.

'Look, Miss Rimmer, it's hard here. We have few funds and a lot of sick children. We have rules and regulations and we run the place like an army barracks. These kids need understanding and patience. They don't like some of things they have to have done to them. They don't like the discipline, or the cold. They play us up,' he said emphatically. 'No one could work here unless they were dedicated. And I'm sorry if I'm misjudging you, but you don't seem too keen.'

Alice looked towards the window. For a moment she was tempted to walk out, but how could she? She could hardly return to Ethel and tell her she had failed. It would be just one more failure on top of all the others. Slowly she turned back to Ray Berry. He was younger than she had expected and blunt. He was also in charge – and she suddenly she didn't want to fail again.

'I'm sorry if I don't seem like the perfect candidate,' she said honestly. 'I don't like institutions – I was in one too long – but I do like children, whatever you think. And I can be kind and patient. It's just that I can't beg you for the job. I just can't.'

It was his turn to be surprised. He hadn't expected her to be so forthright and admired her for it. She was speaking from the heart, not like so many do-gooders that came to see him, looking for work – looking for something to make themselves seem better. He knew the types all too well – the men and women who needed to rule children; or the others who needed to be popular, needed the children's adoration to make them feel important.

But this woman wasn't like that. She was honest and looked as though she hadn't seen much luck in her own life. He also found himself wondering why she hadn't got married.

'You don't have any references, I suppose?'

Alice shook her head. 'No.'

For a moment it was all that Ray could do not to laugh.

'Miss Rimmer, just tell me one thing – why *should* I give you a job?'

Alice thought for a moment and then sighed. Finally she looked him squarely in the eyes and said: 'You shouldn't – but you will. You will, because I know what it's like to be one of these children. I was never sick, but I was always different. Like them. You could hire the best teacher in the country, Mr Berry, and she could teach them Latin and English Literature. She could teach them about foreign countries and dead kings. But she'll never know how they *think*, or what frightens them. *I do* – and that's why you'll hire me.'

Olive McGrath was trying to smoke a cigarette whilst fiddling with her left suspender. The ash dropped off the stub and onto her shoe, Olive cursing. She was late, as always, being the only one of the staff at Greenfields to live out. The others lived in, at what was laughably called The Cottage. She would die rather than stay there, Olive thought, straightening her stocking and then checking her reflection in the lavatory mirror.

'Oh God,' she sighed.

One too many port and lemons the night before with Ed, she thought. Her head thumped. 'It won't be long now,' Ed had told her. 'Soon you won't have to work up there any more. I'm going to get a few of the men together and we're going into business. Our own painting and decorating business . . .' Olive raised her eyes heavenwards. It would never happen. Ed would bugger it up, because he always did. Besides, he was colour-blind, and that was never an asset to a decorator.

'Oh, Christ!' she hissed, as a bell rang in the corridor. She was in such a hurry that she didn't look where she was going and bumped into a tall woman outside. A stranger.

'Oh, hi, who are you?'

'Alice, Alice Rimmer.'

'New?'

Alice nodded. 'Starting today.'

After the bell rang a second time, Olive grabbed Alice's arm. 'Where are you supposed to be?'

'With someone called Mrs McGrath.'

'Lucky you, that's me,' Olive said, smiling. 'You going to be working in the school then?'

'So I was told,' Alice answered loudly as a boy walked past ringing a large brass bell.

'Not the sanatorium?'

'Not at first,' Alice answered her. 'But not many of the children there need teaching, do they? I mean, aren't they too sick?'

Olive raised her dark eyebrows almost to her auburn hairline. 'Not all of them are very sick, most have to have some kind of education. The Board insist on it. And what the Board says, goes.'

The boy turned round and passed them again, ringing the bell enthusiastically.

Wincing, Olive put her hands over her ears. 'Oh God, my bloody head.'

'Are you OK?'

'Hung over, but ready to go,' Olive replied, steering Alice into a classroom and closing the door behind them.

A group of twelve or so children stood up as they walked in, staring curiously at Alice. Quickly Olive wrote the date on the blackboard and then 'Alice Rimmer' underneath.

'This,' she pointed to Alice, 'is Miss Alice Rimmer. She's going to be working here from now on. She's going to be a teacher.'

Unexpectedly, Alice liked the sound of it. *A teacher*. She was going to be a teacher . . . Ethel was right: she *could* make a new life for herself. A respectable life, without revenge or memory. A life totally removed from the home or the Arnolds. A life away from disappointment.

'Miss, miss!' one child called out, hopping from foot to foot.

Olive looked over to him. 'What is it, Graham?'

'I want to go to the toilet.'

'No, you don't, sit down,' Olive replied, winking at Alice. 'Master Graham has a problem with his bowels. He can't hold them once a lesson starts. Mind you, he never has any problem in the playground.'

The class laughed, Alice looking at children one by one. They were all around nine years old. Some looked sickly, most had little colour in their faces and were dark under the eyes; a few had the shaven heads which spoke of a lice infestation. All of them wore their overcoats and mittens to keep them warm, as the windows of the classroom were wide open. Alice shivered in her thin suit.

She watched Olive write some simple sums on the board and then sit down at the teacher's seat. Even though she was wearing a top coat, her hands looked chilled.

Catching Alice's eye, she beckoned for her to bring her own chair up onto the dais.

'Hey,' she whispered, 'you must be freezing. Where's your coat?'

'No one told me to wear one.'

'Well, I'm telling you,' Olive replied. Her face was bright pink with the chill, her green eyes lively. 'You won't last the winter out unless you know how to keep warm. And eat.'

'Oh, I can eat,' Alice assured her.

'Wait until you see the portions!' Olive replied, laughing.

By the time the lesson was halfway through, Alice could hardly talk. The day was cloudy and damp, everyone's breath coming out in little wisps of vapour. It was the policy of Greenfields, Olive explained, that there was always plenty of fresh air. The doctors insisted on it. It was good for the children's lungs, they said . . . Huh, Olive, replied, it was all right for the doctors. They didn't have to work in such temperatures.

At ten thirty the bell rang, the class herded out into the playground. There they were given hot milk and cake. So was Alice.

'I'm not hungry,' she said, pulling on her coat and buttoning it up to her neck.

'Hungry or not, you have to eat,' Olive replied, 'or you get fired.'

Alice laughed. 'Fired for not eating?'

Olive nodded. 'The teachers have to eat everything the children do. It's supposed to set a good example, and besides, they think that by feeding us up we're less likely to catch anything.'

Reluctantly, Alice picked up a bun and chewed on it. 'How long have you been here?'

'Three years,' Olive replied, cupping her hands around her mug of milk to warm them. 'Three long years.'

The playground was full of children, some standing around in groups, others playing half-heartedly. To their left was the dark block of the sanatorium, to their right the wild bulk of the moors, and a way off, a huddle of buildings called Tollbank Farm. No flowers bloomed on the moor's bleak slopes, except for snatches of wild heather – the only vegetation tough enough to survive.

'Why did you come here, Olive?'

'I didn't want to work in a normal school. This seemed like a challenge. Anyway, I had a brother who came here a while ago.'

'Was he cured?'

'No,' Olive replied simply, turning to one of the children and calling out: 'Doris, get moving! I want to see you run round this playground twice.' She turned back to Alice. 'Why did you come?'

'To make a fresh start.'

Olive nodded, then ducked behind Alice. Suddenly Alice heard a match being struck and Olive lit a cigarette, hurriedly waving away the smoke with her hand.

'Tell me if you see Berry coming, will you?' she asked. 'I just *have* to have a fag.'

Alice smiled, her body shielding Olive. Over her shoulder she whispered, 'Is he strict?'

Olive sniggered. 'None more so. He smokes like a blocked chimney himself, but he won't have anyone else snatching a smoke.' Alice could hear her inhale greedily. 'Ed – that's my husband – says that Ray Berry is actually rich – a real playboy once.'

Alice frowned. 'No! Are you certain?'

'Sure I am. He was loaded – well, he still is, I suppose. But now he's got serious and runs this place like a prison. Mind you, he does well by the kids, I'll give him that.'

'Is he married?'

'Why? You interested?'

Alice's face flushed. 'Of course not! I was just wondering.'

Olive was chuckling behind her. 'No, Ray Berry is not married. And if he has a girlfriend, he keeps her bloody quiet. No one here's seen any woman around for over two years.' Olive hurriedly finished her smoke and then ground out the stub, pocketing the evidence.

Smiling, Alice warmed to her. It was a relief to find someone like Olive McGrath on her first day – someone who wasn't too curious, who had a life outside Greenfields.

'Are you going to live in?'

Alice nodded. 'I have to, during the week anyway.'

'At The *Cottage*?' Olive laughed. 'Oh God, I can never say that without laughing! Have you seen it yet?'

Oh yes, Alice had seen it. The Cottage was a large, flat-fronted brick building, with double-barred entrance doors. Over the doors read PER ARDUA AD ASTRA – and its translation underneath – Through work to the stars. Alice wondered how anyone could have put that up as serious motivation on a building which was so off-putting. The house was grim and unwelcoming, segregated into staff quarters. The male teachers – all four of them – lived on the first floor, the three female teachers on the ground floor.

That morning Alice had been introduced to all of them. The average age was fifty, the average build was stout, and the average demeanour was hostile.

'I guess you're a bit of a novelty for them,' Olive said, looking hard at Alice. 'There's not been a good-looking woman around here for long enough – except me, of course. But then, I'm married and I don't live in.' She paused, looking Alice up and down. 'Think you'll cope?'

'With the children?'

'I was thinking more of the teachers,' Olive retorted. 'Some have been up here so long they're moor crazy.'

Alice laughed. 'Oh, come on!'

'Seriously, it gets some people that way. They get used to being cut off from the normal world and after a while they don't want to mix any more. I bet half of them don't even know what's going on outside Greenfields. Oldham could be on another planet.' She sighed. 'Thank God I have a home to go to at night. And a man.'

Silent, Alice mulled the words over in her head. It was so similar to Netherlands: another old-fashioned island in the middle of the modern world. But now she could walk out of the door any time she liked.

'Don't get like the others,' Olive said suddenly. 'You're young. Don't hide away, Alice. It would be too bloody easy.'

Chapter Thirty-One

There would be no more slow looks, no more touches passed between them, each giving life to the other. Victor might have longed for Alice most of his life, but he realised, finally, that they would never be reunited. He was not fully conscious of his decision, but by choosing Hilly, Victor made sure he would marry someone who was the complete opposite of Alice. With Hilly, there would be no reminders, no sexual heat, no intensity, no pain. Instead she would be kind, and he would be protective. He had thought of her as a friend for so long, but now he looked at her as his wife to be.

Because the woman he had wanted had gone. Because the person who had fired him up, inspired him, provoked him, was beyond his reach. Besides, Victor thought, there was another reason why the marriage to Hilly should work – she knew about Alice. There would be no secrets between them. She accepted that Victor loved her more like a brother than a husband, but it was enough. In his turn, Victor was prepared to look after Hilly and devote himself to her. It would be his life's work. It would keep his mind off what had been lost. Better to be secure and safe than tormented.

Passion was for children, he told himself. Maybe if he and Alice had married their attraction would have faded – and then what? With Hilly there was no expectation of passion; with Hilly, Victor could be calm, settle into his work and later, middle age. It was not as though he hadn't experienced real love. Maybe it was never meant to last; maybe it would have destroyed, rather than united, them in the end.

On the morning of his wedding, Victor paused at the front door of the house on Trafalgar Street, then suddenly turned and looked into the kitchen. It was only a memory, but for a moment it lived. Alice was there, smiling at him, her arm resting on the mantelpiece, her hair loose about her shoulders. Longing made a fool of him and Victor stumbled towards her, striking his leg against the kitchen table. As he did so, the image disappeared and he was left staring at an empty kitchen, with Hilly's photograph looking out at him kindly from the wall.

The wedding ceremony was held at the registry office in Salford, Ethel and Gilbert standing as witnesses. There was a rainstorm afterwards, and Victor took off his coat and put it around Hilly as they waited for the bus to take them home. She had won by default, but that didn't matter to her. She had her man.

Watching them, Ethel slid her arm through Gilbert's and frowned up at the sky. 'Always rains on weddings.'

'Not on ours,' he replied. 'It were fine that day.'

She squeezed his arm. 'Any regrets?'

'Like what?'

'Like marrying me!' she chided him. 'Have you ever had any regrets?'

'I wished I'd had more money to buy you things,' he replied honestly. 'You know, take you on holiday and maybe get a car.'

'Oh, what do we want with a car? There's buses every few minutes. And holidays – who needs them? I don't like the heat.'

He was touched and linked his fingers with hers. 'Have *you* any regrets, Ethel?'

'None,' she said firmly. 'I can honestly say that I never wanted anyone but you. I got the man I wanted, Gilbert Cummings. I reckon that makes me a lucky woman.'

*   *   *

Standing with her back to the wind, Alice counted the children in the playground and then followed them back into the classroom. The windows were half opened, the draught ruffling papers on her desk. Within weeks she had graduated from general dogsbody to relief teacher. Her education – cobbled as it was from Netherlands and Mr Matthews – was more extensive than anyone had thought. The girl without a qualification to her name was suddenly a teacher of the little ones.

And she gloried in it. She knew every child's name and history and, without realising it, made them feel important – something no one had ever done for her when she was growing up. Firm but just, Alice could control the classroom without raising her voice, because they wanted to please her. She made learning fun too, and understood that children who were not strong had little concentration.

'You've got the little swines eating out of your hands,' Olive said, surprised. 'Even Geordie Wilks.'

'He was difficult at first, but he's settled down now,' Alice replied, picking up her books and putting them into her bag. 'I just hope it lasts.'

Later she would go back to The Cottage and mark the essays, later still she would make a selection of drawings. The class liked her sketches and could remember history much more easily if they had a picture to relate to. The Battle of Hastings, 1066, Alice thought, that was a good one to draw. Besides, drawing made her feel light-hearted, young again. And it had been a long time since she had known such contentment.

Sitting on the edge of Alice's desk, Olive put her head on one side. 'Well you've settled down to the teaching bit, but what about a personal life?'

'I don't have time,' Alice replied. She knew that the previous Friday Victor and Hilly had married. She had sent them a card, but the wound was still raw to the touch.

'You should get out, get a boyfriend. I'm sure Ed would know someone.'

Alice thought of the bullish Ed and winced. 'I'm OK, Olive, honestly.'

'But it's not natural at your age –'

'*What* isn't?'

'Being stuck with a load of old fossils,' Olive replied shortly. 'You can't tell me they're a bunch of laughs.'

They were far from that, Alice thought. In fact the other teachers did not mix with her at all. They were polite, but distant, set in their ways. If she asked them a question, they would answer her, but they never initiated a conversation. Even having to share a bathroom with the three other female teachers didn't make for cosiness. They hurried in and then hurried out first thing in the morning in silence, one in a nightcap, one in curlers, the last in a hairnet. Why they bothered Alice couldn't imagine. The only men who saw them were the other teachers, and none of them was remotely interested.

'You'll get old before your time,' Olive said, adding wickedly, 'You know what they say – *if you don't use it, you lose it.*'

Alice pulled the bag onto her shoulder and turned. 'What?'

'You know.'

'No, I don't.'

Olive dropped her voice. 'You know what I mean – sex.'

Alice could feel her face flush. Seeing the reaction, Olive laughed loudly. 'I thought so! You're not as innocent as you make out, Miss Rimmer.'

'Keep your voice down!' Alice retaliated, walking off, Olive in hot pursuit.

'I thought you must have had a boyfriend. Who is he?'

'Olive, let it drop.'

But it was too good to let go of that easily. 'I'm just glad you're not one of those goody two-shoes who save themselves for marriage. I said I would, but I didn't in the end. Not that Ed knows, of course. But still,' she smiled her lopsided grin, 'what you don't know, can't harm you.'

Alice was embarrassed and anxious to get away. She liked Olive, but didn't like anyone prying into her private life, especially someone who liked to gossip.

'Wait!' Olive called after her, as Alice hurried down the hall. 'Don't get all huffy. I was just teasing, that's all.'

'Forget it. I have to go now.'

'I thought we could go out sometime.'

Alice hesitated. 'Where?'

'To the pictures. *King Kong*'s coming soon. It's supposed to be terrifying.'

'I'll think about it –'

'Oh, suit yourself!' Olive snapped, suddenly impatient. 'I'm not the one who needs a friend.'

When she thought about it later, Alice realised that she should have gone after Olive and made amends there and then. But she couldn't face it. She hadn't come to Greenfields to socialise, she had come to escape and make something of herself. Olive wouldn't help her with that. She was a married woman, with her life mapped out. She didn't have any obvious ambitions and said repeatedly that she would give up work if Ed made a fortune. Well, no man was going to support *her*, Alice thought. If she wanted to get on, she had to do it herself.

Her thoughts turned back to Geordie Wilks. He was slow to learn, and when he had come out of a long stay in the sanatorium he was well behind his peers. Rather than look stupid, Geordie had decided to be disruptive – the class clown.

Alice had struggled with him for two lessons and then asked him to stay behind. Geordie had been awkward, spoiling for a fight. His clothes were too big for him, obvious hand-me-downs, his feet in clogs. For an instant Alice had seen herself reflected in him.

'Geordie, what's the matter?'

His narrow face had been truculent, his pale eyes sly. There was little colour to his skin, only a familiar waxy pallor.

'Nuthin'.'

'You can tell me – what's wrong?'

'Nuthin'.'

Alice had looked at him for a long moment. He had been flicking ink pellets at the other children and bullying them, his clowning turned nasty.

'I want you to be the form prefect.'

Geordie had opened his eyes wide. 'Wot the 'ell –'

'Don't swear,' Alice had said calmly. 'I need some help. I need your help.'

Frowning, Geordie had wiped the back of his mouth with his sleeve. All the food packed into him hadn't put a spare pound on his bones.

'Is this a lark?'

'No. I'm new here and I need help,' she'd said reasonably. 'I want *you* to help me.'

Geordie had tried to looked indifferent, but couldn't keep it up. If he was form prefect he would be someone; the other kids would have to listen to him.

'Of course, it's a very responsible post – do you think you could do it?'

'Sure,' Geordie had said with certainty.

'You have to be very mature, very much in control.' Alice had paused, as though reconsidering. 'Maybe it wouldn't work after all. Maybe you couldn't cope with it –'

'I could! I could!' Geordie had said eagerly. 'You watch me.'

Smiling at the memory, Alice walked across the gravelled drive towards The Cottage, letting herself in and sighing when the warmth hit her. That was the one good thing about living there: the rules for open windows did not apply.

In her room she saw the letter she'd received that morning on her dressing table.

My dear friend,
      I missed you at my wedding, but I understood. I don't know if I should be writing this or not. If it's the wrong thing to do, please don't hold it against me.
      I do love Victor. But I know that he does not love me half as much as he loved you. I can never repay you for the kindness you always showed me – but I can promise that I will look after Victor and do right by him.
      We three have so few friends, don't let us grow apart, please, Alice. I love him and I love you.
      Always,
      Hilly

Ray Berry was standing watching Alice through the glass partition of the classroom door. She had not seen him. Instead she was writing on the blackboard, her coat sleeve covered in chalk dust, her mouth moving – although he could hear little of what she said.

He had to admit that he was surprised by her. She, of all people, had turned out to be a natural teacher. It was obvious in everything she did. As he looked on, Alice stopped and listened to a child, giving the boy her full attention. When he had finished, she answered. Obviously she said something funny, because the class laughed. Yes, Ray thought, that's what all the children want, someone to listen to them and cheer them up.

Ah well, there was no time to daydream. Hurriedly he

left the building and made for the sanatorium. A bitter late snap had come down fast, bringing with it April snow from the moors. The Ice Saints, he thought, remembering the old saying about saints rising from their graves and walking, bringing a late frost with them.

Running, he kept his head down and then shook off the snow at the doorway.

Sister Mills looked up when he came in, her dark, Romany features puzzled. 'That's not snow!'

'Well, it's not icing sugar,' Ray replied drily. 'Dr Priestly's coming in an hour.'

'He's not due for another week,' Sister Mills replied impatiently, walking on into the main ward, Ray following her.

The ward consisted of twenty beds in a row down one side of the room, facing three huge patio windows. They looked out on to the moors, at this moment freckled with white. In each bed was a child, the more severe cases set apart in isolation. Each child wore pyjamas and was sitting up, washed and tidy.

'Wait until you hear his car and then open the windows,' Ray said, turning back to the sister. 'Not a minute before. It's too bloody cold – I don't care what the doctor says.'

'It's fresh air –'

'It's murder,' Ray said wryly, walking over to the nearest bed and smiling at the occupant.

When he got back to his office he would phone the Macclesfield industrialist again, see if he had reconsidered. Maybe he would even try a bit of pressure to loosen the purse strings. They needed more equipment, Ray thought impatiently, looking round. And the linoleum needed repairing.

His face creased into a frown. No one remembered them because they were too far away. If the sanatorium was in the middle of the town, with people seeing them and passing them daily, it would be another matter. But up here they had no chance. It was hard to get charity out on a limb. After all, who would see a good deed in a place no one visited? Much better to fling around your charity where it can be measured and applauded.

The isolation wasn't so bad for the recovering children in the school, allowed to go home at night, but for the worst cases, who were segregated for weeks, even months at a time . . . Who wanted to know about some place where sickly kids coughed up sputum samples into cracked Petri dishes? A place where poor parents rode buses and then walked for miles to visit? A place people considered to be only one step up from a leper colony?

Exasperated, Ray turned back to the Sister Mills. 'How are you coping?'

'Like I always do – with difficulty,' she replied, her voice tart.

'You're a saint, Sister.'

'And you're a liar, Mr Berry,' she retaliated, smiling slowly. 'Do you want to see Dr Priestly?'

Ray shook his head. 'No, I'll send someone over to take his report. I have too much on at the moment.'

The person chosen to go over to the sanatorium was Alice. Called out at the end of her class, Ray Berry met her in the corridor.

'I need someone to take notes – can you do that?'

'I can try, but I'm not a secretary.'

'But you can write down what the doctor says, can't you?'

She nodded, surprised that she had been singled out for extra responsibility. 'What do you want me to do?'

Ray looked at his watch. 'Go over to the sanatorium in fifty minutes. There you'll see Sister Barbara Mills. The doctor who comes to visit the children every two weeks is due in an hour. It's a surprise visit. He's a good doctor and attends here for a pittance, so we accommodate him.' He paused, noticing how dark Alice's eyes were. Embarrassed to be caught staring, he glanced away. 'Just keep a note of anything the doctor says and then give it to Gladys. She'll type it up when she comes in later.'

Alice nodded, then frowned. 'What about my next class?'

'Someone else will have to do it.' Ray replied, turning round and beckoning to Olive, who was hanging about at the end of the corridor.

She came over to him, smiling. 'Morning, sir.'

'Have you been smoking?'

She shifted her feet. 'Just one.'

'I don't want one, or forty-one. You don't smoke here, got it?'

Reluctantly Olive nodded.

'Now, I want you to take Alice's next class. She's doing something for me.'

The expression on Olive's face veered from surprise to spite in an instant. Glancing at Alice quickly she then nodded and walked off.

'Perhaps you should have asked Olive to do –'

'I ask who I want, Miss Rimmer!' Ray replied shortly. 'I can't do with women's moods.'

Stung, Alice kept her voice down. 'I just meant that Mrs McGrath was senior to me –'

'And irresponsible. I want someone I can trust,' Ray said brusquely. 'Can I trust you?'

Trust . . . The word seemed alien to her.

'Yes, you can trust me.'

'Good, now get on with it.'

Sister Mills was standing in the main ward of the sanatorium when Alice walked in. Looking at her watch, the sister said simply, 'The doctor's always on time. We have one minute to go. Right, all the windows open! Now!'

In an instant the other three nurses leaped forward and opened the huge patio windows on the ward. The wind blew in fierce and cold, snow following.

Incredulous, Alice looked at Barbara Mills. 'What are you doing?'

'Doctor's orders,' she replied, smiling slyly. 'Well, when he comes on his rounds, that it. The medical profession believe that fresh air is good for tuberculosis. The trouble is that the doctor's built like a tram and doesn't feel the cold – not like the children.'

She moved down the ward, Alice following. In every bed there was a shivering child, wrapped up to the neck in pyjamas. Some had dressing gowns on, all had their overcoats on top. And every bed was piled high with blankets, many of them darned with a rash of patches. The temperature was dropping rapidly.

'The snow's settling on the end of some of the beds, Sister,' Alice said, looking round. 'They're going to freeze to death!'

'Never,' Sister Mills replied. 'Those children have about ten layers on. Besides, as soon as the doctor's gone we close the windows again, just leave them open a crack at the top.'

Only seconds later there was the sharp sputter of a car coming to a halt outside, followed by the sound of footsteps running up the steps into the sanatorium. As Alice waited in the ward, she could hear the deep muffle of a male voice and the noise of stamping as the doctor cleared his snow-covered shoes.

'Alice! Can you come here please?' Sister called.

Walking from the ward into the hall, Alice stopped dead in the doorway. Dr Guy Priestly was rummaging through his medical bag, his bearded face flushed with cold. Memory took over: the same doctor coming to The Dower House to see Robin, the doctor Alice had begged to be recalled that night her charge died ... For an instant she wanted to run, but then realised that there was no escape. Running would provoke as many questions as staying.

'Dr Priestly,' Sister Mills explained, 'Mr Berry's secretary is not here today, so this lady will take down your notes.'

He turned, saw Alice, and a flutter of recognition passed over the Celtic features. She saw it and tensed herself for exposure, but instead Dr Priestly merely nodded.

'Well, let's get on with it, Sister,' he said brusquely, walking past Alice into the ward.

What was he wanting for? Would he tell Ray Berry about her later to avoid a messy confrontation now?

'I'll talk slowly so that you can get everything written down, Miss . . . ?'

'Rimmer,' Alice replied, catching Guy Priestly's eye again. And then she saw it, the wink.

Light-headed with relief, Alice opened her notebook and took down the dictation as accurately as she could. From time to time Dr Priestly would spell something for her, and wait until she had written it. From bed to bed they went, the doctor examining the children and complimenting Sister Mills on listening to his advice.

'Fresh air is fresh air,' he expounded. 'Our patients can't have too much of it.'

Alice exchanged a glance with the Sister and then began writing again as Guy Priestly paused by the last bed. His interest in this patient was extensive, and so were the notes. Concentrating, Alice wrote down every word, her hand sticky with effort.

Finally he stopped talking.

'And that's it for today, Miss Rimmer,' he said briskly, turning round. 'Sister Mills, will you get me the file on Norman Ecclestone, please?'

He waited until she had left them alone and then turned back to Alice.

'I'm not going to say a word,' he told her, his bass voice lowered. 'You deserve a chance, Alice. What happened to Robin Tripps was not your fault, whatever the family say. I always believed you – that you asked for me to call again – because I knew how much you loved Robin.' He tapped her arm with his left hand. 'Dorothy Tripps made you her scapegoat.'

Alice kept her own voice low. 'I never lied, Dr Priestly, I swear it.'

'I know that.'

'What happened after I left?'

He shrugged and wrapped a thick wool muffler round his neck. 'Dorothy Tripps turned into a martyr and her parents let her. You did well to get away. Mrs Tripps would still hurt you if she could.'

'But I did nothing to her!'

He sighed. 'I know, but she believes her own lie now. She had to have someone to blame, and it had to be someone she could get rid of, someone who had no clout.' He paused, thinking back. 'I've often wondered about that woman – she's been unbalanced for years.'

Alice said the next works without considering them. 'Since the murder of her sister?'

He frowned. 'You know about that?'

'Yes . . . Charlie told me.'

'Ah, Charlie. A right Charlie!' Dr Priestly said, laughing. 'He's getting married, you know.'

'I'm glad,' Alice said honestly. Her brother getting married. Daft lanky Charlie marrying . . .

'The Arnolds are an odd family, all told. I felt sorry for them for a long time, but after that business with Robin – when I knew his mother had slandered you – that was it. I refused to treat them. Then, or since.' Suddenly, he turned round, 'Ah, Sister Mills, thank you.'

Crossing the hallway, she handed him the file and smiled. 'So we'll see you again in a fortnight, Doctor?'

He opened the front doors, a blast of white cold air hitting him.

'In a fortnight,' he agreed, disappearing into a swirl of snow, the sound of the car door slamming ricocheting out across the courtyard and on to the moors beyond.

Chapter Thirty-Two

Ray Berry was glad that summer was coming. Stretching, he raised his arms above his head and yawned extravagantly. In his old life he would have been doing the season now – Ascot, balls, regattas; he and his friends would drink too much and vie with each other to date the best-looking girls.

He thought wonderingly of his parents in London, and Tommy, his brother. Reckless Tommy, charming to the nth degree, still single. As he was. Strange that – he would never have believed that he wouldn't have married or had children. But here he was at forty-one, childless and wifeless. With only Greenfields to call home.

Still, at least he had done something with his life. But why not a career *and* a family? It was his fault, Ray decided; he hadn't put any effort in to finding a mate. Oh, he had toyed with the idea, even had an affair with Barbara Mills. He smiled to himself. She had been almost perfect: she was a nurse, involved in his work; she was good-looking, she was feisty – so why hadn't he married her? *Why?*

He couldn't blame it all on Toni Palmer. Enough time had passed for him to move on, to stop blaming himself for her death. Yet every time he seemed to get close to another woman some past shadow image of Toni imprinted itself on the film of the present. Or maybe that was just an excuse.

Unexpected homesickness came over Ray in that instant. No one had driven him away, no one had blamed him, he had exiled himself. There was nothing to stop him visiting his parents or his brother, nothing to prevent him going down to London and reviving some of his past life.

Nothing to stop him – and nothing to *make* him either.

The phone rang shrilly beside him.

'Hi, it's Tommy.'

Smiling, Ray shook his head. 'You won't believe this. I was just thinking about you.'

'And you won't believe this – I'm coming up to your neck of the woods on Thursday.'

'What for? You hate the North, Tommy, you know you do.'

'I might hate it, but needs must when the devil drives.'

Ray grimaced. 'Which particular devil this time?'

'Oh, nothing too bad. I just have to sort something out in Manchester.'

A debt, no doubt.

'So you're coming to stay at Greenfields?'

'Only overnight,' Tommy replied. 'I can only take so much excitement. I'll come over to you about five – that OK?'

It was closer to seven when Tommy finally arrived, blowing his car horn as he drove up to the front door of Greenfields and calling out loudly for his brother. Alerted by the noise, Barbara Mills looked out through the sanatorium window, astonished to see a stocky, overdressed man with a wild mass of wiry black hair.

At the same moment Ray came down the steps towards his brother's car.

'Dear God, what happened to your hair?'

Tommy grinned, showing big white teeth. 'I had the top down on the car to feel the wind in my hair.'

'It looks more like you had thousand volts put through it.' Ray replied, leading his brother towards the entrance of Greenfields.

As they approached, Tommy looked round at the massive brick edifice punctuated by bare windows, and then he read the sombre black letting – 'GREENFIELDS' – printed high over the door.

'Jesus, Mary Shelley must have had this place in mind when she wrote *Frankenstein*.'

Ignoring the crack, Ray showed his brother into his private rooms. There were furnished with essentials, no more, his only luxury being row upon row of books.

'So when d'you take your vows?' Tommy quipped. 'I mean, Ray, this is *gloomy*.'

'If you don't like it, you know what you can do.'

Tommy put up his hands. 'Hey, I was just making a joke. Remember I haven't seen this place before and it is a bit . . . stark.'

'It's an institution, Tommy, not a night club.'

The air crackled between them. Ray found the jibes irritating and Tommy thought his brother was too much on the defensive. Not that he couldn't see why. Dear God, how *could* Ray live and work in a place like this? It was isolated, spartan, way out on the bloody moors – and Ray, *his brother Ray*, had once been the biggest playboy of their group.

'You must go mad up here, away from civilisation,' Tommy went on, blowing out his cheeks and looking round. 'Anything to drink?'

'Whisky?'

'Make mine a double.'

'What else?' Ray mocked, and passed him a well-filled tumbler.

'Mother and Father were moaning. Said they hadn't seen you for two years.'

Ray shook his head. 'Never!'

'Honestly, two bloody years,' Tommy replied. 'Ducking your responsibilities, I call it. Leaving me to look after the old folks.'

'Aren't they well?'

'Fitter than I am, I don't doubt,' Tommy answered,

draining half his glass. 'I wasn't supposed to say anything, but I'm on a mission to find out why you're hiding away up here. "What's so compelling about the bloody North?" I think were Father's exact words.'

'Tell them I've gone mad, and that I'm in an asylum, but that you want them to keep it a secret from all their friends.'

'You may laugh, but if you stay up here much longer, it could happen,' Tommy retorted. 'I saw Fiona Gessington the other day. She asked after you, had that look in the eye.'

'Which eye? I seem to remember she had a slight squint.'

'But a big allowance,' Tommy said, pulling a face. 'Sorry, I forgot you'd gone all priestly.'

'Don't be snide,' Ray replied, 'we martyrs do what we can.'

Laughing, Tommy leaned back in his seat and stared into his brother's face. 'So, how are things really?'

Ray shrugged. He was aware of how grim Greenfields looked in Tommy's eyes and was oddly embarrassed.

'I'm busy. How's things with you?'

'You know, same as usual.' Tommy grimaced, looking around him again. 'I admire what you're doing, Ray, but isn't it time you widened your horizons? I mean, running a sanatorium is fine, but – is it catching, by the way?'

'What?'

'TB – is it catching?'

Letting out a long, slow breath Ray looked at his brother. 'Jesus, you don't change. You always put yourself first, middle and last.'

'It's the only way to be, Ray. You fool yourself if you think that anyone really does otherwise.'

Their eyes locked for a moment. In his brother, Ray could see a shadow of his old self, the person he had once been, and now loathed.

'Come on, Tommy, what do our parents *really* want to know?'

With a resigned gesture, Tommy lit a cigarette and gave his brother one. The tobacco was good, better than the usual smoke Ray could afford.

'They want to know why you don't take your allowance.'

'I get a salary here.'

'I can see it must be a big one,' Tommy replied, sitting down and crossing his legs. 'Look, you've done the hermit bit long enough now, Ray. It's time to get back to your roots.'

To his amazement his brother burst out laughing.

'What roots would those be, Tommy? The parties, clubs, gambling? Or the girls? Perhaps the booze, or the drugs? Still enjoying the forbidden, Tommy?'

'When I can get it.'

'Then more fool you.'

'More fool you, more like!' Tommy snapped back. 'No one gives a damn any more, Ray. All your old friends have forgotten you. No one is impressed to see you wearing a hair shirt for the rest of your life. It's a fucking waste.'

Stung, Ray towered over his seated brother. 'Look, I never came down to London to comment on how you live, so what gives you the right to come up here and criticise me? You don't like it, fine – you're not doing it. But this is my home and Greenfields is my responsibility. I'm doing something worthwhile for the first time in my life.'

'Don't tell me it's enough!' Tommy retorted. 'There has to be more to keep you here. A woman, perhaps? Some little nurse who's on hand to help you in work and in play?'

'You know something, Tommy? I dislike you. I never realised how much before.'

'Hey, I was only joking –'

'No, you weren't. You meant it.' Ray sat down in the chair next to his brother's. 'The sad thing is that if you sat there and I sat here for the next year we'd never understand each other. You think I'm wasting my life – I *know* you're wasting yours.' His tone was exasperated. 'What d'you want from me, Tommy? You want me back? Why? So that I'm living the old life, colluding with you again? If I'm with you, I approve of you – is that it? Well, I *don't* approve of the way you live.'

Uncomfortable, Tommy shifted in his seat.

'Christ, listen to the saint speak! It must be hard brushing your hair with that halo on.'

Despite himself, Ray smiled and changed the subject.

'How are our parents?'

'They want to see you.'

'You've already said that. Tell them I'll see them soon.'

'You said that two years ago.'

'This time I'll make more of an effort.' Ray replied, anger abated. 'Are they well?'

'Getting old, you know how it is.' Tommy stubbed out his cigarette. 'Well, I can go now, or I can stay and we can fight a bit longer.'

Amused, Ray punched his brother's arm. 'You're a bastard, Tommy.'

'No sweet talk, I'll get sentimental,' he replied.

Both brothers turned when someone knocked on the door.

As soon as Alice walked in Tommy was fascinated. The woman was beautiful, young, with a fine figure – that was obvious even under the poor clothes. Well, well, well, Tommy thought, so *that's* the reason Ray couldn't be prised away from his fever pit. It *was* a woman, after all.

Hurriedly, Tommy rose to his feet, his hand extended. 'Hello there, I'm Ray's brother, Tommy.'

Alice took his hand. 'I'm Alice Rimmer.'

'Do you work here?'

She withdrew her hand and nodded. 'Yes, I teach the little ones.' Then she turned back to Ray. 'I was just –'

'About to have dinner with us,' Tommy finished for her.

Confused, Alice looked at him and then at Ray. What

on earth was going on? 'Thank you, but I don't think I can. I have some marking to do.'

'But that would wait for once. Wouldn't it, brother?' Tommy asked, his thick eyebrows raised. 'I mean, how often do you get family visiting?'

'Not often enough,' Ray replied sourly. 'We can't go out to dinner, Tommy, there's nowhere to eat round here. We eat in.'

'So let's all three of us eat in.'

Alice could sense the atmosphere and wanted nothing to do with it.

'I really do have work to finish,' she said pleasantly, walking to the door.

Tommy was there before her, his smile winning. 'Please join us.'

'No,' she said simply.

'As a favour?'

She smiled. 'No, not even as a favour. It was nice to meet you, Mr Berry, now please excuse me.'

When the door closed behind her Tommy let out a low whistle between his teeth. Slowly he turned to his brother and smirked.

'Quite an incentive to stay hidden away up North, I would say.'

To Ray's astonishment, Tommy had the look he knew of old, that smitten look. He had seen it so many times – but that had been when Tommy had met a dancer, or one of the girls in their social circle – someone glamorous, sensual, someone he could show off. And yet here he was with that same look – about Alice.

'Don't worry, Ray. Your secret's safe with me.' Tommy smiled his big-toothed grin. 'I didn't know there were girls who looked like that up here or I would have visited more often. Those eyes. Wow!'

Ray was baffled. 'Are you talking about Alice?'

His head cocked on one side, Tommy looked at his

brother slyly. 'Oh, come on, you can tell me. I won't breathe a word to anyone.'

Thoughtful, Ray sat down again. 'You think that Alice is beautiful?'

'She's a stunner! And she'd be even better if she had some good clothes. You're a mean bastard, Ray, you should treat her to some goodies. All the girls like spoiling. There *must* be some good shops around – although God knows where. I walked down Deansgate this afternoon and the shops were bloody awful, nothing like we get in London – but then maybe I'm biased. Can I refresh my drink, Ray?'

'Of course. Do you *really* think that Alice is good-looking?'

Downing a measure of whisky in one gulp, Tommy frowned. 'You're *not* involved with her?'

His expression said it all – if you're not involved with Alice, I might be interested. Suddenly Ray felt an over-whelming sense of jealousy. Would you believe it? he thought. He had hardly noticed her before Tommy started rambling on.

'Well, we have an ... understanding. But,' Ray said cautiously, 'it's early days yet. Things are just beginning.'

He was delighted by the disappointed look on his brother's face.

'Oh well ...' Tommy paused, his mind working over-time. 'Mind you, if things are *just beginning*, I wouldn't be stepping on anyone's corns really, would I? I mean, if Alice isn't spoken for, then may the best man win.'

'The best man already has,' Ray replied warningly. 'You did say you'd be leaving in the morning, didn't you?'

Chapter Thirty-Three

What a difference in her, Ethel thought, remembering Alice's visit at the weekend. She had put on some weight, her face was smooth, her eyes brilliant. A beauty, and no mistake. Excitedly she had talked about the children and the routine at Greenfields; how she waited for the bus which brought some of the recovering children up from Oldham and the surrounding villages. Then, at the end of the day, how she put them back on the bus and saw it start its long, slow curl down into the valley.

Her voice had been animated for the first time in a long while. Suddenly the world seemed sweet to Alice again; she was useful, needed. She had children back in her life and they responded to her. And no wonder. Proudly Alice had told Ethel and Gilbert about the play she had put on, mimicking the children's voices and acting out all the parts herself. By the end, Gilbert had been weeping with laughter. It was obvious that Alice had mellowed. Her weeks were full with Greenfields, her days busy, her evenings at The Cottage passing in a blur of drawings and markings and work.

It was all excellent, Ethel thought, putting some water on to boil. Except for one thing – Alice hadn't got a man. And if she hadn't got a man, how could she ever have children of her own? It was all right looking after the sickly TB offspring from the towns – Alice identified all too readily with the likes of Geordie Wilks – but when would she have her own child? Her own family?

'You're always bothering that girl,' Gilbert said impatiently. 'When she was here you pushed her to get a job. Now she's got a job, you want her to get married.'

'That's a damned lie, Gilbert Cummings, and you know it! I've said for years that Alice needs a good man to settle down with – long before that rigmarole with Victor Coates ever began.'

'Well, I think you should leave Alice alone to find her own man.'

Ethel blew out the match with which she had lit the gas.

'Oh yes? And how will she do that, pray? She works all day up at Greenfields, and at night she works too. At the weekends, she comes to us. When does she go out?'

'I went to the pictures with her only last week,' Gilbert replied, hurt. 'That were going out.'

'I mean with a lad!' Ethel said, flicking the tea towel at him. 'She needs a man of her own.'

'I think you should let her take one thing at a time. It weren't so long ago that Alice was half out of her mind about that Robin boy.'

'But now she's got dozens of little Robins,' Ethel replied, sternly. 'I just want more for her, that's all. She's done well up at Greenfields, I know she has. But there's more to life than work.' She leaned down and picked up the little animal Gilbert was carving. It had taken him nearly four weeks to mark out the rudimentary details of a horse. Ethel's fingers ran over the wood tenderly. 'I want Alice to love someone, Gilbert, and know that she's loved.'

He watched her and then sighed. 'You know something, old girl?'

'What?'

'You're a thinker, you are. And you're wise.' He tapped her arm. 'How did you get so wise, Mrs Cummings?'

'I didn't get wise,' Ethel said thoughtfully. 'I got old.'

Ray had had his neck at such an awkward angle that it was stiff when he moved again. Cursing, he rubbed it with his hand and tried to move his head. Bloody hell, he thought, he'd ricked his bloody neck! Staggering back to his desk, he winced at the pain. Typical, he thought, just typical. He had been trying to watch Alice through the window, but she had been out of range so he had leaned out and twisted his head round to catch a glimpse . . .

Hanging out of windows! He was acting like a bloody imbecile! *Him*, the last of the great seducers, reduced to the comical posturings of a spotty oaf. It was true that Tommy's interest in Alice had sparked his own fascination, but if Ray was honest, he had not been *totally* immune to her attractions before. Her eyes, for instance, were astonishing. Very dark, very intense . . . Ray coughed and rubbed his sore neck. She was only in her early twenties and he was forty-one – what chance did he have?

Yet there was no one else standing in his way. No boyfriend had come calling for Alice, and he had found out that her weekends were spent with the Cummingses in Salford. It was down to him to make a move. If she rejected him, well, so be it. Then again, she might not reject him. But if she did . . . Ray sighed, exasperated with himself.

He couldn't concentrate on work, and had been more than a little short with Guy Priestly, which was a pity as they were becoming friends. For the first time in many years Ray was daydreaming – weaving up fantasies about himself and Alice. God, he was crazy, he must be.

Yet whenever he was near her he felt inebriated. When she moved it was like ballet; when she spoke it was like the Sermon on the Mount. Yet if she noticed his interest she had been very discreet – in fact, it looked as though romance with him was the last thing on Alice's mind. But then again, you never knew with women. Besides, she had had a hard life, and didn't wear her heart on her sleeve. She had had to struggle, had been brought up in an institution. What better wife could there be for him? Ray thought, and then jerked on the word. *Wife* . . .

Unannounced, Gladys came in with a batch of letters for signature. She was miffed, due to his short temper with her that morning.

'Could you sign these please, sir?' She made the word *sir* sound like an obscenity.

Ray bent his head and winced.

'What's the matter, sir?'

'I cricked my neck,' he replied, certain that he caught a flash of delight in her eyes. It would be easy enough to apologise, but he didn't feel like it. He was out of temper and didn't care. 'Anything else?' Ray asked, passing back the signed letters.

'Miss Rimmer wanted a word.'

At the mention of her name Ray accidentally knocked his diary onto the floor. Bending down, he tried to sound nonchalant.

'What about?'

'I don't know, sir. Shall I send her in?'

He wanted to say – *No, no, don't send her in. Send her away. Or send me away.* But he didn't.

'Fine, ask her to come through, will you?'

He hardly had time to compose himself before Alice came in smiling.

'Hello, Mr Berry, I wanted to have a word –'

'Jesus!'

She raised her eyebrows. 'What?'

'Sorry,' Ray said, wincing. 'I've just pulled my neck. It keeps twitching. Sorry, what were you saying?' Smiling wanly, he rubbed his neck with his hand, his head over to one side, his eyes watering with the pain.

'If this isn't a good time –'

'It's fine. Fine,' Ray said, through gritted teeth.

'But your eyes are watering,' Alice replied. 'It must hurt a lot.'

'No, it's nothing,' he managed to say, 'a muscle twinge, that's all.'

'Well, if you're sure you're OK . . .' Alice said, hurrying on. 'I was wondering if I could have some time off.'

'What?' He snapped, his neck going into spasm.

'Just a week.'

A week – he couldn't stand it for another week. He had to know now whether she was interested in him or not. But how could he impress her with his head drawn over to one side with a neck spasm?

Blinking back tears, he found his voice again. 'I wondered –' he began. Then his elbow slipped suddenly, knocking his diary back onto the floor.

Incredulous, Ray watched it fall. He was turning into a freak, unable to control his limbs. Hurriedly he bent down, Alice also bending to pick up the diary. He saw her movement and in order to avoid cracking heads with her, Ray jerked back – and hit his own skull on the edge of the desk.

'Christ!'

Alice winced and handed him the diary. 'Oh, sorry.'

By now seeing flashing lights, Ray nodded. The pain in his temple was building fast, rivalling the one in his neck. Eyes half closed, he straightened up and tried a smile.

Alice smiled back stiffly.

'I was wondering,' Ray managed to say, his head drawn over to one side again. 'What do you think?'

She was baffled. 'About what?'

'What I said.'

'You didn't say anything,' Alice replied calmly.

She should leave, she thought, let him lie down and recover himself. It was so surprising to see Ray Berry out of control. Instead of his brusque, assertive manner he was now babbling and humped over like Quasimodo.

'I wondered if you would like . . .'

'Yes?' Alice encouraged him.

Ray blinked; she was coming in and out of focus. It was like looking through a telescope – now she was near, now she was far away. God, he *couldn't* be living this, he must be dreaming. He'd never had any trouble asking women out before. In the past, he had been a Lothario – others had come to *him* for advice.

'I really do think you should rest,' Alice said, rising from her seat.

Ray was on his feet in an instant, lurching over the desk like a drunk. 'I was –'

'Rest, Mr Berry,' she said soothingly. 'That's a big lump coming up on your forehead. I could get a steak for it.'

'Yes, yes, we could,' he said urgently,

'We could what?'

He was leaning on the desk for support, one shoulder higher than the other, his head twisted, eyes running, and a lump the size of the Roxy rising on his forehead.

'What?'

Alice persevered. 'I said I could get a steak to put on that bruise.'

'That's right! We could go out for a steak,' Ray agreed eagerly. 'So that's settled then?'

'We don't have to go *out* for it, Mr Berry. They've got steak in the kitchen.'

Ray reckoned that he had about thirty seconds before he lost consciousness.

'I don't want any steak for my eye, I want it for dinner!'

'But that's not a problem either,' Alice replied hurriedly. 'The cook can make you one.'

'I want to have bloody dinner with *you*!' he shouted. 'For God's sake, Alice – will you have dinner with me?'

And then he passed out.

It did not escape Olive McGrath's attention that there was something going on. She told Ed about it, but he wasn't listening, just feeding his face with stew.

'That Alice Rimmer!' she said to her husband. 'She didn't waste any time, did she? Now I think back, she asked if Ray Berry was married the first day I met her.'

Ed burped, then scratched his belly. 'Good meal that,' he said happily. 'What was it?'

'Strychnine,' Olive replied shortly. 'Everyone thinks she's so perfect – *Alice this, Alice that* – and now she's the principal's girlfriend she'll be impossible.'

'Oh, leave off. You're a married woman, what's it matter to you?'

Olive regarded her husband thoughtfully. If Ed McGrath ever managed to get out of Sutherland Street, it would be nothing short of a miracle. He would never shape up and he wanted her to get pregnant now. Huh! Olive thought, that would be the day. She wasn't going to get bogged down by a load of little pot-bellied Eds. Not yet, anyway.

It wasn't that she didn't love him – she did. She just wanted her little bit of power back. Before Alice had arrived at Greenfields she had been the youngest, the smartest. All the kids had liked her well enough, but now they all liked Alice. And the newcomer was a good teacher too – which was even more infuriating.

Ed looked at her hopefully. 'Any sign, girl?'

Olive stopped chewing the side of her nail and turned to her husband. 'What *are* you talking about, Ed?'

'You know? This month, are you . . . are you . . . ?'

'Pregnant?'

'Yes.'

She shook her head, all mock regret. 'Not this month, luv. Sorry.'

Not this month, or the next, Olive thought to herself, returning her attention to her fingernail. No, she had other things to think about at the moment . . . She liked Alice. They were friends and it had been a long time since Olive had had anyone of her own age up at Greenfields. She didn't want to argue with Alice, but she was getting left out. Ray was giving Alice all the attention – and more.

Sulkily, Olive chewed her nail and stared at the floor.

A moment later, Ed was standing behind her, his hands on her shoulders.

'We could go upstairs now. Get in a quickie before I go to work. How d'you feel about a bit of slap and tickle?'

Olive shrugged his hands off, her eyes blazing.

'How do I feel about *a bit of slap and tickle*?' she snapped. 'How d'you feel about a fat lip?'

It was clear to Dr Priestly on his next visit that there was a different atmosphere up at Greenfields. It might, he thought, have something to do with the late summer warmth. An Indian Summer, they called it. The days were long, sun-streaked, the evenings mild. In the mellow sunlight, the moors looked benign, the sound of the cows lowing coming over from Tollbank Farm. Water caught on the sweet streams, and the war memorial on the horizon harnessed the late light at its highest point.

Guy had driven his car up to Greenfields and then parked outside the gates. Sitting for a while in silence, he had thought about what he had heard that morning. Alwyn Arnold had had a heart attack and was now confined to bed, her daughter looking after her. Judge Arnold had given up work as soon as his wife was taken ill this last time and Leonard was now running the businesses. Up at The Dower House it would be grim, full of depression and loss – as it had been for as long as he could remember.

But it wasn't grim here, Guy thought. Thank God Alice Rimmer had got away from the Arnolds. There was something almost sinister about the family. Or maybe it was just that too much money and power had corrupted them. That was probably it. Having always kept themselves apart, they were now completely segregated from the rest of the world.

Not for the first time the doctor wondered why the family had stayed in that house. Surely it would have been more sensible to sell it after the death of Catherine? What could it hold but bad memories? As for Dorothy, she had found her murdered sister there, so why keep living in a place which could only remind her of tragedy? Why didn't she move out with her husband? And how *could* she have stayed on there after their son's death? It would have been difficult for the strongest character, but Dorothy had never been emotionally resilient. Did Judge Arnold really think that by taking Dorothy away for a few years after Catherine's death that she would forget? How could she, when every room and every echo of that place must remind her daily of what she had lost?

Guy thought back to Robin's illness. He couldn't have known that the boy had a heart defect – no one knew that until after the post mortem. But it was interesting to hear that Alwyn had had a heart attack now. Admittedly she was getting on, so it wasn't that surprising. But maybe there was a weakness in the family? And if it was left to the Arnolds no one would ever find out . . .

Guy's gaze travelled back to the gates of Greenfields. He had been pleased to see Alice's progress over the year. She had found her feet and her confidence had returned. A lesser woman might have buckled under the weight of the scandal, but not her. She was strong. She had needed to be.

An memory came back to him at that moment. He had called to see Ray a few weeks earlier, only to be told that he was out walking. Glad of the excuse to take some air himself, Guy had set off, expecting to find Ray at one of his usual haunts. But it wasn't Ray he'd found.

It was the wrong moment to intrude, so Guy had stayed silent, watching. Alice had been dancing – turning round and round with her arms outstretched, her hair falling loose on her shoulders, her face flushed. Singing, she had thrown her head back and then suddenly laughed at the clouds. She had been compelling, fascinating, disturbing – all at the same time.

Feeling suddenly like a voyeur, Guy had moved away – backing straight into Ray.

'Incredible, isn't she?'

Guy had nodded. 'I was looking for you, and came across her. She doesn't know anyone's watching her, that much is obvious.'

Ray's eyes had been fixed on the dancing figure. 'It's as though there are two different people inside the same body. The serious teacher, and this . . . this one. This changeling.'

Guy had wondered then if it was the time to confide in Ray what had happened with Alice and the Arnolds. But immediately he had decided against it. Alice had a right to start again – and a right to leave the past behind.

'Why is she dancing?'

'Because she's alive,' Ray had replied, 'because she knows she alive.'

Guy smiled to himself. He wasn't too absorbed in his work to miss the romance that had begun soon afterwards or the glances between them, or the whispered asides. Ray was looking better than he had done for years, his weathered features less tense. If they married it would be a good match for Greenfields. Alice was bright and a good teacher and Ray Berry had more than proved himself. Alone they had each made something of their lives. Together, what couldn't they achieve?

Then, unwelcome as it was, Guy's mind wandered back to Werneth Heights. He had been visiting a patient there only the week before and had slowed down as he passed The Dower House. There had been few lights on, the drive dark and forbidding. Maybe, he had thought then, there had been just too much tragedy to bear. The death of Catherine, then Robin – maybe a family could only endure such losses if they closed ranks against the world.

Now his thoughts moved to David Lewes. Surprised, he leaned against the bonnet of his car and folded his arms. David Lewes had been so handsome, so charming, so likeable. Guy hadn't been the family doctor then, but he knew David Lewes by sight and reputation – a man who laughed a lot. He remembered the image of David Lewes at a ball in Manchester. Guy had been very young, and thought David incredibly glamorous. The latter had been dancing and stopped to get a glass of champagne to quench his thirst. Then this idol, this paragon, had turned and winked at him. It had been a small kindness, but a treasured one. Whilst most people had made him feel small, David Lewes had taken the trouble to put a gangling young man at ease ... Guy could see his face now, the turned head, bright dark eyes, the brilliant smile which made everyone respond.

He'd been a dandy, a poet, an explorer – anything but some staid and predictable Northern businessman. He was exotic, Guy realised. That night, in a dinner jacket, David Lewes had seemed like some admired actor who had stepped down from the stage to move, fleetingly, amongst his audience. He was charismatic. He was kind.

He was a killer. And a coward. A man who had run away from what he had done. A man now presumed dead after so long ... Sighing, Guy shook his head. Then, the memory dislodged, he pushed open the gates of Greenfields and, whistling, walked in.

Chapter Thirty-Four

It was clear to Alice almost immediately how much Ray cared. His brusqueness – unchanged with everyone else – was tempered with her. Little kindnesses, gifts, letters, flowers, were pressed on her. Love, come unexpected and welcome, made a young man of him. He was surprisingly tactile too; always linking arms with her, touching her shoulder, stroking her cheek. As though he could hardly believe his luck he seemed to want to touch her, to remind himself that it wasn't his imagination. He had a lovely young woman whom he loved.

And who loved him. But did she? Alice wondered. She was fond of him, certainly, and found him amusing, attractive. But love? Just what was that? Certainly the blinding heat she had felt for Victor wasn't there, but maybe that was as well. It had only led to heartache, after all.

Putting her books together, Alice left The Cottage and caught the bus down to Oldham. She was due to meet Hilly outside the town hall, and was running late when she arrived to find her friend reading a paper on the corner.

'Hilly!'

She looked up, smiled that slow smile, her fine hair newly washed.

'Alice!' she cried, hugging her. 'I'm so glad to see you.'

'You look well.'

'You too,' Hilly replied, putting her delicate head on one side. 'You're blooming, Alice – what is it?' Hilly fell into step with her. 'You're in love!'

Alice didn't deny it. 'I might be –'

'I'm so glad! Who is it?' Her arm slid through Alice's

and they walked down the high street. 'Come on, tell me.'

'I've been seeing Ray Berry –'

'Up at Greenfields?' Hilly interrupted. 'That's perfect.'

Alice looked at her. 'We're not getting married, we're just going out with each other.'

'And at his age he isn't looking to settle down?' Hilly asked mischievously.

Alice wondered if Hilly's pleasure wasn't tempered with some relief. After all, if Alice had found someone of her own Hilly no longer had to worry about Victor holding any old feelings for her friend. The thought was so uncharitable it made Alice blush.

Hilly saw her colour and misread it. 'Oh, you *are* in love, aren't you?'

A couple of young men passed them, sized Alice up and down, then walked on smiling.

'I like Ray very much, Hilly, but I'm not in love. I don't know that I want to be.'

Hilly's face was puzzled. '*Everyone* wants to be in love.'

'Yes, but everyone wants to be in love with the right person.'

A silence fell between them. Alice could feel Hilly's hand tense against her arm and wondered if she had been too harsh. She was glad they were friends again, genuinely pleased to be able to shop with Hilly and have a confidante of her own age. But the spectre of herself and Victor was ever present and for several months after their marriage Alice had refused all invitations to the Coateses' home.

Then one evening she had called by unannounced. They had been eating dinner, Victor in his shirt sleeves, Hilly with an apron over her dress. Happily she had shown Alice into the kitchen and for one scintillating moment there had been a terrible ache in her gut. Seeing Victor, Alice had suddenly imagined a different scene: Hilly knocking at *her* door; *She* in the apron; Victor, *her* husband. But for a trick of fate it would have been Alice in Trafalgar Street, not Hilly.

Then the moment had passed, Alice had seen things for what they were and accepted them. From then onwards she had been a regular visitor to Trafalgar Street. Mrs Hope listened at the wall and told her husband how it was a disgrace that Victor Coates had a harem. And on the other side the stupidest family in the street, the Booths, were still there. Mr Booth had caused a small explosion at his new job at the gasworks and been laid off, and as for Lettie Booth, she just kept sewing and sewing.

Life went on, Alice thought, distantly envious of Hilly and yet fully aware that she might not have settled down in Trafalgar Street. So where would she settle? Up at Greenfields with Ray? Well, why not? He was a good man, he was ambitious and came from a wealthy family, like her own . . . Stunned at the thought, Alice took in a breath. What was she thinking of? She had to forget the Arnolds, forget that they were related in any way. What good had it done her by trying to get back at them? She had to forget, live her new life.

But it was in her mind, always present even though she tried to suppress it. She wanted to tell Ray who she was, where she had come from. She didn't want him to think of her as some poor orphan – she was from the richest family in Oldham.

Yet if she confessed to her family, she would have to confess to what had followed. And how would that make her look? Revengeful, dangerous. And as for Robin . . . Dear God, Alice thought, she could never tell Ray about the past. He would hate her for it. Better to let him love her for what he *thought* she was – better for both of them.

Suddenly Alice's spirits lifted at the thought of Ray, and she tugged Hilly's arm.

'Why don't we go shopping?'

'What for?'

'Clothes, what else?' Alice replied light-heartedly.

'Oh, I'm not sure. You know I'm not that interested in how I look –'

'Which is why we're going shopping,' Alice said, pulling Hilly towards the nearest dress shop. She stared in the window and then shook her head. 'No, nothing here for you.'

'Oh, Alice, let's shop for you.'

'No, Hilly, we're going to get you a new outfit. It'll be fun.'

Three shops later, Hilly was standing in front of a full-length mirror looking at her reflection. She was wearing a red dress, the shade startling, but flattering her fine colouring. Good Lord, Hilly thought, what would Victor think?

'It's not me.'

'It is!' Alice insisted, putting her head on one side. 'You should wear more colour, and show off your figure.'

'I feel . . . strange.'

'Well, you look wonderful,' Alice replied, glancing at the price ticket and pulling a face.

'How much is it?'

'Not much.'

'How much?' Hilly repeated, trying to see the price ticket which Alice had pulled off and was hiding in her hand.

'I want to buy it for you – as a birthday present.'

'Alice, it's not my birthday for ages!'

'So have it as an early present,' she said emphatically. 'Please, you look so lovely in it. You look like a countess.'

'But it's too much –'

'We're best friends – how could it be too much?'

'I never had another friend like you,' Hilly said quietly. 'I'm so glad we got back together.'

'We'll always be friends.' Alice replied, absent-mindedly, wondering if she could ask the woman in the shop for a discount.

'Victor wants a family.'

Despite herself, the news jolted through Alice like a cattle prod, but she kept her expression serene. After all, she had Ray now; she had no reason to be jealous any more.

'How do you feel about that, Hilly?'

'OK . . .' she replied, trailing off. Her gaze moved over the mirror again. 'This dress makes me look too thin.'

'Most women would kill for a dress which made them look thin. Besides, you don't look too thin. You look elegant, like something out of a magazine.'

'But it's more the kind of thing you would wear,' Hilly persisted. 'I know you want to buy it for me, but it's too glamorous.'

'How about a hair shirt instead?'

'Oh, Alice!'

'You're having it,' she said, her tone suddenly wheedling. 'Come on, Hilly, I want to buy it for you. Let me give you a present.'

'But it's such a big present. D'you remember how we used to dream of things like this when we were little? Do you ever think of Netherlands, Alice?'

'Sometimes.'

'Evan Thomas is running it now.'

'I heard,' Alice said coldly. 'He was a spiteful man.'

'Victor told me what he did. He says that it will all come back on him. He believes that – that the rotten things people do come back to them.' Dreamily, she smoothed down the material of the dress with her fingers. 'Why don't you settle down, Alice? Ray Berry is a great catch. He came from money and he's built up Greenfields, and you love teaching. Oh, please, if he asks, marry him. We could all go out together in a foursome, we would have such fun. Marry him, please.'

'Why the hurry?' Alice replied, turning Hilly round and

scrutinising the back seam of the dress. 'I think the stitching's uneven. Maybe I could get some money off for that.'

'Alice, listen to me! You need to be safe with someone. Things happen to you, they always have. People get jealous and try to hurt you.' She reached out and tapped Alice's hand. 'When you're married everything changes. You feel like you belong, you're not just some poor foundling any more. You're *Mrs* Someone – it's different in shops, everywhere. You know what I mean. We never had anyone before. We were pushed around at Netherlands, Miss Lees was horrible with you and then that Dorothy Arnold tried to ruin you. You're not safe on your own, Alice. You need someone there to protect you. When you get married people can't get at you the same. It's so good, so good. Marry Ray, please.'

Alice was preoccupied. 'I reckon I could get five shillings off this dress –'

'Oh, listen to me!' Hilly said, exasperated. 'I think you should marry Ray.'

'I don't know if I love him enough to marry him.'

'You will in time.'

'I might – but then I might not,' Alice answered, looking round. 'Is the owner that woman over there? God, she doesn't look like she'd be open to haggling.'

'Alice, listen to me!'

'I am,' she replied, 'but you know that I've always wanted to be someone, Hilly, I still do. I can't change how I feel. Take the dress off, I'm going to have a word with the owner.'

Obediently, Hilly pulled the dress over her head, still talking. 'But if you married Ray, you would *be* someone. You would be the mistress of Greenfields.'

'If I married him, I would have to tell him about my past.'

'He'd understand,' Hilly replied with certainty. 'What

have you got to hide? All right, you wanted to get back at the Arnolds, but Robin's death had nothing to do with you – everyone knows that.'

'And how would it look to the Board of Greenfields if they heard about Dorothy Arnold's accusations?'

'They weren't true.'

'I know that,' Alice replied, 'but mud sticks.' She laid the dress over her arm, her voice suddenly serious. 'I'll tell you, Hilly, it would be a nail in Ray's coffin. Everyone would ask how he could hire a woman who had a shadow over her character.'

'But you don't –'

'I know!' Alice snapped. 'But I have to wait until the time is right to tell him what happened with the Arnolds. If it gets serious, *then* I have to let Ray know everything – who I am, and what I did. Let's be honest, Hilly, sneaking into the Arnold family and trying to win over Robin wasn't the action of a good woman.'

'You had your reasons –'

'Which he might understand, one day. But not yet, Hilly. It may just be a romance, and then what would be the point of unburdening myself? I love working at Greenfields, I want to stay there. The romance may or may not last, but I want the job to.'

'Work isn't everything, Alice –'

'No, but it means a lot to me. When I was younger everyone was always telling me to calm down, to think – well, now I *am* thinking. I'm taking things very slowly with Ray. This time I don't want to rush anything and lose it. Now, do you want this dress, or not?'

'I don't know if you're aware of it, but you are the most beautiful woman in Lancashire.'

'Only Lancashire? What about England?' Alice teased Ray.

'What about the world?'

'Or the universe?'

He kissed her on the forehead, then the nose, then the mouth.

'Who are you?'

She blinked, startled. 'What?'

'I thought you were some serious little creature when you first came to Greenfields, but you've changed so much. You're all fire now. Who's the real Alice? Or are there two of you? Miss Jekyll and Miss Hyde?'

She smiled, realising he was teasing. 'Oh, there are a lot more than two of me.'

'Is that right?' he said, smiling in return. 'How many of you are there?'

She pretended to think. 'Six, at the last count.'

'All adorable?'

'Each more adorable than the last.'

'I shall never be bored then. If I get tired of one of you, I shall move on to another.'

She laughed, pretending to punch him. 'But maybe the wicked one of me will come and punish you for being unkind.'

'Oh, so there's a wicked one, is there?'

'There's always a wicked one, a black angel,' she replied, 'like in the fairy tales. The one who does bad things, takes revenge on people. Wishes them dead.'

'That one sounds terrible.' Ray replied, mock serious. 'I think I'll give her a wide berth.'

Suddenly Alice turned and rested her head against Ray's shoulder. They were sitting at the top of Hawkhead's Pike, looking down into the valley and the crowded town of Oldham. Around them it was quiet, the odd kestrel stooping down from the blue spring sky.

'I never thought I would love anyone this much,' Ray murmured. 'I never thought I would care for anyone again.'

Then, slowly, he told her the story of Toni's life and death. It was obvious to Alice that the whole episode had shaken him out of his previous life and forced him to change. Confiding in her implicitly, he talked about his old friends and his brother as though he couldn't understand them, almost ashamed that he had once been a party to their selfishness.

It was the perfect moment to confide in him; but Alice didn't. Instead she held back, wondering why she was being such a coward. He had opened his heart to her, making himself vulnerable. He had laid it all out before her, telling her his dreams and what he wanted for the future. He had trusted her – so why didn't she trust him?

'My love,' he said gently, kissing her on the lips, 'my love.'

Her eyes closed but instead of relaxing Alice could only see images of Netherlands and The Dower House. And Robin.

'There's a new post coming up,' Ray murmured to her. 'A teaching post – and I want you to have it.'

Alice opened her eyes. 'But I'm not qualified.'

'But you're perfectly qualified for this position. The boys who board here need a house mistress, someone who organises the main building. She would be a teacher and matron combined. It's a position of trust. You could handle things your own way, Alice.'

'But there are others who've been here longer than I have,' she answered. 'I mean, Olive McGrath, she would love a job like that.'

He frowned. 'I know she would. She and her husband would live off the hog here. No,' he went on severely, 'I couldn't trust them. I need someone I know is on my side. Someone I know inside and out.'

Alice stared at him, and felt oddly cornered. 'But what about Sister Mills?'

'What about her?' Ray replied. 'She does a great job in the sanatorium.'

'But maybe she would like more responsibility?'

Pulling himself upright, Ray leaned back on his elbows, looking out over the horizon.

'I want you to have the job, Alice, and I'll tell you why. I want you near to me, under the same roof, and I want you to get to know how I run Greenfields.' He paused, his eyes narrowed against the sunlight. 'I want to marry you, Alice.'

'No.'

He looked at her, surprised. 'What? Are you saying no to me?'

'No,' Alice shook her head. 'I mean, *no*, I'm not saying no to you.'

He laughed and drew her down into the grass with him. Idly he flicked her nose with his forefinger.

'You talk rubbish, total rubbish.' His lips moved over hers and then he drew away. 'I want you to be the mistress of Greenfields. I want us to run it together. What easier way to get everyone used to the idea than to promote you now?'

'I didn't know I had to be promoted to wife,' Alice replied, teasing. Ray sat up immediately. 'Oh come on,' she chided him, slipping her arm round his shoulder. 'I didn't mean it like that. I was just teasing.'

'You make me sound as though I'm manipulating you,' Ray replied coldly, 'I wouldn't do that.'

'I know you wouldn't.'

'So you'll agree?'

She stared into his face. Tell him now, a voice inside her said. Tell him now, or he'll never understand why you didn't. How much has he got to do for you for you to trust him?

Alice took in a deep breath and then began: 'Ray, I want to tell you something –'

'It's raining,' he said suddenly, looking upwards. 'God, would you believe it? It was full bloody sunshine a moment ago.' His hands grasped hers as he pulled her to her feet. 'Come on, we've got to make a run for it.'

She felt herself dragged behind him, the rain coming down hard and fast.

The moment had come. And passed.

Chapter Thirty-Five

Sister Mills was standing at the window of her office, smoking a cigarette. It was half-past two in the morning and she was on night shift. She did it only once a month, and usually she didn't mind, but tonight she did. Inhaling, she waved the smoke away with her hand and picked up the book she had been reading about Charlie Chaplin. Her fingers flicked over the pages, but her interest wasn't there.

Idly she stubbed out the cigarette and walked to the ward doors. Everyone was asleep, the patients silent. She then walked upstairs and checked the isolation wards. All three were occupied. It was the policy of the Council to move out contagious TB sufferers and then fumigate their houses to stop the spread of the disease, especially in the crowded slums. Those patients would come to the sanatorium – some for a short stay before they returned home, some for weeks on end.

Sister Mills took off her starched cap and walked back to her office. Normally she would never remove any part of her uniform – but what did it matter in the witching hours when there was no one to see? No one. Lowering herself into a chair she drummed her fingernails on the arms and then crossed and recrossed her legs.

Restlessness, anger, fear – all the feelings piled up on top of each other. She had been at Greenfields for nearly six years; been the sister since she'd started and been in love with Ray Berry for as long. Their romance had been sweet and short. Sweet to him, at least. To her, bitter, because she had wanted it to continue.

He hadn't and somehow that decision had been bearable when he didn't replace her with anyone else. Perhaps, she had told herself over the years, he'll come back to me. I run the sanatorium well and he can trust me – he'll come back, in time. But he hadn't. He'd kept working instead and if he did have any romances Barbara Mills never heard of them.

Until now. Now everyone knew about him falling in love with Alice Rimmer. It was so plain – Ray watching her in the dining room, looking out of a window to catch sight of her.

Barbara stared at the linoleum floor. She was thirty-four years old. Alice Rimmer was about ten years younger. And fresh. Very fresh. Barbara felt the acid taste of jealousy in her mouth.

She was going to marry Ray Berry. Oh, they might not have told people, but it was on the cards. It was the perfect solution, after all. The job advertisement in the staff room didn't fool anyone – they all knew that the post was already filled.

Alice Rimmer had to be stopped, Barbara thought coolly. It was simple – cruel, yes, but simple. After all, she was only protecting herself and her future. But *how* could she get rid of Alice Rimmer? It would be pointless to do the deed herself. She had to remain above it all, untouched, so that Ray would turn to *her* after Alice had gone.

It was obvious that Barbara would have to join forces with someone else. She would have to make the bullet and get someone else to fire it. And there was only one possible candidate – Olive McGrath . . . Silence nuzzled against Barbara, but she wasn't tired. In fact, she couldn't stop thinking of her plan and imagining the outcome. Her eyes were wide open, watchful.

She was waiting for the morning and the chance to strike.

*   *   *

Olive had had a bellyful of Ed that morning and was glad to escape his grasping hands and get to work. Waiting with a group of the kids who were sufficiently recovered to commute to and from Greenfields daily, she got on the school bus and then looked out of the window. Deep in thought, Olive wiped the early morning condensation away with her hand. Bloody Ed was as randy as a rabbit. She would have to watch it or she'd get caught out, and then where would she be? Stuck at home with a crew of kids in tow. Not likely.

'Geordie Wilks, keep down the noise!' she shouted towards the back of the bus.

Then she looked out of the window again. It was a cold morning, but it would warm up before long. The bus coughed up the steep incline, the driver whistling a band tune. Olive tapped her feet. She liked to dance. In fact, she wouldn't have minded having a dance with the driver.

'Geordie!' she snapped again as a paper pellet struck her on the back of the neck. 'I'm warning you.'

Geordie never flicked pellets at Alice, Olive thought irritated, as she settled back in her seat. Oh no, not Alice. She felt a mixture of affection and irritation at the name. Oh, damn you, Olive thought, why couldn't you just be ordinary? Why did you have to make a play for the principal? Now things were different – Alice had the boss's ear. And probably the boss's bed too.

Outside the gates of Greenfields, the bus emptied as the children piled out, Olive catching hold of Geordie Wilks's ear as he passed.

'Flick one more pellet at me, and I will make you eat your catapult.'

'Aw, cum on, Mrs McGrath!' he whined. 'I were only having a laff.'

'We'll see who's having a laugh after I've finished with you,' she replied, letting go of his ear and watching as he ran through the school gates.

'Little bugger,' a voice said above her. Olive looked up to see the driver leaning out of his cab. He had slicked-back black hair and the tattoo of a fish on his forearm.

'You have to make allowances for them,' Olive said grandly, 'they're sick.'

'You weren't making too many allowances for his ear,' the driver replied, jumping down in front of her. 'You on this run later?'

'I might be.'

He put his head on one side, sizing her up. 'What d'you do here?'

'I'm a teacher.'

'Really? I bet you could teach me a thing or two.'

Olive smiled seductively at him. 'Maybe I could, and maybe I couldn't.'

With that, she walked off towards the gates, tossing her auburn hair. Her spirits soaring, Olive smiled to herself. Who in God's name would want to be tied down? She had a lot of living to do yet, she wasn't cut out to be a mother. At the gates, she turned to see the driver watching her. She waved and he waved back, climbed back into his cab and leaned over the wheel, grinning.

'Can I have a word?'

Olive jumped at the voice and turned to see Barbara Mills watching her.

'What is it?'

'We have a problem with Alice Rimmer.'

A child brushed past them, following his peers into Greenfields. The morning bell had rung, hurrying them indoors, leaving Olive and Barbara in the empty playground.

'*What* about Alice?' Olive asked, looking into the sister's face. 'She's a friend of mine.'

'Not for long,' Barbara replied shortly.

'How d'you make that out?'

'Did you hear about the new job?'

Olive frowned. '*What* new job?'

'The big one – live-in matron and house mistress. The kind of job which would be perfect for you and Ed. Just think about it, Olive. You would have somewhere nice to live and Ed would have a proper job –'

'Hey!'

Barbara smiled sweetly. 'I don't mean he *hasn't* got a proper job now, but this would be permanent. You would have a nice home and steady wages.'

Olive was instantly conjuring up thoughts of living at Greenfields. That would show everyone that she and Ed had made something of themselves. Oh yes, it was tempting. Very.

'I've been here a while now, I should be first in line.' she said to Barbara. 'Those old fossils at The Cottage are past it.'

'Of course they are,' Barbara agreed. 'But there's one person at The Cottage who isn't. Alice.'

A bell rang again from inside the building.

Olive spun round. 'Bugger it! I have to go –'

Barbara caught her arm, pinching it.

'Och!'

'Sorry, Olive. I just want you to stop for a moment and think about it. Think now. Alice is having a fling with Ray Berry –'

'Your old love?'

'Listen to me!' Barbara snapped. 'They're going to get married.'

'What?'

'Oh, they haven't said anything yet, but I know Ray. He's going to give Alice the job so that everyone gets used to her running Greenfields with him. The Board wouldn't like it otherwise. She's so young and inexperienced, they would never buy it. But if he introduces her slowly –'

'Alice, running Greenfields!' Olive repeated, her tone shrill. 'She's only been here a year or so.'

'Exactly, and look how far she's come in that time,' Barbara said slyly. 'We have stop her, otherwise you'll lose out.'

'And I suppose you won't?' Olive replied, her voice tart. 'You want to get back in bed with Ray Berry and you can't with Alice around, can you?'

'Well spotted, I always said you were bright.' Barbara said sarcastically, looking over her shoulder to check that no one was listening. 'We both have our own reasons for wanting to get rid of Alice Rimmer. And we can do it – if we work together.'

'But if Ray Berry's in love with her, nothing will work.' Olive's voice had turned into a wail.

'Oh, I think a bit of scandal might.'

'Scandal? About who?'

Barbara moved closer towards Olive and dropped her voice. 'When Alice first came here I overheard a conversation I wasn't supposed to – between her and Dr Priestly.'

'She's having an affair with Dr Priestly?'

Barbara raised her eyes heavenwards. 'No! Alice was talking to him, that's all. He'd sent me off on some errand but I came back more quickly than he thought and I heard what he said. It was about Robin Tripps, the grandson of Judge Arnold.' She repeated the name for emphasis: 'The Arnolds? Of Werneth Heights?'

'Oh, the Arnolds,' Olive said, the penny dropping. 'What about them?'

'Alice worked for them once –'

'She never!'

'And whilst she was there the grandson, Robin Tripps, died. Dr Priestly said something about Dorothy Tripps trying to frame Alice.'

'Frame her? For what?'

'Her son's death, I suppose.'

Olive was goggle-eyed. 'Jesus!'

'Quite. Now do you think that Mr Ray Berry knows

about Miss Alice Rimmer's sordid past? I mean, even if she had nothing to do with the boy's death, the mother thought she did – so that begs some questions for a start. And has she ever mentioned anything about her past? Not a word. We both know why now. And another thing – what's she doing teaching here? She hasn't experience, like you. All she was was a nanny. A negligent nanny, who might possibly have been responsible for a child's death.' Barbara paused, giving Olive time to take it in. 'Now, I ask you, would *you* want a woman like that running Greenfields?'

Olive stared at her suspiciously: 'Why don't you tell Ray Berry about Alice?'

'Why should I? My job isn't at risk.'

'Neither is mine!' Olive snapped.

'No, not yet. But who knows, new brushes always sweep clean, don't they? Oh, think about it, Olive! You and Ed could be on the gravy train here. Don't let some common little nobody cheat you out of it. You love it here, it's your little kingdom. You don't want to go back to some slum school, do you?'

Olive flushed. 'I've been here for years, Alice Rimmer can't get that job over me!'

'Of course she can! She's going to be the boss's wife. Before long, she'll be able to do *anything*.' Barbara could see that Olive's temper was up and running – just as she had hoped. 'You deserve that job, and you would get it if the Board knew that Alice Rimmer should never be allowed to look after children –'

'But maybe she didn't have anything to do with the child's death.'

Barbara raised her eyebrows. 'So why didn't she come clean? Tell Ray all about it?'

'Maybe she has.'

'Oh no, it was obvious from what I overheard that Ray knows nothing about Alice Rimmer's past. Having secrets like that is hardly the way to start a marriage, is it? Maybe someone else should tell Ray. It's only fair he knows. He should be told – by someone he can *really* trust.'

Chapter Thirty-Six

She was shaking from head to toe, unable to speak. Someone knew about her, and they had betrayed her. They hadn't come to talk to her first, they had talked to Ray. Alice rubbed her hands together to try to warm them, then shrank back further into the cupboard. She should have told him, she knew that all along, and yet she hadn't. She'd left it too long and now he hated her.

It was growing dark. Soon she would sneak out and . . . What? Go over to The Cottage and pack? Would she leave? Did she have to leave again? Why was her whole life a series of arrivals and leavings? Why was she never safe anywhere . . . ? If she had just told him it would have been so much better. But she hadn't and his expression when he had confronted her was so hurt, so bewildered.

He'd asked what the truth was and she had told him, but she knew in that moment that something had died. It had been obvious in his responses, his movements. He'd been shaken, because he loved her and he had trusted her – and she had never loved him enough to trust him with her past. Shouting at her would have been better, Alice thought. She could have coped with that, but not the awful silence that had followed.

'Why keep it from me?' he had asked her. 'If you had nothing to do with the child's death, why say nothing?'

'I didn't mean to hide it –'

'But you did!' he'd replied, baffled. 'An innocent person would –'

'I *am* innocent!' she had shouted. 'I tried to tell you

many times, but there was never the right moment. And then it got harder and harder to tell you.'

'But you could have told me anything.'

Turning away, Ray had walked behind his desk and sunk into his chair. The light had been fading, sounds of the school bus coming onto the gravel driveway. She had been a child again, disappointing people. And like a child, she had stood in front of him and waited for the punishment. But she wasn't a child any more and the punishment wasn't going to be anything obvious.

So she had left Ray's office and walked to the staff room and then realised that she couldn't go in there either. Everyone knew about her, everyone would be talking about her. How had she supposed she could bury the past? How could she have believed she'd got away with it? She never had done before.

Finally Alice had gone down into the cellars and wandered around. Pacing the floor, she had tried to work out what to do. Should she go and see Ray and beg him to forgive her? Or was he going to send her away? In moments all her carefully sustained calm left her. She would hide, Alice thought panicking. If he couldn't find her, he couldn't banish her, could he?

So she hid at the back of an abandoned old wardrobe and slid to the floor, her arms wrapped tightly around her knees. There was only a chink of light coming through the door, the smell of camphor balls oppressive. Hours wound by, Alice dozing, tired from crying. Slowly, time passed. The day moved on, the chink of light faded, the wardrobe fell into darkness.

And still she didn't come out.

'Where is she?' Ray shouted, catching up with Olive at the gates as she was about to leave.

'Who?'

'Alice!'

'I don't know,' Olive replied.

Her plan had worked, but only partially. He had been shattered when she told him, but he was more annoyed with her for betraying Alice.

'When did you last see her?'

'This afternoon. I haven't seen her since.'

His face was hard. 'If anything's happened to her –'

'Why should it?'

'Because of what happened today!' he bellowed. 'What d'you bloody think?'

Olive flushed. 'I thought you should know –'

'Oh, don't play the injured party with me! You wanted to shop her, and that's all there is to it,' Ray replied curtly, looking round. 'Go home. Go on, Olive, go home! I can't bear to look at you.'

Affronted, Olive walked off. Her last glimpse was of Ray Berry storming across the playground, calling Alice's name. Biting her lip, Olive climbed on board the bus. The driver winked at her, ready for a little flirtation. After all, she had been more than encouraging that morning.

Smoothing back his oily hair, he grinned at her. 'Well, hello there. How's my favourite teacher?'

'Oh, for God's sake!' Olive said shortly. 'Why don't you piss off?'

Satisfied with the way things had gone, Barbara Mills looked out from the sanatorium window. Oh, Ray might be upset now and running around like a scalded cat, but he would settle down. He hated deceit of all kinds, and Alice Rimmer had deceived him in the worst possible way. And then she had run off. Well, Barbara thought, if that wasn't proof of her guilt, what was? She didn't even stay around to deny the accusations and face her accuser. Even if she wasn't guilty, she was acting guilty.

It was probably better she went in the long run, Barbara thought, soothing her conscience. Alice Rimmer had been a cuckoo too long in the wrong nest. But now she had been ousted. Things would return to normal soon. Before long no one would even remember that there had been an Alice Rimmer around. Greenfields would return to normal, high up above Oldham, a little nucleus which was only ever rocked *temporarily* by outsiders from the world below.

'Oh Christ,' Ray said, pulling open the wardrobe door in the cellar and shining a torch light inside. 'What the hell are you doing, Alice?'

She blinked and covered her eyes as he took hold of her arm and pulled her out.

'I've been looking for you everywhere,' he said, his anger fading as he looked at her and brushed her hair away from her forehead. What had she been doing hiding in a cupboard? he thought. Was she afraid of him? Oh God, no, she couldn't be afraid of him.

'Come on,' he said gently, leading her to the cellar steps. 'Come and get something to eat.'

She went with him obediently. He was calm, kind even. In time he would tell her what he was going to do, and she would obey. That was all she could do.

Back in his rooms, Ray poured her a brandy and watched her sip at it. 'Go on, drink it. It'll do you good.'

All he could see was a child, not a woman. For all her poise and intelligence Alice had been reduced to a cowering child. Jesus, he thought, what's happened to you?

'Is that good?'

She nodded, although the brandy burned her throat.

'Ray, I had nothing to do with Robin Tripps' death. You must believe me. Robin had a heart defect, that's what killed him. His mother wanted me to take the blame, because *she* wouldn't call the doctor out when I asked her. The doctor was Guy Priestly, that's why he didn't give me away when he saw me here.'

'But why were you involved with Robin Tripps in the first place?'

'I was looking after him. I was his nanny.'

'At the Arnolds' place?'

She paused. Go on, she thought, tell him the truth. It doesn't matter now, you've lost him anyway. 'Robin Tripps was my cousin.'

Ray stared at her blankly. 'What?'

'I'm related to the Arnolds. Dorothy Tripps is my aunt, Judge Arnold is my grandfather.'

'So why were you your cousin's nanny?' he asked, obviously confused.

Her voice fell. 'Because they didn't know I was related to them.'

Suddenly suspicious, he leaned back from her. 'You worked for them without telling them you're related to them? Why?'

'Because they sent me away when I was a baby! They sent me to Netherlands. They gave me away!' She looked at him pleadingly. 'Believe me, Ray, I'm not making this up. I was put in the home when I was a year old. No one ever thought I'd find out where I came from or who my family were. When I did, I was so angry I wanted to get my revenge on them.'

'You wanted revenge?'

She paused, aware of how damning it sounded, her face white as chalk. 'Yes . . . I wanted to punish them for getting rid of me.'

Folding his arms, Ray leaned back against his desk, his face hard. 'And did you get your revenge, Alice? Was Robin's death revenge enough?'

'I would never have hurt him. I loved Robin. I admit I wanted to hurt the Arnolds, but I would *never* have hurt him. Never! I just wanted Robin to love me – to love me more than he loved them. *Any* of them.' She could see the disbelief in Ray's face, but continued. 'The Arnolds were so cruel. When I first went there I was my aunt's confidante. Me, a lowly servant. But then she changed, rejected me. Like the Arnolds always did –'

'So you wanted to get your own back by stealing her child from her?'

'I didn't steal Robin!' Alice shouted. 'I *loved* him. All right, I admit it, I hated his mother, I hated all the Arnolds.' Her voice had hardened. She was different to him. Almost frightening. 'Why shouldn't I want revenge on them? They had so much whilst I had so little. I *hated* them for not loving me. They had got rid of me without a second's thought. I was dead to them, so why shouldn't I wish *them* dead?'

'But it was Robin who died.'

She nodded, her eyes dark, unreadable. 'Yes, it was Robin who died. My Robin –'

'He wasn't "your Robin". He wasn't your child.'

'Oh, I know that, Ray,' she said distantly. 'I know that now. But at the time I loved him so much – and I was so sick with jealousy – that I came to believe that he *could* be mine. I had it all planned out, you see. I would become everything to him, and then later – when I exposed the family for what they had done – Robin would stay with me. He would love me enough to choose me.'

Words failed Ray. He had always known that there was another side to Alice, but this was incredible. The fury, the darkness she was showing him was unnerving. He realised then that he didn't know her. And probably never had.

'But Robin's death was *not* my fault,' Alice said emphatically. 'I'm guilty of plotting, of been deceitful, of hating, but I would have died rather than hurt that child. Robin was sick, his death was inevitable . . . but it doesn't feel that way to me. It feels likes a punishment – one I deserved, but not one he did.'

Ray was finding it all too much to take in. He loved Alice, but he was now wary of her, of the black angel whose presence she had once hinted at. Yet with his anxiety was a fascination. He was angry that she had hidden so much from him, but intrigued by her at the same time. Compelled, in love, consumed.

'I'll go away.'

Ray flinched. 'You will not!'

'I have to. I can't stay here. The Board wouldn't want me around – not when they know the full story.'

'We don't have to tell them the full story. As for Robin's death, we'll get Guy Priestly to talk to them. He's a good man; they'll listen to him.'

'I'll ruin you,' Alice replied, her voice flat. 'I'm not lucky, Ray, not lucky for anyone.'

He wondered for an uneasy moment if it was true. His answer would be a risk either way. If he lost her, he would never find another Alice – but if he hung on to her, would he live to regret it?

'I'll take my chances,' he said finally. 'I don't care if the whole bloody world falls down on my head. I don't care if I lose Greenfields – but if I lost you, that would break me.'

Unmoving in her seat, Alice said nothing in reply.

'I love you,' he repeated, touching her cheek.

'Ray, don't –'

'I can't help it. I care about you too much to let you go.'

When she answered her voice was a whisper. 'And I care about you too much to stay.'

Chapter Thirty-Seven

In the kitchen, Ethel was dolly-tubbing the sheets, her face shiny with exertion. Alma knocked on the window and walked in.

'How do?' she said, sitting down without offering to help. 'I've just been –'

'Up the doctors. What's it today?' Ethel said patiently, turning back to her work.

It was getting harder and harder, she thought. But age was like that; it made you slow. Only weeks earlier she had finally finished working at Netherlands, but instead of finding time on her hands she seemed to be working round the clock doing all the domestic chores she hated.

'It's my hands, Ethel. Riddled with rheumatic, and the skin on them's that raw, they could bleed. I got some stuff from the chemist. Oh, you know the one, it's advertised all over. Coopers hand cream, or some name like that.' She waved one rough hand in the air before her as though reading the billboard. '"Makes hands soft enough to sew silk."' Alma snorted. 'Well, I don't know who they think they're kidding, but I couldn't knit a barbed-wire glove.'

Ethel started at Alma. Perhaps if she had had children, she wouldn't be so self-absorbed. All least all her kids were settled. All married, and she'd seven grandchildren at the last count. As for her second family, as Ethel called Alice, that was coming along nicely. Oh yes, Alice would marry Ray Berry and be set up for life. No more worrying about her – things had turned out for the best, after all.

'Oh, and there's a slate off your roof,' Alma said suddenly. 'It could have fallen on my head.'

'At least it wouldn't have done much damage,' Ethel replied shortly. 'I'll get Andy Clough to fix it. He's cheap.' Struggling with the weight, Ethel pulled the wet sheets out of the dolly tub and fed them through the mangle. 'Here, give us a hand, will you?'

'Oh, I don't know, Ethel, what with my back.'

'You wouldn't be using your back, Alma, just your hands.'

Reluctantly, Alma picked up the end of the bed sheet, as Ethel guided it through the wooden rollers of the mangle.

'You need a proper washer, one of those I saw advertised in the paper –'

'Oh, yes, and how much are those?' Ethel retorted. 'A King's ransom, I don't doubt. Hold up that sheet, Alma! It's trailing on the floor.'

'Gilbert said that your Alice will be home tonight,' she said, the sheet only inches off the floor. 'You don't know what loneliness is, Ethel. Nothing's been the same since our Jack went. My health suffered from the loss. Oh, the things I could tell you, would make your hair curl –'

'It'll be to nice have her around, and that's a fact,' Ethel said, damning the flow. 'Nice to have some life in the house. But even nicer to visit her in her own home.'

'Own home? What d'you know that I don't?' Alma replied, the sheet dropping from her hands, Ethel jerking it off the floor, exasperated. 'I did hear about her seeing that Ray Merry –'

'*Berry*,' Ethel corrected her. 'He's called Ray Berry. The sheet's on the blasted floor again! If I'd given you a mop you couldn't have done a better job. Alma.' Hurriedly she folded the sheet and then hung it over the clothes rack. 'I think Alice might have something to tell us tonight. About her and Ray Berry.'

But Alma's attention was wavering as she stared back at her hands. 'The doctor said I wasn't to get them chapped. He said –'

Ethel was preoccupied with her own thoughts and continued blithely, 'I think we might be going to a wedding soon, Alma. You'll need a new hat. Ray Berry, head of Greenfields – that would be quite a catch for Alice, and no mistake. Mind you, he'll be lucky to get her,' Ethel replied, glancing at the door. 'Hush now, here she comes.'

Walking in, Alice kissed Ethel on the cheek and smiled over to Alma.

'How are you, Mrs Tudge?'

'Just leaving,' Ethel answered for her, ushering Alma to the door. 'Put some cream on those hands, luv. I'll see you tomorrow.'

Hurriedly she then moved back into the kitchen and looked expectantly at Alice 'So?'

'So what?'

'Have you something to tell me?'

'Like what?'

Ethel frowned. 'I thought you might have some news, Alice. Something important.' Then she saw that Alice's eyes were puffy. 'You've been crying!'

'No –' Alice said, turning away.

'You have!' Ethel insisted, walking up to her and turning her round. 'What's happened?'

'Nothing.'

'Nothing doesn't make your eyes puffy. What's going on?'

'I've left Greenfields.'

'Left Greenfields? But why?'

'It's a long story.'

'I bet it is!' Ethel countered. 'Why don't you tell me about it?'

Alice tried to speak and then closed her mouth again.

'Are you ill?'

Shaking her head, Alice turned to the door, but Ethel blocked her exit. 'Hey, come on, spit it out. A trouble shared is a trouble halved.'

'There was a job going up at Greenfields. Ray wanted me to have it. He said it would be a way of getting the Board used to me before we married –'

'You're getting married!'

'Not now.'

Ethel shook her head bewildered. 'Why *not now*?'

'Someone told Ray about Robin's death and how I was implicated.'

'But you've explained to him about how it really was? You must have told him about it before.' Ethel paused. 'You hadn't told him?'

'I meant to, but there was never a good enough time. So when he found out it made me look as though I had something to hide. As though I was guilty.'

Ethel stared at her. 'So he *fired* you?'

'No, he loves me.'

'Then it's all OK –'

Alice's eyes flickered. 'I can't marry him! I thought you'd understand.' She shook off Ethel's hands and moved over to the table. 'I'm not sure that I love him. I'm not sure about anything any more.'

'But you care about Ray, you know you do. And it doesn't sound as though he was put off by what he heard.'

'I told him about the Arnolds, how I was related to them and how I'd gone to work for them under false pretences.' Her voice hardened. 'I really let him have it, Ethel. Told him what I was really like, how much I'd plotted and hated them all. How much I'd wanted to take over Robin, steal him from his mother. In the end I came clean about everything.'

Ethel hesitated. Alice had altered, her light-heartedness gone. In its place was the shadow of her old self, the one they all hoped had gone for ever.

'But Ray still loves you. You're a lucky woman. I also think that if you had an ounce of common sense you would love him in return.' She leaned towards Alice impatiently.

'Oh, think about it, girl! You love your work; marrying Ray Berry would mean that you could be the mistress of Greenfields. The two of you could achieve so much. Besides, the man comes from a very good family –'

'He comes from a rich family,' Alice retorted. 'I don't know how *good* that makes them.'

Stung, Ethel folded her arms. 'I despair of you! Even when things go your way, you bugger them up. You've always provoked jealousy and lost out too many times through other people's spite. But now this time, Alice, you're going to cut off your own nose to spite your face.'

Alice coloured. Ethel could see the defiance flaring, all the old heat of her childhood coming back. So she hadn't really changed that much, after all, had she? Just camouflaged herself.

'If Ray marries me, his career will suffer,' Alice snapped. 'You know that, Ethel. The Board will find out about me and my reputation –'

'You were proved to be innocent.'

'But I was *suspected*,' Alice replied coldly. 'And mud sticks, they say. You remember how it was, how people gossiped. You remember what they daubed on your door? Now you tell me, how will that help Ray? Married to some orphan with a past? How could he raise money from the big shots in Oldham with me at his side?'

'Maybe he doesn't think that raising money is the most important thing in his life.'

'Maybe he doesn't think it now – but he will in time. I didn't care about anything when I was in love with Victor. I would have walked through fire for him, just as I know he would have for me. But I don't feel that passion for Ray.' She paused, coolly detached. 'I can't kid myself. You always wanted me to be in control. Now I am, and you're criticising me for it.'

'Being in control and being bloody stupid are two different things!' Ethel hurled back. 'You chose to leave Victor because of the circumstances. That was a noble thing to do, Alice, but don't make a martyr out of yourself a second time.'

'*A martyr!* Is that what you think?' Shaken, Alice moved away from Ethel and stood in front of the fire. Her hair seemed inky black in the darkening light of the kitchen.

'Yes, if you give up Ray Berry on some pretext of helping him,' Ethel snorted. 'Oh, come on, Alice, own up – if you wanted him enough you wouldn't give a damn about his career. It's not him you're thinking about, it's yourself.'

'What if it is?' Alice challenged her. 'It's no crime not loving someone enough.'

'Don't lie to me!'

'What do you want me to say?' Alice countered, her eyes cold. 'That I'm pretending to be noble? Well, maybe I am. And maybe you're the only one who can see through it.'

'Alice –'

'No, you hear me out!' she snapped. 'I've been doing a lot of thinking about the past. I thought I'd left it behind me, but telling Ray about it brought it all back. I'm not an ordinary woman, not the woman he thinks. He thinks I'm kind, good with children, that I would make a loving wife. Well, I wouldn't.'

'You don't know that.'

'I do!' Alice shouted, beside herself. 'The only man I wanted to marry was Victor.'

Taking in a breath, Ethel sat down. 'I thought that was all over.'

'So did I, until today. Until I looked at Ray and realised that he would never understand me, or where I came from. You should have seen his face when I told him how I went to work for the Arnolds, how I planned to win over Robin, how I hated them all. Victor would have understood – he knew me – but Ray didn't. He looked shocked, Ethel. He tried to hide it, but he was shaken. He was wondering why

I hadn't confided in him, probably wondered what else I'd hidden from him.'

'But you reassured him?'

'In a way, but not enough. I don't know if I could marry him, live at Greenfields. I keep wondering about myself, about how I could expect to live a normal life.'

'You are normal!'

'How do you know that for sure, Ethel?' Alice countered. 'You don't know how I feel, the rage inside. I was obsessed by Robin – God knows what would have happened if he had lived.'

'That was the past –'

'The past is what we are!' Alice replied hoarsely. 'The past is what makes us. We can't ignore the truth – what my father did, what *I* did. Think about it – what would have happened if Robin hadn't died? What damage could I have done?'

Angrily Ethel got to her feet and shook her. 'Forget it! It's over. You did wrong, but no one suffered for it but you. You're away from the Arnolds now and the past –'

'I am my father's child.'

'What the hell does that mean?' Ethel replied, troubled.

'I can hate, Ethel, really burn with hate. I hated the Arnolds. I would look at Judge Arnold, or Dorothy, and want to strike out, to smack the smug looks off their faces. All the time I was cleaning up after them, smiling at them, obeying orders, I *hated* them. I used to imagine them dying, or me having The Dower House. If my father hated as much as I did – then I know why he killed my mother.' She paused. 'Now, look at me and tell me that I should marry a good man like Ray Berry.'

Genuinely shaken, Ethel took a moment to reply. 'Have you ever thought that marriage to him might settle you down?'

'What if it doesn't?'

'Dear God, Alice, since when did anything in life come

with a guarantee? You have to take a risk, have to grab at what chances you have. I didn't know that you still loved Victor, but he's taken, he's Hilly's man now. You have to get over that, Alice, and move on. You have to stop running away – from life, from men. From love.'

'Oh, leave me alone!' Alice shouted.

'No! NO! NO! I won't leave you alone. You're being stupid, and someone has to tell you. I don't care if you hate me from now on, Alice, but I won't let you fool yourself. Ray Berry loves you. He'll protect you, he'll give you a good life. Don't throw yourself out into the wilderness again because that's all you think you deserve.'

'I don't love him –'

'You don't *let* yourself love him,' Ethel answered fiercely. 'Dear God, Alice, do you want to go through life carrying a torch for Victor Coates? That's over, done with. You have another chance now, grab it. Why do you want to be the poor little orphan all your life, forever down on your luck? D'you want pity? D'you want to make sure that you never achieve anything? Why? Because your family gave you away and made you feel worthless? Because you think there's some of your father's badness in you?'

Without thinking Alice struck out, but Ethel fielded the blow and slapped her hard across the face. 'Grow up!' she snapped. 'Grow up and live, Alice. You can still make a good future for yourself. If you wreck your life now it's no one's fault but your own. I never thought I would live to see you throw away your good fortune.'

'I'm not lucky for anyone,' Alice replied. 'I'm not lucky.'

Ethel shook her head disbelievingly, then pulled Alice over to the mirror above the mantelpiece.

'You make yourself believe that. No one else does. Look at her – look at that young woman. She has beauty, brains, charm. Look at her, Alice! Now see her twenty years on – alone, worn down, bitter.' Ethel put her hand under Alice's chin and jerked her head round to look at her reflection again. 'Your family didn't want you, but that doesn't mean that everyone else feels the same way. I want you, Gilbert wants you, Ray wants you. We all love you. But none of that matters, because you hate *her*.' She pointed into the mirror at Alice's averted face. 'You'll run and run all your life and you'll never stop and you'll never be happy – until you can look her in the face and say: *It wasn't my fault. My father was a killer, but I'm not –*'

'How do you know?'

'Because I know you!'

'Then you know me better than I know myself,' Alice replied evenly.

Infuriated, Ethel shook her head. 'Let go of the Arnolds and the past, Alice, *let go*. They tried to destroy you as a child, then as an adult – don't let them win. Please God, don't let them beat you.'

Part Three

The past and present here unite
Beneath time's flowing tide,
Like footprints hidden by a brook
But seen on either side.
                    Longfellow,
          'A Gleam of Sunshine'

Chapter Thirty-Eight

The men were marching again, the newspaper said. Where were the jobs promised after the last war? The mills were not hiring, the pits down on their numbers, even the old stalwarts like the engineering factories were restricting numbers. Men used to working locally took to travelling over to Salford and the Stafford Park area around the River Irwell. If there were any jobs going, they would be there.

But all too often the few jobs there were had been filled first thing in the morning, hundreds turned away. For men with families life was desperate. Cheap food bought at the end of the day from the market stalls was fly-spotted in summer and hard in winter. Meat was a luxury; all the working class could afford were the fatty cuts off Tommy Field's market – and fruit was unheard of for them. Children filled themselves up with bread and jam, and rickets and malnutrition became rife in the slums. In Oldham and the surrounding areas like Saddleworth and Dobcross times were difficult, but in the worst hit areas like Salford, existence itself was tenuous.

Since the turn of the century many of the Irish poor had come over from the old country and docked in Liverpool. From there they had graduated to The Bent in Salford where they had congregated in an Irish sector. In the worst slums areas the unemployed poor had created hell holes, unpoliced, and barred to all but their own. Drunkenness, prostitution and crime became the currency of the area.

Only religion was revered, most of the poor of The Bent, Catholic. Slum schools sprang up to cope with the increase in children, the Church opening some of its own schools, run by priests. Others were council run, the so-called ragged schools, where the poorest went. And to St Ursula's, Alice Rimmer came.

Her argument with Ethel had been fierce, but she had stuck to her guns. She was going to leave Greenfields for a whole mess of reasons which might make little sense to Ethel, but they drove her. It was not fair to marry one man when she was still in love with another. And she didn't want another episode of gossip, of the likes of Olive McGrath and Barbara Mills talking about her. She had loved Greenfields, but not enough. She had cared for Ray, but not enough. If he married her he would be for-ever wondering about her. Their childhoods had been too different to reconcile, she saw that now. Victor had been the man for her; they had had a shared history, shared fears . . .

The morning after the row with Ethel, Alice left Cullen Street before anyone else got up. She wrote to Ray and posted the letter in the quiet early morning. It read:

Dear Ray,
    I don't know how to thank you for all the things you've done for me. Your kindness and your love, so generously given, deserve someone better than me.
    I can't stay at Greenfields and I can't stay with you. You would suffer from the gossip. And people would gossip, Ray, I know that for a fact. They would say, 'There's no smoke without fire,' and although I know I wasn't responsible for Robin's death, others wouldn't be sure. And how could you have a teacher in your school with such a shadow hanging over her? How could you possibly have a wife like that?
    There are other reasons I can't stay. I should

have confided in you long ago. I know it must have hurt you that I didn't. There should be no secrets between people who are close.

I told you the truth when I described what I was like. I'm prone to moods, to brooding, to envy – none of them good traits. You need a nicer woman. But I can't hide what I am and I'm tired of trying to. Forgive me.

I don't want to leave you or Greenfields. You are a good man, doing good work. But I'm not good for you. Believe me, I know. And you do too, Ray, if you're honest.

Your love has been precious to me. You have been precious to me. Always in my heart,
Alice

As she let the letter fall from her grasp into the box, Alice shivered. It was over, time to start again. But where this time? Intuition told her that jealousy had prompted her exposure. She suspected Barbara Mills, as Ray's old flame, but never thought Olive had betrayed her. Whoever it was, everyone now knew about her supposed involvement with Robin Tripps' death.

So by running away, didn't she make herself look more guilty? But what was the choice? She had to move on, to somewhere no one would find her. But *where*? Only one thing was certain: she would settle in Salford – well away from Greenfields and Werneth Heights. And she would have to find some place that no one would voluntarily go. But where could she work without a reference and experience? There was only one place, a place no one else went to unless they were desperate.

The poor school – the council-run poor school, St Ursula's, at the back of the old glue works, only yards from the black, imposing Victorian viaduct which spanned the slums. It was the roughest school in town, the roughest in Lancashire. Only the desperate sent their children to St Ursula's. Only the desperate went to work there.

Dressed soberly in a navy suit and hat, Alice caught the bus over to the slums and got out at the stop under the viaduct. The air was dark with soot and grime, the shops sordid. On every corner was a pub, and slatternly ginnels ran off the main street, where huddled figures talked in doorways. As Alice walked into Hatton Row she avoided the curious stares and then stopped outside St Ursula's.

It was blackened with soot, the front steps chipped, an old, wheelless bicycle lying on the pavement outside. Cautiously, Alice walked up the steps and pushed open the entrance doors. They closed with a dull thwack behind her. The hall was dim, the sound of children coming from the back somewhere. Scuffed benches were piled high against one wall, and on the other there was an old fireplace and a crude doodle of a gibbet drawn on with chalk.

Alice looked round for a bell or any sign of life. Then she walked on into a corridor which appeared to run the length of the building. The smell was familiar and unpleasant. The smell of onions – which meant lice.

'Who the hell are you?' a big man said, walking over to her. He had greasy hair parted in the centre and a wall-eye. His hands were thick, the nails grubby and the black suit he wore was shiny with age.

'I wanted to see the principal.'

'That's me, Douglas Schofield.'

'You?'

'Yeah,' he said belligerently. 'Anything wrong with that?'

Alice shook her head. 'No, I wanted to ask if you had any work here. I mean, if you had any jobs.'

'Work *here*?' he said, taking a good look at Alice. 'What for? No one wants to work here.'

'I do. I have some experience with children.' Alice waited

for him to question her more, but he didn't so she hurried on. 'I can work hard.'

His left eye was looking at her, his right in some other direction altogether. 'You'll *have* to work hard here. There's nothing *but* hard work. Can you cook?'

'Cook?'

'Aye, cook,' Mr Schofield repeated. 'Have you got trouble with your ears?'

'No,' Alice said hurriedly. 'What do you want a cook for?'

'We need a cook and a teacher.'

'I could try to do both.'

He looked at her suspiciously. 'What's your name?'

'Alice,' she said, then made her first big decision since leaving Greenfields. 'My name is Miss Alice Cummings.'

'Well, for what it's worth, my wife will help you, Miss Cummings,' he replied flatly. 'She's an odd old bird, but tries hard.' He moved off, then turned. 'Any references?'

'Well, no –'

He sniffed. 'I thought not. You Catholic?'

'Er, no. . .'

'It just gets better and better, doesn't it, Miss Cummings?'

Quickly Alice moved into step with him as he walked off down the corridor. Oh Jesus, she thought as she followed him down the bare-floored hallway. On either side were religious statues. A boy with a placard on his back stood facing the corner. The placard read 'I BITE. KEEP AWAY'. Alice stared and then hurried on. The school smelled of stale food and unwashed clothes, the windows so caked with dirt that it was difficult to see out. No sign of the moors here, no Tollbank Farm.

Homesickness welled up in her, but she kept following Douglas Schofield until he came to a door and walked in.

'Mrs Schofield, Miss Cummings.'

His wife rose to her feet, laughing. Her head was tiny, her eyes darting from her husband to Alice like a nervous starling. The shabbiness of her dress was disguised by ribbons and cheap jewellery, a belt of rhinestones around her diminutive waist.

'Oh, Miss Cummings, how lovely to meet you,' she said, her soft southern voice a curious contrast to her husband's northern accent. 'And why are you here?'

Mr Schofield looked at his wife like a man looks at a blocked drain. 'She's the new cook –'

'And teacher,' Alice added.

Lizzie Schofield blinked slowly. 'Oh, how nice. What do you teach?'

Her husband turned to Alice. 'Yeah, what *do* you teach?'

'A little of everything – for children aged five to twelve.'

Lizzie moved over to Alice and then nuzzled against her shoulder. 'Can you cook sponge?'

Bemused, Alice nodded. 'Yes, yes, I can.'

'I like sponge,' Lizzie went on, 'it reminds me of my childhood.'

'Hah!' Douglas Schofield said simply.

It seemed that Alice was in the Schofields' living quarters. They consisted of one large room with a black iron grate and a mantelpiece covered in faded green velvet. There was no carpet, the chairs torn and patched, the windows covered with cheap market blinds smeared with fingerprints. It was a terrible place.

'It will be so nice to have someone young around,' Lizzie went on. 'When I was a child –'

'Oh, shut up about your bloody childhood!' her husband snapped. He turned to Alice. 'Her father was a dentist, she married below her. Didn't you, Lizzie? You could have married Freddie Isaacs.'

Lizzie stiffened and played with the rhinestone belt around her middle. 'Freddie loved me –'

'Freddie ran off with a doctor's daughter,' Douglas Schofield said, laughing. 'And Lizzie ended up married to the head of the ragged school!'

Mortified, Lizzie smiled at Alice. 'Don't mind my husband, it's just his fun. Would you like me to show you your room?'

For an instant Alice wanted to run, to say, *No, I'm getting out of this hellhole.* But she didn't. No one would find her here, certainly not called Miss Cummings. She could hide away. Anyway, the place looked like it needed a new pair of hands. It was grim, but it would have to do.

'I'd like to see my room, thank you.'

'Show her the kitchen first, Lizzie,' Douglas Schofield sneered. 'She might not stay when she's seen that.'

Lizzie talked all the way down the corridor, but when a bell rang she shrank against the wall as children hurried out of a nearby classroom. Finally, she pushed open a door and let Alice pass through. It was a huge, high-vaulted kitchen, poor-quality food lying around on greasy surfaces, bread grown mouldy on a Belfast sink.

'Is this where you *cook?*' Alice asked, nauseated.

'I do my best,' Lizzie replied. 'This isn't what I'm used to, you know. My people had money, I came from a good family.'

Sighing Alice looked round.

'Oh, please come to work here, my dear,' Lizzie urged her. 'It's not as bad as it looks. You'll get used to it. I know, I did.'

A subdued Alice returned to Cullen Street an hour later. Letting herself in, she made tea and then walked out into the backyard. Calling to Ethel, she passed her a cup.

'Thanks, luv. You been out?'

'Up to Hatton Row –'

'That slum!'

'To St Ursula's ragged school.'

Ethel put down her peg basket and sat down on the back doorstep. Alice sat beside her. The morning was mild, but hardly warm enough to dry the washing.

Alice sighed and pointed to the line. 'It'll never dry.'

'Probably not,' Ethel replied, sipping her tea. 'You going to work at St Ursula's?'

Alice nodded.

'They're all rough as a bear's arse there.'

'I know. I met the principal and his wife.'

Ethel kept sipping her tea. 'So you're definitely not going back to Greenfields?'

'No,' Alice said simply. 'And I've done something else. I hope you don't mind – but I've changed my name. I call myself Miss Cummings.'

'Well, I always think of you as one of my own,' Ethel said calmly. 'You reckon that no one will find you there, with a different name, and all?'

'I hope not.'

'And you don't think running away makes you look like you've something to hide?'

Alice gave her a sidelong look. 'I don't care any more, Ethel. I just want to get away from my past now, as far away as I can.'

'So why go to somewhere as grim at St Ursula's? You thought Greenfields was bad enough when I first suggested it.'

'I know, I know. But no one will come to St Ursula's. No one I knew from Greenfields and certainly not from Werneth Heights. They're separate worlds, Ethel. St Ursula's is a dead end, the last and lowest place you can end up.'

'And you think you'll fit in somewhere like that?' Ethel's voice was even, without emotion.

'Why not? I aimed too high before and it ended in tragedy. Maybe this time I can do something worthwhile.'

'Martyr.' A moment passed between them. 'Look, if your heart's set on it, fine. You have to do what you think is right. But does it have to be St Ursula's? For God's sake, Alice, it's a bit extreme – even for you.'

Extreme or not, Alice began work the following

Monday. At once, she set about trying to get some order in the place. Lizzie had obviously given up long ago. But it was difficult from the start. The caretaker, Paddy, was truculent, and the general cleaning woman, Ada, unhelpful. What, they all wanted to know, was some stuck-up, good-looking woman like Miss Cummings doing in a place like this? Was she hiding from something? A man, perhaps – some violent husband? Or maybe she'd been thrown out pregnant and lost the baby, or had it adopted? Either way, they didn't trust her. And she didn't trust them, suspecting that both Ada and Paddy pilfered the food rations.

Soon Alice had cleaned out her bedroom above the main school and pinned some lace at the window over the boarded-up pane. She had agreed to live in as part of the job, as some of the other teachers did – some glad to have any home at all. Bedclothes, soiled and torn, were boiled and patched up, and Alice bought an eiderdown off Tommy Field's market. The sour smell of the room faded slowly, and at night she pulled the bed away from the damp wall.

Sounds came into her dreams from the streets below: men coming home drunk from the pubs; dogs fighting; the noise of the late trains coming over the viaduct on their way to Manchester Central. They were all night noises, sad sounds in the dark.

At first, Alice did not come into direct contact with the children, only seeing them through the serving hatch in the kitchen. *Her kitchen.* The window was now clean, the floor mopped. The Belfast sink was shiny too, the pans all scrubbed and hanging up on hooks. Mouse traps were scattered around the larder and behind the fridge. At first there had been corpses every morning, but now it was only occasionally that some rodent met its end. Likewise with the cockroaches.

In a welter of boiling water and buckets Alice scrubbed every thought of Ray Berry off the walls and floors of

St Ursula's. Every time she boiled the sheets and disinfected the eating utensils she moved further away from him. There was no trace of the sweet high cold ground of Greenfields in the dank basement kitchen of the ragged school. There was no memory of love in the faces of the Schofields. Every day took Alice further from her past; every day made her forget a little more of Alice Rimmer.

It was impossible that she had once belonged to the Arnold family. How could she, a slum teacher and cook, have come from money? How could she have anything to do with Ray Berry? They were nothing to do with her – not with Alice Cummings. Their connection had been with another woman, in another time.

A woman who had reached for the sun and got burned for her trouble.

Chapter Thirty-Nine

'Books!' Douglas Schofield bellowed.

'Yes, you know, rectangular things with printing on them.'

He pulled a wry face at Alice. 'I thought you were the cook.'

'You said yesterday that I could start teaching next week. I was just doing some preparation, that was all.'

'Well, prepare the bloody food and keep your nose out of my business,' he hissed, walking off.

Lizzie was at Alice's side in a moment. 'He's a pig. You have no idea what I suffer at the hands of that man. As for Freddie Isaacs, he *did* want to marry me. It was only after I turned him down that he married the other girl.'

Alice stared at her employer's wife. Lizzie Schofield had given up long ago. She was married to a slob, a man who everyone looked down on – the head of a slum school. She had no friends and no interests. The cooking she had done before Alice arrived had been rudimentary – boiled, mis-shapen potatoes and hard rice pudding served up to hungry children. She was all too grateful to hand it over to Alice – and Alice had been all too willing to pass it over to a newcomer, Jilly Foster. She knew that Douglas Schofield would create about having to pay for another employee, but after he saw what Alice had achieved he relented, hiring Jilly for a minimum wage.

In such a way, Alice had managed to get out of the kitchen. Now she was ready to teach – something few others seemed to want to do at St Ursula's. Teachers came and went with depressing frequency. Few of them could control the slum children or endure the sordid living conditions.

But Alice was staying, and she knew what she wanted to do next.

'I want to start teaching.'

Lizzie was musing, a piece of worn black ribbon round her neck like a sad choker. 'He was always a pig –'

Alice touched her arm. 'Lizzie, I want to start teaching. Today. Please.'

Forty pairs of eyes looked up at Alice as she walked into the dim classroom. The windows were grimy, little peepholes rubbed clean to look out through, the imprints of dozens of small greasy fingers marking the glass. Alice looked at her pupils one by one. Their faces were unlike any she had seen before. In Greenfields, the children had been sickly, but at St Ursula's they all had the hard, sly look of poverty.

Slowly she walked onto the dais and stood in front of the blackboard.

'Can you tell me your names?' she asked.

Silence. 'Can you tell me what you are called? I'll start at the back. You, what's your name?'

'Pat.'

'Pat what?'

'O'Donnell.' The boy frowned, his hands dirty, the nails blackened. His feet were barefoot. 'Are you our new teacher?'

'Yes, I'm Miss Cummings.'

'And Goings,' he answered back, laughing at his own joke, the others joining in.

Stepping down from the dais, Alice walked between the rows of desks. To her astonishment, the children seemed to be of different ages, and the boys and girls were all mixed together.

'Have you got any books?' she asked one girl.

'No.'

'No, *miss*,'

'No, miss,' the girl replied. 'We don't have books.'

'So how do you learn?'

'Mrs Schofield teaches us sums,' another child replied. 'She writes them on the blackboard. She teaches us about God too.'

Alice frowned. 'What about reading and writing?'

'*What* about it?' Paddy asked.

'Do you all know how to read and write?'

Silence.

'M' mam says it's a waste of time.'

Alice looked in the direction of the voice. A whey-faced girl was staring at her. '*Can* you read and write?' Alice asked.

'Nah.'

'Do you want to?'

Pat chimed up from the back, 'Nah. No one cares 'bout things like that.'

'I care.'

'Yeah, but you won't stay.'

'Want a bet?' she said lightly, folding her arms.

Each face reminded her of faces she had known at Netherlands. Tough little nuts. All of them were children, but they were old for their years. Poverty had done that, poverty and ignorance.

'Put your hands up all those children who are seven years old.'

A score of hands went up.

'Now, put your hands up all of you who are eight.'

Another clutch of hands.

'Anyone nine?'

Three hands went up. It was chaos. How could any of them learn anything at different ages and abilities?

'Right, I want the seven-year-olds to sit over here. Quickly, move,' she said, clapping her hands. 'I want the eight-year-olds to sit here,' she pointed to the central rows, 'and the nine-year-olds to sit on the right. Yes, there.'

Pat's voice came above the muffle of movement. 'What about Daft Dora? She's eleven.'

Alice walked over to him. 'Don't call anyone daft. How would you like it?'

'But I'm not daft and she is, miss, everyone knows that. She just sits over there and wets herself.' He pointed to the corner where a thin girl sat hunched over her desk. 'Her mother's on the game, m' father said so. He said she were –'

'That's enough, Pat!' Alice replied, walking over to the girl and kneeling down by her desk. Dora's mouth was ringed with sores, her nails bitten to the quick. Under her desk there was a pool of urine.

'What's your name?'

She looked at Alice blankly.

'What's your name?'

'Daft Dora!' someone shouted.

Immediately Alice rose to her feet. 'Sit down all of you! Now! I want complete silence.' Surprised, they stopped talking as she moved back to the girl and lowered her voice. 'Now, tell me your name.'

'Daft Dora.'

'No, your name is Dora, just Dora.'

'Dora.'

'That's right. How old are you, Dora?'

There was nothing in her eyes. 'I don't know.'

'All right, it doesn't matter. Have you any brothers and sisters?'

She had nodded. 'Six brothers.'

'Do they come to school here?'

She nodded again.

'Can you read, Dora?'

'Dora can't read!' someone shouted. 'She shows her knickers in the outside lav!'

There was a chorus of laughter, but Alice continued to stare at the baffled girl. Then slowly she took hold of Dora's hand and led her up to the dais. There Alice placed a chair beside her own, helped Dora into it, and then looked back to the class.

'Dora will be sitting with me from now on,' she said calmly. 'Now, I want every one of you to write your name as best you can. If you can't write, I'll teach you how to.'

'What for?'

'Because you need to learn, Pat,' Alice replied, 'and it's my job to teach you.'

Ray could hardly stand the sight of Olive McGrath. He had thought he would get over her betrayal of Alice, but he couldn't. Every time he looked at her, he remembered it. She had been the one who had indirectly made Alice leave Greenfields. Her spite – because he knew it was that – had resulted in him losing the woman he loved.

He hated her for it. Did she really think that he would give her the job he had wanted to give to Alice? Was she that stupid? She was a reasonably good teacher, but nothing more. In fact, in a more conventional school Olive McGrath would have been called to account long ago. She was sloppy, she defied the rules, she let the children cheek her. She was second-rate. But she was one of the few people willing to work up at Greenfields. Beggars couldn't be choosers, Ray thought bitterly.

The very sight of Olive coming across the courtyard to Greenfields made him tense, the sound of the morning bus, which he knew would drop her off, making every nerve ending jangle.

For her part Olive was well aware of the dislike coming from her employer. She had thought at first that Ray Berry might come around to being grateful – after all, if it was true that Alice Rimmer had been involved in the death of a child, surely she wasn't a person to have around in a school? Oh, but he hadn't seen it that way at all.

He had thought that it was just spite. That she had been jealous of Alice and wanted her out of Greenfields. It simply wasn't true, Olive thought. She and Alice had been friends; she had only acted in the best interests of Greenfields. And now here she was, being harassed by the employer she had tried to help.

She almost believed it.

'Mrs McGrath!' She jumped, turning to see Ray beckoning to her. In silence he walked to his office, Olive following.

Finally, he spoke. 'Your class was out of control yesterday, Mrs McGrath.'

'They were a bit high-spirited –'

'They were out of control!' he snapped.

Olive looked down. She wouldn't antagonise him, she would just wait until his temper burned out. When he thought about it he would see that she was actually a loyal employee, someone he should value.

'Sorry, Mr Berry.'

'I saw you smoking too, at the gates.'

This was news. Olive coughed. 'I don't think –'

'That you should smoke in or around these premises. How many times have I told you that?'

Her face flushed as red as her hair. 'You smoke!'

'I'm the principal here! And besides, I never smoke around the children.' He rose to his feet and walked over to her.

For a fleeting moment he wanted to slap her. 'Perhaps you would be better off working at some other school –'

'What?' she snapped. 'You can't fire me!'

'I can do as I like,' Ray replied. 'You're sloppy and getting worse. You set a bad example to the girls with your flirting – oh yes, I saw you with the bus driver.'

'I bet you wish you could flirt!' she hissed back. 'I know

what's wrong with you, Mr Berry. Your lady's upped and left you and you're bad-tempered.'

'Alice left because of you –'

'She left because her secret came out,' Olive retorted, her voice shrill. 'I was doing you a favour. If she's a danger to children, she should never have been here.'

'Get out!'

'No, I won't!' Olive hurled back. 'You can't fire me. If you try it, I'll go to the governors – then we'll see whose side they'll be on. They wouldn't have wanted some murderess working here –'

'Alice never hurt anyone!' Ray shouted, his fists clenched as he looked into Olive's scarlet face. 'You don't know what you're talking about.'

'Neither do you! How can you be so sure that she was innocent? Apparently, the boy's own mother thought she was negligent.'

'How do you know that?' Ray asked, his face white.

'Barbara Mills told me.'

Olive stopped short. She had given her accomplice away. Oh well, Olive thought, if she was going to suffer, so would Barbara. She wasn't going to take the punishment on her own.

'What does Sister Mills know about this?'

Olive shifted her feet. 'Only what I told you.'

'And how did she come about the knowledge?'

'I don't know,' Olive lied. 'Why don't you ask her?'

'I'm asking you.'

She hesitated, then rushed on. 'She overheard a conversation between Alice and Dr Priestly when Alice first came here.'

'And yet she didn't think it was important enough to tell me then?' Ray asked coldly. 'Why now? Perhaps it was because now I wanted to marry Alice and promote her at Greenfields?' He sat down behind his desk, the contempt in his voice apparent. 'So, you thought that by betraying

Alice you and your husband would get her job, and Sister Mills wanted Alice out –'

'To get you back. Yes! Yes! That's right, she wanted you to herself. Now who are you angry with, Mr Berry? Me or Sister Mills?' She paused. 'Can I go back to my class now?'

He nodded. Once.

For nearly an hour Ray brooded before finally walking over to the sanatorium. Briefly he looked in on the patients and then went in search of Barbara.

She was washing her hands in the nurses' kitchen when he found her.

'So you got Olive McGrath to betray Alice Rimmer to me?'

Her hands paused, the towels still. 'What?'

'You heard me!' Ray snapped. 'You waited until you thought the information would do the most damage and then you got peevish Olive to deliver the blow for you.' He propped himself against the sink and touched her cheek. She softened to the caress. 'Barbara, why? Because you wanted us to get back together again?'

'Of course I did,' she murmured, laying her head against his palm. 'We were good together, we could *still* be good together. We could run this place and be happy on our own.' She let her lips brush his hand. 'Alice Rimmer wasn't right for you. She was too young, too inexperienced. I've worked here for years, beside you. She would never have known what to do – not the way I do.'

He leaned towards her, his lips almost touching hers, his voice low.

'Barbara.'

'Yes, darling?'

'I'll never come back to you.'

She straightened up, slapped out of her reverie. 'What?'

'It was over a long time between us and I never wanted it to start again. I want Alice Rimmer, not you.' He saw the pain his words were causing, but didn't stop. She had to feel the agony he was feeling, to suffer as he had done. 'From now on, you aren't even a friend of mine. You can stay here and run the sanatorium for ever, I don't care. But I'll never speak one word to you – other than that of employer to employee.'

Desperately, she caught at his sleeve. 'Ray, please, come on, talk to me. Alice Rimmer was no good –'

'She was!' he shot back, his voice strained. 'And I loved her. But you drove her away – you and Olive McGrath. You drove her away and I can't find her.' He shook off Barbara's hand. 'Get off me! Get out of my sight! You got your revenge – well, now I've had mine. It hurts, doesn't it? Well, I can tell you something, Sister Mills, it gets worse.'

Chapter Forty

Knocking away Ed's hot hands, Olive walked over to the bed and flopped down on it. The ceiling needed plastering, new cracks appearing every week. If only they had the money; if only Ed was more useful around the house . . . Irritable, she rolled onto her stomach. Her threat had shaken Ray Berry all right, but it had been an empty threat. She couldn't go to the governors and expose Alice – no one knew where she was now.

She had gone away. To Huddersfield? London? Who knew? She had just gone . . . Olive picked at the eiderdown with her nails, feathers settling round her. Jesus, she shouldn't have lost her temper with Ray Berry! That was stupid. She was lucky to have kept her job.

But Ray Berry was mad at her. That much was obvious, sickeningly so.

Ed lay on the bed next to her, a man in overalls smelling of oil. Slowly his hand travelled up her thigh and rested on her buttocks.

'I was thinking about you all day, wanting you. Do you want me?'

'Every minute,' Olive said sarcastically.

His hand tightened on her bottom. 'I've got half an hour before I have to go out. We could –'

'No, we couldn't!' Olive snapped, sitting up. 'D'you think of nothing else? Sex, sex, sex – that's the beginning and the end for you.'

'I think about kids too,' Ed said stupidly.

That did it. Olive was on her feet instantly.

'Well, I don't! I don't want children yet, Ed. In fact, I

may *never* want children. I want to see more of life, go places, do things – I don't want some snot-nosed kid in a cheap pram giving me stretch marks and a prolapse.'

He stared at her, crushed. 'You don't want kids?'

'God, give me strength!' she shouted, running downstairs.

He followed her into the kitchen, his hands on his hips.

'Now, listen to me, Olive McGrath, you are my wife and you'll do what I say.'

'Are you off your bloody head?' she retorted, sneering. 'The day I do what you say is the day they take me to the madhouse.'

'We have to talk about this –'

'No, we don't,' Olive replied, her voice calming. 'We have other things to talk about, more important things. Like my job. I thought I might get that new job, Ed. The one which would have meant that you and I could have gone to live at Greenfields. We would have been someone then, shown all these toerags round here. But you're not interested in that, are you?'

'I'm happy wherever you are.'

'*I'm happy wherever you are,*' Olive mimicked back. 'Well, at the moment I'm in the shit.'

'Huh?'

'Ray Berry's bloody angry with me.'

'Huh?'

'Stop saying huh!' she snapped. 'I said that Ray Berry's vexed with me'

'For what?'

'Singing too loud,' Olive replied wryly. 'He didn't take too well to my telling him about Alice Rimmer. He wants to get back at me, so the bastard's making life hard.'

Ed sat down. 'Sorry, luv.'

'Yeah, me too,' Olive replied, thinking of the bus driver. 'I like it up at Greenfields.'

'Still, look on the bright side.'

She glanced at her husband curiously. '*What* bright side, Ed?'

'If you wanted to quit your job you'd have time for children. In fact, we could start now.'

Daft Dora had sat up on the dais with Alice since the day she began teaching at St Ursula's. The girl wet herself every time. Alice never scolded her, just silenced the taunting children and had Ada, the cleaner, mop up the urine. After a few weeks, Dora had fewer accidents, but she was still withdrawn and patently terrified of everything. But Alice didn't know why. Asking Dora directly invoked no response, so finally Alice decided that she would go to see her parents.

The family lived on Bow Lane, one of Salford's worst slums. A narrow street running between high terraces, it was cut off at one end by a makeshift wall. Skipping ropes hung from the broken streetlamp and a blocked drain pooled over the cobbles.

Dressed inconspicuously in her dark work clothes, Alice checked the number of the house on the piece of paper she had brought. The paint on the door of number 125 was peeling, the number chalked on the brick wall beside it. A dog growled from inside. Several people had come out to watch Alice's progress, women with their arms folded, a man spitting on the street by Alice's feet. It was the Irish quarter, and all strangers were suspect.

At Alice's knock, a heavy, coarse-faced woman opened the door. 'What d'you want?'

'Mrs Garland?'

'Who wants to know?'

'I'm Dora's teacher, Miss Cummings.'

'Dora's teacher!' the woman said, laughing. 'Wot you teaching her? Latin?'

'Can I come in?' Alice asked, aware of a small knot of people listening to the conversation.

'Nah, I don't want teachers here. Dora goes to school because she has to. When she's old enough she'll get a job. Do some bloody good around here instead of wasting her time.'

'But, Mrs –'

'Clear off!' the woman snapped, slamming the down in Alice's face.

The gathering of people watched Alice as, embarrassed, she began to walk away, several following her. Her footsteps sounded loud and lonely on the pavement. She had been an idiot to come here! They just thought she was some snot-nosed teacher trying to preach to them. Which was just what *she* would have thought when she was at Netherlands. One more outsider coming to patronise . . . She walked on. The people followed. Then they stopped. Suddenly aware of them, Alice felt her hands grow moist, her heart beating as she glanced over her shoulder. They wouldn't do anything to her, she reassured herself; they wouldn't attack a woman . . . But still she hurried towards the end of the lane, to the well lit main road, about a hundred yards away.

'Oi, teacher!' an Irish voice cried out suddenly.

Alice thought about running – then thought better of it and turned. 'Do you want to talk to me?'

'Yeah, *I want to talk to you*,' the man mimicked. 'Get out of here and don't come back. We don't like your sort.'

Afraid, but irritated, Alice answered him coldly: 'What exactly is *my sort*?'

'Bloody educated bastards,' he replied. 'Bet you came down here to slum it, didn't you? Have a look at the poor people in Bow Lane.'

'I came to talk to Dora's mother –'

'And now you're going home to a nice warm bed, in some frilly-curtained little house?'

'No!' she snapped. 'I'm going back to a cold room and

a hard mattress. I live in St Ursula's – and we don't have that many net curtains there.'

Surprised, the man hesitated. 'Oh, I thought ... well, get out of here, anyway.'

'Or you'll do *what*?' Alice asked, the words out of her mouth before she could check them.

Putting her hands on her hips, she faced the man and the knot of people behind him. Her temper had risen, her old recklessness sneaking back to life. An orphan kid, brought up in the slums, showing everyone where she came from.

'So, what *are* you going to do?'

'Seeing as how you're a woman –'

'Oh, don't let that stop you!' she hurled back at him. 'What d'you want? A fight? You think I'm a stranger to your sort. Well, you're wrong. I came from Salford – not here, but from Netherlands Orphanage. And I don't frighten easily. I teach your kids, whether you like it or not. And I'll do my best for them – whether you like it or not.' She breathed in, then looked each one of the crowd in the face. 'Don't think you can scare me off. I'm coming back and I'll keep coming back. You see if I don't.'

'We don't want you here.'

'You may not – but your children do,' Alice retorted. 'Give them a chance.'

A short woman at the back of the group stepped forward. 'You live at St Ursula's?'

Alice nodded.

'It's a dump,' the woman went on, 'and that bastard Schofield is a thief.'

'I don't know anything about that.'

'Well, I'm telling you. The money he gets from the council ain't going into the school, and that's a fact. He's as crooked as a corkscrew.'

'I knew 'im when 'e were out of Strangeways first time.'

Alice turned in the direction of the voice. An old

man without teeth was leaning on a stick and looking at her.

'If you think you can do any good at St Ursula's, then you've got yer work cut out. It's a pit, run by a thief. You come down here telling us what you're going to do for us – well, others said the same. They left, though, and that walleyed bastard Schofield stayed.'

'I'll help your children –' Alice began, but was interrupted immediately.

'Don't try to pull the wool over my eyes. No one helps the likes of us. We're the bottom of the midden. People don't care whether we get learning, or if we starve. No bugger's interested in Bow Lane or St Ursula's. You'll learn. We're the scum down here, best forgotten.'

'I don't believe that, and I promise I'll help you.'

The old man nodded. 'It's been said before, and nothing were done. You won't be any different.'

Chapter Forty-One

Alice realised early on that there was no point tackling Douglas Schofield about his thieving the funds; he wouldn't admit to any wrongdoing and she would be out on her ear. The way she could best help was to work from within. The two other teachers – Minnie Lomond and William Reynolds – had been at St Ursula's for some years. Their teaching skills were rudimentary, but no one was going to complain and, besides, who else could Douglas Schofield hire, offering such poor wages and sordid accommodation?

Minnie Lomond was brushing thirty and lived at St Ursula's in a couple of rooms at the top of the school, and Will Reynolds was a drunk. The times he arrived to teach much the worst for wear were frequent. His favourite pub, The Lionheart, was used to seeing kids from the school sent down to haul him out. He was tall, dressed in a suit off the market, his moustache trailing over his top lip. If he had any ambitions, he had given them up years ago, and was now an inebriated – if sometimes amusing – bachelor.

The only time Will Reynolds was sober was when the school governors visited on their infrequent checks. They came in a hurry, looked, and got out of St Ursula's as quickly as they could. What could you expect, they said to each other, it was the poorest school in Salford? Sadly, even the Church had nothing to do with St Ursula's. The local priest avoided the place and there were few donations.

So when Alice came with her ideas and hard work she was laughed at – but allowed to do pretty much as she liked. After all, if she was prepared to work like a dray horse, who was going to stop her? Her only ally was Jilly in the kitchen. She was young, easily led, but she admired Alice and was eager to please.

As for Lizzie Schofield, she had no desire to carry on teaching, and encouraged Alice to take over her duties.

'I can't control them like you can,' she said, twisting a row of fake pearls around her thin neck. 'They like you.'

Alice looked at her employer's garish finery. 'Are you going out?'

Lizzie beamed. 'I'm off to church. It's not the usual church – I go to the Spiritualists.' Lizzie dropped her voice. 'Douglas – the pig – doesn't like it, but he can't stop me. He's a –' she dropped her voice still further, '– *Catholic*.'

Alice smiled, not knowing quite what she was supposed to say.

'My mother was a medium, you know. She used to go to the Spiritualist meetings all the time. She was quite well known in her day.'

'Spiritualist church, hey?' Alice mused, fascinated. 'What happens there?'

'We get messages from the other side,' Lizzie said, hopeful of a convert. 'From the dear departed.'

'You believe in life after death?'

Lizzie's eyes were brilliant with the certainty of something better to come. After all, the next life had to be better than the one she was enduring.

'Of course I believe! We've all lived before and when we die we all go on to better things.'

Alice was mystified: 'Where?'

'To the afterlife,' Lizzie replied emphatically. 'All the people we've loved we see again.'

So that was how she coped with her husband and St Ursula's, Alice thought. By living in another world.

Curiosity was getting the better of Alice. 'What do they say, the spirits, when they give you messages?'

Her voice a whisper, Lizzie took Alice's arm. 'They tell me that my parents are watching over me.'

'So they see everything that's going on?'

Lizzie's voice took a harder turn. 'Oh yes, they see everything. They see that that toerag of a husband of mine is a pig. They see that all right.'

Alice was trying not to laugh. 'But *he* must have family on the other side too?'

'I doubt if they would want to know him!' Lizzie said firmly. 'They didn't when they were alive, I can't think they'd want to own him when they're dead. His mother wasn't even married to his father – not that he'd admit it. But I know. When he talks about my family and Freddie Isaacs I think about his family and smile to myself.' She sidled closer to Alice. 'His mother didn't approve of me, you know. She said I was too stuck-up.'

'No!' Alice said wryly.

'Oh yes, said I was a snob.'

'So why did you marry him?'

A pained look came over Lizzie's face. 'I thought that Freddie might be jealous when I got engaged . . .' A moment passed, then she fluttered back into life. 'I've got to go, or I'll be late.'

She had no sooner left the room than her husband walked in, his face suspicious.

'Were she talking about me?'

'No, it was an interesting conversation,' Alice said smartly. 'She was telling me about the Spiritualist Church.'

'Bah! It's all rubbish, stuff they make up for simple minds.' He stared at the books under Alice's arm. 'What are them?'

'Pelicans,' she replied drily. 'They're books from the library –'

'What!'

'It's fine,' she hurried to reassure him. 'They were old and being sold off cheap.'

'I bet they bloody were,' he said sourly. 'How much?'

'Eleven shillings for the lot.'

'Are you mad?' he snapped. 'We haven't got eleven shillings to waste.'

'This is a school. A school is *supposed* to have books in it.'

'You can pay for them yourself –'

'My wage isn't big enough to pay for books!' Alice retorted heatedly. 'You get allocated money for books, *you* can afford them.'

'There's not enough money to go around. I have to run this bloody place as well as I can on what the authorities give me. Don't tell me how to run this school. You've only been here for a few months.' His eyes stared at her, one in one direction, one in another. 'Don't get uppity with me, I can fire you, remember.'

'Oh yes, and who would you get in my place who works my hours?' Alice replied, her tone acid. 'Perhaps you could ask Miss Lomond or Mr Reynolds to give up some of their spare time.'

Irritated, he blustered, 'We did well enough without you. So don't start throwing your weight around.'

Alice bristled. 'I happen to know that the governors were impressed with my class when they came round the other week. They stayed for a while watching me teach and then they complimented me on how tidy the children were.'

Schofield knew it was true and also knew that Alice was working hard enough for three. If he lost her he would be landed with the work himself – and have to get Lizzie involved again. That was the deciding factor. Since Alice had been around, his wife had been blissfully absent, her forays to the Spiritualist church getting her out from under his feet. Oh no, Douglas Schofield thought, he wanted his wife to keep the spirits company, not him.

'I never said you weren't doing a good job.'

'So I can have the books?' Alice countered, watching him wriggle.

'OK, OK, you can have the books. But no more. And make sure the little bastards don't put fingerprints all over them.'

Back in the classroom, Alice set the children a series of sums to do. Dora sat beside her. The girl's hair was matted at the back, neglected, but she hadn't wet herself for over a week. One by one, Alice looked at her pupils. They were a shabby lot. None of these children would ever have a career; they were destined for the mills and pits, and a few would inevitably end up in Strangeways, the prison outside Manchester. The girls would go to work at fourteen, marry young and soon be aged with childbearing. Some would go on the game, some would get out of the slums and get a job in service. But not many. They were ill-educated, ignorant and ill-mannered – not the types people picked to work in their houses, even below stairs.

Alice thought of the lodging house she had passed the previous night. Full of single men, it housed the feckless and the men newly out of prison. If they could find enough money for a bed, they slept there. Some stayed on and off for years. The older men who came – middle-aged or elderly – were out of work and on the margin of destitution. Of the able-bodied men, drink played its part, and desperation. Some were forced into taking the jobs no one else wanted – working in the hide and skin yards, or the slaughterhouses. The work was hard, foul, and few stayed for long.

And how many of her pupils would end up in similar places? Alice wondered, glancing down the rows, her gaze settling on Micky Regan. He was the youngest of a family of ten, all his siblings at work, except for his thirteen-year-old sister, Mabel. His father was a renowned lout, and rumour had it that the new baby had been produced by his eldest daughter, not his wife. Incest wasn't uncommon in the slums but no one cared enough to intervene. The children weren't going to tell anyone in authority and the wife was scared of her husband.

Micky was clever, though, Alice thought. He could do something with his life, get out of the mire and escape. His reading and writing were good, he had a fine imagination and was also quick with figures. If he got the proper education, Micky could go on to college, university even.

In one of her more practical moods, Lizzie had told Alice about the Regans, how the father had been jailed for grievous bodily harm for three years. It had been a peaceful time, she said, and the family had been happy whilst he'd been away. But then he had come out of prison and moved back in, and before long Mrs Regan had lost two of her front teeth and all the furniture in the house had been taken by the bailiffs.

'I've finished, miss,' Micky said, butting into Alice's thoughts.

'Bring it up here then.'

He came up on the dais, a small boy in hand-me-down clothes, with a muffler round his neck. Sores behind his ears spoke of infrequent washing.

'Has everyone else finished?' Alice asked. There was a murmur of voices and then gradually they all nodded. 'Good. Now, we're going to do something different.' Alice rose to her feet. 'Every day, before we start work, we are going to have a wash.'

There was a murmur of dissension.

'Oh, come on now, it's only water,' she said. 'And that's the way it's going to be from now on. You all come to school and get washed, then we'll begin work.'

'But, miss –'

'No buts. If you do this, you'll get a reward.' She knew the bribery would work. And it did.

Forty pairs of eyes stared at her. 'A reward?'

'Yes, every one of you will get some chocolate,' Alice said recklessly. That was expensive, she thought to herself, and she would have to pay for it. Douglas Schofield would hardly cough up for luxuries. 'A piece of chocolate for every one of you – after you've washed.'

Bribed, they responded. The following day the children arrived at St Ursula's and walked into the classroom to find Alice with her sleeves rolled up, a bowl of hot water on the desk and a pile of towels next to her.

By the time Alice had cleaned the first ten children it was getting late, so she called for Jilly and handed her another bowl.

'Scrub behind their ears, then wash their necks and hands, will you?'

Horrified, Jilly stared at her. 'Wash *them*?'

''Fraid so,' Alice said, pulling a face. 'Every scruffy little kid has to be mopped and dried. Oh, come on, Jilly, we'll get them clean today, then they can do it for themselves after that.'

The two women worked side by side, the time passing, children returning to their seats with red ears and pink hands.

Then suddenly Jilly jumped back. 'Oh Jesus, God!'

Alice stared over to her. 'What is it?'

'Fleas.'

'Oh hell,' Alice said, taking hold of the child and bending her over the bowl of water. 'Get me a jug, will you, Jilly? We have to wash her hair.'

Fleas turned out to be on several of the children, lice on many of the others. Alice washed the worst offenders and then used a nit comb on the hair of every other child – washing the comb in between. They could only clean the pupils' heads and hands, but it was obvious from the smell of them, and from the state of their clothes, that many of them needed baths.

Alice studied the child whose neck she was scrubbing.

'How often do you have a bath, Mary?'

The child looked at her. 'Eh?'

'How often do you have a bath at home, sweetheart?'

'I dunno.'

'So how do you wash?'

'We use the kitchen sink and a tub,' she said dimly. 'My Mam washes the clothes in the tub every week.'

But not the bed linen, Alice thought. That would be crawling with bed bugs ... There had to be a better way to clean the children up, she thought; something more practical. At eleven o'clock she and Jilly finally finished. Alice washed her hands, rolled down her sleeves, and set off to see Douglas Schofield.

He scowled when she walked into his shabby office. 'Oh no, not you again.'

She ignored him and hurried on. 'I want to talk about hygiene.'

He looked at her as though she was mad. 'What?'

'The children are filthy.'

'So what d'you expect me to do about it?'

'Some of them are crawling with fleas and lice,' Alice said flatly. 'They sit there scratching their heads all the time – how can they learn anything if they're not concentrating? And how can they concentrate if they're lousy?'

'I'm not nannying 'em kids!' Schofield snapped. 'If they're dirty, let their parents clean 'em.'

'But they don't, do they?' Alice said, exasperated. 'Most of the parents don't give a damn about themselves or their houses. I've seen some of them down on Farrow End.'

'This isn't a bloody nursery –'

'They could use the baths,' Alice suggested. 'There are two bathrooms on the ground floor. I'd like to make sure that every child has a bath and hair wash every week. They'd feel better and they'd work better.'

'Oh aye, and are you going to call round and do their parents' washing as well?' he replied, his voice mean. 'Perhaps we should clothe 'em too?'

Alice acted innocent. 'Well, if you think we could –'

'Christ!' Douglas Schofield exploded. 'What the hell are you talking about?'

'Clothing the kids wouldn't cost a penny. We could pool together all the old clothes and remnants that get left here at the back door.' She paused, her eyes sly. 'I've seen them – people drop them off here for the children every Friday.'

He shuffled his feet. 'Those go somewhere else.'

'Where?'

'Somewhere else!' he snapped hotly. 'What business of yours, is it?'

Alice had already guessed what had happened to the clothes. 'You're selling them on as rags, aren't you? And pocketing the money?' She could see him colour. 'I don't suppose the governors would like to know about that, would they?'

'Now don't you threaten me, girl –'

She faced him squarely. 'Don't *girl* me! I know your type and I'm up to you. Remember where I came from. I know all the wrinkles people pull at places like this. But you're in charge of this school and you're honour-bound to do the best for these children. That's what you were hired for.'

'I suppose you think you could do a better job?' he sneered.

'*Think*? I *know* I could,' she retorted. 'But you're in charge – for now, anyway.'

In that instant Douglas Schofield could see his job evaporating before him. Miss Cummings had him by the short and curlies. If he fired her, she would expose him to the authorities and he would lose his job. And all the little extras he had been sifting away for years. Bugger her, he thought, the smart little bitch had him over a barrel.

'OK, you can do what you want – within reason,' he said sourly. 'But don't mess with me too much, Miss Cummings. I don't like to be pushed around, it brings out my mean streak.'

Chapter Forty-Two

The harder the Depression hit the North, the more everyone suffered. A fund to relieve distress had been set up in 1932 by local do-gooders and numerous calls for help had been made since its formation. Donations of coal, clothing and clogs came to the slums, the league also organising concerts for the unemployed. It was a vain attempt to make idleness bearable, but men wanted to work, not listen to music.

In the homes the women struggled to feed the children. St Ursula's allotted free milk and an apple a day for each child, but it was not enough to stretch the housekeeping at home. The pawnshops did a lively trade, especially on Monday mornings when any wages coming in had been spent over the weekend. Or wasted – as they sometimes were in the slums. Gambled or drunk away.

Yet as the year came to its close, Alice managed to maintain some kind of order at St Ursula's. The children came to school, got washed and were then set to work. They had their weekly baths and the donated clothes were sorted and then given out. But as the winter began in earnest, the classrooms were so cold that the children wore every piece of clothing they could, some even wearing their summer clothes under their winter ones. Poverty was so acute that one child even attended school wearing wellington boots, his legs chafed raw at the back of his knees.

But the children all adored Alice. She was their one fixed spot, never changing, always a ready listener, and by now, totally fearless. It had taken her many years, but Alice had finally found her feet. Nothing disturbed her. She would argue with Douglas Schofield about funds and money, would beg books off the library and even asked some of the local storekeepers for food for the poorest children.

She did it through charm and cheek. And her spirit was indomitable. Alice had found her calling. Yet her social life was nonexistent. She had missed Ray at first, but now she hardly thought of him. She had the children to think about. At Greenfields she had been part of a team; at St Ursula's she was trying to change things single-handed, and she relished the challenge.

It was not difficult for Alice to see herself reflected in many of her pupils. Her own insecurity was mirrored in each one and galvanised her into helping them. They had nothing – well, she knew what that felt like – but they had *her*. And she would never let them down.

She had singled Micky Regan out for special attention, but his father had other ideas. Stanley Regan had heard about his son's extra tutoring and wasn't impressed. Neither did he like the idea of his children being washed at St Ursula's. It made them look like bug-ridden beggars, he said to anyone who would listen. Just who did this bloody Cummings woman think she was?

Matters came to a head one day when Micky came to school withdrawn and silent. Noticing the change in him, Alice waited until the classes were over and then, when he'd shown no sign of snapping out of it, asked Micky to stay behind.

'What's the matter?'

He was surly. 'Nuthin'.'

'Come on, Micky, talk to me.'

He turned his hazel eyes on hers. 'I have to stop school.'

'What? Who said so?'

'M' dad.'

She remembered what she had heard about Stanley Regan and bristled.

'You're doing too well to leave school. Have you told your father that you want to be an engineer?'

He gave her a far-off look, as though it had been a dream and she should never have deceived him into believing it.

'What's the good? 'E won't let me stay 'ere.'

Alice sighed. 'Do *you* want to stay, Micky?'

'Of course I do! I don't want to end up like the rest in m' family,' he said hoarsely. 'I want to get on, do summit with m' life.'

Alice rose to her feet, picking up her coat. 'Come along, Micky. I have something important to do,' she said.

'Please, miss . . .' he protested, dragging back, but Alice refused to listen.

When they came out of St Ursula's, it was past four o'clock, the afternoon already dark with rain. Walking down the cobbled street, Alice crossed with Micky under the viaduct and headed for Durham Road. She could sense him stiffen the further they walked, the nearer they came to his home. The air was damp, Micky pulling his balaclava over his ears, Alice tying a headscarf around her head. Because of the rain, there were few people about, only a group of idle men standing talking on a corner.

At the entrance to Durham Road, Alice paused. 'What number do you live at, Micky?'

'It'll do no good, whatever you say to 'im.'

'What number, love?' she repeated patiently.

'Fourteen,' he whispered, falling into step with her again.

The terrace was like so many others, grim and dark. Doors were closed, some broken windows blocked up with board, others sporting paper blinds. A dog shook itself in the rain and at the entrance to number 14 there was a stack of rubbish left piled against the front wall.

A stench came off the rubbish, Alice trying not to show her repulsion breathed as she knocked. She knocked again when there was no answer, the door finally opening on her third try.

A burly man in a dirty vest, with a leather belt around his beer paunch, stood looking at her. Then he glanced over to Micky.

'You! Get inside.'

Hurriedly Micky ducked past him, his father clipping him behind the ear as he ran by. Smug, Stanley Regan looked back at Alice.

'Who the fuck are you?'

She winced at the word. 'I'm Miss Cummings, I teach your son.'

The rain was pouring down on her. A baby was crying from inside the house. The man stank of sweat and cheap tobacco.

'You the one who made m' kids wash?'

'I thought –'

'How dare you say m' kids need washing?' he said, his voice cold.

To Alice's surprise she was intimidated by him. He provoked fear in her even though she was outside his house. God only knew what a child felt living with him.

'All the children get washed before they start work,' she said, keeping her voice calm. 'I wanted to talk to you about Micky. Mr Regan, Micky is a clever boy, he should stay on at school.'

He moved down off the step so quickly Alice jerked back, threatened.

'I'll tell *you* what my son does. You don't tell *me*. Micky's been playing around too long, I want him out of school *now*.'

'But why?' Alice asked impatiently. 'There are no jobs; he'll just end up hanging around like so many others.'

Stanley Regan moved towards her, and Alice stepped back again.

'My son will do what I say, not what you say,' he growled, jabbing his finger into Alice's shoulder.

Angered, she brushed his hand aside. 'Don't touch me!

You might beat your family up, but don't try it with me.'

His narrow eyes flickered. 'Who said I beat my family?'

'It's common knowledge,' Alice replied, trying to keep the fear out of her voice. 'Everyone knows, and if anything happens to Micky now, I'll report you.'

'Who the fuck will you report me to?' he said, laughing unpleasantly. 'The police? They don't care. They don't care what 'appens down 'ere. They don't come 'ere, they don't dare.'

Alice hurried on: 'Micky could get an apprenticeship if he stays on at school. Please, let him.'

'Apprenticeships costs money,' Stanley Regan replied curtly. 'Look round. There isn't any bloody money 'ere.' He waved his thick arm around the street. 'You know what it's like down 'ere? No work, no change, just day after day the same. A man goes mad like that. Nuthin' to do.'

'So why do you want Micky to end up the same way?'

He stared at her, then ran his thick tongue over his lips.

'Why d'you care?'

'He's my pupil.'

'You got a family of your own?'

'No.'

'Well, when you do, you can do what you like with 'em. But this boy's mine. Got it?' He turned away and then slammed the door behind him.

Wiping the rain out of her eyes Alice stared at the closed door. A moment later she heard Stanley Regan shouting and the sound of a child crying loudly.

Banging with both fists on the door, she shouted out: 'Mr Regan! Mr Regan! Talk to me.' Silence. Again she shouted, 'MR REGAN! MR REGAN!'

He flung the door open so quickly that Alice almost fell inside. She could see Micky in the background, cowering against his mother.

'*I'll* pay for his apprenticeship,' Alice said, her voice contemptuous. 'You won't have to pay for a thing.'

Stanley Regan laughed into her face. 'You want a back-hander, or what?'

'I warn you again, you touch me and I'll have the police on you before you know what's hit you,' she threatened, her voice hard. 'They might not care about you, but they'll care about me.'

He blinked, wrong-footed, then called to his son. 'Micky! Come 'ere.'

The boy emerged by his side, shaking.

In mock affection, Stanley Regan got him in an arm lock. 'Your teacher 'ere thinks you want to go off and be someone. That right, son?'

Micky looked at Alice and then closed his eyes, wincing against his father's grip,

'No! I don't want to go. I don't know what she's talking about, Dad, honest I don't.'

'You sure about that, son?' Stanley Regan asked, his arm still wrapped around his son's neck. 'You sure that this lady has it all wrong?'

'She's lying, Dad, *she's lying*!' he blurted out, wincing against the pain. 'I never wanted 'er to come 'ere. I never did. I never did!'

Satisfied, Stanley Regan let his son go. Micky disappeared into the house without looking at Alice.

'Seems like you had the wrong end of the stick, miss, don't it?' he asked her smugly. 'Now, you go away, there's a good girl. You go away and don't come back. My son loves me, loves his old dad.' He raised his eyebrows. 'All my kids love me. Every one of 'em.'

Defeated, Alice walked to the end of the dark street and then turned the corner, where she leaned against a wall for support. She was breathing heavily and her legs could no longer hold her up. The rain was coming down in torrents, her coat and scarf drenched. Water ran down her face as she finally hauled herself back on to her feet and began to walk again. Her head was down – and her eyes were burning with tears.

She knew that Micky Regan would never leave the slums. He wouldn't be an apprentice, or be allowed to make his mark in the world. And she knew that she would never see him at St Ursula's again.

Chapter Forty-Three

Hilly was just coming in from shopping when she felt dizzy. Doubling up, she leaned against the kitchen table and breathed deeply. A moment later, the dizziness passed. She would have to see the doctor, she thought, then decided against it. Too many doctors had seen her over the years, predicting all kinds of disaster, but she was still here, all this time later. Who would have thought it?

She smiled to herself and began to unpack the shopping. There was precious little choice, food still on ration, the end of the war making no real change yet. But it was a relief it was over, especially as Victor had made it home safe. What else could she want really? Hilly wondered. Her man was home – which was more than many husbands and sons were.

It no longer upset her the fact that they had had no children. From the first they had been warned that she was too frail, and Victor hadn't minded. Or had he? she wondered. He had never shown his disappointment, and he treated her like a countess. Nothing was too much trouble for his girl, he said frequently. Nothing. If he had not loved her when they married, he loved her now. His letters had said as much throughout the war and his plans for the future were clear. Mr Dedlington had died and his widow was willing to sell the business to Victor. He was going to be a businessman, Hilly thought. *A businessman.* Not bad for two orphans who had come from nothing.

Dizzy again, she sat down and took some deep breaths. This was time for celebration: they had come through the war and now they could enjoy peacetime. With luck they would soon be making some good money, perhaps enough to move out of Trafalgar Street. Not that it mattered to Hilly – she was happy where she was, she always had been. Trafalgar Street was her home. Hers and Victor's.

Their part of Salford had escaped the bombing, but other places had fared less well. The Stafford Park area around the River Irwell had been targeted by German bombers eager to destroy the industrial heartland, and many factories had been ruined. Streets around had suffered from the fallout, many homes razed to the ground.

As for St Ursula's, that had survived, but many of its windows had been blown in by a stray bomb, the grim institution merely patched up, as building materials were scarce during the war. Most of the children had continued to attend school, the cellars acting as air-raid shelters, their routines punctuated by panic and sudden evacuations.

Hilly sighed. She could never have done what Alice had in a million years. She would have been too afraid. But Alice had stuck by the school and by her pupils, and gained an incredible reputation. She and Hilly were still friends, even after so long, Alice visiting Trafalgar Street frequently. Yet despite her good looks she was still unmarried and, these days, consumed with the school.

It did Hilly no good to encourage her to look for a husband. Alice had no time for that. She was a spinster, she said, and if it didn't worry her, why should it worry anyone else? Amazed, Hilly had admired her – as she had always done. Alice now, in her thirties, was striking, even more beautiful than she had been as a younger woman. The fire in her, which she had suppressed so long, had leaped back into life. All the old spirit made her fight for the pupils, and when Douglas Schofield was finally fired for negligence it was Alice who took over the running of St Ursula's.

Many times Hilly had heard rumours about Alice going into the slums, dragging children out to attend school, standing up to belligerent parents. How did she dare? Wasn't she ever afraid? But that wasn't Alice's way, Hilly realised. St Ursula's had filled a void in her life. That hideous building had become her husband, family and future.

Her head swimming again, Hilly put her hands to her face. She was overtired, she told herself, she had been rushing about too much. The victory parties held in the street had exhausted her, and then Victor's coming home – it was all too much excitement. She would rest more and then she would be well again.

Slowly Hilly moved over to the fire and began to fold the drying clothes. Victor's shirt was warm as she lifted it and held it to her face. There was nothing else she wanted from life. Just him. No one else. No children, no money, nothing but him. That was all she had ever wanted.

She was a happy woman. Happy and lucky – whatever the future held.

'Well, I would never have expected to live this long, what with all my problems.' Alma paused, glancing over to Ethel for sympathy. 'I said, I never thought –'

'Neither did I!' Ethel replied, exasperated. 'I thought so much bloody hard work was bound to kill me before now.'

'I'll never make old bones and that's for sure.'

'You *are* old,' Ethel replied, staring at the ill-fitting wig Alma wore to cover her thinning hair.

Piqued, Alma took a moment to respond.

'The doctor said I've survived so long because I was so slim.' Her eyes ranged over Ethel's bulk. She had grown fatter over the years, the weight adding more strain to her knees and making her back ache.

'I'll go on a diet the day you stop going to the doctor's –'

'Aye, Ethel. I need treatment.'

'You can say that again,' Gilbert replied from behind his newspaper.

Ethel glanced down at her full stomach. She *would* go

on a diet, she thought, *one* day. Probably the same day they would go away on holiday ... She rubbed her nose where her glasses had pressed. Things had changed so much. The war had altered everything; it was another world out there now. She sighed to herself as Alma asked Gilbert to read her the newspaper headlines 'because I haven't to strain my eyes.'

The old order was over, Ethel thought to herself. Girls didn't want to work in service any more. They had been used to doing men's jobs during the war and having independence. They weren't going to settle for a little uniform and cleaning grates at six in the morning.

'Oh, speak up, Gilbert! I can't hear a word,' Alma said pettishly. 'You mumble something terrible these days.'

'You can't hear me because you're deaf.'

'*Me*, deaf!' she replied, mortified. 'I'll have you know that the doctor said – '

'I'm surprised you could hear him,' Gilbert said mischievously, winking at Ethel, 'you being so deaf and all.'

Smiling, Ethel turned away, still thinking of the changes in Salford. Mill work was slowing down again since the war ended. Before long, gossip went, the old mills would be closing. And where would people find work then? Ethel wondered. In the shops, she guessed, and all the other places which had opened up. Only the other day her neighbour had told her that her daughter was working as a cinema usherette. She had invited Ethel in and showed her the uniform – a short fluffy skirt and little white cap. Well, Ethel told Gilbert later, if you'd worn things like that in my day you'd have been walking Victoria Street. And not selling bloody ice-cream cornets either!

'I've no idea what things are coming to,' Alma said, pointing to a photograph in the paper of a starlet wearing a skimpy dress. 'You'd wear more on an operating table. It's all these movie stars. They wear next to nothing and earn fortunes. And this lack of clothing can't be good for anyone's health. That girl,' she said, pointing back to the newspaper, 'will be coughing like a racehorse by the time she's thirty.'

It was true about the change in values, Ethel thought to herself. As for the old professions – nursing and teaching – they weren't as appealing as they had been before the war. Who wanted to slave away when there was the glamour of London and foreign countries to seduce them?

The new generation of women wanted excitement. They craved new clothes, something not utility, worshipped Errol Flynn and watched *Brief Encounter*, falling in love with Trevor Howard. The amount of girls who got things in their eyes now when there was a good-looking man about was ridiculous. People forgot the past so easily. And although the cinemas showed footage of German atrocities it was obvious that people wanted to move away from the darkness as fast as they could.

And who could blame them? Ethel thought. Only the other day she had walked past Netherlands and seen the old place boarded up, 'CLOSED – DO NOT TRESPASS' on a notice on the front door. She had paused and without effort could hear the ghost sound of the children running down the corridors and smell the ghost odour of Friar's Balsam, steaming in bowls during long, snow-bound winters. Her gaze had then moved to where the railings had once stood which had been requisitioned during the war, and she thought of a young girl and a young boy who had once whispered to each other, looking for comfort in the dark. But not here, not now. Those two children had grown up, Victor married to Hilly and about to start his own business, Alice a force to be reckoned with, a defender of the poor and needy.

Ethel put her glasses back on and pulled her thoughts back to the present.

'Who wants tea?'

'Is it the Co-op brand?' Alma said, looking up. 'I find

the others hard to digest. It's my stomach, you know.'

'If your stomach can stand it, you can stay for a bite to eat,' Ethel replied, moving over to the bread board. 'Corned beef's what we're having.'

Hurriedly Alma rose to her feet. 'I think I should go. I've a little bit of fresh fish at home. For my stomach, doctor's orders. It's not what I would choose to eat, of course.'

'Oh no,' Gilbert said drily. 'I only eat it myself to please Ethel.'

Immune to sarcasm, Alma left, promising a return visit the next day. As the door closed behind her, Ethel sat down heavily.

'What's up?' Gilbert asked.

'You happy?'

'Eh?'

'Oh, God!' Ethel sighed expansively. 'I said – *are you happy?*'

'Like how?'

'Like happy! Like yo ho ho! Christ, Gilbert, don't act numb. You know what I mean.'

He winked at her. 'Yeah, I'm happy. Aren't you?'

She thought for a moment. 'Do you think about the future, Gilbert?'

'Nah.'

'Don't ever worry about it?'

'I don't worry about what I can't change, and I can't change what's coming, can I?'

She was persistent. 'But everything seems so different now – like the world we belonged to no longer exists. I'm happy – don't get me wrong – I've always *been* happy. Oh, I get annoyed with things and worried about money sometimes, but all in all I've been content. We raised the kids, worked hard – but now I wonder, what was it all for?'

Surprised, Gilbert moved over to her and put his hands on her shoulders. 'That's not like you, luv.'

'I know,' Ethel replied shortly. 'You don't want to listen to me, Gilbert Cummings! Misery loves company.'

Uneasy, he comforted her as best he could. 'Things will settle again, luv. It's just with the war and everything . . . Things will settle down and it'll be like it was.'

She shook her head emphatically. 'No, luv, whatever happens now, one thing's for sure. It'll *never* be like it was.'

Pushing the old pram up the street, Olive McGrath paused and retied the wool scarf round her head. Bloody rain, she thought, bloody lousy rain! A bus passed, throwing water over her shoes. Olive cursed and ducked away too late. Jericho Street was foul. It had been foul before the war, and it was worse now. She would never have expected to end up in a place like this. But that was the way life went – it surprised you. Surprised the hell out of you.

Like Ed dying. That had been a surprise all right. He had died in action in France. Funny, she had wanted him away for years, almost been glad of the war at first. Even had a brief fling with an American in Manchester, but she hadn't wanted Ed to *die*. Even after giving her three children under ten. Even then, she didn't want him dead.

'Hey, Gerry!' she said, jerking her son and putting his hand on the bar of the pram. 'Don't you go off wandering now. I've enough on my mind without looking for you.'

Her son dropped into step beside her, putting his tongue out at the little girl in the pram.

It was incredible how things could change so much in a few years. Olive had clung on to the job at Greenfields for nearly ten months after Alice Rimmer left, and then that bastard Berry had finally found some reason to fire her. Well, it was a *good* reason, Olive thought. He had caught her with the school bus driver behind the bike shed. The bloke's pants round his ankles and not a punched ticket in sight.

She smiled to herself, momentarily light-hearted. Oh, but that knee-trembler had cost her a lot. Her job, for one thing. Not that she could have kept it for long anyway. Berry had been out to get her from the day Alice Rimmer left. He was always going to fire her the first chance he got. But after she'd been sacked, everything went belly up for Olive. Ed was delighted to have her home, promised he'd look after her. Oh, and he did – she was pregnant within two months. First baby. Then pregnant again. Second baby. Then when he came home from leave she got pregnant again. The third.

Well, it was either his or the American's. Either way, it didn't matter much now, did it? It was still one more mouth to feed. And that was rough. Rough, living off charity, in second-hand clothes, with no job. Her, a trained teacher – how the hell had she ended up this way?

She could see that people had gloated, they had all wanted her brought down a peg or two. *There goes Olive McGrath, always thought she was a cut above the rest of us. Well, look what happened to her. Three kids, no man, and no bloody figure left. Lucky if she ever got a man again. Still, she'd had enough in the past to make up for it.*

It was all Alice Rimmer's fault, Olive thought. She had set everything in motion. It had been her who had caused Olive's bad luck. If she could get her hands on Alice Rimmer now, Olive thought, she would knock her bloody teeth out. After all, hadn't it been she, Olive, who had taken Alice Rimmer under her wing when she came to Greenfields? She needn't have done that, Olive thought self-pityingly. And what had been her reward? Sacking. For warning Ray Berry about Alice Rimmer's past.

Olive stopped again and retied her scarf for the second time. Gerry was wailing beside her, cold and hungry, the steep street unwelcoming under the cloudy rain. Barbara Mills was still up at Greenfields. *She* had managed to hang on, but Olive was out in the cold. To think of a qualified teacher ending up this way! Without a job and no reference, and three kids in tow. The one thing she never wanted.

And all because of Alice Rimmer. If she had never met the bloody woman she would still be up at Greenfields, earning a good salary and getting some fun where she could. No kids, no working in the house day and night. She had had freedom, but that had gone. And now what had she to look forward to? Struggle, and more struggle. She'd never find a man again, not with no money, shabby clothes and tits down to her waist from feeding babies.

Alice Rimmer had ruined her life, Olive decided. And she could do nothing about it. Alice Rimmer was probably married now with a nice house – a woman who had been careless with the child in her care, a *murderess* for all she knew – and *she* was prospering whilst Olive was struggling. It wasn't fair, it wasn't bloody fair.

'Oh, come on!' Olive snapped, dragging Gerry along behind her.

'I want m' dad,' he wailed. 'I want m' dad.'

Yeah, and so do I, Olive thought for the first time in her life. So do I.

Disappointment and spite threatened to choke her. Her life had been ruined and it had nothing to do with her. Someone else was to blame for her failure and it was obvious who that was. Jesus, if she ever saw that bitch Alice Rimmer again she would get her own back. Somehow she would punish her – make her suffer as much as she had.

One day their paths would cross again. And then God help Alice Rimmer – because Olive McGrath wouldn't.

Chapter Forty-Four

Leonard was laughing to himself as Charlie read a long poetic piece he had written the previous week. It was appalling, Leonard thought; good to see that the lad hadn't lost his touch. Concentrating deeply Judge Arnold sat watching his grandson, his heavy features lined, his head jutting forward on his shoulders.

Alwyn's death had hit him hard, Leonard thought, changed him. But not softened him. Judge Arnold might be old, but he was more vicious than he had ever been. It was as though Alwyn had checked his excesses, and now she was gone his spite had full rein.

Charlie paused, and with a look Leonard encouraged him to continue his monologue. His nephew was beginning to lose his hair! God, Leonard thought, that was a shame. Then, smugly, he felt his own head. His hair was thick at the back, luxuriant, the bit of him which had aged best. Sadly, his face had not matured well; become bloated, his jowls flaccid, his skin too pink. He was, Leonard had to admit, an unprepossessing man, but what did that matter? He was rich.

'And that's the end!' Charlie said with a flourish. Leonard clapped; Judge Arnold cheered distantly. 'I should get home now to the little lady,' Charlie added.

His wife had refused to enter The Dower House for years. She said it was *spooky*, but Charlie pooh-poohed her. It was his home, he said, what was spooky about it?

'Anything published yet?' Judge Arnold murmured from his seat.

'I'm working on it,' Charlie replied. 'Soon, soon.'

Staring at his nephew as he talked to Judge Arnold, Leonard flinched when he felt a hand touch his shoulder. Turning, he saw Dorothy, her face winsome, her slender figure dressed in an expensive French gown. She was stunning, he thought, but totally unappealing.

Her lips parted in her strange smile, her teeth showing for an instant. Small teeth, white, like a child's. Gliding into the chair next to him, she took his hand. Leonard froze. He could get used to anything but this affection. Even his wife's outbursts, her instability, were nothing like as unsetting as her sudden devotion.

'Darling,' she cooed, her eyes dark, 'will you be long?'

He blushed, yes, *blushed*! 'Ch-Ch-Ch-Charlie's here, m-m-my dear –'

'But I'm off in a minute,' his nephew said happily, immune as ever to the strained atmosphere. 'Back to the little woman at home. She worries more now than she did during the war. Thinks I'll get killed on my way through the park.' He laughed lightly. Leonard wasn't surprised that Charlie had survived the war. It was typical of him. A fool's luck.

'Oh, st-st-stay for a while longer,' Leonard urged him. 'The p-p-place gets boring with just us three.' He could feel Dorothy's grip tighten on his hand.

Why did she want him *now*? Why, after so many years of indifference? It was out of character. After all, even when Robin died she hadn't turned to him – went to her parents instead. Talked to them in their rooms, shutting Leonard out. What they talked about he never knew, just that when she came to bed she was cold, distant, her back turned to him.

Years passed like that. The hated November anniversaries came and went. Sometimes they were difficult, Dorothy agitated for weeks before and after. Other times they were quiet, and that was worse. Luckily, it had become easier for Leonard to get out of The Dower House, because since

Alwyn's illness Judge Arnold had retired and handed over the running of the businesses to his son-in-law. It was not that he trusted Leonard to do a good job, it was just that his wife took precedence over everything.

So Leonard had spent more time at work, and had been glad to. And Dorothy – always devoted to her mother – had nursed Alwyn for two years until her death. There had been professional nurses hired to help out, but most of the care had been undertaken by Dorothy. She had exhausted herself frequently and had been forced to rest, but as soon as she could, Dorothy had returned to the sickroom. Often Leonard had wondered if his wife believed that her mother could *not* die whilst she was there. If she was present Alwyn would hang on. And hang on she had done, Judge Arnold growing quieter and quieter, sitting by the bedside, sometimes drunk on port, inebriated just enough to sleep for a while.

But it had never been enough to *keep* him asleep for the night. He would wake instead and talk to Alwyn, and Leonard had sometimes felt Dorothy creep into bed beside him in the early hours. But she had never woken him up; never turned to him for comfort. She had been there, but not there. Always present, but always absent.

Then in the days which followed Alwyn's death Leonard had waited for the disturbing signs that Dorothy might have a breakdown. But her anticipated mood swings had never come. She'd been quiet at first, frighteningly so. Then a sea change had taken place; all the withheld confidences pouring out of her without restraint. It was as if – her mother gone – Dorothy had finally been able to confide in her husband.

The only matter Dorothy would never discuss was the death of Robin. That was too painful, too disturbing. Leonard wondered sometimes if she talked to her father about it; indeed he had come upon them chatting together intensely and then breaking apart when they saw him. Furtive whispers and quick looks had been a part and parcel of his life at The Dower House so he took little notice, but as time progressed Leonard wondered just what his wife and her father had to talk about so earnestly.

If Leonard had had a jealous nature it would have been impossible for him to live with his wife and his father-in-law under one roof. But Leonard was nothing if not canny. He had learned over the years when to speak and when to keep silent. Judge Arnold's contempt for what he perceived as Leonard's weakness was misjudged, but invaluable to his son-in-law – because he never saw his greatest rival under his very nose. In the end, Leonard had managed by sleight of hand to achieve a perfect victory. He had the business and the power.

And Dorothy. Which – when she had been distant – was bearable. But since Dorothy had grown more affectionate, life had become uncomfortable for Leonard. If she had loved him when they'd first married, he would have willingly returned the feeling, but time and tragedy had distanced him too. He felt love, but not for his wife. For his mistress, Frances.

'Darling,' Dorothy said huskily, 'talk to me.'

Charlie was chatting to his grandfather, both indifferent to Leonard and Dorothy's conversation.

'L-l-later,' Leonard urged her, 'later, my d-d-dear.'

'But –'

Leonard sighed. 'I thought you were going to b-b-bed early?'

He could see her wince. 'Don't you love me?'

It was the last question Leonard expected and it left him floundering. Judge Arnold had heard the question too and was staring at his daughter curiously.

The only person who had noticed nothing was Charlie, still engrossed in telling a story: '. . . And you'll never guess who I saw the other day . . .'

Leonard stiffened in his seat as Dorothy moved closer to him.

'I want you to love me, Leonard. I love you so much.' She rested her head on his shoulder unexpectedly. 'I couldn't live without you. I would die.'

At once Judge Arnold was on his feet, pushing Charlie aside and moving over to his daughter. 'You look tired, Dorothy, go to bed.'

'. . . There she was, lovely as ever . . .' Charlie continued blithely, although no one was listening to him.

'I said you should go to bed!' Judge Arnold repeated, Dorothy staring up at him.

Well into his story, Charlie continued behind them. '. . . And I thought, *I know her*. And you'll never guess who it was . . .'

Judge Arnold's face was flushed. 'Dorothy, it's time you retired for the night. Go upstairs now!'

'. . . Alice Rimmer.'

The name engulfed them like an avalanche. Opening her mouth to speak, Dorothy gaped at Charlie. Leonard was startled into immobility. But it was Judge Arnold who reacted first. Quickly, he turned, almost losing his footing as he did so.

'What did you say?'

'I said,' Charlie went on uneasily, 'that I saw Alice Rimmer the other day. She was in Manchester, looking –'

'*Alice Rimmer?*' Dorothy repeated the name dully, as though for an instant she couldn't remember who it was, but knew it was important. Then her hand went over her mouth. 'Oh God.'

'Charlie, you b-b-b-bloody fool!' Leonard snapped, for once losing control as he stood up. 'W-w-why the hell did you h-h-have to mention that?'

Charlie looked from one to the other, blustering, 'I just . . . I just –'

'Didn't bloody think!' Judge Arnold hissed, taking Dorothy's arm and leading her to the door. 'Go up to bed, Dorothy. Get some rest.'

She was baffled, her eyes unfocused. 'But he said that he saw Alice Rimmer –'

'I know,' Judge Arnold said, his voice hard. 'I heard. Now, go to bed. There's nothing to worry about.'

But Dorothy wasn't going to be pliable. 'Alice looked after Robin.'

Leonard nodded. 'Yes, yes, she d-d-d-did.'

'And Robin *died*,' Dorothy said, her hand touching her cheek. 'I called for the doctor. I called for the doctor, you know. She didn't, she –'

Judge Arnold was holding on to her arm tightly. 'Dorothy, we know –'

'No, no you don't!' Dorothy snapped. 'None of you knows. I'm the only one who knows. Me, just *me*.'

'You did everything you could –'

'Shut up, Father!' she snapped, unexpectedly forceful. 'I want to see her. I want to see Alice.'

He rocked at the words. 'No, you don't. That was a long time ago.'

'I want to see her!' Dorothy repeated. 'I want to see her!' Angrily, she shook off her father's arm and walked back to Leonard: 'I *need* to see Alice Rimmer. Please, darling, please. Bring her to see me, David, please.'

Gently Leonard led his wife out of the drawing room and up to bed. As though exhausted, Dorothy soon quietened down and fell asleep, one arm under her head, her face exquisite. She looked like a child, untroubled, young. Finally, when he was sure she would not awaken, Leonard turned off the light and walked out.

It was only then that he allowed himself to think back over her words. And the fact that she had called him *David*.

Chapter Forty-Five

Hilly never knew that it was she who gave Alice away.

It was coming up to Christmas, the shops trying their best to look festive although everything was still on ration. Dressed in a new swing coat, Hilly hummed as she walked along, to catch the bus to Oldham town centre. She would go to Dudley and Proctor's, she thought. They would be sure to have the ideal present for Victor. It was worth the journey.

Sitting down in the only free seat, Hilly looked around the bus and nodded to a neighbour of hers. Then suddenly she was tapped on the shoulder. Turning, she saw a red-haired woman with a baby on her lap, two scruffy children sitting beside her.

'Hello there. Aren't you Hilly?'

She nodded, surprised. 'Yes, but I'm sorry, I don't know you, do I?'

Olive smiled. 'Not really. But we have a mutual friend, Alice. I saw you with her once.'

Put at her ease, Hilly smiled back. 'Oh, yes we've known each other for years. In fact, we're good friends.'

'So were we, once. But I've lost touch with her,' Olive said, her tone regretful. 'We moved from Oldham and I forgot to send Alice my new address. I know she moved on from Greenfields, but I don't know where to. Can you tell me? I'd love to see her again.'

Hilly was innocent, but she wasn't stupid enough to fall for the line. Alice hadn't wanted to keep in touch with *anyone* from Greenfields. In fact, she had been determined that no one should ever find her.

'I don't know where she went –'

Olive's eyes narrowed. 'You said you were good friends. You must be in touch with her.'

'Not for years,' Hilly lied, threatened. She felt suddenly like a child again, cornered. Her hands grew clammy as they held on to her basket.

Seeing that Hilly was not going to be tricked, Olive changed her tune. 'Alice was a good friend to me. I'd like to repay her for her kindness.'

Hilly didn't like the look of the woman, her baby crying on her lap, one of the other children picking its nose. She looked shabby, but worse than that, she looked sly.

As the bus turned a corner, Hilly got to her feet. 'This is my stop,' she said, lying clumsily. 'I have to go.'

'Fine,' Olive replied, smiling craftily as she watched Hilly clamber off the bus.

A moment later the bus moved on, Olive waving at Hilly through the window. Uncertainly, she waved back, relieved that she had not given Alice away by anything she had said.

But then she hadn't had to *say* anything. Whilst Hilly had struggled to her feet Olive had looked into her shopping bag and – by chance – seen some Christmas cards, ready to send. The top one was addressed to *Miss Alice Cummings, St Ursula's School, Salford*.

Olive smiled to herself. She was ready to bet that Miss Alice Cummings had been Miss Alice Rimmer. Humming a Christmas carol under her breath, Olive jiggled her baby on her lap. She was going to give Alice Rimmer a Christmas to remember.

Chapter Forty-Six

Pulling another face, Alice mimicked the sound of a pig, then an owl, then finally she stood up and pretended to be a wet dog, shaking itself dry. She was teaching the class how to communicate without using words, trying to draw them out by play-acting. It worked, the children giggling, then copying her. Laughing, Alice walked back to her seat and sat down – then noticed one of the children fast asleep at the back of the classroom.

She walked over, kneeled down and touched his shoulder. He woke slowly, blinking and looking around him.

'What . . . ?'

'Declan, are you tired?'

He nodded and rubbed his eyes, shadows mauve beneath them, his skin grey with lack of sleep. Alice had been watching him for weeks, noticing how he never mixed with the other children and seemed permanently exhausted. He was behind with his work as well, slow to learn.

'Don't you get enough sleep at home?'

He mumbled, 'I'm OK, honestly, I'm OK.'

Unconvinced, Alice approached Will Reynolds in the staff room later. His bristly black moustache was flecked with cigarette ash. He was sober, but only just.

'You've taught Declan O'Connell, haven't you?'

He knocked some more ash off his cigarette, his thumb and forefinger nicotine-stained. 'Had him last year,' he said, in a broad Yorkshire accent. 'Why?'

'He keeps falling asleep,' Alice went on. 'I wondered if he was ill.'

Will looked at her, his tone cynical. 'You'd not get much

sleep if your mother was on the game and brought her clients home every night.'

Alice sighed. 'Why didn't you tell me before?'

Once she would have been embarrassed, but no longer. Experience had taught Alice that this area of Salford housed many such families. There was no order to the slums. She had been to see some of the worst families, offered extra tuition to a couple of the brighter pupils, and argued with more than one parent who had kept their child off school. Sometimes it worked, but all too often it didn't. The child sided with its parents out of duty or fear – Alice could seldom make out which.

Why bother? It was hopeless work, Will had told her from the start, but Alice disagreed. If she managed to educate one slum child it was worth any amount of trouble.

'Forget Declan O'Connell,' Will went on, snatching a glance at Minnie Lomond, marking books on the staff-room table. 'He's a lost cause.'

'Oh, save it!' Alice replied shortly. 'There *are* no lost causes. Except you, perhaps.'

He blew her a mock kiss. 'I always knew you cared, boss.'

'It's a passion I fight daily,' she replied lightly. 'You pretend to be such a cynic, Will, and you're not like that at all.'

'I have hidden shallows.'

She laughed, punching him on the arm.

'Alice, I don't want to depress you, but your little crusade will fade out. Mine did. Everyone's does, here. We're voices crying out in the wilderness. It's very important to you now, but when you get married you'll move on.'

'But I thought *you* wanted to marry me, Will,' she said, teasing him. 'That's the only reason I've stayed here so long.'

He smiled, then pulled a serious face. 'Don't make this place your life, Alice. Don't waste yourself on children who'll never amount to much. The parents don't care, so why should you?' He leaned towards her. 'Get out whilst you're still young. Work's not everything. You don't want to end up an old spinster with no home of her own, do you?'

Overhearing him, Minnie Lomond looked up, her features sharp with bitterness.

'And what would a drunken sot like you know about anything?' she asked, her voice deadly. 'Your bloody brain's pickled, William Reynolds. And you can talk about getting married – there's not a woman in these parts who'd have you.'

Needled, he sidled over to the desk, looking down at her. She was plain, thin, still young and patently disliked him.

'I wasn't always like this.'

'I'd need to talk to your mother to be sure of that,' she replied smartly.

'I was the best pupil at teacher's training college. I could have done better than this.'

'Yeah, if you'd taken your head out of the bottle long enough.'

Normally Alice would have walked off and left them to it. They always bickered. But this time she watched them; saw Will's tense shoulders and Minnie's aggressive features – and winced. How *would* she end up? Sitting in some grim, green-painted staff room, smelling of dust?

Would the years go past outside the school walls and then, suddenly, would she look up and know that *her* time had passed? Alice swallowed. How long had it been since a man touched her? Too long. She thought of Victor, the warmth of their bodies together, thought of how she had burned for him. How he had ached for her. It had been beyond reason, beyond anything – but living.

Then she thought of Ray Berry, of his kindness, his determination to love her. Would any man love her again?

Shaken, Alice walked out into the corridor, deep in thought. Where had that girl gone, that reckless, high-spirited girl who had sneaked out into the town at night just to look at the streets? Where was she – that beautiful creature who had fought to keep her wildness controlled? Where was that *life*? That danger? That sensuality?

Was it me? Alice thought. *Was it really me?* She ran up the two flights of stairs to her own bedroom. Closing the door and locking it, she moved over to the mirror and looked at her reflection. A dark woman looked back at her soberly, her navy suit neat, her black shoes functional. The heavy wavy hair had been tied back, her face free of make-up. She was Alice Cummings of St Ursula's. Sensible, a woman who had her life in control. Respected even, not the excitable foundling who had been pushed around for so long.

Shaking her head, Alice turned away from the mirror. What was she thinking? She didn't want to go back to those giddy days. She didn't want to be at the mercy of her own emotions. God knows where they would have taken her. Her world was St Ursula's, her pupils were her children, her charges. She was useful.

She was lonely. Suddenly galvanised, Alice searched through the top drawer of her dresser, pulled out the second drawer and emptied it onto her bed. Her hands flickered over the objects frantically and then she found what she was looking for. Slowly, she walked back to the mirror and carefully applied an old, red lipstick onto her full mouth. Then she undressed herself, letting her clothes fall onto the floor, her naked body white in the daylight. Untying her hair, Alice shook it around her shoulders and, fascinated, touched her breasts.

Alice Rimmer came back to life in that instant. In one tantalising moment she looked soft and sensual, welcoming. A woman who had kissed and been kissed. A woman who would welcome a man. Staring blindly at her face,

Alice smiled. A cat smile, the smile of a beautiful woman who was fully aware of her allure.

Then the smile faded. Startled, Alice turned away from the mirror and pulled on her clothes, shaking with cold and surprise. What was she doing? What the hell was she doing? Savagely she scrubbed off the red lipstick. Her mouth swelled, her lips bruised as she rubbed away the colour and all trace of the woman she had once been.

The woman of whom she was so afraid.

Christmas was going to be difficult, Leonard thought. There would be days when he wouldn't be able to visit Frances, and that saddened him. She was so loving, so stable. No temperament there. He would miss her whilst he had to stay at The Dower House with Dorothy and the old man, playing at happy families. The servants would put up a tree and wrap parcels and the tiny family which was left would act as though Christmas meant something.

After Dorothy's outburst Leonard had waited for her to mention Alice again, but unpredictable as ever, she hadn't. It was becoming more and more difficult for him to cope with her moods, the sudden switches terrifying. He even suggested to Judge Arnold that they get a psychiatrist in to see her.

The old man was enraged. 'A bloody head doctor! No one in our family has ever needed someone like that.'

Leonard persisted. 'Dorothy is getting no b-b-better. She should h-h-have treatment.' He paused, wondering whether to say it. 'She called m-m-m-me *David* again the other day.'

The old man winced. 'I told you a long time ago that she was in love with Catherine's husband. She never got over it.'

'Well. She sh-sh-should have done! After all, it's b-b-been years. The m-m-man's dead. He must be – or s-s-someone would have found him by now.'

'I don't want to talk about David Lewes! It's all over

and done with. The man was a bastard who killed my child and then ran off like a bloody coward. Probably committed suicide somewhere. He was always weak. I never knew why Dorothy loved him so much.'

Leonard couldn't let the matter rest. 'She s-s-seems to be b-b-brooding on it more and m-m-more. She said the other day that D-D-David could still be alive.'

'Rubbish!'

'B-b-but what if he is?'

'He isn't! Of that I'm sure.'

'But she's g-g-going on as though he is. She's slipping back into the p-p-past.' Leonard persisted, cursing the stammer which made eloquence impossible. 'I think Dorothy's getting really ill. I'm w-w-worried about her.'

'Dorothy was always highly strung!' Judge Arnold snapped. 'You know that. She's just tired, that's all.'

But Leonard was not about to be fobbed off. He was dreading Christmas and the uncertainty of Dorothy's behaviour. And he missed Frances already.

'M-m-medication might help her,' he persisted.

'My daughter doesn't need medication!' Judge Arnold retorted hotly. 'She needs a supportive husband.'

Stung, Leonard sprang to his own defence. 'I've always b-b-been supportive.'

'To your wife or your *mistress*?' the old man countered, his aim deadly.

Colouring, Leonard looked away.

'Oh, I know all about her! Nothing escapes me. I have known about her for a while. It doesn't matter – as long as Dorothy doesn't find out. If she does, Leonard, she'll *really* be ill. And it will be all your fault.'

'Why? Dorothy n-n-never loved me!' Leonard snapped. 'Any wife who can c-c-call her husband by the n-n-name of her former l-l-lover –'

'David Lewes is dead!'

'How d-do you know for sure? She acts as though

he was alive,' Leonard shouted. 'I think she s-s-still loves him.'

'And why not? Why wouldn't she prefer him to a stuttering fool like you?'

Leonard reeled. 'David Lewes k-k-killed your daughter! He k-k-killed his wife!'

'He was provoked,' Judge Arnold replied, his voice cold as slate. Then he turned away, leaning against the mantelpiece. 'Catherine was always hounding him, hanging around him, baiting him. Especially after Dorothy told her sister that she was in love with David.'

The words stopped Leonard in his tracks.

'*Why would she do that*? In G-G-God's name, why?'

'I told you a long time ago, Catherine was always jealous of her sister. And Dorothy played on that. They were rivals from childhood. The trouble was that Catherine turned vicious when she knew that David and her sister were lovers. I don't know what happened that night, but I always thought that Catherine *drove* David Lewes to kill her because of Dorothy's involvement with him.'

'N-n-no wonder she's unbalanced,' Leonard said, his tone sharp. 'Why d-d-didn't you tell me this before? I should h-h-have known about this long ago.'

The old man shrugged, his head down. 'Which father would admit that his child engineered her own death?'

'You r-r-really think that Catherine *wanted* h-h-her husband to kill her?'

'How do I know?' Judge Arnold snapped, still formidable even in old age. 'Time passes and things get less clear. It would have been the perfect revenge on Dorothy, though, wouldn't it? What a thing to have to live with for the rest of your life – your own sister's murder.' He sighed. 'You think you know what happened, but after you think about it over and over again you're not so sure. I loved my daughters, but I knew they were difficult, complicated women. I should have sent Dorothy away as soon as I suspected something was going on with her and David Lewes. I was to blame. It was my fault.'

The confession caught Leonard off guard. 'What happened to D-D-David Lewes? You know, d-d-don't you?'

Judge Arnold shook his head. 'Not for sure. But personally I think he died soon after the murder. There was a body found in the Manchester Ship Canal, but it was too decomposed to identify.'

'But you never t-t-told Dorothy this?'

'Did I hell as like! And I don't want you to tell her either.'

'But if she knows David Lewes is dead, she m-m-might forget him.'

To his astonishment, Judge Arnold burst out laughing.

'*Forget him*? Are you *that* big a fool, Leonard? If she knows David is dead she'll give in. You think she's unstable now – well, you have no idea what she would be like if she knew the truth.'

'I d-d-don't understand,' Leonard replied, baffled.

'Of course you don't! But you know your wife isn't in love with you, never has been really. You must have wondered why, Leonard. Even *you* must have wondered why that was.'

He was stung into anger. 'How can you b-b-be so sure that you know all about my marriage?'

'Because my daughter tells me everything,' Judge Arnold replied smugly. 'I know her better than anyone. Much better than you'll ever know her. There was always the possibility she was unbalanced by the murder. Then when Robin died I thought she'd go over the edge.' He paused, weighing Leonard up. 'I keep my daughter sane *because I understand her*. She'd lost a sister and a son, so when she started talking about David Lewes again, I let her. Better to live in a fool's paradise than give in.'

'But she has m-m-me,' Leonard said helplessly.

'Exactly,' Judge Arnold sneered. 'Not much, is it?'

'B-b-but she's living a lie!'

'Dear Leonard, don't you know that that's how most people live? Like you. Your marriage is a lie. You have a mistress you love far more than your wife. Be honest now – man to man – if this family hadn't been so rich, so good for your continuing fortune, would you have *stayed* married to Dorothy?'

The question was distasteful, as was the unspoken answer.

'I thought so,' Judge Arnold replied, turning away from his son-in-law. 'Well, whether you approve of it or not, I'm keeping my daughter alive the only way I know how. The memory of David Lewes keeps her going. That's the one thing I can thank him for. The *one* thing he did of value.'

Leonard walked up to the old man, beside himself.

'And I'm s-s-supposed to stand around w-w-whilst my wife loves a g-g-ghost?'

'You've done well enough out of his family, Leonard Tripps! You've got more money and power than you could ever have achieved yourself. I even turn a blind eye to your mistress – but if you ever leave Dorothy, or tell her the truth about David Lewes, I will kill you. I'm an old man with nothing to lose. Wherever you ran to, I'd find you and I'd kill you. Remember that.' He tapped Leonard's shoulder with his hand paternally, his voice softening. 'We're a family. We keep our own secrets. You married into us and now you have to stay with us.'

Leonard could feel his mouth dry. He might be old, but his father-in-law was as powerful as ever. Stupidly, he had underestimated him. There was to be no future with Frances, Leonard thought hopelessly. His future was locked into the Arnolds, tied to The Dower House for ever.

And it was his own fault. He had wanted power and he

had got it. It was too late to go back. The price he had paid was higher than he could ever have imagined. His father-in-law was ruthless, without conscience, and his wife was in love with a dead man.

Chapter Forty-Seven

When Alice called round at Trafalgar Street that evening, she found Hilly packaging some Christmas parcels on the kitchen table. Alice took off her coat and threw it over the back of a chair, then, smiling wryly, she took the ribbon from Hilly's hands.

'Here, let me. You never could tie ribbons.'

Hilly stood back, smiling too. 'You used to spend hours trying to teach me. I was always a lousy pupil ... I saw Ethel this morning, she said you were going to spend Christmas Eve with them. Where are you going Christmas Day?'

Alice finished tying the bow and then stepped back to admire her handiwork. 'I'm not sure yet.'

'Good, you can spend it with us then.'

Alice pulled her face. 'You don't want me around. Have Christmas on your own.'

'We're hardly newlyweds!' she said, gently mocking. 'I want you to come.'

Alice put her head on one side quizzically. 'What's up?'

'Why, should there be something wrong?'

'You look different,' Alice said, staring into Hilly's face.

To Alice's surprise, Hilly turned away. 'I want to talk to you.'

'That sounds ominous,'

Taking a deep breath, Hilly sat down, her hands on her lap. 'Funny, it's not as easy as I thought it would be. I kept running it over in my head earlier and I thought I had it all worked out, but now it's going to be difficult.'

'*What* is, Hilly?'

She looked up, her eyes huge, fringed with long pale lashes. 'I'm ill.'

Shaken, Alice sat down beside her. 'Is it bad?'

'Yes,' Hilly replied, all icy calm. 'I went to see the doctor yesterday afternoon. I hadn't been feeling well for a while, but I thought it was just too much excitement. I thought I was tired, that was all. But then I started to feel worse and I saw Dr Michael. You know him – he has a practice up on Westfield Street, next to –'

'I know where he is, Hilly. What did he say?'

'That I was sick . . . Oh, why can't I just come out and say it? I'm not going to be around for much longer.'

'No!' Alice replied emphatically. 'The doctors were wrong before, they can be wrong again. If we'd believed what they said years ago, you wouldn't be here now. Besides, everyone knows that Dr Michael's a blundering old fool.'

Hilly tapped the back of Alice's hand and pulled a face.

'Not this time. This time it's bad. I need you to help me, Alice . . . Oh, I know you always have. You were the one who looked out for me at Netherlands, the sick kid in the sanatorium that no one else gave a damn about.' She paused, resting her head against the back of her chair. Her skin looked tightly drawn over her features, the loss of weight apparent. 'You were in love with Victor then, weren't you?'

'Hilly, that's all in the past.'

She studied Alice's face carefully. Was it *really* in the past? 'It still hurts, doesn't it?'

'Some things always hurt. But this isn't the time to talk about it –'

'It's the *perfect* time,' Hilly replied with certainty. 'I've been thinking very seriously, ever since yesterday evening. We have to plan this, Alice, plan it to help everyone in the best way possible.'

'Plan what?'

'When I die Victor will be lost; he won't know how to cope. I know I rely on him, but he relies a lot on me too – more than he thinks. He won't be able to make sense of things when I'm gone.' She paused. The daylight was fading, the room growing dimmer. Firelight played along her cheekbones and the pale line of her eyebrows. 'I want you to look out for him –'

Alice cut her off. 'Hilly, you have to see another doctor.'

'Oh, the time for doctors is over,' she replied, exhausted by the topic. 'I know what's going to happen and the only way I can bear it is if I make things right beforehand. I love Victor too much to let him suffer. And I love you, Alice. A long time ago you were in love with him –'

'We were children then, Hilly. It was different.'

'No, it was more than that. You and I both know that it was no flirtation,' she said, her breathing laboured.

Her weariness surprised her, coming so suddenly. Within days she had gone from being tired to being exhausted. Even the slightest effort left her breathless. Panic had followed. If it was to be so soon, she would have to sort things out quickly, have to put her life – what was left of it – in order. And Victor's. Just give me enough time, she prayed, just a little longer.

'Victor loved you very deeply, Alice. He still loved you after he married me. But I was lucky – in the end he grew to love me more. But I know his feeling for you is still there. Don't get me wrong, I *want* it to be.'

'Hilly, don't –'

'Oh, hear me out!' she replied, uncharacteristically impatient. 'There's not much time. When I'm gone I want you two to get together again.'

Alice shook her head. 'I'm not going to talk about this any longer,' she said, her voice wavering. 'You're going to see another specialist, Hilly. We'll find someone who can do something.'

'I'm not seeing another specialist,' Hilly replied calmly,

'and I want you to sit down and shut up for once. *Listen to me*. I *have* to talk to you. I always relied on you in the past and now I have to again. I don't have the strength to do this alone. *I need you*.' She tightened her grip on Alice's hand. 'I never achieved very much, but I've been a good wife. Well, now I need to find my husband a new partner – and you're that person.'

'Hilly, listen to yourself,' Alice said gently. 'You can't plan things like this. Life isn't like that; love can't be manipulated.'

'No, but men can,' Hilly replied phlegmatically. 'God, for a clever woman, Alice, you certainly are stupid about men. Victor will need someone's shoulder to cry on – and I want it to be yours. I don't want some other woman to move in on him when he's vulnerable.' Hilly looked up, almost exasperated. 'You still love him, I know you do. Look at me! Tell me you don't still love him.'

'I love him like a brother.'

Hilly tapped her on the shoulder. 'Now look at me and say that again . . . Oh, Alice, I know you. You wouldn't love him any other way whilst I was around. But soon I won't be.'

'I can't let you go,' Alice said suddenly.

'You have no choice.'

Hilly was scared, but afraid to admit it. Now, at night, when she closed her eyes she wondered if she would wake. Or where she would wake. Was there a Heaven, a Hell? Where would she go? And to go alone, without Victor . . . The long night hours lying next to him passed so slowly, with only her thoughts for company whilst he slept. She hadn't asked for much in life, only her man, and she hadn't had him for long. Not that long.

Not long enough to see him grow old. They had never been on holiday even – never been enough money, but she hadn't minded, and the Christmases had always been so good. Every year Victor had brought home a fir tree and put it in the window: 'It's the biggest tree in Trafalgar Street,' he'd say. 'An angel could land on the top, no problem.'

They had grown to know each other so well. Maybe that had been the blessing of beginning as friends, then developing into lovers. No other man would have held her when she was sick, Hilly thought, no other man would have rubbed her back and brushed her hair when she was in pain. Victor had been her guardian angel – and suddenly she couldn't bear the thought of leaving him behind.

'I'm scared,' she admitted quietly.

Alice squeezed her hand.

'I need to leave this life knowing that the people I love are safe.'

'Oh, Hilly –'

'Yes, "Oh, Hilly",' she repeated gently. 'Poor Hilly, who never had that much . . . But I did.' Her eyes shone. 'I had a wonderful life. Because I got the right man. The years pass quickly, Alice, remember that. You think you'll live for ever, but it's over so soon. So soon . . . Take Victor. Take the opportunity I'm offering you.'

'Hilly, I have the school –'

'And when you retire, then what? Who'll be there for you then? Your pupils will be grown up with their own families; they won't have time for you. If you're lucky they might come to call on you once in a blue moon, go to see their poor old teacher because they feel sorry for her. But they won't *care* about you.'

'I never thought you felt sorry for me.'

'I don't, because you have the chance to salvage something precious. How many people can say the same? I'm giving you my blessing, Alice. I want you to love Victor. Look how easy I'm making it for you. Now, make it easy for me.'

She *couldn't* really be dying, Alice thought. They had been saying that Hilly was seriously ill for years and yet she had always recovered. She would this time too. And yet there was a difference in Hilly's face. She *was* moving on – only this time she was moving on alone.

Sighing, Hilly moved her position in the chair, her hand gripping Alice so tightly her fingers whitened.

'I want you to marry Victor when he asks you.'

'He may not ask me.'

'Of course he will! Love doesn't die of its own accord. But if we're fools, we kill it.' She smiled conspiratorially, her eyes bright in the firelight. 'I was never clever, but I was good at love. Really smart, in my own little way. I look at Victor when he sleeps and think, *This is my man*, and it's quite a feeling. I came from nothing, Alice. God knows where I'm going, but no one can take my marriage away from me. Or the love I have for him. When I'm gone . . .' she put her hand gently over Alice's mouth to silence her, 'when I'm gone, tell Victor that his wife adored him, will you? I can't seem to find the words. Tell him I always loved the Christmas tree in the window. *The biggest one on Trafalgar Street.*' Her eyes closed. 'Tell him to keep putting one up every year, bigger and better, so his angel can land on it.'

Chapter Forty-Eight

Checking her reflection for the third time, Olive McGrath smiled. It was important that she looked the part – not like some no-hoper that no one would take any notice of. So she had borrowed a suit from her sister in Huddersfield and dumped the kids on her next-door neighbour – in return for a home perm next week – and made her appointment with the governors of St Ursula's.

The suit was a bit tight, but it would be OK if she left the jacket open, Olive thought, staring at herself in the mirror. Before she had had the kids the damn thing would have hung off her. Still, no point thinking about the past, she had other matters to attend to. Like Alice Rimmer.

Or Alice *Cummings*, as she liked to call herself now. Probably thought no one would find her if she changed her name, but Olive had found her. By accident admittedly, but she had been lucky there. Which was more than that bitch was going to be . . . Olive smoothed her hair down, spitting on her palm and trying to make it look tidy at the back.

It didn't matter to Olive that St Ursula's was a dump, a ragged school filled with the rubbing rags of the slums. What mattered was that Alice was running it. Olive had found that out by asking a few questions in Salford. Oh yes, people knew Alice all right. Thought she was a wonderful woman, so caring. *D'you know, she even goes down the slums like Docker Row and takes on the fathers?* someone told her admiringly. *That takes guts. The bloody coppers only go down there in threes. Such courage for a woman, and a good-looking one at that; she could had have her pick of the men if she'd gone another way.*

An hour after setting out, Olive was in Salford, walking towards St Ursula's and then making a right turn at the back gates. She was worried that she might run into Alice, and hoped she would manage to tell her story to the governors before their paths crossed. Pulling down her jacket over her hips and breathing in, Olive rang the bell.

A worried-looking, portly man answered, showing her into what seemed like a seldom-used office. At a worn desk sat two other men, one thin and hard-looking, the other never once meeting Olive's gaze.

'Sit down,' the fat man said, showing Olive to a seat opposite the table. 'I'm Mr Appleton, this is Mr Falmer, and this is Sir Herbert Jordan. You wanted to come and have a word with us I take it?'

Olive nodded. 'It was good of you to see me. I know you must be busy –'

'The governors of St Ursula's are always busy,' Mr Falmer said shortly. He didn't like the look of the hard-faced redhead in front of him and wanted to get the whole complicated business out in the open. 'What do you want to tell us?'

'I believe a Miss Cummings runs St Ursula's?'

Mr Appleton nodded. 'She has been principal here for some four years, since Douglas Schofield was moved on. She's done a good job too.'

'Well, she's not quite what she seems,' Olive said, shifting in her seat, but relishing the moment. 'Alice Cummings isn't her real name, for a start.'

Sir Herbert Jordan stared at her and then took off his glasses, coughing under his breath. Meanwhile, the expressionless Mr Falmer studied Olive. He was automatically suspicious. Was this just another sacked employee trying to settle an old grievance?

'What is her real name?'

'Alice Rimmer.'

'How do you know that?' he asked coldly.

Olive found herself unexpectedly cowed. 'We worked together once. She was up at Greenfield, with me. I was a teacher there . . .' She paused waiting for the reaction, but no one seemed the least impressed. 'Well, anyway, Alice had a past – and it came out.'

'This all sounds very dramatic,' Mr Appleton said nervously, smiling as though he didn't want to believe a word she said. 'And what kind of *past* does Miss Cummings have?'

'She was involved in a child's death.'

All three men winced at the words, Mr Falmer staring hard at Olive. 'That's a very serious allegation, madam. I hope you can substantiate it.'

'It was common knowledge!' Olive blustered. 'She was working for the Arnolds –'

'Of Werneth Heights?' Sir Herbert asked. 'I used to know the family quite well. What did you say her name was?'

'Alice Rimmer. She was looking after Robin, the grandson of Judge Arnold – and he died in her care.'

Sir Herbert turned to Mr Falmer. 'I remember something about this. It was a long time ago, a tragedy. The boy had been neglected by the nanny they said. His mother was out of her mind with grief –'

'No, wait a minute,' Mr Falmer replied, his sharp face alert. 'There was a follow-up to that. The Arnolds' doctor came forward and said it wasn't negligence, that there had been something wrong with the boy all along.' He tapped the table with his forefinger. 'The doctor was called . . . Oh, what *was* his name? Priestly, yes, that was his name, Dr Guy Priestly.'

Olive didn't give a damn about Guy Priestly, she just wanted to know what was going to happen to Alice.

'But the boy's mother thought it was Alice Rimmer's

fault. And if it wasn't, then why didn't she tell you about it when she came here?' Olive paused, her face sly. 'You didn't know about it, did you? And why would she hide it unless there was some truth in the matter?'

'And what business it of yours?' Sir Herbert asked, his thick hands fingering his watch chain. 'What have you got to gain by exposing this woman, Alice –' He looked over to Mr Appleton for prompting.

'Rimmer!' Olive said impatiently. 'Alice Rimmer.'

'Yes,' Sir Herbert said, 'Alice Rimmer. What's in it for you, madam? If you pardon my vulgarity.'

Nettled, Olive looked down at her hands. 'I just thought you should know about her. I mean, if she's in charge of children at St Ursula's, she should be above suspicion, shouldn't she?'

Mr Falmer narrowed his eyes. The woman was right and yet he disliked Olive McGrath enough to want to make her uncomfortable. Of course the matter was serious – why had Miss Cummings changed her name? And why had she never mentioned working up at Greenfields? When she came to St Ursula's she gave everyone to understand that she had no previous experience. So why had she lied?

Sir Herbert was thinking along the same lines. He didn't doubt for one moment that Olive McGrath's humanitarianism extended only to settling an old score, but the matter had to be investigated. It was different before the war – time was when they had been glad to get anyone to teach at St Ursula's, but things had changed. Now there were governing bodies, do-gooders who wanted to make sure that places like St Ursula's were monitored. Oh no, Sir Herbert thought, he would certainly have to look into the allegation; show that he had his finger on the pulse. Besides, he was up for election as mayor soon. It was imperative to make an example of the woman – and show his dedication to the education of the working class.

Meanwhile plump Mr Appleton was watching the cogs turn in Sir Herbert's brain and thinking of Miss Cummings. She had worked miracles at St Ursula's. The school, which used to be a byword for slatternly teaching and incompetence, was transforming. She cared so much about her pupils that she spent her own time protecting their welfare. Not one child was considered too stupid or too poor for her to bother with.

And just exactly where would they ever find a woman like that again? Mr Appleton thought. If Miss Cummings – or whatever her name was – left, they would be forced into hiring someone else, possibly some monstrosity like Douglas Schofield. Oh, Sir Herbert might fool himself into thinking things had changed, but they hadn't changed *that* much. St Ursula's was a slum school for slum children, in a slum area. They would be lucky to get *anyone* to work there.

'Mrs McGrath, what else do you know about Miss Cummings –'

'Miss Rimmer.'

Mr Appleton signed. 'For the time being we will continue to refer to her as Miss Cummings. Now, what else do you know about her? Why did she leave Greenfields?'

Olive swallowed. She hadn't been prepared for an interrogation, thinking the governors would simply take her at her word and banish Alice. But now *she* was the one on the spot.

'There was a rumour going around about the Robin Tripps child. She left Greenfields when people found out about it.'

Mr Falmer looked up from his notes, his narrow face hostile. '*How* did they find out?'

'Someone told the principal.'

'Ray Berry?'

Olive nodded, too choked to speak for a moment. Finally she said, 'You know him?'

'Oh, yes, I know him,' Mr Falmer replied. 'Are *you* still teaching?'

'No, not now. I have three children to look after, and I'm a widow.' Olive played the sympathy card. 'My husband was a war hero.'

Like hell, Mr Falmer thought.

'So why did *you* leave Greenfields, Mrs McGrath?'

'What?'

'I asked you why you left Greenfields. You see, it seems to me that you know a lot about Miss Cummings – so maybe you have taken it upon yourself to *protect children's interests* before? Perhaps it was *you* who told Mr Berry about Miss Cummings?'

'I never –'

'Come now!' he said sharply. 'You're not going to tell me that you didn't, are you?'

'I was doing it for the right reasons!' Olive blurted out, leaning forwards, the borrowed skirt tight over her stomach. 'It wasn't right for her to be around children.'

Mr Falmer's face was impassive. 'Did Ray Berry fire her?'

Olive laughed, replying without thinking, 'Hardly! He was in love with her! He would *never* have fired her. He wanted to promote her. And marry her. You think she's such a saint? Well, whilst she was educating the poor kids by day, she was warming the headmaster's bed by night . . .' She trailed off, her face crimson against the red hair. 'Not that that has anything to do with it –'

'I would say it has a lot to do with it,' Mr Falmer replied acidly.

'I'll say it does. I mean, is the woman moral? We need people who set an example,' Sir Herbert said pompously.

Giving him a sidelong look, Mr Falmer waited for him to speak again.

'I mean, aside from her . . . acquaintance with Mr Berry

. . . *why* did the Cummings woman lie? Why *didn't* she tell us about her past? It looks shifty. Very shift indeed.'

Olive was trying hard not to appear triumphant. It had been touch and go back there for a while, but she was sure that Sir Herbert was on her side.

'Maybe she just wanted to move on.'

Sir Herbert shook his head at his neighbour. 'No, no, that's too pat. Too pat. We should call the woman in and ask her what she's playing at –'

'She's playing at making this school less of a hovel!' Mr Falmer barked.

Mr Appleton clapped his hands together urgently. 'Come now, gentlemen, let's not lose our tempers. We should sort this out in a calm manner.'

'I'm not saying another word in front of that woman!' Mr Falmer replied, pointing at Olive whose flush was now turning her neck scarlet. 'I know her type. Always causing trouble because they're jealous –'

'I beg your pardon!'

'You should!' Mr Falmer snapped back.

Sir Herbert glided between them. 'Mrs McGrath, we want to thank –'

'Hah!'

' – thank you for your interest. The matter will be dealt with in due course.'

'Alice can't stay on here though, can she?' Olive said, suddenly panicked. 'I mean, you have to get rid of her.'

'Like Ray Berry got rid of you?' Mr Falmer said. It was a guess, but it was deadly accurate.

Getting to her feet, Olive walked to the door. She was indignant, outraged.

'I came here in good faith,' she said piously. 'Alice Rimmer shouldn't be allowed around children. She's a menace. If you keep her on here, I hope you can live with your consciences.'

Sneering, Mr Falmer looked Olive up and down. 'You

hope *we* can live with our consciences? Probably a lot easier than you can live with yours, madam.'

It was late in the afternoon when Dr Priestly called up at Greenfields to see Ray. Yawning, he got out of his car and stretched his arms, then walked in through the gates. He was tired; it had been a long day. And now this. He thought of the letter he had found waiting for him in his surgery that morning.

> Dear Dr Priestly,
>   It has come to my attention that a certain teacher in our employ – a Miss Cummings – was known to you as Miss Alice Rimmer. Apparently you were acquainted with her when she worked as a nanny for the Arnold household at the time of Robin Tripps' death. You then were reacquainted with her when she found work at Greenfields Sanatorium.
>   We would like to talk to you, as a matter of some urgency, concerning this lady. Perhaps you would telephone me at the above number.
>   Yours sincerely,
>   Mr Giles Falmer

The address and telephone number were private. There was no hint of where Alice was working.

Dr Priestly had read the letter again and then picked up the phone. After a moment he'd put the receiver down. Why should he telephone this Mr Falmer at his request? Perhaps there was more to this than was immediately apparent. Perhaps Mr Falmer had been in touch with Ray Berry too.

Knocking loudly on Ray's office door, the doctor walked in. Ray was sitting at the desk looking into a magnifying mirror.

'What are you doing?'

'I've got some grit in my eye!' Ray barked. 'Can't get the bloody thing out.'

'Let me look at it,' Guy said, staring at the pupil and then stepping back. 'Nothing there any more. You must have scratched it. Bathe it with salt water and it'll settle down.'

'Thank you, Doctor. How much does that set me back?'

Guy smiled and sat down, crossing his tweed-clad legs. 'I had a letter today about Alice Rimmer.'

He thought that Ray was going to drop the magnifying mirror. '*Alice*? What about her?'

'I think she might be in trouble,' Guy said, certain from Ray's reaction that there was still affection there. 'Some man called Falmer wrote to me.' He pushed the letter over the desk to Ray. 'Go on, read it.'

A few minutes later, Ray looked up. 'What the hell does this mean? She changed her name? God, no wonder I could never find out where she went. And this man's address is in Salford – d'you suppose Alice is working there?'

'Probably. It's a long way away from Oldham or Werneth Heights. A good place to hide – especially if you've changed your name as well.'

Ray stared at the letter and then looked back to his old friend.

'You know about the Arnolds at Werneth Heights?'

Guy leaned his bearded face towards Ray. 'Yes, and I know about Robin's death. I saw how Alice was made into the scapegoat. I heard all the rumours spread by Dorothy Tripps and it was me to tried to scotch them after the post mortem.' He paused, seeing relief in Ray's eyes. 'I believe Alice. She loved that child, she would never have hurt Robin.'

'And you never thought to tell me the story when Alice came here to work?'

Guy hesitated then shook his head. 'No, I didn't. I

thought that Alice deserved a fresh start and I didn't want to jeopardise her chances. She had had enough people putting spokes in her wheels.'

Cautiously Ray said nothing. Did Guy know the rest of the story? That Alice was related to the Arnolds? That the reason she loved Robin so much was that he was her cousin, her own flesh and blood?

'What else?'

Guy shrugged. 'Nothing really. Alice went away. Well, she was *driven* away from Werneth Heights by Dorothy Tripps and all the gossip – and then she came here. Then that bitch Olive McGrath exposed her to you.'

Ray looked back at the letter. 'Looks like someone else can't stop dragging her through the mud.' He fingered the paper thoughtfully. 'Why did you show me this, Guy?'

'Because you still love her.'

'That obvious, hey?'

'The girlfriends you've had over the last few years were a good cover, but I know the truth, Ray. You fell in love with Alice and you've never forgotten her, have you?'

He shrugged. 'To tell the truth, I don't know any more. If you'd asked me that question this morning, I would have said that I was over her. And yet when I hear her name and read that letter and know that someone is out to get her – then I can't stop the feelings. I love her, yes. But I don't want to. I don't want to miss her. But I do. I don't want to think about how she left me. How she hurt my pride . . . But yes, I love her.'

'Well,' Guy said, his voice resigned, 'you're buggered then, aren't you?'

When Guy Priestly phoned Mr Falmer he was asked to attend a meeting at St Ursula's in Salford. *St Ursula's*, he thought, what a dump. Surely Alice wasn't working there now?

'I'm one of the governors of the school,' Mr Falmer

went on, 'along with Mr Appleton and Sir Herbert Jordan.'

Herbert Jordan! That puffed-up windbag, a born politician, Guy thought. 'What's the meeting about?' he asked.

'We want to call Miss Alice Cummings – or Rimmer – whatever her name is to explain herself. I have to tell you now, Dr Priestly, I personally think that Miss Cummings has done a wonderful job at St Ursula's. She runs the place now, has done for years since the last principal left under a cloud, but Sir Herbert seems hellbent on making a spectacle of her.'

'Courting votes,' Guy replied coldly. 'He wants to be mayor, doesn't he?'

There was a snort down the phone. 'This isn't about Sir Herbert –'

'Then why tell me he was being antagonistic?' Guy countered. 'If you need someone to vouch for Alice, I will.'

'Thank you, doctor. Your medical knowledge will also be useful. And we need a character witness for Miss Cummings.'

At once Guy seized his chance. 'What about Ray Berry? He was her old employer at Greenfields.'

'More than an employer, I heard,' Mr Falmer said grimly.

'Whatever you heard, it wasn't how you're making it sound!'

'So you wouldn't say that Miss Cummings has rather loose morals?'

'Don't try to use that as a stick to beat her with!' Guy replied heatedly. 'Ray Berry was in love with Alice, but she never used that as a lever to get what she wanted. In fact, quite the reverse. She could have been Mrs Berry now, running Greenfields with Ray – but she chose not to, and it's your gain that she came to St Ursula's.'

Surprised by the vehemence over the line, Mr Falmer altered his tone. 'You appreciate that we have only heard one side of the story –'

'And whose side was it?' Guy countered, his temper sparked. 'Although I think I could make a guess.'

'A Mrs Olive McGrath –'

'Hah!' Guy shouted. 'That bloody woman is eaten up with jealousy. She wanted promotion at Greenfields and was furious that Alice was going to get it instead of her. To try to discredit Alice she went creeping off to Ray Berry and told him all about Alice's background. That blasted redhead was responsible for Alice leaving Greenfield.'

'But why *did* she leave, Dr Priestly? If she had nothing to hide, why run away?'

Guy paused, cautious. He did not know how much of Alice's background Falmer knew and was not prepared to divulge anything.

'Why don't you ask her?'

'I intend to,' Giles Falmer replied. 'That's why the Governors wish to call a meeting. We want to confront Miss Cummings with what we have been told and listen to what she has to say. That's why we would like you to attend, Dr Priestly, and that's why we would like someone to stand as a character witness for Miss Cummings. Ray Berry will do nicely.'

It was dark when Alice arrived at Trafalgar Street. Hilly answered the door smiling.

'Come on, we're going out,' said Alice.

Hilly frowned at her. '*Out?* It's past six.'

'I have a surprise for you. Tell Victor you're going out with me, then he won't worry,' Alice answered. 'And get yourself wrapped up warmly, Hilly. Go on! Hurry up.'

Linking arms, they walked down the street, passing Lettie Booth, who waved through the window and then carried on sewing. She wore even thicker glasses now. Her husband was cutting out a dress pattern on the table – and cutting through the table cloth at the same time.

Grinning, Alice hurried Hilly along, hailing a bus at the High Street.

'Where *are* we going?' Hilly asked, her hair covered by a woollen hat, her hands in thick gloves. She was losing weight, now frail, but her eyes were bright with interest. 'Come on, Alice, where are we going?'

'We're doing something mad,' she replied mischievously. 'Something completely crazy.'

'Oh God,' Hilly sighed, slipping into silence.

But she was intrigued. Alice was lit up, like her old self. It felt good sitting next to her on the bus seat, Alice tapping her toe with impatience. Her hair was loose around her face, her skin glowing with the cold air. Suddenly Hilly's mind went back to Netherlands, to a young girl who had come sneaking into her sickroom at night, a girl who had lain next to her on the bed and stared up at the ceiling, talking out her dreams. This was the Alice she remembered of old.

'Where are we going?'

'You'll see,' Alice replied. 'It's somewhere you like.'

Together they rode the bus, until Alice pulled Hilly off at Park Road, Oldham. As the bus drew away, they looked at each other, Hilly putting her head on one side quizzically.

'What on earth are we doing here?'

In reply, Alice looked her up and down. 'Are you sure you're warm enough?'

'Sweltering,'

'Good,' Alice said simply, leading Hilly through the gates of Alexandra Park.

The lamps were lit, illuminating the various curling pathways, the huge stone lions glowering in the semi dark. In silence, Alice steered Hilly down a narrow pathway and then paused.

'Look.'

Hilly's eyes fixed on the scene in front of her. It was her

favourite place, the place where Victor had taken her the day he proposed. The place she had come as a child on one of her rare outings from Netherlands. It was magic to her, fairyland. The park lake was twinkling under the lamplight, the place deserted, the water still and dark as velvet.

Hurriedly, Alice flicked on a torch and then guided them towards the lake.

'What *are* you doing now?' Hilly asked, laughing and watching in astonishment as Alice pulled a boat out from its hiding place behind the boating shed. 'Oh, Alice –'

'Come on! Hurry!' Alice urged her. 'Before someone stops us.'

Hilly stared, mouth open.

'Come *on*!' Alice repeated.

'But we *can't* take a boat out at night!'

'Why? Who'll know? Hurry up, Hilly. Get in!'

Without another word, Hilly climbed into the boat, the water lapping around its brightly painted sides. Then she watched, mesmerised, as Alice felt under her seat and drew out a large cardboard box.

'What's in that?'

Smiling slyly, Alice took off the lid and took out a flask and some wrapped sandwiches. Then she set out some candles and lit them, the pockets of light flickering on the water and shining up into Hilly's face. She looked for a moment like a child caught up in the magic.

With sure strokes, Alice rowed the boat out into the middle of the lake and then lifted the oars in. The silence around was absolute, their whispered voices darting like fireflies over the water. Laughing, Alice poured out some tea for both of them and then handed Hilly the sandwiches, the candle flames shuddering as she moved.

'This is perfect,' Hilly said at last. 'Thank you.'

Alice raised her mug in mock salute. 'I thought we'd have a picnic.'

'At night?'

'No crowds,' Alice replied, smiling. 'Are you warm enough?'

Hilly nodded. 'You keep asking me that. I'm fine.' Her glance moved across the water, memories flooding in.

The smell of the hot tea and the warm bread seemed sweet to her, the thought of Victor unbearably moving. This was her special place, and Alice knew it . . . Sighing, Hilly smiled at her, Alice smiling back with her eyes. They both knew that there was only a little time left.

'There'll be a ruckus if we get caught.'

Alice shrugged. 'Why should we? Besides, even if someone sees us, they're hardly likely to swim out to capture us, are they? The water's freezing.'

'You're in a good mood.'

'I *feel* good,' Alice admitted, surprising herself. 'Suddenly I feel content. It might not last, but tonight I think that the world's kind.' She glanced at the lit pathways on the shore. 'We could stay here for ever, Hilly, just you and me. Nothing could touch us.'

Hilly smiled indulgently. 'We'd run out of food.'

'We could catch fish.'

'In Alexandra Park?'

Alice pulled a face. 'Well, maybe we could beg people to throw things to us from the bank?'

'I could sing for our supper.'

'Then we'd starve.'

Alice could feel the gentle rocking motion of the boat, and smell the sweet water. For a moment she wanted nothing more than to stay there, suspended in that moment. Hilly would never die and nothing would ever change.

They would just rock on the water for ever and ever, two foundlings huddled together under an indifferent moon.

Chapter Forty-Nine

It was two days later that Alice was called to see the governors. She was teaching and suddenly a message came, via Jilly, that she was wanted. Surprised, she left the class in Jilly's care and walked out into the corridor. There were few signs of neglect indoors. St Ursula's might still look grim from the outside, but inside the floors were scrubbed and polished and the distempered walls had been whitewashed. Posters and drawings that the children had made were pinned up along the corridors and pasted on the high windows. The kids liked to see their handiwork displayed – it seldom was at their homes – and Alice had seen to it that above their coat hooks were printed labels with their names on. Often it was the only thing a child had of its own.

Alice checked the formal black worsted suit reflected in a window, and smoothed her hair, neatly tied back into a French plait. Then she walked towards the staff room where the governors were assembled.

Entering, she stopped dead. They had rearranged the room, moving the staff table to a central position where the three governors sat positioned behind it, like JPs behind the bench. To their right was Dr Guy Priestly.

Dear God, Alice thought, why was he there? It could only mean trouble; he knew so much about her. And yet, Alice thought, he hadn't betrayed her before, so why would he now?

'Please, take a seat,' Mr Appleton said, embarrassed.

Sitting down, Alice looked at her hands to try to steady her nerves.

The harsh voice of Mr Falmer was the next to speak.

'Some allegations have come to light. For one, that your real name is Alice Rimmer.'

Alice's head jerked up at the ghost name, the shadow woman who never really went away.

'That's true.'

Sir Herbert glowed at the admission. The woman was a liar: time to bring her to book.

'You admit it then?'

'Yes.'

'So why did you change your name?'

'Circumstances,' she replied, keeping her gaze averted from Guy Priestly.

Sir Herbert leaned forward. 'Someone has informed us that you used to be the nanny for Robin Tripps, grandson of Judge Arnold.'

Robin. Alice could see him in her mind's eye, the turn of his head, the way he tried to wink at her for mischief. Robin, her charge, Robin, her cousin. Robin, her flesh and blood.

'I was his nanny, yes.'

'There was a rumour that you were negligent.'

Guy was on his feet in an instant, his quick temper flaring. 'I told you, she was *not* responsible! The night Robin died, Alice asked for me to be called out again, but his mother overrode her wishes. It was not Alice's fault, and she was not negligent. Robin Tripps had a heart condition which was discovered on post mortem. In all likelihood, he would never have survived long past childhood.'

Sir Herbert sniffed, Mr Falmer turning to Guy with a curious expression.

'What *kind* of heart condition, Dr Priestly?'

'Does that matter?'

'It might. I know we're not doctors,' Mr Falmer replied, 'but I would appreciate it if you would humour us.'

Guy took in a breath, obviously irritated. 'Robin Tripps

had a congenital heart defect which proved to be fatal. Possibly it's a condition which passes down the female line in his family.'

Mr Falmer had lost interest, but Alice was transfixed in her seat. *Robin had a condition which might be passed down the female line. A fatal condition.* And that meant that *she* might carry it. That she might pass it on to any offspring of her own.

She bowed her head, Sir Herbert misreading the action.

'You do well to hang your head, young lady. This is very serious.'

Guy was outraged. 'Don't you listen? I've just explained the situation! Surely even an idiot could see that Alice changed her name to protect herself from scandal?'

'But she was still called Alice Rimmer when she went to Greenfields after leaving the Arnolds' employ. Why was that?'

'If you knew Greenfields, Sir Herbert, you wouldn't have to ask,' Guy said irritably. 'It's a world of its own. No one mixes much with the townspeople. And they don't have time for gossip – usually. But Olive McGrath –'

Stung, Alice looked up at the name.

'– was always jealous of Alice. Jealous because she was the better teacher and up for promotion. Jealous because she was popular and because Ray Berry had fallen in love with her. If Alice Rimmer had been ordinary, she could have stayed hidden away for years. You wanted to know why she went up to Greenfields? Because she thought that she'd picked the place most people would shun.' He paused. 'Have *you* been up there, Sir Herbert?'

The last comment was an obvious barb and found its mark.

'Dr Priestly, I should remind you that you are supposed to be here to *help* Miss Cummings.'

Alice wasn't reacting to anything being said around her. All she could think of was Robin, a heart condition she might carry, and the fact that Dorothy Tripps' accusation – although false – was upturning her world again. She thought of Dorothy, of the sly slow smile, the instability, the craftiness. And she hated her.

Mr Falmer asked the next question: 'Why did you change your name when you came to St Ursula's? And why did you not tell us about Greenfields?'

Alice didn't hear the question. She was stupefied by what she had just learned.

'Miss Cummings, please answer,' Mr Falmer said shortly.

Alice looked up. 'What?'

'Can you explain why didn't you tell us about Greenfields?'

There was a momentary hesitation. Alice looked from one man to the other and her anxiety suddenly gave way to fury. They were questioning her as though she was a criminal, putting her on trial. And she was tired of being judged.

'Tell you about Greenfields?' she said bitterly. 'You want to know? Well, I'll tell you everything, gentlemen, everything you want to know. I was born Alice Rimmer and I was abandoned at Netherlands Orphanage. I worked for the Arnolds in Werneth Heights. I looked after Robin, and I did my best for him.' They were all listening, Guy sitting down and staring at her. 'He died in the circumstances Dr Priestly described, but Robin's mother, Dorothy Tripps, used me as a scapegoat. She was a vicious liar who tried to ruin me.' Alice paused, to let the words have effect. 'So I ran away to Greenfields and I worked my way up, teaching. When I was exposed at Greenfields, I left.'

'Why?

'Why *what*?' Alice replied, her fury obvious.

They could do what they liked with her – drop her, throw her out, who cared? She would cope, she always had . . . Her thoughts turned back to what Guy had said.

Did she carry the medical defect too? If she had had children, could she have passed on it? And then she thought of Dorothy Tripps, lying, conniving Dorothy.

'Why did you leave Greenfields, Miss Cummings?'

Her eyes blazed. 'Ray Berry had done such incredible work up there – he didn't need anyone to soil his achievements. And I would have done, wouldn't I? If I had married Ray, people like you –' she glanced at the three of them in turn – 'would have judged me like you are doing now. *What's she like? What's she done? Did she have an affair with the principal before she married him? Is she moral? One of us?*' Her voice was molten. 'Well, I'm *not* one of you. And I don't want to be. You're hypocrites! You're moralising, sanctimonious asses!'

'How dare you?' blustered Sir Herbert.

Alice turned on him furiously. 'Because it's true! When I disinfected your school, scrubbed your walls, cleaned up your slum children, it was *Thank you, Miss Cummings*. As long as I stayed where I belonged, where you thought you could bully me, then I was doing a good job. After all, it wasn't a place any of *you* would have wanted to work, was it? All right for the likes of me, but not you.'

Hardly breathing. Guy glanced at the three governors and then he noticed the door open behind Alice and Ray Berry walk in, pausing just inside the room.

Mr Appleton was staring at Alice. 'We have to ask these questions –'

'So ask!' she snapped. 'I've nothing to hide any more.'

'Were you and Mr Berry anything other than employer and employee?'

'Yes,' she said, tossing her head back.

'You were going to get married?'

Guy held his breath, Ray transfixed behind Alice.

'We might have married. If things had been different. But when my past was exposed, I ran away. I thought he would be better off without me.'

Nervously, Mr Appleton tried a question: 'But why change your name?'

'So I could be doubly sure that no one would know me, no one would find me. After all, gentlemen, who from Oldham, Greenfields or Werneth Heights would come to a place like St Ursula's? I admit that I lied to you about my name. I lied to you about my past, but I had reason to. I was afraid that someone would spoil things for me again. And I was right. They did, didn't they?'

Looking over to the doorway, Sir Herbert saw Ray standing there and snapped, 'We're in a meeting!'

Surprised, Alice turned, saw Ray, but then turned away from him.

'It's Ray Berry,' Mr Falmer explained to Sir Herbert. 'It's good of you to come.'

'*Why* did he come?' Sir Herbert asked curtly.

'As a character witness,' Mr Falmer replied.

'Seems to me that he may well be biased.'

Ray winced. 'Biased enough to know that if you fire Alice, I'll give her a job tomorrow at Greenfields. She was the best teacher I ever had.'

'And more –'

Ray's eyes flickered. 'Sir Herbert, as a political animal you should know when to talk and when to keep your mouth shut.' Out of the corner of his eye, he could see Giles Falmer smile. 'I can say no more than that I would trust Alice with my life – and the life of any under my care.'

Wrong-footed, Sir Herbert blustered. 'No one said anything about firing Miss Cummings ... Miss Rimmer – whatever she's bloody called!'

He was frantically backtracking. It wouldn't look good for him to be seen penalising the woman who had done so much for St Ursula's – a woman who appeared to be guilty of little more than provoking jealousy. That McGrath woman had been the one who had caused all the trouble – and what did her word count against the likes of Ray Berry and Guy Priestly?

But Ray was not about to be mollified. He had heard what Alice had said and was suddenly galvanised. Maybe she still cared about him. Maybe she would come back.

'Alice has had more than enough bad luck. She deserves her second chance. I suppose I can guess who stirred things up again – Olive McGrath?'

'Mrs McGrath was trying to help –'

Mr Falmer cut across Sir Herbert immediately. 'She came to us with a story we had to investigate. Speaking for myself, I feel that there is nothing more to be said on the matter. Miss Cummings is welcome to stay at St Ursula's, if she would like.'

Alice's voice was deadly. 'Maybe I *wouldn't* like.' Ray touched her arm, but she shook him off.

'Maybe I'm tired of doing the dirty work. Tired of visiting sluttish parents who don't care if their children learn or die ignorant. Do you know what the Salford child-mortality rate was last year?' she asked Giles Falmer, then turned to Sir Herbert. 'And what about incest? Have I shocked you, Sir Herbert? I'm so sorry, but you see incest, prostitution, venereal disease, homelessness, drunkenness, violence – that's the currency of my world. That's what I deal with at St Ursula's daily –'

'I think you've said enough!'

'Not nearly enough!' Alice snapped back at Giles Falmer. 'You want an upright, moral woman without a stain on her character – well, good luck! I hope you find her. But let me tell you, gentlemen, you wouldn't get a woman like that to walk through the doors of St Ursula's. I can work there, and endure it, because I came from Netherlands, in the slums. I understand those children, because I see myself in them. I admit I lied to protect myself and my own interests – I imagine every one of you has done the same, not in slum schools, but law courts, council chambers, in your private clubs and homes.'

Sir Herbert was grey-faced with outrage. 'You have no right to speak to us this way!'

'I have every right! And I've only just realised it. We live in a free country, and that means free for everyone.' Her voice hardened. 'You won't break me, or make me apologise. Those days are over. From now on the only person I have to explain anything to is myself.'

With that she rose and, without speaking, left the room. Ray hurried after her.

The day was overcast, threatening rain as Alice moved down the staircase and out into the yard of St Ursula's. She heard Ray call for her, but kept walking away towards the viaduct, moving back against the wall when a lorry roared past her.

'For God's sake!' Ray snapped, catching hold of her arm. 'Do you want to kill yourself?'

He was pale, confused, the lines around his eyes more pronounced. Do I look so much older to him? Alice wondered.

'Alice, come back to Greenfields with me. I'll look after you, keep you safe. You don't want to stay here.'

'I don't know *where* I want to be!'

'There are children up at Greenfields who need you,' Ray insisted. 'You can do more there. There's money, facilities. I've raised more funds now; you could do what you liked.'

'Greenfields is yours.'

'It could be *ours*!' he snapped, then softened his voice. 'I never stopped thinking about you. I thought I would, I tried to, I really did. There have been other women, but they weren't you.' Alice moved off, but he ran after her. 'I can't get you out of my blood! You're in me. Everything and everyone is nothing to me if you're not there.'

'I can't come back,' she said, turning to face him. 'There's no future for us, Ray.'

'Why not? Can you honestly tell me that you don't feel anything for me?'

'Ray, just hold on for a minute,' she said, confused. 'There's so much to think about. I can't just jump back into a relationship with you. I have to work my life out –'

'Work it out with me.'

'I can do it myself!' she replied heatedly. 'Stop trying to take care of me, Ray. I can take care of myself. I have done for years.'

He hung back, stung. 'I think you love me, Alice. I think you always did. You just couldn't let yourself believe it. I can make you happy.'

'But can I make you happy?' she countered. 'You know me, you know what I'm like – a loose cannon. Is that what you really want? Anyway, you heard what Dr Priestly said – Robin died of a condition passed down the female line. I'm part of the Arnold family. If Dorothy passed it to her son, I might well carry the same defect.'

He shook his head. 'I don't care. I don't want children. We *have* children, Alice. Hundreds of them. Pupils, kids who need us, children who are sick or poor – why do we need more of our own?' He gripped her arms. 'Don't walk away from me again. *Please*, stay with me. We can work together, make a difference. Think about it! Apart we have done so much, what could we do as a team? Don't tell me about your past, Alice; don't use that as an excuse this time – I know all about it.' He paused, looking at her and holding her gaze. 'I'm the *only* person who knows everything about you. And now ask yourself – have I ever betrayed you?'

'No,' she admitted, 'never.'

'And I never will. There's only one place on earth which is safe for you.' He touched his heart, then took her hand and rested it against his chest. She could feel the rhythmic heartbeat.

'It's not that easy, Ray.'

'What isn't?'

'Life isn't,' she replied, then smiled wistfully. 'I gave them hell in there, didn't I?'

'No more than they deserved.'

'I was angry –'

'You were incredible.'

'Oh, Ray,' she said, touching his cheek gently, 'we weren't meant to be a couple. It wouldn't work. I once said that I thought I was unlucky for you, remember?'

'I remember. But I didn't believe it then, and I don't believe it now. You are unlucky *without* me, Alice. And I am unlucky without you.'

Part Four

You have been mine before, –
How long ago I may not know:
But just when at that swallow's soar
Your neck turned so,
Some veil did fall, – I knew it all of yore.

Dante Gabriel Rossetti,
'Sudden Light'

Chapter Fifty

The weather had changed suddenly for the worse, catching Ethel out as she came back from town, her coat drenched, her woollen hat brim out of shape. She was more annoyed about the waste of a good hat than the fact that a day later she was in bed with a severe chill. As someone used to looking after people, she made a bad patient. Gilbert – unused to the change in role – made endless cups of tea and fussed around her.

'It's freezing up here,' Ethel grumbled, pulling a cardigan around her bulk as she sat up in bed. Sneezing, she blew loudly into a handkerchief. 'Don't come too close, Gilbert, we can only have one patient at a time.'

He smiled tolerantly. 'Do you want me to fluff up your pillows?'

She grunted. 'Nah.'

'What about having a look at the paper?'

'It's a full of the Nuremberg trials. *Trials!* I'd try them with a bullet! As for that Goering – I heard he wore women's clothes. I ask you, the man's sick in the head.' She shifted her position, her legs moving under the mountain of blankets.

'We'll go and see *Brief Encounter* when you're better –'

'I hate romances!' Ethel replied irritably. 'And besides, you talk about Ada, but you're deaf. You can't hear a flaming word they say.'

He sighed and then pushed the tray over to her with his arthritic hands. He had made toast – slightly burned – and tea – slightly weak.

Ethel eyed it suspiciously. 'You'd never have made a

nurse, Mr Cummings,' she said, winking. 'I'd have been fired if I'd given a patient that.'

'Well, if you don't want to eat, look at the paper,' he urged her again. 'It'll take your mind off things.'

Sighing Ethel looked round. 'You seen my glasses?'

He shook his head. 'I thought you had them.'

'If I had them, I wouldn't be looking for them!' she said, sneezing three times. 'God, I hate being ill.'

'No one would have guessed,' Gilbert said wryly. 'Maybe you're sitting on your specs.'

'If I was sitting on them they would be no good now, would they?' She felt under her. 'When I get rid of this bloody cold, I'm going on a diet.'

'Nah,' Gilbert said, tweaking her cheek, 'I like you plump.'

'I was plump, now I'm fat,' she replied, sneezing again. 'An old fat lady with a snotty nose.'

'And red eyes,' Gilbert teased her. 'Don't forget the red eyes.'

She gave him a sidelong look. 'I suppose you think you're some kind of Lothario?'

'I've had my chances,' he said archly.

'Oh yeah?' Ethel replied, her voice nasal. 'With whom, may I ask? No, don't tell me, Enid Warburton.'

He pretended to be thinking of her and sighed. 'Ah, Enid, what a girl –'

'She was fifteen stones if she was a pound,' Ethel replied, still feeling round the bed for her glasses. 'She married and buried two husbands. Probably rolled over on them in bed.'

'What a way to go,' Gilbert mused, Ethel bursting out laughing and throwing a pillow at him.

'Of course, I could have had a fling or two myself.'

'I bet you could.'

'I could, I'm telling you,' she said, still searching the bed for the lost spectacles, then pushing Gilbert to one side as she felt around the eiderdown. 'There was Gilbert Cummings, for one.'

'Or you could have married Sol Wakeman.'

She sneezed loudly. 'Or Harold Fernshaw. He was a nice bloke – but he had a crazy father, pity that. Oh, move over, Gilbert, I can't find my specs if you're sitting on them.'

He got off the bed and then, kneeling down painfully, felt under it.

'Nothing here.'

'I can't think where I put them,' Ethel replied, blowing her nose again. 'And I can't read a bloody word without them.'

'Hey,' Gilbert said suddenly, 'I knew I had something to tell you. I bumped into Ernie Cox yesterday and he told me something you'll never believe. He looked bad, but didn't say if he was poorly –'

Ethel raised her eyebrows. '*What* did he tell you?'

'It was about Evan Thomas.'

Galvanised, Ethel sat up, wheezing. 'What about that toerag? I've not heard a word about him since Netherlands closed. That was a sly bugger. If you shook hands with him you had to count your fingers afterwards.'

'Ernie said that he was dead.'

'Nah, I bet he's faking it.'

Gilbert nodded vigorously. 'Yeah, he's dead all right. He was thieving at a jewellery shop in Wales and dropped off the roof when he was trying to escape.'

Ethel eyes widened. 'Well, I knew he was a bad 'un, but out and out thieving . . . He must have been a bit old for that. No wonder he bloody slipped.' She paused, thinking back. 'Well, well, well, Evan Thomas, with all his swank, so smarmy, so sure of himself. A real snake. But who'd have thought he'd have ended up like that? Still, at least he had the decency to go back to Wales and die.'

Gilbert sat down on the bed again and glanced at the

morning broadsheet. 'Well if you can't read the paper and you won't listen to the radio –'

'It gives me a headache –'

'– we'll have to talk instead.'

She stared at him, smiled at the familiar ageing face. 'We've been married for nearly fifty years, Gilbert Cummings, what the hell have we got *left* to talk about?'

'The kids?'

'Boring,' she teased.

'The grandchildren?'

'Boring.'

'Politics?'

She gave him a burning look.

'OK, not politics,' Gilbert agreed. 'What about the past?'

'I've been there.'

'D'you remember when we met?'

Sneezing again, Ethel cursed under her breath and then leaned back against the pillows, wheezing.

'You were supposed to be marked down for my sister. She was so annoyed with you when you took me out,' Ethel mused. 'You came round on a Saturday in a starched collar which rubbed your neck raw. My father swore they were rope burns.'

'It was a bugger, that collar,' Gilbert agreed. 'You were wearing a lilac dress with little lace cuffs, your hands peeping out. I thought you were the most beautiful girl I'd ever seen.'

'Apart from Enid Warburton, that is?'

'She was never in your league,' he said gently, touching Ethel's cheek. 'When you laughed you had two dimples – there and there.' She rested her head against the palm of his hand. 'And the day we went out for the first time you were upset about your mother having lost her bird.'

'Aye, Gilbert, fancy you remembering that,' Ethel replied, touched.

'We went looking for the bloody thing all around the town – that was before it was built up so much and there were still fields. I kept calling, "Billy, Billy," and felt a right fool.'

Her eyes misted. 'I thought you were wonderful. There's not many men who would have gone out calling for a budgie.'

'I wanted to impress you.'

'You did,' Ethel said softly. 'We went back later that night and had tea at my house. My dad was off work and cleaning out the coal shed. It was a hot day, wasn't it?'

He nodded. 'Hot day and hot evening. We sat on the back step of your parents' place, talking until after midnight, and then your father came down and shooed me off home.' Gilbert paused. 'But I never went home that night.'

'You what?'

'Nah, I was in love,' he admitted, flushing. 'So I just wandered around, looking at the stars and thinking about you and those little lace cuffs ... When I finally *did* get home – around dawn – my mother was waiting for me and gave me a thick ear as I walked in.'

Ethel laughed and then took his hand. 'I was so slim then, so pretty. I've changed.'

'Nah,' Gilbert said, touching her cheek again. 'You've got a bit of upholstery on you, but that's what you've got to expect. You got bigger because you had our kids, and because you had to work hard and eat to keep yourself fit. But it's made no difference to me, and never will. I'll tell you this, our girl, no one could have had a better wife. Yeah, you were pretty and little when I met you – but I like you big, Ethel. It gives me more to love.'

Trafalgar Street was dim with rain and cold under a threatening winter sky. November had come round again, Anna Hope watching her husband snooze in his chair. Although past retirement age, he was still working part time for the council, still name-dropping and pretending to be important, both Hopes still certain that they were a cut above their neighbours.

In fact, Mrs Hope was surprised that the impressively stupid Booth family was still living in the street. Surely the man was unemployable? He had had more jobs than was decent and was a well-known menace. His stupidity had cost many a firm money. Only the other month he had gone to work for the council in Salford park gardens and managed to pull up every newly planted cutting. He thought, he explained later, that they were poor-looking little things, obviously weeds.

Age did not dim his stupidity. Neither did it slow down his wife. Somehow they had managed to keep the old sewing machine going and Lettie Booth worked it all day and some of the night. Unfortunately – as it was old and exhausted – every fifteen minutes it made a juddering noise before it righted itself. In the daytime the sound was hardly audible, but at night Mrs Hope lay in bed, her teeth clenched, as she waited for the intermittent gasping of Lettie's machine.

Sighing, Mrs Hope glanced at her husband again and then heard noises from next door. The Coateses were moving about! she thought delightedly, turning her wheelchair and gliding noiselessly over to the wall. Checking that her husband was still asleep, she then slid the hidden glass from behind a large photograph, pressed it against the wall, and put her ear to it, sighing with pleasure

At that precise moment, Lettie was trying to teach her husband how to sew. Jug-eared Terence was looking at the machine with what passed, for him, as interest, his head bent low down over the Singer.

'It's simple, Terry,' she coaxed him. 'You just feed the material under the needle. Easy.' Always eager to encourage her husband, she slid off her stool and let Terry sit down. 'Now when you're ready, you just put your foot lightly on the pedal and the material will go under the needle and get stitched.'

'How do I get it out again?'

'You lift the needle and pull it out. When you've cut the thread.' She smiled, pleased to see that he was taking notice. No one had any idea how smart Terence really was; they always misjudged him. 'Now, go ahead, slowly put your foot down on the pedal. You have to drive it.'

It would have done Lettie some good if she had remembered Terry's ill-fated attempts to drive the cart for the brewery. He was, people were never slow to point out, the only man who had backed the beer cart into the canal – horse and all.

'Go on, Terry, have a go.'

He did, putting his size twelve down on the pedal, the machine giving a disgruntled snort, like a horse mounted by an unfamiliar rider.

Blinking behind thick glasses, Lettie watched her man. The cloth was running nicely under the needle, his hand guiding it smoothly through. He was a natural, she thought, seeing visions of Terence making bridesmaids' frocks by the dozen.

Unfortunately he then put his foot down a little harder – the material running under the needle as quickly as a rat up a drainpipe.

At once, Terence panicked.

'Take your foot off!' Lettie shrieked, the machine growling and chewing up the cheap cotton. Into the machine went the sleeve of Mrs Little's youngest daughter's dress, Terry mesmerised by the flashing of the needle going up and down, up and down.

'Terry, take your foot off the pedal!' Lettie shouted again. 'Please, luv.'

But he was too caught up with the drilling needle and the sudden – and ominous – sound of the Singer's machine barking. To the astonishment of both of them, it then reared up unexpectedly, like a bucking bronco, Terry's foot slipping off the pedal as the sewing machine continued alone across the living-room floor.

Finally it stopped. Terry looked at Lettie and Lettie looked at Terry. The machine was muttering to itself, the needle dribbling thread, the remaining part of Mrs Little's youngest daughter's dress sleeve mangled under the metal plate.

'Oh, Terry,' Lettie said simply, her husband turning to look at her.

'Have I killed it?'

'It's a machine, Terry, you can't kill a machine.'

She regarded it thoughtfully, then moved closer. The Singer was silent, malevolently quiet. Gingerly she nudged it with her foot. Nothing. Then she touched the pedal, the needle coughing a couple of times and then juddering to a halt.

'I can fix it,' Terry said happily.

Lettie moved quickly between her husband and the injured Singer. Putting up her hands, she smiled wanly.

'No, my dear, no, you go and have a pint with your friends. This is women's work, after all.'

'But I was just getting the hang of it –'

'Really, Terry, leave me to it.'

'OK, if that's what you want,' he said happily, moving to the door. 'If you have any trouble just give me a call.' He winked. 'We make quite a team, don't we?'

Next door, Victor and Hilly had heard the commotion and been laughing. The machine was silent for once. Victor said it was almost sad. They were sitting up in bed, Hilly having retired early because she was tired. She had been getting a lot weaker lately, but seldom referred to her condition and had never let Victor know how serious it was. It was just weakness, she'd told him, you know how feeble I am at times.

'Not a sound,' Victor said, jerking her head towards the partition wall. 'The Singer appears to have sewn its last frock.'

Hilly giggled. 'We couldn't get that lucky. They'll have it mended, they have to. The only money that comes into that house is what Lettie makes with her sewing.' She rolled over onto her side, her head cupped in her hand as she looked at Victor's profile. 'I do love you.'

'What brought that on?' he asked, surprised.

'I just wanted to say it.'

He studied her tiny face, the long fair lashes, and thought her some pretty elf. Something real and not real at the same time.

'I love you too, Hilly. I always will.'

'As long as I'm here.'

'What kind of a thing is that to say?' he asked, suddenly alerted. 'Are you all right?'

She wasn't sure how much to tell him, but she had to say something. For months she had managed to dodge the issue but before long he would guess. Because there wasn't that much time left. The doctor had told her that she might die quickly, within weeks, and Hilly had asked him if she would deteriorate physically. 'You see, I don't want my husband to know until the end. I want to spare him . . .' The doctor had replied that Victor *would* know before the end came. Sorry, he said, but it was unavoidable.

So Hilly's quandary was – should she tell Victor now, and give them time to say the things they wanted to say? Or should she wait and hope that she had enough time later?

'Hilly,' Victor repeated, 'are you all right?'

She was tiny in her nightdress, her neck as slender as the top of a man's arm. 'I'm not well,' she admitted at last.

His eyes fixed on hers. 'Is it bad. Hilly?'

'Not good,' she said quietly. 'I didn't want to tell you, but I didn't want to go suddenly –'

He put his hand over her mouth and leaned towards her.

'Don't say it. If you don't say it, it can't happen.'

Gently she moved his hand away. 'It *will*, darling,' she said. 'We have to accept it.'

Shaking his head, Victor sat up.

'No, we don't! We'll go and see another doctor. Plenty of doctors. We'll sell the business and go to see a specialist abroad. We'll live abroad, that'll help you. You need warmth and sun –'

'I have leukaemia,' Hilly said quietly, watching Victor take the word in and react by putting his hands over his ears.

'No. NO!'

Immediately she pulled his hands away. 'Aren't you worried that you might miss hearing something doing that?'

'I don't *want* to hear anything else, Hilly,' he replied. 'I don't believe it. I won't let you go.'

'You can't stop it. It's out of both our hands.' She paused, then tucked her nightdress around her knees. 'We've been so lucky –'

'LUCKY!' he exploded. 'How can you say that?'

'Because we have. We found each other, we've been so happy. How can I not think that was lucky?'

'And now you're leaving me – how lucky is that?' Victor asked, brokenly. 'Jesus, Hilly, you're my life. Tell me what to do, tell me what I can do to save you.'

She held out her arms and he folded against her body, his head against her heart.

'I can hear your breathing, Hilly. You're alive.'

'And so are you, but your heart will go on beating long after mine, Victor.' Her arms tightened around him. 'I know you love me – thank you for that – but don't stop living when I do. I couldn't bear that.'

He was sobbing against her, his hands balled into fists.

'Don't Hilly, *don't.*'

'Victor, shhh, listen to me, listen to me, darling,' she said, her tiny frame like a child's in the large double bed. 'I want you to promise me something. I want you to marry again –'

He jerked upright. 'What are you talking about?'

'Not straight away,' she teased him, 'I want you to miss me a bit first. But after a while, Victor, please marry again. Please don't get bitter and be alone.' She pulled him towards her and rested her cheek against the top of his head. The smell of wood chippings and polish came like a perfume to her and her heart turned. 'Alice is alone, and you will be alone.' She held on to him as he winced. 'You loved each other once, you can again.'

'I don't want to talk about this –'

'Of course you don't,' Hilly replied. 'Neither do I, but I have to. You see, I have to look after you now, just as you've always looked after me. It's my turn to be the strong one. When I was a child, Alice protected me; when I grew up, you protected me – well, now I have to stand on my own two feet. Because this is something I *have* to do alone.'

He stared at her, his eyes reddening. 'Hilly, please –'

'Victor, my darling, my love.' She stroked his hair, his face. 'My dearest husband – how I've loved you. How I've thanked God every day for you. I've been so happy – don't let all that go to waste. Don't miss me so much that you can't love again. That wouldn't be worthy of you.' She kissed him gently, her lips cool on his. 'When I'm gone –'

'No.'

'Ssssh,' she urged him. 'When I'm gone, love again. I love you and Alice more than anyone else in the world. You were the only two people I ever had. We three came from the same place, with the same fears – only you and I found each other, but Alice is alone. You loved her once. Take my blessing, Victor, and love her again. When the time comes, love her again.'

Chapter Fifty-One

The November chill came in full blast, Guy Priestly hurrying towards his car and clambering in, rubbing his hands together as he started the engine. The snow had started early, falling on the high ground of the moors and working itself down into the valley. Before long he knew that Oldham and Salford would be hard into the frost, and the bleak heights of Greenfields would be more unwelcoming than ever.

He'd get himself home, Guy thought, and have a whisky to warm himself. Slowly he edged down the steep road towards Oldham, driving carefully, the wipers making arcs in the snow-covered windscreen. With luck his housekeeper would have a hot meal waiting for him, and with a bit more luck no one would call him out to deliver a baby or write a death certificate. He would go to bed early, get some sleep in.

He braked as a rabbit darted suddenly across the road. Cursing, Guy started the car moving again and headed home to Dobcross. Thirty-five long minutes later he got out of his car and hurried into his house.

Mrs Clough was waiting for him in the hall. 'Hello there, Doctor, how was your day?'

'Hell,' he said simply, picking up a stack of messages and flicking through them. 'The roads are terrible, snow's falling and it's going to freeze hard. What's this?' he asked, showing her a note.

'You had a call about an hour ago from that gentleman.' She looked at the paper. 'Mr Leonard Tripps. He said he wanted to see you and that it was urgent.'

Guy raised his eyebrows and stuffed the note into his pocket. 'What's for dinner?'

He was tempted not to return the call. Certainly he wasn't going to venture out on a night like this. A long time ago Guy had told the Arnolds that he would have nothing more to do with them. He was no longer their family doctor, so why had Leonard Tripps suddenly contacted him after so many years?

Having lit his pipe, Guy poked the fire in the grate and stared into the flames. He was glad he had never married; it would never have worked. He wasn't that keen on women – found them too complicated, too exhausting. Give him a good case of croup and he was fine, but women left him baffled.

He thought then of Dorothy Tripps. That was a complicated woman, he thought, just the kind to make a man mad. Her face rose up before him unbidden, the strange slow smile, the lightning changes of mood, the brilliance of her eyes. Guy then thought of her sister, Catherine. They had been very similar, only eighteen months between them. Catherine had been beautiful, but troubled, jealous of her elder sister. Why she should have felt jealous, Guy didn't know; on the few occasions he had seen her Catherine had seemed a beauty to him.

It was natural that Guy then thought of David Lewes, so adored, and then so maligned. God, what a shadow to fall over anyone's life, he thought. No wonder Dorothy was unstable. Of course, Judge Arnold had tried to take care of everything. It was wise to take the family away for a few years, wise to attempt to put distance between themselves and The Dower House. But then why did he bring his daughter back?

Stretching, Guy rubbed his neck and glanced round, looking for where the draught was coming from. Stuffing an excluder behind the door, he then regained his chair and turned his thoughts back to the Arnolds. Why did

Leonard Tripps want to see him now? Whatever the man said, he wasn't going to treat the family again, especially not Dorothy.

The phone rang suddenly in the hall outside. It stopped, then after a few moments Mrs Clough came into the snug.

'It's Mr Leonard Tripps again. He would like a word with you.'

'Did you say I was home?' Guy asked shortly.

'Well . . .'

Irritated, Guy leaned over to a side table and picked up the extension. 'Hello, Dr Priestly here.'

'This is Leonard T-T-Tripps. I w-w-would like to see you.'

'What about?'

'It's p-p-private.'

'Can't you tell me over the phone?' Guy asked impatiently.

'N-n-no.'

'All right, why don't you come over to see me in the morning?'

'Dr Priestly, this is important. I n-n-need to see you at once.'

'Is someone ill?'

'No. I-I-I'm calling f-from the office.'

'Then it can wait, Mr Tripps –'

'It c-c-can't. Please, w-w-whatever you think of us, hear m-m-me out,' Leonard said emphatically. 'I'll be round in h-h-half an hour.'

It actually took Leonard nearly an hour to get from Werneth Heights to Dobcross, the roads were so bad. Inching along, he wound down the car window and stuck his head out to see the road more clearly. At last, tired and cold, he came into Guy's snug.

Taking off his right glove, he extended his hand.

Guy took it with little enthusiasm. 'So, what's so important, Mr Tripps?'

418

Sitting down, Leonard accepted the offered whisky and unbuttoned his coat.

'It's about D-D-Dorothy. You know w-w-what time of year it is. This t-t-time is always b-b-bad for her.'

'I understand. If she's getting upset, I suppose you want to have her sedated?'

Leonard glanced up. His hair had greyed, his face ruddy. But his eyes had lost none of their keen intelligence.

'It's n-n-not that. D-D-D-Dorothy has it in m-m-mind that she wants t-t-to see Alice Rimmer again.'

That *was* new. 'I would have thought that she'd be unable to look her in the face,' Guy said bluntly, 'after what she did to her.'

'My w-w-wife has just told me all about h-h-how she lied. She t-told me that Alice wanted to c-c-call you out again that night and that she had lied when she said Alice was n-n-negligent. Robin's d-d-death wasn't her fault.'

'I've known that all along,' Guy said bitterly. 'I was the one who tried to undo the damage your wife caused. You have no idea the pain your wife's accusations cost Alice Rimmer. She was hounded because of them, and now you say that your wife wants to see her. Why?'

'I d-d-don't know for sure,' Leonard admitted, 'but I have to f-f-find Alice Rimmer. This h-has b-b-been on my w-wife's m-m-mind for months now, she s-says.'

'So why come to me?'

'I thought you might know w-w-where she was. You st-st-stuck up for her; I thought you m-m-might still be in touch.'

Guy studied Leonard Tripps carefully. He wasn't sure if he was telling the truth, or lying. *Why* did Dorothy want to see Alice again? To apologise, or what? And would Alice want to see *her*?

'I might know where Alice is –'

'Tell me, p-p-please.'

Guy smiled sardonically. 'You belong to a very rich

family, Mr Tripps, you have a great deal of power. But not over me, or over Alice Rimmer. I *will* contact her and let her know what you said. If she chooses to get in touch, she will. But I will not let you have direct contact with her.'

Leonard blinked, but knew he was snookered. Guy Priestly was not a man to push around. What he had suggested would have to do.

'If you w-w-would contact Alice as soon as you could,' he said, 'I w-w-would be grateful.'

Guy stood up, indicating that the meeting was over. Surprised, Leonard finished his whisky and followed Guy to the door.

'Oh, and Mr Tripps, I warn you – if you make trouble for Alice Rimmer again, you won't get away with it. She was a nobody before, with no protectors. She's a woman of stature now, with support. Remember that, won't you? That's if you – or your lady wife – ever feel like bullying her again.'

'Dr Priestly, I c-c-can assure you –'

'Mr Tripps, if you will forgive my saying so, your assurances count for nothing.' Guy opened the door in Leonard's astonished face. 'Good night.'

Chapter Fifty-Two

When Leonard returned to The Dower House he parked the car in the converted stables at the back and then walked round to the front door, letting himself in. The hall was lit by two standard lamps, light also coming from under the library door. Upstairs he could hear footsteps and a far-off radio playing a dance tune. It sounded mournful, sad.

For the first time for years he looked at the surroundings where he had lived for so long. This was his home, or was it? Actually it was Judge Arnold's home, the place where, many years earlier, Leonard had moved in to live with his wife. But it was not *his* home, not a place he had bought and furnished to his own taste. He was just a lodger, paying his way by running the businesses.

Silk damask wallpaper lined the walls, the floor was black and white tiles. Paintings of ancestors, and others bought from auctions in Manchester, looked at him gloomily, as if they too wished to be somewhere else. Leonard glanced up the staircase, at the suit of armour on the landing. Armour, he thought, how apt, how typical of Judge Arnold.

The days of believing that things would change were over, Leonard knew. There was to be no happy ending with Frances, no little nest in which to end his days. He was locked into The Dower House and Dorothy, just as he was locked into the business. And who was to blame? No one. It had been his own choice.

But the choices one makes as a young man and the choices one makes later are different, Leonard decided. His wife's instability and the looming presence of the old man hadn't seemed too unbearable before, but now he was older, they was insufferable. He was slower too, his own body starting the winding-down process of age. The optimism and guile of youth was fading; the belief in bright futures and endless opportunities had proved to be a sham.

The house seemed to press down on him at that moment, every piece of furniture and stained glass making its presence felt. The walls were choking him as thoroughly as a ligature. For a moment Leonard wanted to run, to leave before he saw Dorothy. To hide before another meal, another hesitant conversation, another awkward pause sapped what little life there was left out of him.

But he didn't leave. He couldn't. It was too late. He was caught by them and, although certain they would devour him whole, he almost welcomed the release.

'Leonard,' Dorothy said suddenly, running down the stairs to meet him. She was in one of her girlish moods, he realised, pecking her on the cheek.

She smiled, a long slow smile. 'Darling, did you have a good day?' she asked, taking his coat off him and linking arms. So this was to be the dutiful wife role, was it? 'I missed you. I went shopping today.'

They walked into the drawing room together. Judge Arnold was slumped in a chair. The lower lids of his eyes had dropped, the blood-red linings showing. Heavy jowls and a flabby, overweight body made a ghoul out of him.

Slowly he moved his head round to look at them

'Hello there, Leonard, everything all right at work?'

'Fine, s-s-sir,' he replied, sitting down, Dorothy snuggling up to him on the sofa.

'Did you find out?' she asked.

'W-w-what?'

She pulled a child's face of annoyance. 'About Alice! Did you find out where she was?'

'Alice? Alice who?' the old man barked, his heavy shoulders heaving as he moved round in his seat.

'Dorothy w-w-wants to s-s-see Alice Rimmer –'

'Oh, grow up!' the old man snapped at his daughter. 'The past is the past, let it go.'

Her eyes fixed on him. Anger, like a heat haze, smouldered from her.

'I want to see Alice –'

'Never!' her father replied. 'You have too many fancies, girl. You don't know what you're talking about.'

'I do!'

Judge Arnold's voice was thunder. 'I said no, and I mean no!' he barked. 'I'll hear no more about it. I thought you had more sense than to encourage her, Leonard. I thought you understood.'

Leonard was suddenly past understanding anyone in the Arnold family. He was tired and missing Frances; he was exhausted by the bickering and the threats with which the old man kept his remaining family in line. *I bet there are more than a few things that keep you awake at night, Leonard* thought, *I bet your conscience chews a hole in you.* Loathing welled up in him as he looked at his father-in-law. Judge Arnold had known about his two daughters' rivalry; he had even known about Dorothy having an affair with her sister's husband – and yet he had done nothing, just covered up when the damage was done.

'If Dorothy w-w-wants to s-s-see Alice –'

'She doesn't!' the old man snapped. 'She doesn't know what she wants. She never did.' His daughter's face had clouded. 'Oh for God's sake, Leonard, look at her. She's not in her right mind.'

Leonard was on his feet in an instant. 'H-h-how can you say that about your own c-c-child? How could any father say something like that about his own flesh and blood?'

Judge Arnold fixed his gaze on Leonard. 'Because she *is* my flesh and blood, that's why. Dorothy and I have secrets – old secrets – which no one else knows. Not even you, Leonard. You married into this family, but that doesn't make you belong.'

'I don't want to belong to your b-b-bloody family!' he retorted fiercely. 'This place is a m-m-morgue and you're turning into a tyrant.'

With a sinister smile, Judge Arnold relaxed back into his seat.

'Poor Leonard, out of your depth, aren't you? Not tough enough to take it, are you?' You were never man enough for Dorothy. She needed someone stronger, someone with nerve.'

'Like D-D-David Lewes?'

The name was out before Leonard could stop it. Dorothy put her hand up to her mouth; the old man slammed his hands down on the arms of his chair.

'I won't have that name mentioned in this house!' he snarled. 'How dare you bring David Lewes into the conversation? He ruined our family.'

Leonard was beside himself. 'Your family w-w-was ruined long b-b-before David Lewes came into it. I've lived w-w-with you for years – and if he f-f-felt as trapped and as much of an outcast as I do, then I pity him.'

'He murdered my child!' Judge Arnold hollered.

'You s-s-said that Catherine *drove* him to it,' Leonard shot back, suddenly aware of what he had said as he turned back to Dorothy, aghast.

She was staring at him, her blue eyes fixed. He thought for a moment that she might spring up and hit him, but instead she glanced over to her father. There was an exchange of looks, some understanding passing between them.

Leonard, seeing the exchange, went in for the kill.

'What is it?' he snapped. 'I've lived f-f-for years with all these poignant l-l-looks and silences. What the h-h-hell is going on? Or what *went* on?' He stood up, towering over his wife. 'I want to know. I w-w-want to know once and for all – w-w-what happened in this house that made David Lewes kill your sister?'

When Dorothy looked away, Judge Arnold answered for her.

'You know what happened. David Lewes killed Catherine in an argument and Dorothy found her sister afterwards. Isn't that bad enough, Leonard? Isn't that gruesome enough for you? I've spent my life trying to protect my surviving daughter, by trying to keep the world at arm's length. Dorothy has suffered enough. Let it go.'

But Leonard was unwilling to let anything go. He felt used and was willing to risk anything.

'You t-t-told me that Dorothy was h-h-having an affair with David Lewes –'

His wife made a mewling sound and looked down at her hands.

'I told you not to talk about it!' Judge Arnold retorted. 'Do you want to upset her any more than she is already? Do you want to drive her mad?'

'Mad? Why all the talk of m-m-madness, Judge? Your conversation is l-l-littered with it: *Dorothy is unstable, Dorothy doesn't know w-w-what she means, Dorothy is erratic.* If you were really worried about her believing it you w-w-wouldn't keep bringing it up. Especially in f-f-front of her. Not if you really loved your daughter.'

'And you love her better, do you?' the old man retaliated. 'I don't think so. I don't think that a man with a mistress loves his wife that much.'

The words struck Dorothy like an axe blow. She flinched and then pressed her hands to her stomach, rocking herself on the sofa.

Incredulous, Leonard glanced over to Judge Arnold.

'Why d-d-did you have to tell her that? You old bastard! W-w-why did you have to tell her?'

Judge blinked slowly at the insult, then smiled. 'You can blow off at the mouth all you want, Leonard, it'll make no difference. Dorothy and I know the world better than you think. So don't try impressing us with your talk about morals. Don't act scandalised about how she could love her sister's husband when all the time *you're sleeping with another woman*.' He stared at Leonard defiantly and then at his daughter, who was ghostly pale. 'I think we should go in to dinner now.'

'Go yourself!' Leonard replied, as the old man walked out of the room. 'I'm g-g-getting out of here –'

He was stopped by Dorothy grabbing his arm. 'No, don't go,' she pleaded. 'Don't leave me alone with him.'

I loved you once, Leonard thought, but that was so long ago.

'Dorothy –'

'Don't leave me,' she urged him. 'Not now, please. I don't care what you think of me, I don't expect you to love me like you used to, but don't leave me here.' She glanced over her shoulder as if to check that her father wasn't there. 'I can't stay here alone. I rely on you. You're the only one I can trust –'

'D-Dorothy, this is –'

'Sssh!' she warned him, looking round again. 'It's all wrong, it has been for a long time. My father won't die, he'll live for ever, watching this house, watching me.'

'Be reasonable. He's an old man, he'll d-d-die one day.'

She shook her head impatiently. 'Leonard, listen to me! I need you now. I know you think I'm crazy. He's made you think that – he's made *me* think that. But I'm not as unstable as I seem. I know the truth, you see. I know the truth about the past. *Everything that happened*.' She clung to his arm. 'Please, I can't sleep, I can't think. My father doesn't care, but I do. I have to make things all right again. I need to see Alice. *I need to see Alice Rimmer*.'

Sighing, Leonard hung his head. He wanted to go and yet he couldn't leave her. Not with her father; not after so long. Not after all they had endured together. It wasn't fair, and although he was a weak man, he wasn't cruel.

'I w-w-went to see Dr Priestly. He's passing a message to Alice Rimmer that you want to s-s-see her.'

He saw the look of gratitude in his wife's face and was moved by it.

'Dorothy, *why* d-d-do you have to see her?'

'To explain,' she said simply, 'just to explain.'

Chapter Fifty-Three

'I know, I couldn't believe it either!' Ray said happily. 'Tommy's getting married!'

Alice raised her eyebrows, her chin cupped in her hands as she looked across the table at Ray. 'I thought your brother swore he would never marry?'

'So he said, but he fell like the rest of us – hook, line and sinker. Oh yes, it'll hit him hard, after all these years of dodging marriage. Serves him right, I say.'

'You dodged marriage long enough.'

He pulled a face at her. 'I wanted to marry you a long time ago, but you wouldn't have me. It wasn't my fault. I was just left dangling on a string whilst you toyed with me.'

Laughing, Alice shook her head. 'You are impossible! I never left you hanging about –'

'You stole my heart and then walked off with it,' he teased her. 'I had nothing beating in my chest for years. It's a miracle I survived.'

Interrupted by the phone ringing, he picked it up and began talking to Barbara Mills. She had stayed on at the sanatorium, having long since given up on Ray Berry as a potential suitor, but clinging frantically to her status as matron. The sanatorium was her kingdom; she might have liked to have run it as Mrs Berry, but she had never pushed her luck. After all, she had to make sure that she wasn't banished like Olive McGrath.

Whilst she half-heartedly listened to his side of the conversation, Alice watched Ray. He had wanted her to return to Greenfields with him, but she hadn't. Her kingdom remained St Ursula's. To her amazement the governors hadn't fired her after her outburst; maybe they realised the truth of what she had said; maybe after they saw Ray Berry and Guy Priestly defend her, she grew in status in their eyes . . .

Ray had been baffled by her insistence on staying at St Ursula's. 'Why work at that dump when you could work at this dump with me?' he had teased her.

'Because St Ursula's is mine, and Greenfields is yours,' Alice had replied, 'I want to stay there, Ray. I can't give up now.'

'But –'

'But nothing,' she'd teased him. 'You have your little kingdom and I have mine.'

And so it remained. They saw each other a few times in the week, and every weekend, Alice trying to convince herself that Ray was the perfect partner. After all, she was very fond of him. He was attractive, amusing, and he was interested in the same kind of work as she was. They would make a great pair. And she would have the status of being Mrs Berry.

If she didn't long for him as she had longed for Victor, maybe that was a good thing. Maybe it was time to settle down, to curb that wildness of spirit. And Ray would help her do that.

He was raising his voice at Barbara Mills suddenly, his heavy eyebrows drawn together in a frown.

It had been made clear to Alice that Ray didn't want children, so that wasn't a problem, no chance of her giving birth to a damaged child. A child who might die, like Robin. It was lucky, Alice thought, jarring on the word.

If she had married Victor they would have had children before she knew anything about her inherited condition. They might have lost those children, or they might have survived. No one knew – but Alice wondered what it would have been like to hold a child of her own, and thought momentarily that knowledge could be a bitter advantage.

Ray was shouting again now and Alice leaned her head back against the chair, her eyes closing. An image of Hilly flared up, the little figure sitting in the boat on the park lake, eating a ham sandwich, the candlelight flickering on her pale hair. Hilly . . . Her one friend from so long ago, her confidante in the days when she was no one, a cast-off, a nothing. In the days of Netherlands and hand-me-down clothes and corridors smelling of thin gravy and cheap soap.

Hilly in her sickbed, laughing in the sanatorium; Hilly talking to Alice in the dead of night; Hilly, as gentle as a child; and Hilly, now dying . . . Alice winced at the thought, and the one which followed. *Marry Victor and look after him*, Hilly had said. Marry Victor . . .

But how *could* she marry Victor? She was with Ray now; they had an understanding. Their interests were so similar, their obsessions with their jobs so equal . . . She would explain it to Hilly, Alice thought – and then realised she couldn't. It was too much to expect Hilly to take on. Instead, she would simply let the matter rest. When Hilly died – she flinched at what was to come – she would comfort Victor, but no more. They *could* have been a couple once, but that was another time, and that time had passed.

'Stupid cow,' Ray said thoughtfully as he put down the phone. 'She makes so many unnecessary calls these days.'

'It's an excuse to talk to you,' Alice replied, smiling.

'Oh come on, I don't think Barbara's lovesick any more.'

'Maybe not lovesick, but she still loves you. She can't help it, Ray. If you've loved someone very much you never turn the feeling off. You don't want it, but it's there just the same.'

Who was she talking about, Alice wondered suddenly – Barbara Mills or herself? Before she had time to think it out, Guy Priestly knocked and walked into Ray's office. He smiled when he saw Ray and then turned to Alice.

'I'm glad you're here.'

'Why?'

'I have a message for you. Lionel Tripps came to see me.' Alice's face paled. 'He said that his wife wants to see you, Alice. I told him I would pass the message on. Don't worry, I didn't tell them where you were.'

'Dorothy Tripps?' Alice said bitterly.

Ray was on the defensive at once. 'What the hell does that damn family want?'

Guy shrugged. 'I've no idea, just that Dorothy Tripps wants to see Alice urgently.'

'To cause trouble, no doubt,' Ray replied curtly. 'You don't have to go, Alice.'

'I know I don't *have* to go.' She glanced over to Ray, Guy catching the look and tactfully moving to the door.

'I have to call in the sanatorium and check on the patients, I'll call back later when I'm done.'

They both waited for the door to close behind him before Ray walked over to Alice and looked down at her.

'Don't go –'

'Don't tell me what to do!' she said shortly. Ray flinched. 'I'm sorry, I didn't mean to be sharp. Dorothy Tripps . . .' She mused on the name. 'I hate that woman. I hated her when I was at Netherlands and I hated her more when she tried to implicate me.'

'Alice, forget it, you owe her nothing.'

'Of course I owe her nothing,' Alice replied, her tone steely. 'I just wonder how she has the nerve to summon me after so long. After what she did, did she think I would come running? I'm not a servant now. She was always crazy. I wonder why she wants to see me now?'

Ray hesitated before uttering the next words. 'Do you want me to come with you?'

Alice knew that if she said yes, he would go with her to The Dower House. He would stand by her side and face the Arnolds and protect her if there was any nastiness. He would say that she was his fiancée and – if there was trouble – demand to know how they dared to talk to her like that. He would have all the confidence of a moneyed background, a man talking to people of his own social standing.

But she *wasn't* going to go back like that, Alice thought. She had gone into The Dower House as a no one. She had arrived there with a bitter heart, looking at the house and the grounds and the furniture and thinking – *This should be mine, all this. I should have had this place, these curtains, these clothes, these paintings. Whilst you had so much, I had nothing. And I'll take it away from you.* And all that plotting and bitterness had achieved precisely nothing.

But the experiences at The Dower House, and since, had taught Alice courage. She could go back with a partner, an ally, but equally she could, and *would*, do it alone. Not as some man's fiancée, protected by him. Nor as the principal of a school, protected by her rank. No, she was going back as Alice Rimmer, the woman she had tried so hard to bury. The woman she had shunned as successfully as the Arnolds had once shunned her.

'Whatever they say can't harm me,' she said coldly. 'Whatever Dorothy Tripps does can't hurt me now.' She smiled that hard smile of the past. 'So they want me now, do they? God knows why.'

'Leave it, Alice, they're bad luck for you.'

She was staring ahead, remembering. He was right, they *were* bad luck, but they were also blood. It might be madness, but she was going back. To her family, to her home.

Judge Arnold was eating some cheese on a tray on his lap. He had developed a sudden odd fetish – he could bear no one watching him eat. So his food was brought to him when he was alone in the drawing room or his study, his thick hands pulling the bread apart, his eyes fixed on the cheese and cold meats.

He was halfway through his rice pudding when he heard the doorbell. The butler came to tell him who the visitor was.

'There's a Miss Alice Rimmer at the door.'

Judge Arnold's head shot up. That bloody fool Leonard had given in to Dorothy. 'I'm eating!'

The butler blinked. 'She asked for Mr Tripps. I thought he was in here with you.'

Awkwardly, the old man put the tray on the table next to him and leaned forward in his seat. His eyes were reddened and rheumy. 'I want to see her. Send her in here first.'

'But –'

'Don't argue with me! Send her in here.'

A moment later Alice was shown into the study. She stood for an instant at the door, taking in the musty smell of old books and the dim fire in the grate. Nothing had changed since her days there – except for Judge Arnold. A man deserves his face, she thought, and now the old man's exterior looked what he had always been on the interior. A sinister bully.

'Long time no see,' he said, wiping his mouth with a napkin and then tossing it onto the tray. 'Where have you been hiding?'

My grandfather, Alice thought. Dear God, I wish you weren't. I wish you weren't in that chair, breathing, living. I wish you were dead.

'I haven't come to see you. Mr Tripps asked me to come here and see your daughter –'

'My daughter's sick. Unhappy woman, very confused,' Judge Arnold said, slurring his speech slightly. The empty glass beside him explained why. 'She has fancies – well, you remember that, don't you? You saw enough of them.'

'I saw enough of everything here.'

He was stunned by her tone. Where was the little maid he could intimidate?

'Don't get uppity with me –'

'I can do what I like and talk to you any way I like,' Alice replied curtly. 'There's too many things I should have said long ago.'

She turned to go, but the old man called out to her.

'Wait!'

She turned back, looking him full in the face.

'I want to know something. And I want an answer now – who are you?'

'What?'

'I said – *who are you?*'

'Who do you *want* me to be, Judge?'

He stared at her avidly. 'I never bought that story about your being found outside on the road, the little lost sheep. You worked your way through our family very cleverly, Alice. Don't think I didn't see it all. My wife was your first ally, and then Dorothy – then Robin.' His voice was thick, muffled with booze, age and spite. 'You encouraged that child to love you, not Dorothy. You came between them deliberately.'

'He was fond of me because I was his nanny.'

'You were more like his bloody mother!' the old man spluttered. 'But it all went wrong, didn't it? You lost in the end.'

'I didn't lose anything, apart from Robin.'

'He's probably better off dead than living here.'

'How could you say that, you vicious old man?' Alice hissed. 'I hated you then and I hate you now. Robin deserved a good life. He died because he was sick – and you know that, whatever your daughter told you.'

Judge focused on her, dangerously sly. 'I don't believe everything my daughter tells me – just as she doesn't believe everything I tell her. You're going to have a very difficult life, Alice, if you think that people always speak the truth.'

The irony of the remark was not lost on her.

'I came to see her, not you,' Alice replied, moving to the door.

'You came back for something,' the old man replied, 'whether it was to see Dorothy or cause trouble, I don't know.' He stood up, weaving slightly on his feet. 'There's something about you, Alice Rimmer. I felt it from the start and I can sense it now. You're no common nanny, no scrubber.' He moved unsteadily towards her. 'I think you're dangerous – and unlucky for this family.'

Boldly, Alice faced him. 'Oh, I've been unlucky, that's true. But any bad luck that's come to this family was not down to me. You had tragedy long before I arrived – and you'll have it long after I leave.'

He winced against the bitter words. 'Now look –'

'I came back because I was curious. But this time I can go when I want. You can't fire me, Judge Arnold, or injure me in any way.' She took hold of the door knob. 'You don't scare me either.'

'We'll see,' he said malevolently as she left. 'We'll see.'

In the hallway Leonard was waiting patiently. He saw Alice and coloured, remembering how he had made a pass at her so many years before. Yet there was little of the young Alice in this poised adult. She was still dark, still striking, but there was a confidence about her which was daunting and left him momentarily cowed.

He had expected the frightened girl who had been driven away, not the mature woman who looked at him with cool hostility.

'You sent for me.'

Her voice was calm, and made him stammer more.

'I w-w-was asking for you to c-c-come and see my wife. D-D-Dorothy has been asking for you.' He paused, but there was no response. 'She's v-v-very distracted.'

'Am I supposed to feel sorry for her?'

He blinked, wrong-footed. 'She's sick –'

'I don't care,' Alice replied, her cruelty shaking her. This house, these people, made her into someone she disliked, someone she had walked away from. And should have stayed away from.

'Alice, I know we w-w-were unfair to you.'

'Unfair!' she snapped. 'You have no idea *how* unfair.'

He wilted under the attack. 'Will you see my wife?'

'Why now?'

'I d-d-don't know,' Leonard replied honestly. 'Maybe it's because it's November. Dorothy w-w-was usually distressed around this time. It's the anniversary of . . . w-w-well, you know . . .'

'Her sister's death. Yes, I remember.'

Leonard was fascinated by the accuracy of Alice's recall. Surely a nanny from so many years ago would have little reason to remember such a date so clearly?

'C-c-can you see m-m-my wife? Please, Alice, c-c-can you?'

The hallway was cold, Alice chilled as she stood on the black-and-white tiled floor. Slowly her gaze travelled up the stairs to the suit of armour glinting in the dim light, and on the landing – tucked in a corner – stood Alwyn's wheelchair. It was as if at any moment its owner would call for it, then be lowered down to the ground floor in the now-silent lift.

Memory, clammy and unsettling, made Alice hurry. 'I can't stay long.'

'I'll t-t-take you to D-D-Dorothy now then,' Leonard replied, guiding her to the stairs.

She wanted to say, *I know the way. I walked up these damned stairs a thousand times. With food, with clothing, with Robin. I watched your wife call over the polished banister and you run down in the mornings when you were late for work. I know each spindle, even the one that Robin carved his initials into – have you found the sad little memento yet?*

Silent, she followed Leonard up the stairs and paused on the landing.

'We m-m-moved rooms,' he said, by way of explanation. 'D-D-Dorothy sleeps b-b-better alone.'

And you? She wanted to ask, do you sleep better alone?

He knocked, then opened the door and stood back for Alice to walk in. The curtains were drawn, lamps lit, a fire in the grate. Above the marble mantelpiece was a painting of Dorothy done many years earlier, and beside it several photographs of Robin in silver frames, but none of Leonard or her parents. The room had been refurbished in pale-coloured silk, but there was no lightness to the chamber, and the thick carpet underfoot muffled every sound.

She was beside her before Alice realised, making her jump as Dorothy whispered in her ear, 'You came.'

Alice turned to face her aunt. Dorothy was dressed in champagne-coloured silk, her hair piled on top of her head, her strange smile welcoming and yet hesitant. This was the woman who had driven her away, Alice thought, the woman who had made her a scapegoat for her son's death. A liar. A bitch. *A relative.*

'Mrs Tripps –'

'You can call me Dorothy,' she said, moving over to a sofa and sitting down. Quickly she patted the seat next to her. 'Come here, Alice. I have to talk to you.'

Reluctantly Alice moved over to her and sat down. A scent of gardenia came off Dorothy strongly, a curiously listless perfume.

'I need your help.'

Alice stared at her. 'My *help*? Why?' Her tone was incredulous.

Dorothy looked round. 'Where's my father?'

'In his study.'

'My husband?'

'I heard him go back downstairs,' Alice replied. 'Why?'

'They spy on me,' she answered, her tone reasonable. 'I know they do. I want you to help me.'

'You already said that.'

She frowned, surprised. 'Are you angry? Are you cross with me?'

'What's the matter with you!' Alice snapped. 'You know what you did to me. You blamed your son's death on me and it wasn't my fault. You've known that all along. But you said nothing. You herded me out of this house and let everyone think I was some kind of monster –'

'I know!' Dorothy said frantically. 'I know! What I did was wrong, very wrong. You see, I thought he'd leave me if he knew –'

'Who would leave you?'

'I thought that if Leonard knew the truth he would leave me. I couldn't face that.' Her voice dropped to a confidential whisper. 'My husband has a mistress.'

Quickly, Alice got to her feet. 'I don't care, Mrs Tripps. And frankly I'm wondering why you would tell me something like that.'

'Because you know about me,' Dorothy replied, staring up into Alice's face and nodding. 'Yes, you do. You know about me. *And I know about you.*'

Alice could feel her mouth dry. Did Dorothy know she was her niece? Had she known all along? Was that the reason why she had been called to see her?

'Know what?' Alice asked suspiciously. 'What do you know?'

But Dorothy's attention had drifted. 'I need you to stay with me on the twelfth.' Her tone was perfectly composed. 'I can't be here alone.'

'You're not alone. Your husband and father are here.'

She laughed abruptly. 'You and I know they aren't any help to me. Stay with me on Saturday. I can't get through the night without you.'

Alice had a sudden memory of a woman in a white dress scrubbing at the carpet in the drawing room, the moonlight making a corpse out of her.

'I can't,' Alice said, moving away.

Immediately Dorothy grabbed at her sleeve.

'Was I *so* cruel to you? I know I was, but I've suffered for it, Alice, more than you know. I was so jealous of you, so jealous of the way Robin loved you.' She paused, tightened her grip. 'He loved you more than he loved me.'

Bitterness made Alice cruel. 'I know he did.'

'Because you made sure he did!' Dorothy replied heatedly. 'I may not be innocent, but you're not without guilt. You came between me and my son – I don't know why, but you did. Yes, I hurt you, but you'd hurt me.'

'I owe you nothing,' Alice said coldly. She looked into her aunt's face, into the crafty eyes. 'I don't know what you're up to, but I want no part of it.'

'I'm not up to anything!' Dorothy shouted. 'Alice, I need you. What d'you want me to do? Beg you? Go down on my knees to you? I will, if that's what you want. Shall I beg you, Alice?'

Alice kept staring at her, wanting to see Dorothy Tripps on her knees, wanting to watch her humiliation.

'I want you to beg, yes.'

Discomforted, Dorothy kneeled down, but in the instant she did so, Alice turned away, disgusted.

'Come back on the twelfth of November, please,' she cried on her knees. 'Please, come back. I have something to tell you, Alice. Something important – something I should have said a long time ago.'

Alice turned back to her, her heart thumping. 'What do you want to tell me?'

'Come back on the twelfth,' Dorothy whispered. 'I'll tell you everything then.'

Chapter Fifty-Four

That Saturday Alice called to see Ethel, who had recovered from her chill, and then visited Hilly. She was quiet, peaceful, Victor sitting by the bed reading to her. Somehow Ethel had managed to get some extra meat, and a stew was simmering in the cooker downstairs. After being pressed to eat with them, Alice left around eight thirty. She never mentioned where she was going.

She had meant to. After all, Hilly and Victor knew about her background, what would have been easier than to tell them? But the moment never came, and Alice felt like an intruder as she watched the quiet affection between the two of them. A jug of water by the bed, the evening paper on the coverlet, a card from Ethel on the fireplace were all unbearably sad reminders, Victor brushing Hilly's hair as she laughed at something on the radio.

It was time to leave, Alice realised, walking out and catching the bus which went from Trafalgar Street all the way to Oldham Mumps. There she would change and catch another to Werneth Heights, walking the rest of the way as she had done all those years before.

Looking out of the bus window, she noticed posters advertising Vimto and Capstan cigarettes. The colours were bright, the mood cheerful after the long dull years of the war. Yet her mood did not lift. She was bound for The Dower House, where nothing had changed. A sudden memory of Charlie made Alice smile. He had made it through the war and was now married to his sweetheart, Emily. A girl with enough sense to settle them in Lytham St Annes, far away from Werneth Heights. My brother,

Charlie, Alice thought. I wish I'd got to know you better; I wish I could have told you the truth.

Changing buses, she waited at the stop for the number 34, her hands dug deep into her pockets. A child passed, holding tightly on to its father's hand and suddenly Alice wondered about David Lewes, *her* father. She had never held on to his hand, never walked with him. He was an enigma to her, a person without a face or voice. A man whose flesh and blood she shared, but about whom she knew only the most damning facts. On the rare occasions she *had* thought of him it was like thinking of some stranger, some character from a book or film. She was, Alice had to admit, ashamed of him. Ashamed of being the child of a murderer, a coward. He had done nothing for her. In fact, his actions had caused her banishment . . . Alice stared at the child holding its father's hand and, moved, turned away. Why should she care about David Lewes when he had cared so little for her?

The bus arrived, Alice getting on and paying her fare. She might struggle not to think of her father and yet, here she was, on a bus going toward Werneth Heights and the Arnolds. Going back to the past. Soon she would enter The Dower House on the very night her father had killed her mother. She was to stand watch with her aunt, and through the dark hours give comfort to a woman who was desperate to confide. But confide *what*? Alice wondered. Was it to be this night when she would finally be recognised for who she was?

The bus juddered to a halt just as it left the town centre.

'What's happening?' Alice asked the conductor.

He shrugged. 'This bus is old; had trouble with it on and off all week.'

'Will it start again?'

'Might, or it might not. The driver's looking at it now. If anyone can fix it, he can.'

'What's wrong with it?'

'It's not running.'

'I gathered that,' Alice replied.

The man in the next seat leaned over to her. 'I were born on a bus.'

'I might die on one if they don't get it moving soon,' Alice replied drily.

There was nothing for it but to wait for the bus to be repaired, or for another bus to be sent to ferry them on the last leg of their journey. Half an hour passed. Alice asked the conductor what was happening.

'We'll get her up and running again,' he said cheerfully, although he sounded less hopeful now. 'No hurry.'

'Not for you, maybe,' Alice replied. 'Is there another bus going to Werneth Heights?'

'Nah, you're stuck with the old number 34, luv.'

Looking at her watch Alice realised it had stopped. 'What time is it?'

'Nine fifteen.'

Time was getting on and she still had to cross the rest of the town. Then there was the walk at the other end. She hadn't given a time of arrival to Dorothy, but she had wanted to be there for the evening, not turning up late.

Maybe Dorothy would think she wasn't coming. Serve her right, Alice thought and then looked down at her hands. She wanted to be there tonight. This meeting wasn't just for Dorothy ... Tapping her foot impatiently, Alice wrapped her scarf around her neck. It was cold, getting colder by the moment in the stalled bus. If she had had any sense, she would have asked for a lift from Ray in his battered Vauxhall. But then she would have had to explain where she was going – and he would have tried to stop her.

She instead she had kept quiet and told no one where she was headed. And now she was sitting in a freezing bus on a bitter night.

'Like I said, I were born on a bus. It were a cold evening,' the man next to her suddenly chirped up.

'What happened?'

'My mother missed the train she were going for!' He laughed. 'She called me Dermot, after the bus conductor.' He laughed again. 'So where are you off to? Going dancing?'

'No, visiting . . . Relations.'

'Where?'

'Werneth Heights way.'

He blew out her cheeks. 'It's dear up there. Your folks must work for some posh sods.'

Alice winced. It had been immediately presumed that any relation of hers would be a servant at the house, not its owner. Irritation bit into her and she turned away, wiping the condensation off the window. She had been put in her place again. Not meanly – the man had meant nothing unkind about it – but she had been made to feel her position. And that night of all nights it rankled on her.

It was nearly ten forty when the bus finally dropped Alice off at the boundary of Werneth Heights, her travelling companion waving merrily to her as the bus drew away, its lights twinkling for only a few moments before it turned round the bend. When it had gone the road was dark, the only illumination coming from the widely spaced streetlamps.

Slowly Alice walked along, her footsteps dragging. She could turn round, she told herself, turn round and never go in. Never find out what her aunt wanted to tell her. But she knew she wouldn't. *She had to know.* Whatever it was. The drive to The Dower House was lighted, her way clear as she crossed the lawn and stood looking at the great stone mansion. The next house was only twenty yards away and yet it seemed that The Dower House was deserted, cut off from the world.

Finally Alice walked up to the front door and rang the bell.

Leonard let her in, his manner agitated.

'Dorothy said y-y-you were coming. Thank you.'

He glanced up as Dorothy walked out onto the stairs. She was wearing a dark evening dress, her hair in a French plait. Around her shoulders was a silk shawl, her hands winking with diamonds. She was, Alice realised, quite beautiful. And strange.

'Alice, thank God! I thought you weren't going to come.' She glanced at the clock. 'It's nearly eleven o'clock.'

'I was held up,' Alice replied. 'The bus broke down.'

Leonard flushed. 'You s-s-should have c-c-called me. I would have come to p-p-pick you up.'

Ignoring him, Dorothy called down the stairs eagerly, 'I'm having some food sent to my room. Alice will eat with me tonight.'

Leonard was pale, his lips bloodless. 'I'll come and j-j-join you.'

'NO!' she snapped. 'Leave me alone, Leonard. I have Alice with me now.'

Together they walked into Dorothy's sitting room, off her bedroom. A copy of *Vogue* was lying on a chaise longue, two photographs of Robin on a side table. Transfixed, Alice stared at them, her fingers running over the image of his face.

'He was handsome, wasn't he?'

Alice nodded.

'Not like Leonard at all,' Dorothy went on. 'Robin had my looks.'

Moving away, Dorothy took the cloth off a tray and exposed a light supper. So genteel, Alice thought, little sandwiches cut into shapes, delicate cakes. The war had only been over for a few months but there were no shortages here. There never had been.

'Are you hungry?'

Baffled, Alice stared at her, wondering why she had been asked here. She had thought Dorothy was distressed, but she was acting like a hostess as a cocktail party. There was no logic to it – but then there never was with Dorothy.

'I'm not hungry.'

Idly Dorothy stared at the food and then dropped the cover over it again. The clock chimed the hour. There was the sound of footsteps coming up the stairs, then passing by the door. Alice watched her aunt, fascinated. She was rigid in her seat, her eyes unblinking. Apparently she was listening, the tension about her morbid.

'I should never have lost my son,' she said at last, getting to her feet and beginning to pace the room. 'I've lost so much – my son, my sister, my mother now. There are so few of us left.'

Alice said nothing. She could see Dorothy's agitation rising by the minute, panic setting in, a slow and suffocating despair coming with it.

'I'm getting older now, Alice. Getting older . . . I don't sleep, not much. Bad dreams.' She moved over to the mantelpiece and picked up a cigarette. Her eyes lighted up momentarily in the lighter's flame. 'I have to talk.'

'About what?'

'The past. Don't you think about it, Alice?'

Her tone was cold when she answered. 'Should I?'

'I think about the past all the time,' Dorothy replied, inhaling deeply. 'We were very popular – my sister and I. We had everything, money, clothes, the best holidays. We were alike, very similar. Did I ever show you a photograph of my sister?'

'No, I never saw any of her.'

'They were all moved after she died . . . There are so many things hidden here. So many secrets. My father likes secrets, likes to keep his family in check. He always did.' She wasn't talking to her, Alice realised, she was talking to herself. The time was passing; Dorothy was more distant, detached. The night was working its evil on her. 'I've lived on the edge for so long, and I've got so tired.'

'So rest.'

'I don't rest!' Dorothy snapped, grinding out her cigarette. 'I heard the bombs in the war. Heard them fall – it was a long way away, but so much noise. Charlie went off to fight, but he came back. He didn't stay here, though, he moved away. Left us. He was so simple, but then stupidity has saved many a man from madness.'

Alice could hear the quarter-hour chime. Eleven fifteen. What time had Catherine been murdered she wondered? What time had Dorothy found her sister's body?

'I know you saw me.'

'What?' Alice asked, startled.

'That night so many years ago. You came and found me in the drawing room. You were kind to me.'

'You repaid me in a strange way,' Alice replied coldly.

She winced. 'You can be very cruel –'

'You have no right to talk about cruelty!' Alice retorted. 'What you did to me was wicked.'

'And you'll never forgive me, will you?' Dorothy said, her tone strange. She stopped pacing suddenly. 'I think I can sleep now.'

'I thought you wanted to talk?'

'There's all the night to talk. It can wait a little longer. What I have to tell you has been waiting for so long.'

For a moment Alice wanted to hit her, to slap the distant face. You're playing games with me again, she thought. Well, this time we'll see who comes out the winner.

'Stay here, Alice. I won't sleep long.'

Within minutes the building was quiet. Obviously the old man and Leonard had retired. A far-off church clock chimed, the sound of a car horn echoing dreamily in the distance. Pulling a rug over her, Alice lay down on the chaise longue and closed her eyes.

Her anger kept her awake. Why had she bothered to

return? Was Dorothy going to tell her anything, or just have her on call, a servant to the last. She felt no pity for her aunt. In fact, if she could have done she would have shaken the truth out of her. But Dorothy was going to do it her way. All Alice could do was to wait.

The night swung on. Dreams came and went as Alice slid in and out of chilly sleep. Outside, winter foxes crossed the lawns and by the gate a cat brought home its night's kill.

A sudden noise woke Alice in the small hours. Then Dorothy was shaking her shoulder.

'Get up! Get up!' she whispered. 'And come with me.'

Alerted, Alice followed Dorothy downstairs. The house was in darkness, the drawing room shadowed as they walked in. Noiselessly, Dorothy moved across the floor and then paused by the window.

Her voice was calm, unnaturally so. 'My sister was lying here when I found her.'

My mother, Alice thought.

'I heard noises and came down. Walked in. Saw the window open. He was running. Over the lawn, to the wall. I stopped and looked down. She was here,' Dorothy pointed to the floor, 'on her side. One arm under her head. I walked over to her. She was dead. There was blood on the tip of my shoe.'

Alice could feel the hairs rising on the back of her neck as Dorothy continued, 'My father came in, turned on the light. He knew then. It was arranged. All arranged.'

'What was arranged?' Alice asked, her voice hoarse.

'I knew about them, you see.'

'Knew about who?'

'David and her.'

The moon shifted suddenly from behind a cloud and fell across Dorothy's passive face. Her eyes were distant.

'He loved me. He loved me best.'

The moon was lighting her, making her real. Her arms

were folded, her hair loose around her shoulders. Her years aged her cruelly and suddenly.

'You have to listen to me,' she pleaded. 'I have to talk.'

'Then talk,' Alice urged her.

'What if someone hears?'

'No one will,' Alice assured her hurriedly. 'No one's about. Tell me, tell me now.'

She had to hear. Dorothy was talking about her mother and her father.

'She loved David, tried to steal him from me. I heard them talking. She had made him crazy, made him think mad things, agree with her.' Dorothy leaned towards Alice, her expression bewildered. 'She wanted him to kill me. She hated me, she wanted me dead.'

'Why?' Alice asked, her tone harsh. 'I don't understand.'

'No one does. Only I know why – oh, and my father. My mother knew, but she's gone now . . . David thought it would be me here that night, that she would send me. He came here to kill me. But I outsmarted them.'

Alice's voice was soft, encouraging, as though talking to a child.

'What did you do?'

'I wrote a letter, supposedly from him, to her. It said that David wanted to see her. A lovers' meeting. I sent her here to wait for him. It was secret, in the dark. I heard him come in here.' She paused, as though listening to the memory.

Alice was staring at her, transfixed. This woman had engineered her own sister's death . . .

'What happened then?'

'I heard David come in and walk to the window – I heard him hit her, over and over again. He stabbed her, but it didn't sound like a knife going in, more like a series of blows.'

'Jesus . . .'

'He was going to kill me.'

'But he killed her.'

'Yes,' Dorothy said hungrily, 'he killed her instead. He killed the one he loved. He killed *her*.'

'Why tell me?' Alice asked, instinct warning her, tipping her off.

'You had to know.'

'Why me?' Alice pressed her. Tell me, she thought, tell me.

'You must know the truth.'

Gripping her arm, Alice shook her. 'Dear God, *who are you? Who are you?*'

'I'm Catherine.'

'Catherine?' Alice replied incredulously. 'No –'

'I am. I'm Catherine.'

'No!' Alice repeated, backing away. 'You're not Catherine. You can't be!'

Her legs buckled and she leaned against the window-ledge for support. The woman she had taken for her aunt, was her mother. The woman for whom she had looked for so long, then mourned, was not dead after all. The pretty Catherine she had wondered about, the mother she had presumed would have kept her, was *this* woman. The same woman who had planned the death of her own sister and assumed her identity.

'You can't be Catherine!' Alice snapped.

'But I am –'

'You can't be!' Alice repeated, pushing her away and moving towards the door.

Hurriedly Dorothy intercepted her. 'You were so kind to me. I wanted you here because you were so kind to me before. But I wanted to say sorry too, for what I'd done to you. I was so jealous of you and Robin.' She rubbed her temples. 'I've spent my life being jealous, and nothing came of it, except tragedy. I'm so sorry for what I said, so sorry for trying to blame you for my son's death.'

'Get out of my way!' Alice shouted, trying to move

Dorothy away from the door. This couldn't be real, she was dreaming. This wasn't her mother. Not *this* woman, who had been betrayed by her father and then taken revenge in the most sinister way possible.

'I don't believe it!'

'Don't believe what?' Dorothy asked, puzzled.

'If it was true, why would you pretend to be Dorothy?'

'Because I always wanted to be her,' she replied, as though it was reasonable.

'But you didn't have your husband any more? What good did it do you?'

'I didn't *want* him any more after what he'd done,' she snapped. 'How *could* David want her more than me?'

'Because he loved her –'

'But he lost her in the end! He killed her – now what better punishment than that?' Dorothy said viciously.

'You're no better than he was!' Alice replied, turning on her. 'You murdered your own sister.'

'I had no choice –'

'You did! You sent your sister to be killed. You knew what you were doing. Why did you do it? WHY?' Alice shouted.

'I was jealous.'

It was the motivation which had driven Alice to The Dower House all those years earlier.

'Oh, come on, Alice, don't look at me like that. You're no stranger to that emotion.'

'I never killed because of it.'

'Maybe not,' Dorothy replied deftly, 'but you must have wanted to. Everyone hates at some time.'

She was picking into her thoughts, Alice realised. Because she knew her. As a mother knows its own child.

'What you did was wicked. No amount of talking will make it less wrong.'

'I know that,' Dorothy replied. 'That's why I wanted to

make amends. I wanted to say sorry to you. To do one good thing after all the bad things I've done.'

Alice found it difficult to speak. 'Was there nothing else?'

'I thought you'd understand. You seemed to have something about you, Alice. There *was* something different about you. My father saw it, so did I. He mistrusted you. He thought you were out to harm us.'

'I was,' Alice said flatly. 'I wanted to destroy this family.'

She could see her mother blink, monitor the words.

'Why? Why would you want to do that?'

The clock chimed suddenly, one, two, three. Moonlight, white and cold, shuffled over their faces.

'Why did you think I'd understand you?'

Dorothy stared at her.

'Look at me!' Alice commanded her. 'Look at my face. Does it mean *nothing* to you?'

Obediently Dorothy stared at her, at the dark eyes, the white skin in the moonlight. Understanding came and then clouded.

'*Who are you?*'

'I'm Alice, Alice Rimmer.'

She frowned. 'I know. But who *is* that?'

'You had two children. Charlie and a little girl, a baby. You kept the boy but the girl was sent away. She grew up a foundling. No one told her about her past, no one knew anything. She grew up, this foundling, and then she discovered who her family was. The Arnolds, living off the fat of the land. Living in Werneth Heights, whilst she lived poor in Salford. Look at me!' Alice commanded her again, turning her face back to the moonlight. 'That orphan came back. She came back burning with jealousy. She came back to get what was hers. Her rightful name, her rightful inheritance. She came here as a maid, then worked her way up to become a nanny. She loved the little boy she looked after, because he was her cousin. And when he died they said it was her fault. But how could it have been? Why would she have murdered her own flesh and blood?'

'I don't believe you!'

'*Believe me!*' Alice said hoarsely. 'I was that child. I was that woman who came to hurt you. I was eaten up with hatred and bitterness. I wanted to destroy you. I wanted to drive a wedge between you and Robin. I wanted this house. I wanted to hurt you as much as you had hurt me. I hated you.' Alice paused, the naked moonlight on her face. 'Now, look at me again. *Look at your child.* I am that daughter you gave away.'

She could see her mother reel and then Alice winced as she cupped her chin in her hand, turning her face to the moon.

'I *thought* I knew you,' she said, her voice faint. 'Once, when you turned and smiled at me, it made me think of someone else. Of David . . . I thought I was imagining it, of course. I was never stable – perhaps it was just another fancy of mine, one of the many that my father talks about.' She relaxed her grip and touched Alice on the cheek, studying her. 'My daughter . . .'

The revelation tingled between them.

'And what will you do, daughter? You have the power now. Your revenge is in your hands. You can expose me and watch me suffer. It would be justice, after all.'

A moment passed between them, the moon shifting again, the light less fierce.

Holding her mother's gaze, Alice said simply, 'I want to know one thing. Did you ever love me?'

'Of course. You were my baby.'

Her voice wavered. 'Then why did you give me away?'

'You would never come to me, Alice. You loved Dorothy, always cried when I picked you up. Everyone commented on it. The nurse, everyone who ever saw you. After Dorothy was killed my father said that you were the only one who could give me away. Then everyone would know I was Catherine and that it was Dorothy who had been murdered . . .' She slumped suddenly. 'What have I done? God, what have I done?'

'But did you think of me?' Alice said. 'Did you *ever* think of me? Wonder how I was? Where I was? I have to know that I mattered to you. I was so alone for so long. How *could* you do that to your child? You gave me away.'

'I wasn't in my right mind!' her mother said dumbly. 'It was all so confused, so hurried. My father took us out of the country for years so that the scandal could die down. When we came back any change in me would be put down to time and shock. He organised everything, just as he organised your adoption –'

'I was never adopted!' Alice cried. 'I was left at an orphanage. There *was* no family for me. No brothers, no sisters, no home.'

'But he told me he had you placed with a good family! He said you were going to be loved and looked after.' She gripped her daughter's hands. 'I would never have let you go if I had known the truth. Please, believe that, I would never have let you go. I understand now, Robin's death was a punishment –'

'He was ill!' Alice said firmly. 'You've been punished enough –'

'I can *never* be punished enough! I engineered my sister's death.'

'But you said she would have killed you if you hadn't,' Alice replied coldly. 'She wanted your husband. They betrayed you.'

'David loved me so much before she got her hooks into him. He was so handsome.' There was a pause, a dip into memory. 'I was so jealous of my sister. She was the calmer one, the more beautiful one. But when I married David I thought I'd won. I had the prize. But she took him away.' Another memory tugged at her. 'Dorothy stole him – just as she had stolen everything from me.'

453

'But she didn't steal him in the end, did she?'

'I saw his face when I walked in that night. I saw his face in the moonlight. He saw me in the doorway and then looked down and realised what he had done. I thought he would collapse. He just stared at her, bewildered. I walked over to him – but he backed away. And then he ran. Ran away.'

'Where to?'

'No one knows. They tell me he's dead, but I don't believe it.'

'Tell me about my father,' Alice said.

'He was handsome, charming, but weak. But he wasn't the only coward,' she added softly. 'The thing is, that even after what he tried to do to me, I still love him. I always will . . .'

Still, Alice pushed her. 'But you married again.'

'It was my father's idea that I marry Leonard. It looked right, he said.'

'But if David Lewes is alive it would be bigamy.'

'My father doesn't believe he is,' Alice's mother replied quickly. 'But I do.'

'You can't think he's still alive, not after so long.'

'Of course he is!'

'Then where is he?' Alice pressed her.

'I don't know!' she snapped. 'I just know that he is, Alice. And that's the reason I am.' Her voice dropped, hardly audible. 'They try to convince me that David's dead, but I know otherwise. I can *feel* him breathing; I know he lives. That's the only thing that's kept me alive – knowing that he's out there somewhere. I loved him so much, you see. That kind of love is dangerous, out of control. It makes madness. Every day I think of him, hear his voice, the sound of his laugh. They took all his clothes away, but I kept something.' She rose to her feet and rummaged at the back of a drawer, bringing out a small package and passing it to Alice.

454

She unwrapped it slowly, a man's handkerchief lying amongst white tissue.

'It's all I have left of him.'

Alice stared at the square of white linen, the only contact she had ever had with her father.

'But he *betrayed* you.'

'That changes nothing! He could have killed me a thousand times and I would have forgiven him. The only thing I couldn't forgive was the fact that he loved my sister.' She gazed at Alice, mystified. 'Are you really my child? You're very beautiful, though not like any of us. Just a little bit of David.' She touched Alice's forehead, her hand cool, the gesture infinitely gentle.

Without thinking, Alice jerked away.

'Don't touch me!'

'You're my child –'

'I wish I wasn't! I've believed for years in some mother I could have loved. Not someone like you.' She stared at her unblinking. 'It was bad enough knowing what my father had done, but this . . . I don't want anything to do with you.'

'But I could make it up to you –'

'Never!'

'Then I have nothing left to live for.'

Alice shook her head in disbelief. 'You never cared about me before, don't try to manipulate me now, Mother.'

'But I can't go on living with all this guilt. And I can't live with you hating me too.'

Alice paused. What should she do now? Walk away? She had found her mother, but what comfort had that been? Walk away, she told herself, walk away.

'I want to hate you –'

'I understand.'

'You don't!' Alice shouted. 'You have no idea how I feel. I want to wish you dead. I want to hate you for the rest of my life. But I can't.' She paused, bewildered by her own feelings. 'I was as jealous of this family as you were of your sister. Maybe I belong here.'

'No. You *should* have destroyed this family, Alice. We're no good, no good to you, no good to anyone. My father's corrupt and as for me . . . well, I am what I am.'

'You are my mother,' Alice replied. 'And you will always be that, whatever you've done.'

'And your father?' Catherine countered. 'What of him? Will you own up to him, be proud of him? Was it worth it? Now you know who – and what – your parents are? Will you wonder now if it wouldn't have been better *not* to know?'

'I've lived all my life as an outsider. I never belonged anywhere, to anyone. You're the only family I have. You are my mother and David Lewes is my father,' Alice replied. 'For better or worse, you're all I have.'

Bending her head, Catherine reached for her daughter's hand and then pressed it to her heart.

'I know it's too late in the day, but I'm here for you, Alice, and your father *is* alive. Somewhere. Don't believe what they tell you – he's alive. I know it. Whilst he breathes, so do I. And only when he dies, can I let go.'

Chapter Fifty-Five

Back at St Ursula's the following morning, Alice walked into her rooms and shut the door behind her, sinking onto the old bed. It creaked, had done she since had come there so many years before. Idly she looked round. Was it just a hectic schedule which had meant that she had never decorated? Perhaps just a lack of money? The school had been cleaned up and homely little touches added, but not in her own rooms. Why was that, Alice wondered. Because she had never really wanted to stay?

She loved the work and the children, but knew that her home was never going to consist of two square rooms lined with cheap paper, and a bathroom down the hall. The cracked tiles around the little alcove where Alice cooked her meals on an old stove were clean, but old-fashioned. There were no paintings on her walls, no photographs, no little lifters to the spirit. Or reminders of home.

Will Reynolds and Minnie Lomond had decorated their rooms. The latter even had needlepoint cushions and chintz curtains inherited from God knew when, but Alice had never made any impression on the place she had lived so long. It was where she ate, slept and worked, but if she left tomorrow there would be no trace of her remaining. No impression of her ever having been there.

It was a sombre thought. Rolling over onto her back, Alice stared at the cracks in the ceiling and thought about her mother's rooms. The opulence, the size and plushness of the furnishings. *Her mother's* rooms. She breathed quickly at the thought. She had found her mother at last.

She was alive. Everyone had been wrong: Alice Rimmer had a living, breathing mother.

But who could she tell? No one. If she did Catherine would be exposed, and that was not going to happen. She had a mother, but she was a secret. Like so many others . . . Alice covered her face with her hands, her eyes closed. The memory of the previous night came back in all its disturbing clarity. But despite everything Catherine had done, it was Judge Arnold that Alice despised.

He had planned everything. She could imagine how he would have bullied her mother, distressed and bewildered at what had happened. How like him to keep control, to spirit his wife, grandson and daughter away. How carefully carried out everything was, to the last detail. People would gossip after the tragedy – but what could be more natural than a father taking his daughter away from the scene of the murder? After a couple of years any change in Catherine *would* have been put down to trauma. It would have been so simple to make her swop places, to make an unstable girl into her dead sister.

Alice was certain that her mother had never planned the swopping of roles. She knew that Catherine had plotted her sister's death, but doubted that she had the foresight to see further than the murder itself. What thoughts had gone through her mind when she saw her dead sister – and the look on her husband's face when he realised what he had done?

And what did *he* think? Seeing Catherine, did David Lewes hope for a moment that he was mistaken? How long were those few seconds in which he looked from Catherine to Dorothy and knew that he had killed the wrong woman? And how quickly did he realise that Catherine had planned it that way?

How his world must have spun round in his head, despair and guilt making him run – away from his wife, from The Dower House, down the dark lawns and into the town. What did he feel then? Alice wondered, her hands pressing her eyelids. *What did he feel?*

How much had he loved Dorothy that he could have killed his own wife for her? And how much did Catherine love him that she would have sacrificed her sister? In the name of love, Alice thought. Jesus, not in the name of *love* . . . She sat up suddenly, queasy with distress. The envy she had seen in her mother, the jealousy which had caused death, were in her too.

Hadn't it been jealousy which had driven her? Made her infiltrate the Arnold family, set child against mother? Hadn't she burned with spite and longed to hurt? Quickly Alice paced the room, her footsteps tapping on the bare boards. Who were her people? She looked round the shabby room. The poor? Or the rich up in Werneth Heights? Where did she *really* belong? . . . She kept pacing the floor, distressed and restless. Catherine had begged her to stay, to move back into The Dower House, but Alice had hesitated. Her mother needed her, that much was obvious, but did she need *her*? There was much more she needed to find out; things that her mother couldn't tell her.

Hurriedly arranging for another teacher to take her class, Alice pulled on her coat and ran down the back stairs and out into the courtyard of St Ursula's. A cold wind was blowing as she left the school grounds, moved under the dark viaduct, then caught a bus out to the moors. Head down, she then walked the remainder of the way to Greenfields, pushing open the heavy iron gates and hurrying towards Ray's office.

He opened on her third knock. 'Alice! Why didn't you call me? I'd have come to pick you up.'

'I have to talk to you.'

He put his arms around her. 'You're freezing. Come and sit by the fire.'

Hurriedly he then stoked up the fire and made them

both a mug of tea, passing Alice hers and then sitting down beside her.

'It's putrid, but it's hot,' he said, frowning. 'What's up?'

'I don't know how to tell you. It's all so incredible . . .' She fought to find words. 'Ray, it's . . .'

'What?' he coaxed. 'What is it, darling? Tell me. You know I'll help you.'

Encouraged, she explained everything that had happened the previous night, leaving nothing out. His face altered from incredulity to frowning displeasure. But he never interrupted her once.

Finally, Alice finished.

'Jesus,' Ray said thoughtfully, emptying his mug and lighting up a cigarette.

She stiffened. 'Is that all you can say?'

He was tired from a bad night's sleep, his face deeply lined. The confidence was unwelcome. He had hoped that Alice would shrug off the Arnolds and settle down with him, but it was apparent now that she had been drawn back, her involvement increasing, not decreasing.

Of course he couldn't blame her. Every child wanted to know its parents, but at what cost? It was dynamite. If the truth came out Judge Arnold would be pilloried, and as for his daughter – God, what would happen there?

'I just need a while to think,' Ray said.

'To *think*?' Alice echoed incredulously. 'What is there to think about?'

'I meant . . .' He paused.

What did he mean? She was beautiful, bright, brave, the perfect consort to work with him at Greenfields. A woman who had never shown any instability in her own character, nothing to give away her lineage.

'Ray,' Alice said urgently, 'talk to me.'

God, what's the matter with me? Ray wondered guiltily. He was looking at Alice differently, searching for any sign of her parents' vices. Would he *always* think that way now?

Wonder about any flash of temper, any subtle guile? She had proved that she could be deceptive, Ray thought, remembering how she had left Greenfields, moving away and changing her name. But that had been merely self-preservation. Hadn't it?

'Don't look at me like that!' Alice said.

He blinked. 'Like what?'

'Like you're looking at a stranger,' she replied, her eyes blazing. 'I should never have told you! It's all changed for you now, hasn't it?'

'Alice, let me just sort out my thoughts.'

Turning away from her, he rubbed his eyes. Alice was the woman he loved, he *had* to trust her. And yet, and yet ... Hadn't she come to Greenfields under a cloud? The business with Robin Tripps – why had she been singled out to be the scapegoat? And what a coincidence it was that her *cousin* should die under her care? Ray had thought all along that Alice had been a victim, but suddenly he wasn't so sure. Maybe she was more like her parents that even she realised.

'Look at me!' Alice urged him, getting to her feet and walking over to him. She was desperate for his comfort. 'I've not changed, I'm still Alice. Your Alice.'

He froze at her touch. Alice backed away. 'What is it?'

'I slept badly last night, that's all.'

'No, it's not that,' she said blankly. 'You're different.'

He had changed in the time it had taken her to tell him the story. Suddenly Ray Berry doubted her. The realisation left her stranded, bereft.

'Ray, talk to me, tell me what you're thinking.'

He shrugged, ashamed and mute.

'Ray,' she pleaded, then dropped her hand from his arm, her tone suddenly cold. 'I see.'

'You see what?'

'You're like the rest.'

'Alice, come on –'

461

'I don't want to talk about it now, Ray. The moment's past. I know what you're thinking. I wish to God I didn't.'

'It'll just take some time to sink in.'

'Take all the time you want,' she said bitterly. 'In the meantime, will you could give me Guy Priestly's number? I want to call him.'

Confused, Ray was clumsy, eager to help.

'I have it here somewhere,' he said, rummaging through his desk. His heart was heavy. 'Here you are.'

Alice took the number. 'Can I ask him to come here? I want to see him.'

'Of course, of course,' Ray reassured her, passing her the phone. 'You're welcome.'

An hour later Guy arrived to find two people he thought he knew sitting in silence. Disturbed, he looked from Ray to Alice and then sat down, his bearded face quizzical.

'So, what's the mystery all about?'

'Anything I say to you will be in confidence, won't it?' Alice said. 'Forgive me, but I have to ask.'

Guy nodded. 'Naturally.'

Then taking in a breath Alice told him what had happened the previous night. His face betrayed nothing, but he was shaken. Fancy Alice Rimmer being related to the Arnolds ... She spared him nothing, admitting her own spite and infiltration of the household, and then waited for Guy's reaction.

Leaning forward he tapped her on the knee. 'You all right?'

She swallowed, touched by his concern. 'Yes, I'm fine.'

'Good.' He looked over to Ray. 'This is a story and a half, isn't it? Poor Alice, what she's been through.'

His reaction was so opposite to Ray's that the latter flushed, awkwardly turning away. Guy saw the reaction and then realised what had caused the tension he had felt when he arrived.

'Guy,' Alice said, 'I want to ask your help.' She could

sense Ray stiffen behind her, but carried on. 'I want to find my father.'

Guy blew out his cheeks. 'Alice, the man's dead.'

'But *is* he?' she queried. 'I'm not sure, Guy. My mother thinks he's still alive. She says she's only living because of him – and for once, I believe her. She'll give up if she knows he's really dead. Besides, I want to know for my own peace of mind.'

'But David Lewes would have come forward by now.'

'Why? He would have been tried for murder. Why come back? Judge Arnold arranged everything, my mother said: the swopping of roles; the going away after the death. Maybe he arranged my father's disappearance too?'

Guy shook his head. 'Alice, I hardly think –'

'He's capable of it,' she interrupted. 'He has contacts everywhere. You know that, Guy. He could have spirited my father away. He could have had him killed.'

'That's a bit extreme, Alice.'

'Is it?' she countered. 'Who was there to look out for David Lewes? He had no family, no one to miss him. Besides, after what he'd done, who would give a damn about him? No one would care about a murderer, would they?'

'But to stay hidden for so long would be impossible.'

'I agree, but what if it wasn't his choice? What if someone had had him hidden away somewhere?'

Guy frowned. 'Alice –'

'I always loathed my father for what he did, but now I'm not so sure he wasn't just another victim of the Arnold family.' She leaned towards Guy, her face pale. 'Please help me. I *have* to find him. It can't be that hard, surely?'

'I wouldn't know where to start,' he replied honestly.

'But think about it – if my father wasn't killed, where would someone hide him?'

'Abroad?'

She nodded. 'I thought about that. Judge Arnold had

463

the money and the contacts. But the police would have been looking for my father at the time of the murder. So why not hide him somewhere nearer home?'

'Like where?'

'A mental institution.'

She could hear Ray gasp behind her, but didn't look round.

'What better place to have someone committed, put away, out of sight for ever. Judge Arnold *could* have arranged it, couldn't he?'

Guy paused to consider before replying. 'It's possible. Unlikely, but possible. He would have to have had a doctor in his pay.'

'And if he did, where could they have taken my father?'

'There are a few places.' He shook his head. 'Alice, I don't think it would work. I mean, people would have recognised David Lewes.'

'If he was held in isolation? Judge Arnold has ruled his family – and a large part of this town – for many years. I don't doubt he could organise this: have his son-in-law locked away, put it about that he was dead and make his daughter marry again. He would cover his tracks well. After all, if anyone found out there would be a scandal and my mother would be a bigamist.'

She had got Guy thinking.

'There *are* a few institutions around here. Summertown, Lark's Height, Rain Hill –'

'And Judge Arnold is always donating money to medical funds, isn't he?' Alice asked.

Guy looked thoughtful. 'That's true. He's always had an interest.'

'So he might well be able to pull it off?'

Hurriedly Ray interrupted them. 'Look, even if all of this is true, do you think you should pursue it? I mean, what's the point?'

Alice stared at him, astonished. Where had Ray Berry

464

gone? she wondered. That good kind man who had always been there for her? Where was he now, when she needed him the most?

'But I *have* to know, Ray. Surely you can understand that?'

'I understand that you should forget the Arnolds and the past!' he retorted. 'Walk away from it, Alice. Come here with me and forget it all.'

She stood up, bewildered. 'It's gone too far. I can't forget it. And you shouldn't ask me to.'

'I don't understand you!' he snapped. 'I'm offering you a good home and you're chasing around digging up the past and all kinds of scandal.'

Her voice hardened with bitterness and disappointment: 'I'm sorry if this is embarrassing you, Ray –'

'You're embarrassing yourself. Acting like a fool.'

Her voice was steely. 'How dare you talk to me like that! This is my family –'

'Something they conveniently forgot when they gave you away!' he hurled back furiously, tiredness and confusion making him reckless. 'What's really drawing you to the Arnolds, Alice? Love or *money*?'

Without any warning, she struck him with all her force, knocking him off balance. He fell against the chair and then landed heavily on the floor.

Guy got to his feet and looked down at him. 'You asked for that,' he said curtly. 'If she hadn't hit you, I would have.' Extending his hand, he pulled Ray to his feet. 'I think maybe we all need to calm down a little. Ray, sit there. Alice, you sit down too, and let's talk.'

Her face was ashen, her lips bloodless, Guy looking at her and seeing something he had never seen in her before. *Rage*. She was composed, the lovely face unreadable, but around her there tingled a pulsating aura. It was then that Guy saw it. In the moment Alice turned and glanced over to him he remembered a night a long time ago. He had been in a ballroom, watching a tall, handsome man, a man who had been kind to him. *David Lewes*. It *was* there – that turn of the head, that dark glance. By God; Guy thought, she really *is* her father's child.

'I'll find out what I can, Alice.'

She nodded. 'Thank you.'

'You know that if I can help you, I will.'

Sullen in his chair, Ray looked at his friend and then at Alice. Suspicion had sunk its teeth into his heart and his shame was threatening to choke him.

Guy moved to the door. 'Do you want a lift home, Alice?'

She nodded. Then left without saying a word to Ray.

Chapter Fifty-Six

After his surgery the following morning, Guy secreted himself away and made a few calls to the three institutions he had mentioned to Alice. And drew a blank, which was what he had expected. Logic told him that it was a wild-goose chase, and yet the longer he thought about it the more he wondered about just what *had* happened to David Lewes.

It had been presumed by everyone that he was dead. After all, he'd run away from his crime; no doubt he had committed suicide. And then there was the body they had found. So convenient, Guy thought, and so lucky that it had been sufficiently decomposed to make identification impossible. Alice had been right when she said that no one would have cared about her father. He was a criminal; all the interest and sympathy would have been concentrated on the family. So after searching for him for a while, the police finally gave up and were willing to accept that the drowned man was David Lewes.

And Judge Arnold would have wanted his son-in-law dead. After all, if he was still alive, his daughter would be a bigamist. He *had* to keep David Lewes out of sight. So *had* he arranged for him to be put away? Under a different name, in one of the discreet, isolated private institutions?

The phone rang beside him, making Guy jump.

'Hello?'

'It's Ray.'

A pause.

''Lo, Ray, what d'you want?'

'Look, I was out of line yesterday, but this idea of Alice's is crazy.'

Once, Guy would have agreed with him, but now he wasn't sure. And he disliked mysteries.

'It'll cost me nothing to check it out.'

'Guy, let it drop.'

'Why?' he countered, surprised. 'If it was my father I'd want to know what happened to him. Besides, if Judge Arnold *did* arrange something illegally *I* want to know. I don't like the idea of corruption in medical circles.'

'Guy, I'm begging you, leave it be. Alice will settle down, forget about it –'

'You *are* joking!' he countered. 'The one thing I would put money on is Alice *never* letting this rest until she's found out the truth.'

Enquiries at the records office of Oldham and then Somerset House yielded nothing. There was no record of the death of a David Lewes. But then that didn't mean he was still alive, Guy thought. He could have been buried under a different name . . . He sighed to himself, scratching his beard and thinking of Ray.

What a bloody fool he'd been, Guy thought. He had shown his hand good and proper. God knew if Alice would ever feel the same about him again. And it was unworthy of him. Ray had never been vicious, or a coward, usually more than ready to stand his corner. But he had failed this time.

Guy was glad that he didn't love anyone. It was easier that way. He had his housekeeper and his patients and had long since bedded himself into bachelorhood. Love was such punishment – he thought of David Lewes and what Alice had told him about her mother – love tore your guts out, befuddled your brain, made every fact a puzzle and every puzzle a fact. It was insanity – and it *caused* insanity.

Sighing, Guy leaned back in his chair, his hands behind his head. If David Lewes *was* still alive, someone had to know where he was . . .

Guy liked Alice and was pleased to help her, but there

was another motive for his involvement – his loathing of Judge Arnold. Every mean thought he had ever had about the old man had been vindicated. Arnold had ruled and ruined his family, but had he done more? In his list of victims, professional and personal, had Judge Arnold managed to manipulate the medical fraternity too?

Guy thought of The Dower House and shivered, uncharacteristically spooked. Then he thought of a man dancing; a man with dark eyes and elegant clothes. A man everyone envied, then shunned. And then lastly Guy thought of that man's daughter – waiting to know if he was dead or alive.

Ray phoned Alice at St Ursula's several times that day, but her secretary told him she was busy. He then penned a note and put it in the post, regretting it immediately. If the truth be known, his shortcomings had come as a shock to him. He had never been spiteful before, or prone to suspicion. But a malignant force had come down between him and Alice and no amount of charm or persuasion could lift it.

Years of struggle and commitment to Greenfields had tired him. He was getting on, weary of problems. But he was in love with Alice – and Alice had always had troubles. Stupidly Ray had believed that she would marry him and settle, be the dutiful wife, their future lives together steady, on a even keel. He had been fooling himself, he thought bitterly, lighting another cigarette and staring at his hands: nicotined fingers, the hands of a worker, not an ex-playboy.

He would have aged better if he had stuck to his old life, Ray thought idly. But that was the way it went, he couldn't regret what he had done, even if it had been hard. He remembered Toni Palmer suddenly, and her death, the way it had changed him, driven to him to do something worthwhile. Which he had. But that social conscience was all but exhausted. He had been looking forward to a comfortable middle age and now here was Alice, trawling up all manner of unpleasantness.

It wasn't *impossible* to ride it. But Ray had lost the appetite for the fight. His love affair with Alice had been stimulating, their lovemaking tender – but she had changed in his eyes now. She represented doubts, an unsettling presence in his life. He loved her, but he was suddenly afraid of her. Of what she might do to destabilise him – and of what she might become.

Shaking, Ray dialled her number again, fighting his instincts. Then, defeated, he replaced the receiver on the third ring.

Burly in a heavy overcoat, his trilby pulled down over his forehead, Guy ran up the steps of Rain Hill Hospital and then stamped the snow off his shoes. The place was quiet, with an air of subdued tension. A nurse hurried over to greet him in the hallway.

'I've come to see Dr Morris Johnson,' Guy explained, shaking the snow off his hat and undoing his coat.

A few minutes later, the doctor appeared, his hand extended.

'Good to meet you, Dr Priestly.'

'Likewise,' Guy replied to the small, fastidiously neat doctor. 'Where can we talk?'

Dr Johnson led him into a side office and then closed the door. He was smiling triumphantly.

'It was a long shot, but as I said on the phone, I think I might have discovered something about David Lewes.'

Guy leaned forward eagerly. 'What?'

'There was an old doctor who was here twenty-odd years ago. He lives nearby, a bit dotty in the head now,' he wiggled a finger at his temple, 'but not *that* dotty. No one takes him seriously any more, but I thought he was worth seeing. I went to visit him after we talked.'

'And?'

'He was a bit weird, made tea and talked about the First World War, how he had been a field surgeon. He'd developed an interest in shell shock, apparently, and that was why he remembered David Lewes and the murder, even though it was ages ago. Old people do that, don't they – remember the past better than the last few minutes?'

Impatiently, Guy raised his eyebrows. 'What did he say?'

'That he thought he had seen David Lewes at Sutton Bridge Hospital –'

Guy felt the hairs rise on the back of his neck. 'He saw him?'

'So he says. At Sutton Bridge Hospital.'

'Which bloody closed ten years ago!' Guy snapped exasperated.

Dr Johnson was looking smug. 'I know, but the old doc remembered something else. He'd been working on another ward when he saw this man hurried in with a couple of people holding on to his arms. He was reminded of how shell-shocked men staggered and so he took particular notice. Because of that he followed the little entourage and caught a very brief glimpse of the patient through a window, before he was bundled away. Well, the old man says that he thought there was something familiar about him – and then remembered the murder case and seeing David Lewes's picture in the paper.'

'But he didn't follow it up?'

'Oh yes,' Dr Johnson replied, 'but he was laughed at. You know the kind of thing – *You're getting as nutty as your patients. David Lewes here? Are you joking?*'

'So he let it drop?'

'No, that's the interesting bit.' Dr Johnson was warming to his theme. 'This old doctor wasn't sure *what* he'd seen, but he was curious. So he tried to get another look at the man, but he was held in isolation and a day later he was moved.'

'Bugger it!'

'Oh, hold on, that's not the end. Our curious doctor sneaked out to have a look when the ambulance arrived late at night. He had no chance of seeing who the patient was, but he *did* see the luggage being packed into an ambulance. And he saw the name tags.'

'Christ! Are you joking?' Guy said, leaning further towards the doctor. 'D'you know that name?'

'There was no name, only initials – one set of initials on a bag – D. L. The old man remembers that well because they were the same initials as David Lewes. But when he looked up the man's discharge papers they were under the name of Donald Logan.'

Guy exhaled impatiently. 'Well, it was hardly likely that they would use his real name.' He paused. 'But it's no bloody good to us, nothing but a dead end. We don't know where David Lewes – if it was him – was taken after he left Sutton Bridge.'

'You want to have a word with the doctor. He's old, a bit forgetful, but he remembers it all very well.'

'But not enough to pursue the matter further?'

Dr Johnson looked Guy straight in the face when he answered. 'I think he would have done. But he was ambitious and his superiors told him that he would be moved onto another – less salubrious – hospital if he ever asked questions again.'

'Jesus!' Guy said with disgust.

'Hang on a minute. As I said, the old doctor was ambitious, but he had a conscience, and it nagged at him. He spent nearly a year tracking him down, but in the end he found *Mr Logan* again.'

'Where?'

'Rain Hill Hospital,' Dr Johnson replied, 'and for all the old doctor knows *Mr Logan* is still here.'

Before she left The Dower House Alice had promised to return. When she arrived one night later that week, the butler showed her straight to Dorothy's rooms, avoiding old man Arnold and Leonard, who were downstairs.

When she saw Alice, Dorothy stood up and held out her arms. 'I missed you.' When Alice stepped back, Dorothy flushed and crossed her arms awkwardly. 'I'm sorry, I shouldn't expect you to treat me like a mother. I don't deserve it.'

You can't be my mother, Alice thought again. Not you.

'I think we should keep everything a secret for the time being,' she said, trying to sound calm. 'We can't tell anyone what really happened. People still have to think that you're Dorothy.'

'But I'm Catherine. I'm *Catherine*, your mother – and David's wife.'

'But I have to think of you as *Dorothy* and call you *Dorothy*, or I might slip up and give everything away,' Alice explained. 'We have to hide the truth.'

'But I want everyone to know what went on.'

'Why?' Alice asked, bemused. 'Why now? After you've managed to keep it a secret for so long? Why confess everything now?'

'I want it to be over – the hiding away, watching every word, every glance. I've been looking over my shoulder for years, too many years. I'm getting older, Alice, careless. Maybe my father's right, maybe I'm a little mad. I know I keep slipping back, thinking and dreaming about the past. *I don't have a future*, I just want to go back to when I was happy. When I was with David.' She looked appealingly at her daughter. 'You have to help me find him.'

'You're not thinking clearly,' Alice cautioned her. 'If all this comes out, what will happen? You'll be pilloried, people will crucify you. You might also be a bigamist – think about that. And your father's part in the whole charade will ruin him – not that I give a damn about him. As for Leonard – how will he feel when he discovers what his wife's done? Or that she might still be married to David Lewes? *If* my father's still alive.'

'I know David's alive.'

'But I don't.'

'Alice, you have to find him. I want David to come back to me. Then things would be as they used to be.'

'*As they used to be?*' Alice repeated, bewildered. 'How can they be? Think back, think about how it was. My father would have killed you. He only killed your sister by mistake, he wanted to kill you . . . How on earth can you think that he would come back to you – even if he could?'

Dorothy turned her head wearily, as though the action exhausted her. 'David loved me before he loved my sister. If she had never come along, he would have always loved me. She made him turn against me, it was her fault.'

'You're fooling yourself!' Alice snapped. 'It's a dream, nothing else. It's stupid, impossible. You *have* to realise that it can never happen.'

'Of course it will! David will come out one day –'

'He will not!'

'He will!' Dorothy shouted back. 'He will. He *has* to – that's all I'm living for.'

'Isn't there something else worth living for now?' Alice asked, her tone cool. 'You have your children. You have me, you have Charlie –'

'Charlie's wife has taken him away from me. He has his own life now.'

'But no one's taking *me* away,' Alice said, then stopped.

The words had come from her lips before she had had time to check them. What was she saying? That she would *help* this woman? This woman whom she had hated for so long? Why? What had changed? Not the past, not her actions, only one thing. *She was her mother*. And, knowing that, nothing would ever be the same.

Dorothy's gaze focused fully on Alice.

'Will you find him? Will you find your father for me?'

'I've already starting looking for him,' Alice replied dully. Why was *she* never enough? Why was she always running second to someone else? 'I've asked a friend to help me.'

'When you find David, we'll all go away together.'

Alice took in a breath to steady herself. It was lunacy, pure madness.

'It can never happen. My father can't come back to you . . . You have to face the fact that he might be dead.'

'No, David's not dead.'

Impatiently, Alice caught hold of her mother's arm. 'But what if he *is*? What will you do then?'

'I can't live without him.'

Still holding her mother's arm, Alice stared into her bewildered eyes. 'But if he's dead, you'll *have* to live without him.'

'No, if he's dead, I'll die. I told you before, I *can't* live without him.'

'You've been living without him for years!' Alice retorted. 'You've been living and eating and sleeping without him for a long time.'

'He's with me always. He's in my heart.'

Alice's face flushed, disappointment making her unexpectedly cruel. She felt rejected again. It wasn't enough that her mother had done it once, now she was repeating the injury.

'It's always *you*, isn't it? Your father protected you, Leonard protects you, they are always at your beck and call – and now you want me to do your running around for you.' Her voice hardened. 'No, Mother. No! You gave me precious little before, don't expect me to act as your servant now.'

'I don't expect you to be my servant! I just thought you would want to help me.'

'Why?' Alice snapped back. 'You never helped me much, did you? You let the old man send me away –'

'I thought you were going to be looked after! I thought you were going to people who would care for you.'

'Why couldn't you?' Alice shouted, her eyes dark with fury, all control gone. 'You were my mother and you let me go. And why? Because I might give you away. You would sacrifice your own child to save your own skin. You're selfish, cruel, hard. You might hate your father, but you're like him. Things didn't go your way in life – your husband didn't love you – and so what did you do? You tricked him into killing the woman he *did* love. And then you let your father tidy everything up . . . Just tell me how much of your distress is real and how much is an act?' She paused, looking at her mother with contempt. 'When you told me who you were it was a shock, but I thought I had someone at last, *my own mother*. But since then all you've done is ask me to help you. Never once – *once* – have you asked how you could help *me*.'

Her mother opened her mouth to speak, but Alice had already moved to the door.

'I'll find my father if he's alive. But not for you. For *myself*. I want to look him in the eyes and understand what drove him to kill.' She wrenched open the bedroom door and then turned. 'We share the same blood, Mother – I just hope that's *all* we share.'

'But I love you,' Dorothy blustered helplessly. 'I want to make it all up to you –'

'You *don't* really love me, Mother,' Alice replied, her tone icy. 'And I doubt that you ever loved my father half as much as you love yourself.'

Chapter Fifty-Seven

Guy was surprised at the change in Alice when he came to collect her at St Ursula's. Lessons had finished for the day and she was standing at the entrance, waiting for him. As he opened the door to let her in, Guy could hear the sound of a tune being played in the next street and smiled.

'The jitterbug.'

Alice looked at him. 'What?'

'Don't you know it? It's a dance.'

Fascinated, he studied her and remembered the young woman he had come across all those years earlier on the moors. Alice was now in her thirties, a beautiful woman, yet divorced from the world. When had he ever heard about Alice going out? Going to the pictures? Going on holiday? Never. Other women of her age had families, children, but Alice's children were the slum kids, her family the huge forbidding mausoleum St Ursula's.

Had she never been in love? He was sure she didn't really love Ray, not with passion. But had there never been any others? If there hadn't, what a waste, Guy thought suddenly. What a bloody stupid waste.

'Do you never go dancing, Alice?'

'Dancing! Oh, come on, Guy, I don't have the time.'

'No hobbies?' he asked, suddenly curious as he drove the car away from the school.

'Like what?'

'Sewing, music, catching butterflies.'

She laughed, the sound melodious and haunting. 'We don't get many butterflies in Salford.'

'No, but there are plenty up on the moors,' he replied,

driving under the grim viaduct and heading out of town.

She was silent for a while, looking out of the window.

'Alice?'

'Yes?'

'Will you forgive Ray? I know he didn't really mean what he said. He was tired, overwrought.'

'There's a lot of it about,' Alice replied poignantly. 'People are saying all kinds of things they don't mean. Maybe it's a new illness, Doctor.'

'He loves you a great deal.'

'Maybe,' Alice said, glancing down at her hands.

'Ray Berry's a good man,' Guy went on. 'Give him another chance.'

'Why are you pleading his case for him?' Alice asked, almost amused. 'I never thought you were a great believer in love.'

'I'm not – for myself,' he smiled, 'but for you two it might work out. You have the same interests, the same ambitions. Ray won't expect you to give up your work and you won't be the demanding, helpless type.'

She flinched at the words. 'Maybe I might like to be the helpless type? To rely on others for once.'

'You?' he said, surprised. 'You're a coper, Alice. The world is divided into two sorts – the helpless and the helpers. You come into the latter category.'

'Like you.'

He nodded. 'Like me – and like Ray.'

Winding down the car window, Alice leaned her face into the wind. It was cold and stung her skin.

'What if I said you were wrong, Guy? What if I said that I *wanted* to be helpless, looked after, carried about.' She turned, her dark hair blowing in the chill wind. Suddenly she looked wild, exotic – and startled him. 'What if I said I didn't want to help people? That I had been forced into that way of life? Persuaded to care? What if I said it had been my *duty*, not my choice?'

He stopped at the traffic lights and turned. The wind was still ruffling Alice's hair; her expression was confrontational.

'What if I told you that the composed, reliable, caring Alice wanted to kick over the traces? Wanted to please herself? What would you say then, Dr Priestly? Would you want to help me then? Would you want to help that kind of woman?'

'I don't understand you,' he said cautiously. A van blew its horn behind them as he ground the gears. 'What are you saying?'

As if to answer him, Alice wound up the window, the wind closed off, her face became composed again. All the wildness, the fierceness of spirit had been extinguished. God, he thought, why was there *always* something disturbing about her? Something secret. Almost dangerous.

For another hour they drove, Alice soon talking again, Guy relaxing and wondering what – if anything – he had actually seen. Gradually Alice became quieter as they left the outskirts of Manchester and finally arrived at the gates of Rain Hill Hospital.

Stopping the car, Guy noticed that Alice's hands were clenched together so tightly that the fingers were white.

'You know what this place is, don't you?'

'Where they put the crazies,' Alice replied. 'That's what the kids say. Are you sure it's my father?'

He nodded. 'Are you ready to see him?'

She nodded, but couldn't find words.

Together they were admitted through the grim, barred entrance doors, Alice biting her bottom lip. The smell was not dissimilar to the smell at St Ursula's, a place long disinfected and scrubbed, but still carrying the old sour odour of neglect.

Automatically Guy turned to her. 'Are you OK? I can go in without you.'

'No,' she said simply, 'he's my father. I promised my mother I would find him. I promised myself.'

She walked on with him, a slim woman, looking delicate next to his bulk. Moments later a nursing sister came to greet them.

'Dr Priestly?'

He nodded.

'Mr Logan is through here,' she said, leading the way.

Guy had explained to Alice about the change of her father's name. Judge Arnold had organised everything thoroughly. Except that he had never expected a doctor to notice the name tags on some luggage. Such a little detail, but so important, forgotten for over thirty years. It was sad, Guy thought, how lives hang on such trifles.

The sister halted outside a side ward, then pushed open the door, showing them in. The light was bright from the windows, blinding Alice for several seconds as she stood on the polished floor. Finally she could make out two beds, one empty, the other ruffled, its occupant sitting in a chair beside it.

Taking her elbow, Guy led her towards the bed. The figure in the chair then came into direct focus, the light playing full on his face. This was an old man! Guy thought. What the hell was the sister doing bringing him in here? There had been a mistake . . . Irritated, Guy leaned closer towards the seated figure.

He was sitting perfectly still, his back rounded, a little covering of grey hair stretched over the yellow scalp. Hands like crumpled paper lay on the top of his immobile lap, his eyes looking down, the lids crepy and threaded with veins.

'Oh my God,' Guy said hoarsely.

'Is it him?' Alice asked, her voice barely audible.

He wanted to say no, no, David Lewes is not this man. This is some cadaver propped up in a chair. Someone who doesn't know he's dead. Breathing doesn't make him human, Guy wanted to say, it's just a reflex action. Because the life is gone, vigour, spirit, charm, all gone.

'Is it him?' Alice repeated, her throat constricting with pity. 'Is *this* my father?'

It can't be, Guy wanted to insist, this is not the man I remember. He was dark and handsome, a dancer, a charmer, with all his world in love with him. He was the man everyone looked at, admired. The man who was glamorous and kind. Because kindness became him. But not this man, not this corpse.

'Guy, tell me! For God's sake, *is it him*?'

He nodded. Once.

Slowly Alice moved towards the figure. There was no reaction, even when her shadow fell over him. A worn cardigan and a shirt several sizes too big drowned the shrunken frame, a pair of old glasses sliding down the wasted nose. All the anger she had felt evaporated, all the bitterness lifted. Judge Arnold had incarcerated her father. Taken him out of the world, hidden him. If he wasn't mad when he was put away, she had no doubt that he soon would have been. Too crazy to protest, too mad to be listened to. Just one more victim.

She could honestly tell her mother that David Lewes was not dead. But he was dying. And obviously he had been for years, ounce by ounce, his heart beating, his eyes blinking in reflex. Nothing more. This was her mother's husband. Her passion, her obsession. Her love.

It had begun with him and would now end with him. *Her father*. She had found him – and lost him – at the same time.

Chapter Fifty-Eight

December came in cold, and stayed cold. The moors grew densely white under snow, the sky opaque as a blind man's eye. At Tollbank Farm, the cows were brought in, the windows still left open at Greenfields, the children muffled like mummies in their clothes.

It had been two weeks since Alice had seen her father. Two weeks in which she had avoided her mother and put off visiting The Dower House. She had tried to put off seeing Ray too, but he was persistent, coming down to St Ursula's and waiting patiently for her outside her office.

He asked for forgiveness, and she gave it. But from the mouth, not the heart. Their closeness had taken a beating, Ray knew, but he was certain he could recover their affection. What he had said, he explained, was disgraceful. He was so sorry, so sorry. He hadn't meant it. What could he do to show her how sorry he was?

And Alice listened to him and told him about her father and thought that, somewhere along the line, they would settle back together. They were so suited, after all. But she couldn't talk about it at the moment, she told Ray. She had too much on her mind – her mother and now her father.

The pain of seeing David Lewes had been beyond anything Alice could have imagined. That hopeless figure in the chair hadn't been alive. When she was younger Alice had wanted to confront him and hate him for what he had done. But how could she hate anything so beaten?

The passion which had caused her parents both so much heartache seemed like a wicked joke. Surely that man in the old chair, with the blank eyes and the stooped back, wasn't the same man who had provoked such envy? Had this really once been David Lewes, the glamorous success-ful businessman married to his beautiful wife? How every-one must have envied them in their early days – and how much they had once been what Alice had imagined her parents to be.

But time and circumstances, envy and malice had destroyed them both. Her father was a stranger and would always remain so. Her mother, for whom Alice had longed, was a woman she despised and could barely bring herself to pity. It was a cold time of year. Cold in the streets and in every cell of Alice's heart.

At St Ursula's, the term ended, the children going home for the Christmas holidays.

'It won't be Christmas for some of them,' Jilly said idly. 'I heard that Paddy Riley's sister's got TB. Going up to Greenfields.'

'I know, Ray told me,' Alice replied, looking down the bare corridor through her office door. All her achievements seemed small to her suddenly, almost pointless. 'I thought the governors might have let us have some money for dec-orations. You can bet their homes won't be without trees this Christmas.'

Her bitterness caught Jilly off guard. 'Are you all right?'

'No,' Alice said bluntly, slamming some papers down on her desk. 'No, I'm not.'

'Feel poorly?'

'Sick to the heart,' she said, pulling a face. 'Do you ever wonder why we bother, Jilly?'

'No.'

'I do. I wonder if anything matters much.' She sighed. 'Oh, don't listen to me. Ethel would say I was cranky, out of sorts. When I was a kid, I would have got a dose of castor oil for moaning. Anyway, it's the end of term, you should be on your way home now.'

Jilly hesitated in the doorway. 'If you're sure there's nothing else I can do?'

Alice shook her head. 'No, go home.'

'But I could –'

'You could go home,' Alice repeated, smiling.

'But what about you?'

'Me? I'm going home too,' Alice replied thoughtfully.

There was a bell-ringing practice on at St Anne's, the melodic pealing spreading over the cold terraces, out towards the city centre and the smutty slums beyond. Under the snow, the town echoed to the sound of the bells, the advertising posters for vanishing cream, OXO and Dunn's Outfitters gazing down benignly from sooty brick walls.

Victor was walking slowly, his head down, snow on his hair and shoulders. He could smell fish being fried and hear a bus brake as it rounded the bend behind him. Somewhere a baby cried, and as the viaduct came into view he could see the vast dark outline of St Ursula's lighted by the yellow streetlamps which ringed its perimeters.

He would go in. No, he wouldn't. He would . . . Victor hesitated, felt hunger, unexpected and sharp, gnaw at him. How long had it been since he had eaten? That morning, yes, it would be that morning. Ethel had come round and made some breakfast for him and Hilly. They had sat on the bed and eaten it, Ethel telling them about how the circus had come to Manchester and a monkey had got free. Took them over half an hour to catch it, she had said, and the audience had thought it was all part of the act.

Hilly had laughed. *Hilly had laughed* . . . He kept staring at the black outline of the school, then moved nearer, approaching the gates. Hurriedly, he tried to open them, but they were locked, snow falling on the black iron railings. Suddenly desperate, he rattled the gates, the snow falling off in icy clumps, his hands burning against the cold metal.

Somewhere he could hear screaming, but didn't know where it was coming from. It seemed behind, in front, and around him. Victor shook the gates, felt his fingers chilling, his head banging against the ironwork as the entrance doors opened and Alice came running down the steps toward him.

'Jesus, Victor,' she said helplessly.

The screaming stopped. It had been *his* screaming, all along.

'Victor,' she repeated, trying frantically to unlock the gates.

She knew what had happened. She had known as soon as she heard that unearthly screaming outside. *Hilly was dead.* Frantically, she scrabbled with the keys, finally unlocking the gates and then grabbing Victor's arm and drawing him in. The snow was falling on both of them, Alice staring, speechless, into his face. He was older now, she thought, so much older. Where was that boy she knew? Where was that young boy who meant so much to her?

He stumbled against her, his head against her shoulder, the icy snow scorching her skin. Together they moved towards the entrance doors, Victor mumbling under his breath. Alice took him inside to her office. Settling him in a chair, she forced him to drink some brandy and then kneeled beside him. He was numb with cold and shock.

'Hilly died.'

Alice closed her eyes for a brief moment, then urged Victor to finish the brandy.

'I loved her so much,' he said blindly, wiping his mouth with the back of his hand. 'Ethel came. They came to the house. Took her away. Took my Hilly . . . She's gone now. Gone.' He stopped, stared ahead. The full magnitude of what had happened passed over his face and panicked him. 'I have to get back!'

'Ssssh! Rest awhile,' Alice coaxed him. 'Hilly's not at home any more, Victor.'

'I never thought she'd die,' he said at last. 'She said it, but I didn't believe her. Not Hilly.' He touched his face, wincing as though his skin hurt. 'She said that she felt so well. Said she wanted a sleep, that she was going to get dressed later on. Ethel was there. We left Hilly, went downstairs. Ethel was still talking about the circus.' He was reliving it. 'Hilly was still warm when I went up to check on her. She was still warm . . . I should go back. She might not be dead –'

'Victor,' Alice said firmly, 'Hilly's gone now. She was always very ill, you know that. But you made her so happy that she lived a lot longer than anyone expected. *You* did that, Victor, you kept her alive. No other man could have done that for her. Only you.'

He was watching her face, reading her lips, as though hearing the words wasn't enough.

'I loved her,' he said, his eyes blind with tears, his nose running. 'I loved her so much. Much more than I ever expected to.'

Gently, Alice put her arm around his shoulder. 'I know you loved her. I loved her too. It was easy to love Hilly.'

Outside the bells were still ringing, the snow still falling. Outside somewhere children were rehearsing Christmas carols, somewhere men were returning from work, and somewhere else lovers were hurrying to secret meeting places. The world was going on. Somewhere. But not there. Not now.

Hilly had held on as long as she could. She had died at the dying down of the year. Slipped away, a good angel finally gone home.

Chapter Fifty-Nine

The year 1947 came in cold and solemn. The children returned to St Ursula's and Dora – previously Daft Dora – called by after school one day to tell Alice that she was getting married. For a girl who had been unable to talk or function normally, it was a triumph. Other pupils of Alice's did not fare so well. The Gorlands were pulled out of school by their parents, and Birdie Riley was back up at Greenlands, her TB making her trips more and more frequent.

In Salford, the bomb-damaged areas had long been cordoned off. Some had been rebuilt, but not that many. Others were simply out of bounds, placards erected – 'KEEP AWAY. DANGEROUS' – but the kids went to play there anyway and Kate Halligan broke her ankle falling off a wall. St Ursula's won some extra funding, and Greenfields managed to raise enough to have the roof of the sanatorium repaired. As for Micky Regan, rumour had it that he had skipped town. Certainly no one had seen him for years. His father was back in jail, but that was no surprise.

All in all, life went on pretty normally. Ray had gradually managed to win back Alice's trust and they were a couple again. As for Victor, he was bent into his grief. Work was the only thing which comforted him. There would never be anyone like Hilly, he said to anyone who would listen, he was lucky he had had her so long.

Anxious about him, Alice often visited the business on Fernshaw Street, Victor always stopping to talk when she called by. He had long since altered the premises, moving all trace of Mr Dedlington, his own name now over the door: 'VICTOR COATES – Carpenter'. As Alice had always believed, his talent had been recognised. There were more than a few pieces of Victor's furniture in some of the North West's finest houses. He wasn't rich, but he was further than he believed he could have come as an insecure orphan, and a hell of a long way from Netherlands.

Alice had invited Victor to spend New Year with her and Ray, but he had declined. He wanted to be alone, he said. He wasn't fit company for anyone. Alice was disappointed, but Ray wasn't. He knew that they had been in love once, and was well aware that Victor Coates was good-looking, still young and a widower. In short, a rival. Yet he needn't have worried. Alice didn't think of Victor as a potential lover. She was well aware of Hilly's hopes for them to marry, but it was never going to happen. Victor had his work, and Alice had Ray.

On 11 January, Alice received a note from her mother.

My dear daughter,

Why don't you come and see me any more? I know we quarrelled, but I don't hold what you said against you. You were right in many ways. Except that I do love you. And I want to prove that to you.

Come and see me, Alice. We could be friends. We should be friends.

Your loving mother,
Catherine

Alice stared at the name. *Catherine*. She had written it for anyone to see. Didn't her mother have *any* idea of caution? She couldn't start calling herself Catherine and not slip up. She was being reckless, stupidly so. You can't be Catherine again, Alice thought helplessly, you have to keep living as Dorothy. You have to keep living and lying . . . It was for her own good. It was for everyone's good.

Alice was also fully aware that if she visited her mother she would want to know about David Lewes. Had Alice found her father? How was he? Where was he? ... Oh God, Alice thought, what could she say to that? She should have visited her mother earlier, but had dodged the duty – and the news she was reluctant to pass on.

Leonard would have liked to sneak off and see Frances, but there wasn't going to be a chance that evening. Work had kept him longer than expected and then the old man had called him into the study and demanded to know about the three shops the Arnolds were opening in March. His brain, Leonard thought ruefully, was as acute as ever. To look at him anyone would think him a bloated old soak, but he was still sly, still keeping his spies on the lookout. Leonard knew who they were; the old stalwarts who had been hired by Judge Arnold and who still felt loyal to him; the ones who watched Leonard, and, no doubt, the ones who first reported the existence of Frances. God, Leonard thought, the old bugger has eyes and ears everywhere.

'You forget how much you owe me,' Judge Arnold said, sinking his bulk back into the bergère seat. 'I'm not ready for the knacker's yard yet.'

He was interrupted by the sudden appearance of the butler. 'Miss Rimmer is here to see you, sir.'

'Alice?' Leonard queried. 'Sh-sh-she hasn't been around f-f-for –'

'Oh, stop bloody stammering!' Judge Arnold barked. 'One day I'll die before you finish your bloody sentence!'

We live in hope, Leonard thought bitterly.

'Show her in!' Judge Arnold snapped at the servant. His eyes fixed on Alice as she walked into the room. 'So, you're back. What for this time? You upset my daughter when you were last here. I don't want her upsetting again.'

It was the wrong thing to say. Alice was out of patience and on edge. The day was bitterly cold, The Dower House gloomy as she walked in. There was no spirit of the New Year, and if it hadn't been for her mother, Alice would never have set foot in the place again.

'I'll leave the upsetting her to you – it's what you're best at.'

Judge Arnold blinked, his eyes narrowing. 'What the hell d'you mean, coming into my house and talking to me like that?'

Alice's aim was deadly. 'I saw David Lewes a few weeks ago.'

The old man's mouth slackened. Leonard gaped at her. 'D-D-David Lewes?'

Alice ignored him and kept her eyes on Judge. 'You knew he was still alive, didn't you? You had him moved to Rain Hill under a different name –'

'You're talking rubbish!'

'You know it's the truth,' Alice replied, standing up to him.

Baffled, Leonard looked from Alice to his father-in-law.

'B-b-but I thought you told me that David Lewes w-w-was d-d-dead?'

'He is! The woman's off her bloody head,' Judge Arnold snapped. 'What the hell are you playing at anyway, Alice Rimmer? Poking your nose into business that doesn't concern you? Why d'you keep coming here and upsetting everyone, telling lies?'

'I'm not the one that's telling lies, Judge.' Her voice was steely. 'You wanted everyone to think that David Lewes was dead. It was *vital* that everyone thought that, wasn't it?' Her eyes bored into his. She could feel the malice coming off him.

'What the hell has our family got to do with you?'

'More than you can imagine.'

Struggling to his feet, the old man faced her. He was livid with fury, his bloodshot eyes narrowing.

'I don't want you here. You have no business in this house. You bring nothing but trouble –'

'*Is* D-D-David Lewes st-st-still alive?' Leonard persisted, looking at Alice. 'Well, *is* he?'

She nodded.

The old man snorted with derision. 'No wonder Dorothy likes you – you're as mad as she is.'

Stung, Alice turned on him. 'Dorothy isn't mad. Dorothy never *was* mad.'

The words kicked out at him. He heard them, understood them, and then seemed to catch himself. Slowly Judge Arnold turned back to Leonard. 'I want to talk to Alice alone.'

'B-b-but –'

'Don't argue with me!' Judge snarled. 'Now, get out.'

For several moments after Leonard had left the room, the old man stood by the fireplace, one arm supporting him as he rested it against the mantelpiece. On the wall above him hung the vast oil portrait, a carriage clock ticking by his hand.

'So,' he said at last, 'what's all this about?'

Alice frowned. 'What in particular?'

'I suppose you want money?'

'I don't want money,' she replied, taking off her gloves and running her fingers through her hair.

'So, what *do* you want?'

'You'll know – in time.'

Judge Arnold flushed, then struggled to control his temper. 'For an ex-nanny you have a lot of nerve.'

'For a man who's broken the law, so do you.'

'*Broken the law!* What the bloody hell are you talking about now?'

'David Lewes,' Alice replied coldly.

She wanted to blow the whistle then, to say: David Lewes is my father. The man you tried to pretend was dead is my father. The granddaughter you tried to get rid off is *me*. All your old corpses and ghosts are rising up now. I know everything, and I know that the woman upstairs is my mother . . . She wanted to throw the words at him and see him rock. But she didn't. It wasn't the right time. She'd waited too long to bugger it up now.

'What do you know about David Lewes?' the old man blundered.

'He was your son-in-law, the man who killed your daughter.'

'His wife.'

'Was it?' Alice asked, feigning confusion. 'I thought . . . Oh, but of course you must be right. You were there, after all. And Dorothy and Catherine were your daughters.'

Judge's eyes were fixed on her. He was aware that she was baiting him, but at first he had thought her simply guessing, an opportunist on the make. Now he wasn't so sure. *Did* she know about his daughters? About the murder? He could feel himself sweat for the first time in years. Who was this little bitch who had been a thorn in his side, on and off for years?

'Spit it out!'

'What?' Alice asked. 'I don't know what you mean.'

'I want you to tell me,' the old man said, leaning towards her. 'What do you know?'

At once Alice turned away. 'I have to see your daughter now,' she said, walking to the door and then pausing. '*Dorothy*, I mean.'

'Who else?' he bellowed blindly as the door closed behind her. 'Who the bloody hell else?'

Having tried to listen at the door, Leonard was waiting for her in the hallway. As soon as Alice saw him she moved swiftly over to the stairs, but he followed her and grabbed her arm.

'What d-d-do you m-m-mean about David Lewes?'

'Why don't you ask your father-in-law? I imagine you couldn't hear that clearly enough through the door.'

He flushed. 'You're n-n-not here to cause t-t-trouble, are you?'

'Oh, Leonard,' Alice said despairingly, 'how much *more* trouble could there be?'

Reaching her mother's bedroom, Alice walked in and then leaned against the door, taking in a deep breath. Had she gone too far? Maybe she should have said nothing. But why should she keep holding her tongue? She was Judge Arnold's granddaughter. It was *her* father at Rain Hill, and *her* mother standing only feet away from her.

'You came, Alice. Thank you.'

Hurriedly she took out her mother's letter and passed it over to her. 'You put your real name on this. You mustn't do that, Mother. You still have to think of yourself as Dorothy –'

'But –'

'No!' Alice snapped. 'You're *Dorothy*.'

Her mother blinked slowly, like someone waking from a drugged sleep. 'Can I *never* tell anyone the truth?'

'No.'

'But,' she paused, struggling to understand, then latching on to another thought, 'did you find your father?'

The question caught Alice off guard. 'No,' she said hurriedly, playing for time. 'No, not yet.'

'But you will?' her mother pressed her.

And then what? Alice wondered. Then I come to you and say: Your husband is an old withered-up man, who can't move, or think, who hardly breathes. He is dead, but breathing. *And he will never come back for you . . .* What a perfect revenge, she thought. I could tell her now and destroy her. If I tell her, all hope will be gone. There will be nothing for her to live for. No promise of a future – however unlikely and ridiculous – to keep her alive. In a house of secrets, it was the most dangerous.

The truth was like acid on her tongue. Go on, she willed herself, she deserves it. Go on, tell her. No one would blame you . . .

But she couldn't.

'Alice, will you keep looking for him?' her mother urged her, desperation in her voice.

The moment stretched out its arms. Malignant, vengeful.

'Alice, will you keep looking for him?'

'Yes,' she said at last. 'I'll keep looking.'

Breathing in a sigh of relief, her mother sat down on the window seat. Snow was falling again, resting on the panes of glass before slipping to the earth below.

'What was he like?'

She turned to Alice. 'He was handsome,' she replied, smiling, but not that faraway smile – something warmer. 'I look at you now and see a little of him. He had dark eyes and hair and he was very tall.'

He is grey now, with dull eyes, and shrunken.

'I loved him so much. Once he bought me a little silhouette of myself, in a gilt frame. I have it somewhere . . .' she trailed off. 'No, I *did* have it, but my father took it away when he took away all of my things. Catherine's things. No, *my* things.'

Alice steered the conversation back. 'Did he propose to you?'

'Oh yes! He asked me to marry him in a friend's house. I was in the garden and David came out.' She focused far away, watching the scene again. 'The sun was very hot that day and he teased me about my face being brown. "It's not fashionable," he said, "but you look lovely to me." I thought he liked me, but not like that . . .'

The snow is no longer falling outside the window. It is summer and the trees are heavy with the cooing of wood pigeons.

'. . . There was a splash, someone had thrown someone else into the garden lake, and we turned, laughing. I couldn't stop looking at David. His jawline, hair, his mouth – I wanted whoever it was to keep squealing in the water, just so that David would never move. I wanted

494

the afternoon to fix itself: keep us locked there. Nothing to think about, to worry about, to lose. Nothing to change . . .'

She can smell the heavy summer roses and see the grass, dry in places from the long heat. She is staring at this man and loving him.

'. . . Then, just like that, David looked back to me and said, "It's you I want. Marry me, Catherine. We could go away, have a life that no one could ever have." I said yes, but I didn't say then that I didn't want to leave The Dower House. I thought I would just keep quiet and David would come to accept it. He would want to work in the business, and settle down . . .'

But he doesn't settle down, he hates The Dower House. The girl he fell in love with changes, and he looks elsewhere, for someone who understands him more.

'David made everyone laugh, and he was so kind. Full of ideas, of things to do. He was always bringing me presents.' She looked at Alice. 'When you were born he gave me a sapphire ring. We called you Amy.'

'Not Alice?'

She shook her head. 'No, you were Amy to us. When Charlie was born your father gave me a diamond pin. He was always kind . . . It was a long time ago, but I know he won't have changed. People don't. Not people like David.' She whimpered suddenly. 'I couldn't go on without knowing he was out there. I've done so many wrong things, so many. I gave you away, I let my father take over. He made me mad.' She shook her head. 'Or maybe it was Dorothy who made me mad. She drove me insane, running after David, stealing him from me. She knew how much I loved him – she didn't love him half as much. She just wanted him, because, for once, she was envious of me.' Her voice faltered. Confusion and guilt made her nervous, agitated. 'Every year I wanted to speak out, to say what had really happened. To tell everyone about the murder.

What I did. What Dorothy did. How I wish now that David *had* killed me and not her . . . But I never said anything. My father knew what I was suffering – but he told me to be quiet. He said, I didn't want to go into a madhouse did I? Somewhere with the crazy people? Because that was where they would put me, he said . . .'

Alice was watching her mother, transfixed.

'I didn't want them to take me away from home, from my parents and Charlie. I should have kept you, Alice. *I should have* . . .' She trailed off, recognising what she had done. 'But I did. I gave you away. *My child.*'

'It was a long time ago. It doesn't matter now.'

'It does! It does! It all matters. Every day it matters more and more. I can't stop thinking about it. I don't sleep . . . Have you told him?'

'Have I told *who*, *what*?'

'Have you told my father about your being my daughter?'

Startled, Alice put her hand over her mother's mouth. 'Sssh! People will overhear. No, I haven't told him. Or anyone. It's *our* secret.'

'But you should tell them –'

'If I do, everything will come out. Once the ball starts rolling it won't stop.'

'No,' her mother assured her, 'they can keep secrets here. My father keeps so many secrets.'

'But what about Leonard?'

He has a girlfriend, Alice thought, what better way to get rid of his wife: annul a bigamous marriage and then wed his mistress? If Leonard knew the truth Alice was almost certain that he would feel no compunction in exposing the old man, or his wife. After all, Judge Arnold had bullied and ridiculed him for years – now here was revenge and freedom in one fell swoop.

'We must keep quiet. You and I know the truth,' Alice said, 'that's enough.'

'*Is it?*' her mother asked, confusion lifting, her tone perfectly lucid. 'Is it really enough? This should be your home, you should have our name, our status, our money. We treated you so badly – I treated you so badly – and after all that happened, you *still* can't say who you are. You should have so much. But you have nothing.'

'We have to stay quiet.'

'Alice,' her mother said earnestly, 'it can't go on for ever. It has to come out one day. You do it, you blow the whistle. Let it be my present to you. Your revenge. You've earned it.'

Outside the window a breeze started up, ivy tapping against the pane. It was an eerie sound.

'I don't want it,' Alice said at last.

Again the ivy tapped against the glass.

Her mother's voice was barely a whisper.

'*Go on, do it.* I know how you feel; you're my daughter, my child. I know you, Alice. I understand you. You're like me, like your father. We knew what we wanted and we were hellbent to get it. You want revenge – so go on, strike back! I would if it was me.'

She was suddenly frightening, ruthless. In that moment Alice saw what so easily she could become. The knowledge terrified her.

'No.'

'Take it!' her mother urged her. 'We all deserve justice. Fight back, Alice. Show them you're one of us.'

The words echoed in the room and in Alice's head. They yawned, became huge, rippled on the still air. The bedroom was suddenly suffocating, the shadows thick with malice. Outside the ivy tapped against the window, the wind starting up.

At that moment Alice knew where she finally belonged.

Chapter Sixty

Ray was watching Alice as she reached for her shoes. Her hair was loose, the firelight making it shine like polished wood. The deep dark scent that she wore lingered around her, and when she tossed back her hair her eyes closed momentarily and she looked like an empress.

He was, quite simply, besotted by her. But marriage was still a subject Alice avoided.

'Don't you want what other women want?'

She smiled flirtatiously at him, pulling her jumper back over her head. Their lovemaking had been tender and she was drowsy with pleasure.

'What *do* other women want?'

'A husband.'

She laughed, turned back the cuffs of the sweater and then kissed him on the tip of his nose.

'What a puritan you are, Mr Berry.'

He caught hold of her and nuzzled her neck. 'We *should* get married, Alice. It will stop people talking about me.'

Laughing, she punched him lightly in the stomach and then rested her head on his shoulder. 'I don't need to marry you –'

'You're supposed to *want* to.'

'I do, but marriage is not that important to me.'

He sighed. 'But you're not setting a good example to your pupils.'

'They don't know what I get up to in my spare time,' she said archly. 'I'm the very prim spinster Miss Cummings to them.'

'But wouldn't that not-so-prim spinster like to settle down?'

Sitting upright, Alice looked at him, her head on one side.

'Why? I don't have to do what other people do. I've never lived a normal life. If I had, I would have married and had children already.' She paused, thinking back. 'Which, as you and I both know, might well have turned out to be a disaster.'

Ray changed the topic deftly. 'But we decided that we didn't need to have children. We could still marry, though. It's quite a put-down for a man to be refused, Alice,' he teased her. 'I was considered to be quite a catch in my prime.'

'You're a bad-tempered, work-obsessed, wrinkled old bore,' Alice said, kissing his jawline. 'I'll never believe you were a playboy. You don't have the charm.'

'Listen who's talking!' he mocked her. 'You're hardly in the running for Miss Tact 1947. Your idea of diplomacy is to talk, and if they don't listen, smack them in the mouth!'

'It's a lie!' Alice replied, chortling, 'I *never* resort to violence. I just stand my corner, defend my rights . . .' Her voice softened. 'It's not that I don't want to marry you, Ray, it's just that I don't see a need to marry. People have talked about me for as long as I can remember – gossiped about me, rumours flying around like wasps round a jam tart. I can't ever be respectable because of my past, because of what I am. Because of where I came from. You know about the Arnolds, but no one else does. To the rest of the world, I'm a nobody, a slum teacher who hauled herself up to principal in a school that no one else would even enter.' She ran her forefinger around his mouth gently. 'Besides, think what your parents would say – You could do better for yourself, Ray.'

'Oh, for God's sake!' he snapped, exasperated. 'What

have my parents got to do with this? I'm middle bloody aged – a bit long in the tooth to need their approval.'

Alice raised her eyebrows and leaned back against the settee. 'You and I are so similar, Ray. We both love our work. We live for it. Could we really live together, in each other's pockets day in and day out? Like Ethel and Gilbert? You've never been married, and neither have I – could we live in the same house without getting on each other's nerves? Maybe we could, and maybe we couldn't. I don't want to stop loving you because you're tired of me, or I'm tired of you. We're loners, you and I. But we're *lucky* loners, because part of the time we have each other. Let's leave it that way, hey?'

Ray nodded, but although he understood what she was saying, he wasn't totally convinced. Alice might make love with him, might share his problems and confide her own, but there was a part of her that she always held back. Maybe she always would – or maybe another man would gain access there. The thought shook him.

'So you won't make me respectable?'

She smiled, kissed his lips, her mouth lingering on his for a long moment before drawing away.

'Nothing's ideal in life. Most of the time we make the best of what we've got.'

'Funny,' he said, his voice hushed, 'but I never think I'm making do with you. I think I've got lucky, won the jackpot, hit the heights – not that I'm *making do*. Jesus, Alice, is that what you think of me – that'll do?'

Mortified that she had hurt him, Alice blustered. 'You don't understand, I didn't *say* that –'

'You didn't say it with your lips,' Ray replied sadly, 'but you said it with your heart.'

It had been a long time since Catherine had left The Dower House. She had been too protected, too scared, to venture out alone. But now she had to. Lack of sleep and anxiety had made her dizzy when she rose, but after a long cool bath she had dressed and gone downstairs to the kitchen. Hardly able to remember where anything was kept, she drank some milk and gobbled down some dry bread spread with jam. The butter she couldn't find.

It was early, the kitchen still empty. If anyone came in she had rehearsed what she would say. But Catherine knew that the kitchen didn't come on duty until eight, and she would be gone by then. With trembling hands she held the glass and then drained it, turning back to wash it out and replace it in the cupboard. Don't leave traces, she told herself. Be careful.

The cool of the morning startled her as she came out of the back door. For a moment Catherine stood in the winter sunlight, trying to remember the details of her plan.

It was simple. All she had to do was to get to Oldham. Breathing in deeply, she moved down the drive, certain at any moment that her father would stop her. But she made it to the bend unhindered, paused before hurrying on, and then turned out into Werneth Heights. The early dew shuddered on the green, throwing light shadows on the cold ground. Many years earlier she had come to play here with her sister, the nanny following behind them. Dorothy had been high-spirited, turning cartwheels, her hair spinning around her head as she spun round and round in the summer sunlight.

Blinking, Catherine turned away from the green and walked on. She had no idea which bus to catch, but she knew that there would be many going into Oldham. Almost in a trance, she walked on. Her heart was hammering, her mouth dry, panic only just under the surface. But this time Catherine wasn't going to let herself down. She would hold on, hold on long enough to do what she planned.

It was justice, after all. It was something she had to do, a way to make amends . . .

Oh, who was she kidding? This had nothing to do with

making amends, and everything to do with revenge. Leopards don't change their spots; what we are, we remain. She paused, sniffed at the morning air. *She was going to get her own back on everyone.* And who cared if she ruined herself in the process?

Her feet moved very quietly on the street. The sudden noise and press of people alarmed her. She had not been out for so long without being guarded, watched. But here she was, on her own, facing the world again . . . Catherine liked that idea. She wasn't quite as helpless as they thought, or as stupid. She had been pushed and pulled in all directions for years. She had been tutored, lied to, made to lie. She was Catherine. No, she was Dorothy. She was *who* exactly?

She was no one now. Out on that early cold street she was just one of many. The town had changed so much – bombsites in clusters. *Bombs*, Catherine thought; of course, there had been a war. The world had changed whilst she had been hiding . . . But she wasn't going to hide any more. She wasn't mad, she wasn't confused, but she was guilty. Guilty of the death of her sister. Guilty of the abandonment of her daughter. Guilty of lying. Guilty of hiding. Guilty of so much.

It had been worth it whilst she believed David lived. Strange, Catherine thought, how so much can change in one night. Her husband and father had thought that she was in bed, doped with her usual sedative to keep the dreams locked out, but instead she had come downstairs and paused by the drawing-room door, listening to the voices inside.

Quiet voices, then raised. Her husband stammering out his questions, his indignation rising with each jamming syllable. Her father shouting back, the rough voice barking one sentence twice. 'David Lewes is dead. I'll say it once more – David Lewes is dead . . .' Oh, to hear it from him, Catherine thought. From her *father*. She could have borne it from Alice – even Leonard – but not from him.

The future had fallen at her feet with the words. It had shattered on the floor and flown into a thousand mean pieces which had lodged in her brain and heart. *David was dead* ...

Almost dazed, Catherine climbed onto a bus and paid what the conductor asked for the fare. Her eyes were staring ahead of her, her expression poised. She was very clear all of a sudden. The shock had done that, slapped her back into reality.

Then Catherine felt her concentration lapse. Memories of stuffy rooms and hot, unsleeping nights swam in front of her; followed by the sight of Robin; and then Alice walking towards her and smiling with David Lewes's eyes.

Be calm, Catherine told herself. This is the most important thing you will ever do. Don't mess it up. You aren't stupid or crazy. Be calm ... Having forgotten that she had asked the conductor to tell her which was her stop, Catherine felt the touch on her shoulder and froze.

'High Street, ma'am.'

At the sound of his voice, Catherine let out a sigh of relief. It wasn't her father, it was only the conductor. Slowly she rose to her feet and got off the bus, several passengers watching the elegant, well-dressed woman with blatant curiosity. Now, Catherine told herself, walk until you find number 237. Look for it, look ... Moments later she walked up to the shiny black door. On a plaque by the bell was written: 'Holland, Graham and Benning, Solicitors at Law.'

She had found them! Catherine thought with triumph. Now came the next part of her plan. Placing her finger on the bell she pushed, the sound echoing inside, footsteps following.

'Good morning, madam,' a dapper middle-aged man said, smiling his greeting. 'Can I help you?'

Catherine wanted to laugh, wanted to say, Yes, yes, you can help me. You're the *only* one who can help me now.

But instead she kept calm, her voice composed. 'I'm Mrs Tripps. I have an appointment to see Mr Benning. It's about making a will.'

Rubbing oil into her stiff knees, Ethel sat on the bed next to Gilbert and muttered under her breath. That was the thing about getting old, she thought. Your body slowed down so much that even doing little things was like running barefoot after someone on a motorbike. Your body never caught up with your brain. Not that men suffered the same way, she murmured impatiently, they just collapsed into a heap at seventy and stayed there.

'Oooo, my bloody knees.'

'I'll give them a rub, lass,' Gilbert said.

Ethel slapped his hands away, grinning.

'I don't want you getting idea, Mr Cummings.'

'Just looking at your bare legs is giving me ideas,' he teased her.

'Yes, well, I'm too old and my legs are too bad,' Ethel replied shortly, pulling the stocking of her right leg up and fastening it with metal suspenders. 'It's worse if I don't keep moving. One day I'll be found in bed, my legs as rigid as two pegs. Oh, it's no good laughing! I'd like to see how you'd cope without me.'

'I wouldn't,' Gilbert admitted, getting serious again. 'I were thinking about Victor –'

'Me too! I dreamed about him last night.'

'I think we should have him round for tea, what d'you say, old girl?'

Ethel sighed. 'It's not tea he needs, it's someone to care about him. You know, I used to think that Alice and he would get fixed up after Hilly died, but there you go – she's back with Ray Berry and looks set to stay the course with him.'

Gilbert blew his nose loudly before replying. 'They've a lot in common.'

'Victor and Alice had a lot in common. *Once.*'

'Aye, but that were a long time ago and people change. Victor's got his little business, but Alice has done well for herself. Really well. If she marries Ray Berry she'll be fixed up at Greenfields.'

Thoughtful, Ethel fastened the suspenders on her left leg and remembered the file she had read that night so long ago in Clare Lees' office. She wondered – not for the first time – if things wouldn't have been better for Alice if those few pieces of paper had been destroyed. Long before Evan Thomas or anyone else saw them.

'I think we *will* have Victor over,' Ethel said at last. 'That's a good idea of yours, Gilbert. He's too young to waste his life. Too young to think that there's nothing for him but pain and trouble.' She stood up, suddenly lively. 'Oi, out of that bed, Gilbert Cummings! I've work to do and you're not adding to it.'

The winter light was coming through the window in Mr Benning's office. It slanted across his desk and rested on his right shoulder like a golden epaulette. Mesmerised by it, Catherine stared and then shook her head slightly. She had to think clearly, keep to her plan.

His head bent down, a flustered Mr Benning was reading the notes he had made. Ever the professional, he was not going to show how shocked he was, but what his client had told him was explosive. The town would be rocked by it. He could remember the case quite well. The murder had been the talk of the county for months. But no one had suspected that there was more to it.

'I have to ask you, Mrs Tripps, why do you want to expose yourself and your father now? Surely you must realise that it would put you both in jeopardy? Are you really sure that you want this information to be made public?' Dear God, the stolid Mr Benning thought, this is unbelievable.

Catherine looked at him passively, then nodded. 'I do. In four days' time. But not before.'

'But there will an uproar; the police will, in all probability, be involved. I mean, you said that everyone thought that *you* were the woman killed, and from all accounts you organised the death of your own sister –'

'I did, yes.'

He swallowed. 'You'll need legal representation –'

'No, I won't,' Catherine said calmly.

'But you'll have to answer all kinds of questions about assuming your sister's name and life. About how you managed the cover up for so long.' A sudden thought occurred to him. 'Did your father know everything?'

She nodded again. 'Oh yes, he knew.'

Mr Benning rubbed his forehead, suddenly at a loss. Judge Arnold was respected, still feared. His family had been hidden for years behind high walls, their lives cut off from the outside world. Who would believe what had gone on? Who would believe that he had colluded in it? But then again, was it *that* remarkable? Judge Arnold had power, money, and considerable influence. So had the old man paid people to keep their silence? Whom had he involved? The medical world? The law? Oh God, Mr Benning thought, this was too much for him to handle.

He stared at the calm woman in front of him. She had endured her husband's adultery, engineered her sister's death, then taken over her sister's identity.

'I'm doing this for revenge. And for Alice.'

He frowned. 'Alice?'

'What I've told you isn't everything, Mr Benning.'

'There's *more*?' he croaked.

'Oh yes,' Catherine said quietly, 'a lot more. I have been guilty of many things, Mr Benning, and now I want to put the record straight. Let the guilty take what's coming to them.'

Nodding, Mr Benning picked up his pen again. He was

wondering just why she had chosen to come to him. Why not go into Manchester, to one of the high-profile lawyers who handled the big cases? Why pick on him? He didn't like bother; he enjoyed a quiet life, with as little aggravation as possible. He had hoped that he could glide into retirement without anyone even much noticing. And now this.

'Are you ready, Mr Benning?'

No, I'm not, he wanted to say, but smiled patiently instead. 'Ready when you are, Mrs Tripps. Ready when you are.'

Chapter Sixty-One

Mr Benning didn't know what to think, but he didn't like the area one bit. Salford, he thought, glancing round suspiciously, what a hellhole. He had heard rumours about the slums and the rats – big as cats, someone had said. He had also heard about the notorious Field Lane, a euphemistically named Gorbals of brothels, boarding houses and murky pubs. Not unlike The Bent, only the latter had now gone, a bad memory nothing more. Time all those places were cleaned out, Mr Benning thought. Progress was finally moving things along; the old days of slums and sickness were coming to an end.

Mr Benning walked down Salford High Street, his neat, bowler-hatted figure attracting some interest. He should have driven, he thought, but then someone had told him that they slashed tyres in Salford, or worse, set fire to any stranger's vehicle. All in all Mr Benning was beginning to wonder *why* he had come down here at all, except for the fact that he had to. God, he thought, would anyone choose to work or live here?

Stopping outside St Ursula's, he looked up at the windows. A child was standing at one and put his tongue out. Mortified, Mr Benning glanced away and then pushed open the wrought-iron gates of the entrance. They were rusty and creaked, his sleeve catching on the bolt. Cursing under his breath, the fastidious solicitor moved towards the front door, several children watching him.

'Oi, mister! What the 'ell's that on yer head?'

Mr Benning flushed, but did not reply. A pellet hit him

on the back of the neck suddenly, his hat falling off as he spun round.

'Who did that?'

'It were me!' one called. 'No, it were me!' another cried out, a group of lads suddenly aiming a barrage of catapults at the flustered little figure.

Huddled against the door, Mr Benning nearly fell in as it was opened, Jilly staring at the ambushed figure.

'You kids, stop it! Stop it now! On your way!' She looked back to the visitor. 'I'm sorry about that.'

Mr Benning was long past being mollified. Brushing down his coat and feeling the swelling on the back of his neck, he said stiffly: 'I want to talk to your principal, Miss Alice Cummings.'

'Does she know you're coming?' Jilly asked, watching a lump rising on the side of Mr Benning's cheek.

'No, but tell her anyway, will you?' he replied testily, glancing towards the door. 'Are those boys pupils of yours?'

'Some are.'

'You might try to teach them manners –'

'We do our best,' Alice said suddenly, walking into the hallway and looking at the dishevelled stranger. 'Did you want to see me?'

'They fired pellets at me,' he moaned, touching his neck. 'I've never been treated like this before.'

'Jilly, get some ointment, will you?' Alice asked, turning back to Mr Benning, 'I'm sorry about this, but these kids aren't brought up to respect anyone.'

'That's obvious.'

She raised her eyebrows and then led the solicitor into her office. 'How can I help you?'

The sting was going out of the lumps. Mr Benning relaxed a little. Purposefully he lifted his briefcase onto his lap and took out some papers.

'I have to tell you something of the utmost importance, Miss Cummings,' he began. 'It's about your mother.'

Mother? Alice stiffened in her seat. How did he know that she had a mother? And besides, did he mean Catherine, or Dorothy?

'I don't understand –'

'Let me explain,' he said patiently, back in his stride again. He was no longer under siege, but a professional in charge.

'Two days ago I was hired by your mother, Mrs Catherine Tripps –'

'Oh God,'

He looked up, startled. 'Are you all right?'

'Yes . . . Go on, please.'

'I was hired by your mother, Mrs Catherine Tripps, who came to tell me exactly what had happened in her past. I take it you know about the murder?'

Alice sat there, without responding.

'Well, yes, of course you do. Your mother told me. As you know – this is very odd, quite the most difficult and extraordinary case I have worked on – your mother was responsible for her sister's death. She also tried to implicate you in the death of her son, Robin Tripps, many years ago. Until recently she did not realise that you were her child, but she is very anxious to make amends now. She feels that you have been treated badly by herself and the Arnold family. She feels that you have been cheated out of a name, status and money. Your mother would like to rectify that.'

Alice was still staring at him, mute.

'As I was saying,' he went on, 'your mother has asked me to make known the true facts of the murder –'

'No!'

'– in three days' time.' Please, let me continue. In three days' time I am to inform the press. You are to be then recognised publicly as her child, and the granddaughter of Judge Arnold.'

'She can't do this!'

'She *can*, and she *has*,' Mr Benning replied. 'Naturally I advised her that such an action would expose her and her father to a police investigation –'

'Then don't let her do it!' Alice snapped. 'My mother obviously didn't understand what she was saying.'

'Oh, but she did,' Mr Benning replied. 'She brought with her a medical document, signed by a local doctor, which confirmed that she was in her right mind and that I had to adhere to her requests. Including the directions of her will.'

'You don't understand, Mr Benning,' Alice said hurriedly. 'Mrs Tripps has not been well for some time. You can't agree to what she asks.'

'I have to do as she requests.'

'But if you expose her, she'll be crucified.'

'She asked me to give you this,' Mr Benning said in reply, passing Alice an envelope. He watched as she opened it, her face averted as she read the few written lines. Then she dropped the paper and got to her feet.

'I have to go, Mr Benning. I have to go now.'

Rushing out, she knocked into a startled Jilly on the way. 'Get his address and tell Mr Benning that I'll be in touch, will you?'

Out on the street, Alice looked round. She could catch a bus, but that would take too much time. Should she ring Ray? But how long would it take for him to drive down from Greenfields, collect her and then drive over to Werneth Heights?

The answer came to her unbidden and Alice ran round to Victor's shop and knocked repeatedly on the door.

He came out smiling, then frowned as he saw her face. 'What is it?'

'Can you drive me over to Werneth Heights now?' Alice said frantically. 'I have to get over there, Victor. There's a crisis.'

Driving as fast as his old van would allow, forty minutes

later Victor pulled up outside the front entrance of The Dower House.

Alice was already half out of the van, before she turned to him. 'Will you come in with me, Victor? Please?'

Surprised, he nodded and fell into step with her.

Without bothering to ring the bell, Alice walked in, an apprehensive Victor following her. The hall was gloomy, late afternoon light making it dull, the suit of armour on the landing looking sinister in the half-light. Calling out her mother's name several times, Alice had already run halfway up the stairs when Judge Arnold walked out onto the upper landing and blocked her way.

His head was bowed, his hand gripping a stick. Age and bitterness had made his face bloated, the bloodshot eyes fixing on her with stark dislike. Behind him, Alice could see Alwyn's old wheelchair, the spokes of the wheels catching the dying light.

'You,' he said simply. 'Of course.'

Alice looked up at him. 'Where's my mother?'

'You want to see her?' Judge Arnold asked, waving his stick down the corridor. 'Be my guest.'

Hurrying past him, Alice ran down the passageway and pushed open the door of Catherine's room. She was lying on the window seat, her hair styled, her make-up delicate. In a dark green cocktail dress she looked extremely slim and fashionable. Only the string of pearls falling to one side spoilt her perfection.

'Mother?' Alice whispered, moving over to Catherine and kneeling down beside her.

Gently she touched her hand, then her cheek. She had known before she did so that they would be unresponsive and cold, that every little tired ounce of Catherine Arnold would have finally let go. Her hand trembling, Alice touched her mother's face, rubbed her hands uselessly and whispered to her, words that neither Judge Arnold nor Victor could hear from the door.

'You should have kept quiet,' Alice whispered into her mother's ear. 'Why did you do it? We could have kept it all a secret. We could have pulled it off.'

Crying, she touched Catherine's face again. Finally she placed the pearls straight on her mother's chest. She was, Alice thought blindly, quite beautiful. Funny, she had never really seen that before. Whilst Catherine had been alive she had been so chockful of pain and confusion that her face had never relaxed. Now she was calm. It was over – and her features were hers again.

'There's never been a suicide in the Arnold family before –'

Alice was on her feet in an instant, hurling herself towards her grandfather, her hands outstretched. Only the intervention of Victor stopped her knocking the old man to the ground.

Caught in Victor's grip, she fixed her grandfather with a look of real hatred.

'*You* killed her.'

'She killed herself –'

'She never would have done if you'd behaved more kindly to her,' Alice snapped, her eyes running with tears, her mouth a gash of hatred. '*You* did this to her. She sent me her suicide note. She told me that she did this for me – for *me*, her child. She said she had heard you talking to Leonard, heard you say that David Lewes was dead.'

Alice struggled to get free, but Victor held on to her. He was afraid that if she got to the old man she would kill him.

'But you knew my father wasn't dead! I found out about him, about how you had him moved under a different name. I found my father!' She was almost screaming. 'You knew that my mother was only alive because she thought David Lewes was. You *knew* that!'

The old man looked away. 'How did I know she'd over-hear us?'

'You didn't care enough to keep your voice down!' Alice snapped. 'You just didn't care about *her* any more. You'd got lazy, indifferent to her. And telling Leonard that David Lewes was dead wasn't true. *He isn't dead.* Don't you realise that my mother killed herself because you lied? But then, you never do much else, do you?'

'Don't preach to me! You came here to try to ruin this family –'

'This family was ruined long ago because of you!' Alice hurled back, throwing Victor off, and moving towards the fireplace. To his astonishment, she then picked up the poker lying there and turned to Judge Arnold.

'You bastard!' she hissed. Victor moved towards her. 'Kept out of this!' she told him. 'This has nothing to do with you.'

The old man was watching her, the poker in her right hand.

'You knew about your daughters, about how they were rivals. A loving father would have put a stop to that, not encouraged it. You knew that Dorothy was having an affair with David, and you knew what that would do to Catherine.'

Suddenly, without warning, she lunged at him. At once Judge Arnold was pushed out of the way by Victor. Only just missing the old man, the poker came down hard on a chair arm.

'She's mad!'

'If I am, it's because of you,' Alice hurled back at her grandfather, the poker still in her hand, her eyes blank.

'Put it down!' Victor said sharply. 'Put the poker down, Alice.'

'Why should I?' she countered. 'Why should I let him live? He as good as killed my mother and my father –'

'And you're just like them,' the old man replied, 'just as out of control.'

'I'll kill you!' she said, moving towards him again. Victor

grabbed the poker from her hand and pushed her into a chair.

'STOP IT!' he shouted. 'This has gone too far.'

'I hate him! I want him dead. He should be dead.'

'You act like slum fodder,' the old man said contemptuously.

At once, Victor turned on him. 'She would never have been in the slums if you hadn't put her there.'

'Is this your boyfriend?' Judge Arnold asked sourly. 'A *workman*?'

Immediately Alice was back on her feet, her temper making her terrifying. 'Leave him alone! Victor Coates is worth ten of you.'

Catching her by the arms, Victor whispered into her ear, 'Stop now, Alice, stop. Don't do this. You're better than this. You're not like them. Stop it now.'

His legs shaking, Judge Arnold moved over to a nearby chair and sat down. Behind him was the body of his daughter, but he didn't even glance at it. Instead he looked back to Alice.

'My daughter left me a note too, a very pretty piece of writing. I see now where Charlie gets his talent from. Catherine wrote that she had organised for the whole sordid business of the murder and deception to be exposed in three days' time.'

Victor could feel Alice's body stiffen.

'*You'll* be exposed then too,' she said gleefully. 'Everyone will know what you really are. And what you've done. The whole world will know what went on behind these walls. You won't be able to go anywhere without people pointing at you, talking about you. Your status, power, will all be gone. And won't the police be interested to know about David Lewes? About how you lied, passed him off as dead? And how you let your daughter marry *bigamously*.'

Alice's dark eyes were black with fury, reminding Victor

of the girl she had once been, that fiery, wilful girl he had loved to distraction.

'You organised everything,' she continued, 'and soon all your lying and covering-up will be exposed. I want to see that. *I want to see you suffer*.'

'You have all the temperament of your father,' Judge Arnold replied evenly. 'You even look like him now, all fired up. He looked like that the night he killed the wrong sister – I saw him. You didn't know that, did you, Alice? Well, neither did Catherine. I never told her. But I was in the garden and I could see what happened. I wasn't in time to stop him killing Dorothy, but I was in time to see David's face when Catherine came in and he knew he had killed the wrong woman.'

She was white with fury. 'You *saw* it?'

He nodded. 'I saw it. David had run off by the time I got in to the room. I knew at once what Catherine had done. I covered up for her. What father wouldn't?'

'What father would have goaded her to it?' Alice countered. 'And what grandfather would get rid of one of his grandchildren?'

'You had to go. You were always trouble, never got on with your mother. For some reason you loved Dorothy instead. Always cried when Catherine picked you up; people commented on it. You would have given her away sooner or later, so you had to go.'

Alice felt her head spinning, Victor holding her upright now.

'That was it – I just *had* to go?'

The old man nodded. 'Most of life is that simple if you don't let emotion get the better of you. That was where David Lewes and Catherine lost out – they were so emotional, so out of control. You're a lot like them.'

'Now, watch it!' Victor warned him.

Waving his interruption aside, the old man looked at Alice. 'Catherine told me who you were in her letter. It

516

seems so obvious now. So you're my granddaughter.' He paused, organising his thoughts. 'You really can't want all this to come out, Alice. Not now. Not now that you have a chance to get what you want. You could live here, have the protection of the Arnold name, money, power – all the things a *nanny* longs for.'

'I'm not a nanny any more. I'm the principal of a school now.'

He smiled thinly. 'Hard work? I imagine it is. Not like the lives the women live in this family. They don't have to work, they can have holidays, buy clothes, jewels. You'd like that, wouldn't you, Alice? Think about it – the last thing you want is more hardship, gossip. If it comes out, everyone will be talking about you again, about your father, your mother, tittle-tattling over your life. You don't want that, do you? You want it easy now.'

Releasing Victor's grip, Alice walked over to her grandfather and stood, looking down at him.

'In return for *what*?'

'Silence.'

Victor was watching them both, wondering what Alice was doing. Was she *really* going to get into league with the old man? The man she had hated for so long?

'You want silence from me,' Alice said calmly. 'What about Leonard? He'll be delighted to know that his marriage was a sham. He can marry his mistress then. He won't want to keep this quiet. He'll want to make his escape, and get his own back on you for all the times you've bullied him.'

The old man nodded. 'You have a good head on your shoulders, Alice, I can see that. We won't tell Leonard.'

'But Mr Benning has been instructed to carry out my mother's orders. How can you stop him?'

'I know his firm, I know the senior partner,' the old man said evenly. 'A little pressure brought to bear on Mr Benning will silence him nicely, I think.'

The expression in Alice's eyes was unfathomable. 'And what about me? Will you still recognise me as your grand-daughter?'

The old man laughed hoarsely, leaning forward.

'We can't let that particular cat out of the bag, can we? I mean, if you're recognised as one of us it will come out about *why* we had to put you into Netherlands – and that would mean exposing the reason.' He paused. 'No, I can't do that, Alice – but I *can* make your life a lot easier.'

She appeared to be thinking it over. Then she leaned down towards him, her voice iron.

'Now I'll tell you what's *really* going to happen. You have three days, Judge Arnold, to leave this house. After that, all hell will break loose. You have a home abroad and more than enough money to live off. Go there.'

'You can't throw me out of my own house! This is my home. I've been here all my life. I'm an old man,' he wheedled, suddenly pathetic. 'I wouldn't survive anywhere else. You can't send me away.'

'Why not? You sent me away,' Alice countered merci-lessly.

'Don't do this –'

She cut him off. 'My mother's wishes will be made public in three days. She left me her jewellery and her money, to do with as I pleased. And I think she gave me the three days to sort out what to do with you – whether I chose to let you sink, or swim. You should be glad I'm so emotional, Judge, because I'm letting you off lightly. I could have thrown you to the lions. Instead, you have three days to get away from here. You can hide away and live out your life in comfort. In secret. But then you like secrets, don't you?'

He was livid with rage. 'I'll fight you –'

'And you'll lose,' Alice replied, gesturing to Victor. 'I have a witness to what you suggested about Mr Benning, and besides, when your actions become common knowledge, your name will be dirt. No one will believe anything you say.'

He blustered, then a slow look of cunning came into his face. 'Don't you feel *anything* for me? I'm your grandfather, your own flesh and blood.'

Alice looked at him with disgust. 'You forgot that for thirty-six years. Thirty-six years when you never thought about me. Thirty-six years when you never wondered if I was alive or dead. Well, I'm not as cruel as you. I'm giving you a way out. But in return I want you to leave this house.'

'I belong here,' he almost screamed, flustered for the first time. 'I've been here all my life. I've never lived alone. You can't do this to me. This is my home!'

'This is no one's *home*,' Alice said chillingly. 'This is a tomb. This is a place that breeds madness, jealousy and murder.' She looked into his bloodshot eyes, her voice resigned. 'There's never been any happiness here. Just secrets, dark dates on the calendar, silences, exchanged sly glances. Remember I lived here a long time ago as a servant. I watched this family, I watched *you*. I saw the traps, the fear, suspicion, power. This place was never a home. No family could live here.'

'You can't throw me out,' he blustered, suddenly feeble and panicked. 'I'm not well. I'm old –'

'But you're still alive. Which is more than my mother is.'

Chapter Sixty-Two

Sir Herbert Jordan was finding it difficult to breathe as he coughed on his whisky and soda, Norman Appleton slapping him anxiously on the back. Beside them sat Giles Falmer, his angular face looking unusually smug. It had been his pleasure to bring the evening copy of the *Manchester Guardian* into their club, leaving it casually lying on the table between them. For nearly ten minutes Giles listened to Sit Herbert grind on about his arduous duties as mayor, whilst Norman Appleton sat stupefied, hugging his gin like a miser's cash box.

Finally, Sir Herbert, pausing in his pompous diatribe, spotted the headline. Giles could see him read it and waited for the response. It was better than he could have hoped.

ARNOLD FAMILY SCANDAL – DAUGHTER KILLS HERSELF AND REVEALS HIDDEN SECRETS AND ABANDONED CHILD

'What the . . .' Sir Herbert trailed off, reading the front page and then beginning to cough, his face the colour of a plum.

'Oh, steady,' Norman Appleton said, patting Sir Herbert's back. 'Go easy, old man.'

'Oh, get off me!' Sir Herbert snapped, stopping coughing and collapsing back into his easy chair. 'What the hell are you smirking at, Giles? Why didn't you say something about this?'

He was all cool innocence. 'Oh, I was going to mention it –'

'Alice Cummings, Alice Rimmer – oh, whatever the bloody woman's called – *she's an Arnold*!' Sir Herbert snatched up the paper again. 'Her mother's Dorothy Tripps! And she's committed suicide!'

He was talking in exclamations. It was poetry, Giles thought to himself. Sheer poetry.

'Dorothy Tripps wasn't Dorothy Tripps, she was Catherine all along –'

'Oh dear,' Norman Appleton said, draining his glass, and signalling for a refill.

Sir Herbert was still gawping at the newspaper. 'Judge Arnold knew all about it. He had his granddaughter adopted. *That grandchild's Alice Rimmer!*'

'I think the people over there missed it,' Giles said drily.

Sir Herbert lowered his voice. 'I always said that Judge Arnold was a crook. He was too bloody lucky in business to be above board. It says here –' he jabbed at the paper with his forefinger – 'that the old man's done a bunk. Gone abroad, no one knows where. I bet they bloody don't!' Sir Herbert blew out his cheeks. 'My God, Catherine wasn't murdered, after all, she –'

'Thanks for the summary, but I've already read it,' Giles said smoothly. 'It seemed that you misjudged Alice –'

'I always knew she had class.'

Giles laughed into his drink. 'Oh yes, Herbert, of course you did. Weren't you the one who was going to make an example of her to help your running for mayor?'

Sir Herbert stared at Giles with sudden, surprised dislike.

'Don't get snide with me! I don't recall you treating her like an empress.'

'I wasn't as biased as you were. You know that. I was quite prepared to give her the benefit of the doubt.'

Sir Herbert's colour was hardening into dull red as he continued to read down the front page. Then he stopped, crumpled up the paper in his fists, his eyes bulging.

'She's been left a pot of money and the house. Jesus, she's worth a bloody fortune!'

'Yes, I read that too,' Giles said benignly. 'I don't suppose she'll want to stay on as principal of a slum school now.'

'You're enjoying this, Falmer, aren't you?' Sir Herbert snapped. 'You're relishing it.'

'I just think it's strange how life works out,' he replied, 'how one minute someone's a nobody, and the next they have one of the biggest houses in the county. Might even be *the* biggest, actually.'

Bigger than yours, he was implying.

Stung, Sir Herbert caught the drift and tried, awkwardly, to smile. 'Well, good luck to the young lady. You know, I always liked her.'

'Goodness me . . .' Norman Appleton murmured, hypnotising his gin again.

'Oh, I know I never showed it,' Sir Herbert went on, 'but I felt we had something in common.'

'Yes, a slum school,' Giles said tartly.

'*Breeding*, is what I meant. I was only saying to my lady wife the other day, that you can always tell real class.'

'The Borgias had the same type of class. Both of Alice's parents were instrumental in murders,' Giles replied, 'and as for old man Arnold, tut, tut, tut, he *was* a naughty boy, wasn't he? Quite the music-hall villain. You knew him rather well, didn't you, Herbert?'

'He was no friend of mine!'

'I thought you and your wife used to see the Arnolds quite often in the past?'

'Only at social functions,' Sir Herbert blathered, 'you know, times when you meet so many people. Just one more person in the crowd.'

'But I thought Judge Arnold seconded you for admittance to this club?'

Breathing heavily, Sir Herbert pushed his face inches

away from Giles Falmer's. 'Enjoy it whilst it lasts, old man.'

'Oh, I intend to,' Giles answered, gesturing to the mangled newspaper. 'Seems like there was a lot going on up at Werneth Heights, lots of secrets and cover-ups. Lots of greasing of palms to keep people quiet. Judge Arnold must have paid a lot of people off for a lot of years – and no one suspected a thing.'

'How could they?' Norman Appleton said timidly. 'I mean, no one went near that house. It was off-limits. As for Dorothy, she never seemed to go out.'

'What about her husband? Leonard Tripps? He can't have known about his wife. Oh no, not Tripps. He was way too ambitious to get caught up in something like that,' Sir Herbert went on, half delighted, half aghast. 'He must be feeling a bit shaken up. Marrying a bloody bigamist!'

'But his wife's death does free him. I imagine his mistress will be delighted,' Giles said wryly.

'Mistress!' Sir Herbert bellowed, then glanced round and dropped his voice. '*What* mistress?'

'The one he's had for years.'

'You never said a thing! You sly bugger, you kept *that* quiet.'

'I thought you were the one who knew everything,' Giles retorted, his face impassive although he was enjoying himself immensely. 'You always said, "Nothing happens in this town, that I don't know first."'

'You're a bastard, Falmer.'

Giles raised his glass in mock salute. 'Thank you. Praise from Caesar is praise indeed.'

It was out of this world, Ethel thought, staring at the paper and then watching Gilbert open his tin of St Bruno tobacco. Slowly he filled his pipe, then lit it, then inhaled. She watched him, mesmerised.

'So, what do you make of it?' she asked finally.

He looked up, an aura of smoke haloing him. 'I think it's

justice,' he replied, glancing upwards. 'Is Alice still asleep?'

'Dead to the world,' Ethel replied, chopping some carrots on the worktop.

Alice had come to the Cummingses' just after her mother's suicide. Shaken, she told them about her argument with Judge Arnold and warned them that the whole story was going to break in the press. With her, came Victor. He stayed for a while, and then left. Then returned. He was, he told Ethel, a friend, someone Alice could always rely on.

Yet his manner was subdued. Her anger had startled him. He had watched her stand up to Judge Arnold and been reminded of the young girl he had first known – the Alice at Netherlands, before she had learned to control her feelings and spirit. She had been terrifying at The Dower House, and yet exciting, her fury at once awful and compelling.

Suddenly Victor had found himself thinking of the past, the way they used to meet secretly, their fingers touching through the iron railings, their longing innocent and yet intense.

'Has she been back to St Ursula's yet?' Victor asked, reaching for a newly made rock bun.

'She left word that she wanted some time off. Hey! I've just made those,' Ethel said, slapping his hand away and pushing a tin over to him. 'Eat the old ones first.'

'It makes a good read,' Gilbert murmured from his chair, his arthritic hands struggling to turn the pages of the newspaper, 'almost like something you'd watch at the pictures.'

Ethel rolled her eyes. 'The neighbours are having a field day, and that's a fact. All those people who looked down their noses at Alice for so long are suddenly either cutting her dead or eager to meet her.' Exasperated, Ethel slammed the pan of chopped carrots on the stove. 'She's rich now – and that makes all the difference. Even the news about her mother isn't going to put people off. Money, hah! It's the only thing that people care about.'

'She doesn't,' Victor said quietly. 'She's upset about her mother, but she's not bothered about the money.'

Was it true? Or was he fooling himself, trying to pretend that Alice wasn't going to change? But how could she *not* change? She now had a vast house, money and position. The scandal couldn't touch her because she had grown up as an outsider. Only this time she was an outsider up at Werneth Heights – a long way from Trafalgar Street.

'God knows what she'll do with that pile,' Ethel said, wiping her hands on a tea towel. 'That old bugger Arnold cleared off, but as for Leonard Tripps –'

'She's going to see him this afternoon,' Victor replied.

'Is she now?'

He nodded. 'She asked me to give her a lift up there. And then drop her at Greenfields.'

Ethel paused. What did *that* mean exactly? That Alice was going to see Ray Berry? Well, of course she was. She had to talk to him. They had spoken over the phone these last few days, naturally, but not met. And now Alice's past and all the Arnold secrets were splashed over the press for everyone to pick over.

It would be interesting to see what Ray thought of it all.

'You'll be staying up at Greenfields and then bringing Alice back?' Ethel asked, with an effort to be nonchalant.

'No,' Victor replied, his tone even. 'I'll just drop her off –'

'Aye, lad, why don't you speak your mind?' Ethel asked abruptly.

Gilbert shot her a warning look. 'Now, leave off, Ethel. It's none of our business.'

'If it's not our business, I'd like to know whose business it is!' she hurled back. 'I've known this lad and Alice since they were children. I've seen them love and lose each other and I'll be damned if I'll not have my say. Too many people suffer from not speaking their minds.'

'Well, that's something you'll never have to worry about,' Gilbert replied, refilling his pipe.

Victor moved over to a red-faced Ethel. 'Alice has to make-up her own mind –'

'You'd risk losing her again?' Ethel countered. 'Well, more fool you. I've been watching you over the last couple of days, Victor Coates, and whether you know it or not, you still love Alice.'

'Oh, come on, Ethel –'

'Shut up, Gilbert! Men know nothing about love. It always comes down to the women to sort it out.' She looked back to Victor. 'You *do* love her, don't you?'

He hesitated. 'She's rich now, with power. What she always wanted –'

'Do you love her?'

'She's out of my league, Ethel. Alice isn't the poor girl she was, she's –'

Ethel's voice was steely. '*Do you love her?*'

Before Victor could answer, the kitchen door opened and Alice walked in. Immediately Gilbert disappeared behind his paper and Ethel turned back to her chopped veg.

She wasn't sure if the pain around her chest was indigestion or a heart attack. It was probably the latter, Olive McGrath thought as she let the newspaper fall from her hands onto the bare floor. She couldn't believe it! At first she had read the piece with slavering interest – the Arnold family brought to book. Murder, mystery, bigamy – it was fantastic – until the fifth paragraph when she read that Alice Rimmer was Judge Arnold's abandoned granddaughter, who had now inherited The Dower House and a fortune.

If it wasn't a heart attack, it must be a stroke, Olive

thought. Certainly she would never get over this. Alice Rimmer, bloody Alice Rimmer, come into money. How was it possible? How? she asked herself. The bloody woman must have known all along, laughing at everyone, just biding her time.

In the next room Olive could hear the dull thunk of Gerry belting his little brother. She had never remarried – never been asked – and the kids had worn her down to a muscular wraith. I'm forty years old, Olive thought, and burned out. And as for Alice Rimmer – she's hit the jackpot. It's not fair, not bloody fair, she wailed inwardly. Hadn't she been kind to Alice when she first came to Greenfields? Even though it was clear from the start that she had been determined to sink her hooks into Ray Berry?

But would she want him *now*? Olive thought, hoping against hope that Ray Berry might get dumped by Alice, as Olive had been so unceremoniously dumped by him. After all, now that Alice had the big house she could afford to pick and choose a husband – not have to marry the head of some TB outpost to think herself well done by.

Brooding, Olive ran the details of the newspaper piece over in her mind. Disgrace had forced old man Arnold out of the country, but disgrace wasn't likely to affect Alice Rimmer. After all, she had withstood the gossip about her background, Robin Tripps' death and even managed to cling on when Olive had exposed her to St Ursula's governors. She was incredible, Olive thought helplessly. There was *no way* the woman could be stopped.

Suddenly overwhelmed with self pity, Olive started to cry, making gulping sounds at the back of her throat. Then, in a fit of pique, she stood up and kicked the newspaper round the room, her Cuban heels crushing it underfoot like a huge black-and-white moth.

Catherine's body had been taken to the chapel of rest in Oldham. Laid out in her coffin, she waited for the visitors who never came. No friends of her father's, no contemporaries, no Charlie, not even her husband came to sit by her or think well of her. She was an outcast. She was also beyond reach of temporal punishment. Just as she had arranged it.

Yet her words lived on in the newspaper, every column inch spelling out the long list of her vices, and the corruption of her father. In death, Catherine had owned up. She had branded herself a calculating, evil woman – and no one wanted to think any the less of her.

So she waited in the chapel of rest, the light from the stained-glass window falling on the coffin and her closed face. And every day the single lily she held between her hands was changed by the one person who came. Alice. The child Catherine had given away was, at the end, her only apologist. The child to whom she had shown no love, was the one who offered love at the last. It was Alice who organised the funeral, and Alice who arranged for the headstone to be carved, and Alice who picked the words to be written upon it.

CATHERINE LEWES
1887–1947

She had thought long and hard about what to put, but Leonard didn't want his name associated with Catherine's, and Charlie was being kept well away by his social-climbing wife. As for Catherine's maiden name, Alice knew it would have been an insult to put *Arnold* on her headstone. So in the end she chose the name which had always meant the most to her mother.

And so let it stand, Alice thought. And if there's a kind God, and a heaven, one day she'll meet my father there.

All the suitcases were sitting in the hallway of The Dower House as Leonard looked around one last time. He half expected to see Dorothy come down the stairs to greet him in her uncomfortably clinging way, or ignore him as she had also done at times. Whoever knew how she would react? He had often thought that being married to her was like living with two women – and he had been right. There was always Catherine intermingled with Dorothy.

He knew he should feel sorry for her death, but he wasn't. It was so dramatic, so unexpectedly vicious. But then his wife had suffered for a long time, and was entitled to her revenge. Momentarily Leonard felt guilt for not loving her enough to enable her to confide in him. When they'd first married he would have been shaken by the revelations, but he would have stood by her. But time killed the love between them – time and distrust and the everlasting presence of the old bastard Arnold.

Leonard was glad that his former father-in-law was gone. Exiled. He had hated him for a long time, and despised the way he treated his daughter. Ashamed, Leonard coughed and tucked his silk scarf in the collar of his overcoat. He should have stood up to Judge Arnold and defended Dorothy more, but he had always felt so excluded by them.

And he had always been weak … A sudden glint of sunlight drew Leonard's gaze upwards. On the landing stood Alwyn's empty wheelchair, the suit of armour huge and forbidding beside it. Where had all the years gone? Leonard wondered suddenly. Where had Alwyn, Judge Arnold, Dorothy, Charlie – where had they all gone? And Robin, his son. Where had *he* gone? It was his own fault, Leonard realised: he had wanted money and worked for money. He had dreamed and planned for nothing but money.

And when he realised it wasn't enough, it was too late. Too late to call anyone back, to apologise, to defend. Too late to change. Or hope. He would walk out of The Dower House and leave his dead behind him. If Frances would have him, he would marry her and try to be a husband, if he still knew how. His stilted relationship with his stepson, Charlie, would stagger on and finally fade out. And then what?

He didn't care that Alice would get The Dower House – he hated the place. Leonard didn't mind her inheriting Catherine's money and jewellery either. He was surprised how *little* he minded. He thought suddenly of a night many years earlier, when a beautiful young woman had stood next to him and left him momentarily dazed. Yes, Leonard thought to himself, he could see that Alice could be the child of Catherine and David Lewes. There had always been a heady, dangerous spirit clinging like a scent around her.

Sighing, Leonard buttoned up his coat and then walked upstairs. As he reached the wheelchair on the landing he pressed the button of the lift and listened as it creaked and rattled upwards. His mind played tricks on him, taking him back to his younger days when that sound had heralded the descent of Alwyn, come down for dinner, or Robin playing from floor to floor. *Look, Dad, look*, he had called out, his child's face smiling from behind the metal grille. *It's me. Look at me . . .*

Look at me, see me. They had all said that to him. Look at me, your child; me, your wife. Look at yourself now, Leonard Tripps. What do you really see?

Spooked, Leonard turned abruptly away and hurried to the landing. Then he kicked the heavy suit of armour and watched as it fell onto the black-and-white flagged floor below, its metal limbs smashing against the marble with the deafening sound of every unspoken word and every unheard cry for help.

Chapter Sixty-Three

Carving an elaborate dining chair, Victor paused and picked up his sandwich off the workbench. He was lonely, the house on Trafalgar Street far too empty, memories of Hilly paining, not comforting him. God, I miss her, he thought, putting aside the sandwich and looking at the chair. He had done a good job, the owners would be pleased. And pay him well.

But what did that matter? What would he do with the money? Put it away? For what? He didn't go on holidays and bought little. Indeed, the house was virtually unchanged since Hilly had died. So what was he working *for*? It was madness – he was still a relatively young man – but the world seemed dull to him. Dry as sawdust.

I thought I could live without you, Victor mused. I thought I would adjust, Hilly, live with memories. But it's not enough . . . He was ashamed of the thought and picked up his tools again, trying to work. But he was uncharacteristically clumsy, his thoughts replaying the night at The Dower House.

Dear God, she had been incredible, he thought. For a moment he had even believed that Alice would kill the old man. All that fire, that temperament. And in the midst of the shouting, the insults, she had stood up for him. *Victor Coates is worth ten of you*, she had snapped at Judge Arnold. Worth ten of you . . .

He hadn't allowed himself to enjoy the pleasure of those words. Hadn't wanted to brood on them, to admit the excitement they evoked. But he couldn't stop himself. She still cared about him, she still loved him. Just as he still loved her.

'Sorry, Hilly,' he whispered, shaking his head. He would work and not think about it. Alice was rich now, and she was going to marry Ray Berry. They were well suited. After all, what could a woman in her position see in a carpenter?

He paused again, leaning against the worktable, his hands gripping the chisel. At once he could feel her body as she had struggled against him, could remember the scent of her. He loved her – not as he had loved Hilly, but as a man wanting a woman. To make love to, to touch, to feel against him. They had been lovers before and he wanted her again. God, how he wanted her again.

'Jesus,' Victor said softly, turning back to the chair. He should have spoken out before, Ethel was right about that. Now it was too late: Ray Berry was going to get Alice. Ray Berry was going to sleep next to her, touch her and wake up to her.

But I want it to be me, Victor thought desperately. *Dear God, I want it to be me.*

The door opening behind him made him jump as Alice walked in.

''Lo there, Victor. How's things?'

He turned away, his face burning.

Surprised, she went over to him and touched his shoulder.

'Are you all right?'

He turned quickly, catching hold of her, his mouth moving over hers. His hands ran over her face, her body, his breath burning her cheek.

'Alice, God, Alice –'

Hurriedly she pulled away, looked at him. 'Victor, what are you doing?' Then she stopped, her eyes fixing on his mouth, her arms going around him.

Years fell away. Everything turned over and over in the dusty workshop. They were children again, hiding away from Netherlands, touching hands between the bars, laughing under the viaduct. He kissed her and nothing remained of Hilly, or the Arnolds – or Ray Berry.

He knew then that he would never give her up. He would, quite simply, die for her.

Having finished his visits for the day, Guy Priestly called by to see Ray up at Greenfields. He had read the newspaper – like everyone else – and was curious to know how Ray would react. Guy knew that Alice had forewarned him, but now that the news was available for public consumption he wondered how the private Mr Berry would take it.

Badly, as it turned out.

'That crazy woman,' Ray said bitterly as Guy followed him into his office, 'what a flaming thing to do to your family.'

'You think that Catherine Tripps should have stayed quiet?'

'She was still Catherine *Lewes*,' Ray snapped, 'and yes, I think she should have stayed quiet.'

Surprised, Guy watched Ray fiddle with some papers on his desk, making himself busy. But he could tell he was preoccupied, uncomfortable.

'Alice is coming over here later. To talk.'

Guy answered carefully. 'You both have a lot to talk about. I imagine she'll need your support. The gossips are having a field day.'

'We can't save her this time,' Ray said quietly, sitting down again. 'Not like we did at St Ursula's.'

'She doesn't need saving. She just needs support.'

Ray looked over to him. 'I'm not sure that she does. D'you remember when we had that argument before? When I said she was out for the money? It was a lousy thing to say, I was tired, but I wonder now if it wasn't something I suspected all along.'

Guy frowned. 'You're not serious, Ray?'

'Alice *is* somebody now. A woman of stature. She has

The Dower House and money. She can do anything she chooses: keep teaching, or give up the lot. She might travel, spend – no one could blame her. After all, the money is hers by right. She's only getting what was due to her a long time ago.'

'You come from money, Ray – why is this needling you so much?'

'I didn't say it was needling me!'

Guy sighed. 'You didn't have to, it's obvious. What's the matter really? Alice hasn't changed, it's just her situation which has. She's the same woman she always was.'

'Money changes people,' Ray said darkly. 'I've seen it happen too many times to fool myself.'

'So you would rather that she was poor?' Guy asked. 'A woman who could look up to you and be impressed?'

'I never said that!' Ray replied hotly.

Silent, Guy scratched his beard and then glanced at the paperwork on Ray's desk. They were two of a kind, he thought, two men who liked their work and liked to be of use; liked serving people. But that meant that there always had to be people who needed them. Their lives were populated with the sick and often inadequate – not equals. Guy had accepted that he would never marry, but Ray – what did he *really* want? A wife or an admirer? Alice as she was, or Alice as she had been?

'When Catherine killed herself, Alice went to The Dower House with Victor Coates,' Ray said at last. 'Not me. She said it was because he was close by, and willing to drive her over there.'

'They're friends, they always have been,' Guy said cautiously. 'But she gave him up long time ago, Ray, and she never got back with him when his wife died. She had plenty of opportunity, and so did he. But nothing happened. Surely you can't think that she wants him?'

'I don't know who she wants.'

'You mean that you don't know if *you* want *her* any more?'

Wearily Ray lit a cigarette, Guy watching him.

'You smoke too much.'

'You talk too much.'

Silence fell between them. It was Ray who was the first to speak again.

'I love her, I always will. I think she loves me. But there's something about Alice, some part of her that I can't get close to. I thought it was because of her past, but now I'm not so sure. There's a world between Greenfields and Werneth Heights, a whole lifetime between poverty and wealth.'

'So why should Alice feel more comfortable with Victor Coates than you?' Guy countered. 'Victor has very little – you have your work and this place. You and Alice have so much in common. You could work together; she might want to involve herself more at Greenfields –'

'I don't want charity from her.'

'Who's talking about bloody charity?' Guy snapped. 'When people love each other there *is* no pecking order, no keeping track of who gave this and who gave that.'

'For a bachelor, you talk a hell of a lot about love,' Ray replied sourly.

'For a man in love, you talk a hell of a lot about money. But then – *are* you in love, Ray?' Guy put his head on one side, looking at his old friend. 'Think about it very carefully. Are you using this as an excuse to finish the relationship with Alice? Or are you just frightened that it will end because of the change in circumstances? You can't afford to get it wrong this time. Alice came back to you once, but she won't do it twice. If you don't want her, be big enough to let her go. But if you *do* want her, then bloody fight for her.'

Alarmed by what had happened, Alice left the workshop and hurried back to St Ursula's. She had to think, she told herself. God, she *had* to think. She was supposed to be going up to see Ray that afternoon. She had to calm down, control herself. But was it *Ray* she wanted to talk to? Perhaps she should talk to Victor first. Yes, Victor. She had better see him after he finished work.

Victor was just answering the door to her in Trafalgar Street when Terry Booth came out of the next house, flapping a dusty mat into the street. He saw them and blushed as he remembered what he had read in the paper. Uncertain whether he should talk or say nothing, he blustered.

'Oh, 'ello there,' he began, smiling at Alice. 'We were all reading about you in the news. You must be right pleased.' He blundered on, 'I mean, sorry about yer mother, and yer father. Is yer father still in that nut house? I mean, it must be nice having a big house left to you. Up in the posh area. Even if you were put away as a kid . . .' His face was waxy with strain as a voice from the back room thankfully called him in. 'Oh, sorry, have to go now. Nice talking to you.'

Embarrassed, Alice exchanged a glance with Victor, then looked away. What had happened earlier had taken them both by surprise. She had lost control, they both had. What now?

'Come in,' he said, taking her arm.

Immediately the door of the Hope house was opened. Wheeling herself onto the step, Anna Hope put on her best accent.

'Afternoon, Alice. Lovely day.'

'Yes, it is,' she replied, feeling the grip of Victor's hand through her sleeve.

'I was just talking to my husband. Don't be a stranger and forget your old friends, now that you've gone up in the world.'

Alice could feel Victor's grip tighten.

'We have to go, Mrs Hope,' he said hurriedly, steering Alice over to his van.

Silently she slid into the passenger seat.

'Where to?'

She paused, anxious what his reaction would be. 'I said I'd call by and see Ray today. Up at Greenfields.'

He nodded, cut to the guts. 'I suppose you have to.'

'I promised,' Alice replied quietly

Pulling away from the kerb, Victor jerked his head towards Mrs Hope.

'You've never been so popular.'

'Not with everyone. I got snubbed at the greengrocer's yesterday. Someone was talking loudly about Judge Arnold being a crook.' Alice looked ahead at the quiet street. 'I went to see Leonard earlier, but he'd already packed up and gone. Didn't even leave a note . . . Everything's changing so much, Victor.'

'You can say that again,' he said quietly.

'Not just us.'

'*What* about us?' he queried. 'We could make a go of it this time, Alice.'

'Victor, what we did –'

'Christ!' he said, stopping the van and turning to her. 'Please don't say it was a mistake.'

'I don't know –'

'Well, I do,' he replied. 'We should be together, Alice. We know each other better than any two people do. You can't say we don't want each other, you can't say that –'

'I wasn't going to!' she said hurriedly. 'I was just . . . I don't know what to think, Victor.'

'I suppose you *could* have your pick of anyone now.'

'Don't be so dense!' she snapped suddenly. 'It's got nothing to do with money, you know that.'

'Then what *has* it got to do with? Are you saying that you love Ray Berry more than you love me?'

'It's different,' she said quietly.

It was. There was little passion with Ray. But there was safety, security, shared ambitions. She wanted Victor, her body wanted Victor, and he was right: he knew her, every inch of her. Every nuance, the good and the bad. She had no secrets from Victor. But the tie was so strong, the feelings so intense – where did that lead? Love like that, passion like that, always burns.

'What will you do with the house?' Victor asked, changing the subject and starting up the car again.

She was surprised by the change in tack. 'I used to long to have that house –'

'I remember.'

'– but now I've got it, it's frightening. The place is too big, too full of memories.'

Staring ahead, Victor drove them down the street, a couple of women pointing at Alice as they turned at the corner.

'Do you mind taking me up to Greenfields?'

'I'm delighted,' Victor said bitterly, 'wouldn't any man be?'

Silence fell between them. Both of them wondered what the other was thinking, but neither dared to broach the subject.

'I didn't like what they wrote about your father,' Victor said at last. 'The paper was hard on him.'

'I suppose they think that a murderer deserves everything that's coming to him.'

'I suppose we all deserve what's coming to us,' Victor said coldly.

What would happen now, Alice wondered. Would Victor drop her off at Greenfields and walk away? Would they revert to being friends? Maybe he would be glad, when he thought about it. Victor had a happy marriage behind him; she had only a murky past and a lover in Ray Berry. It was obvious that Victor would marry again one day, and have a family. Be happy, be normal . . .

Cautiously, she stole a look at him. Victor had aged, but the good-looking young boy was still there in the iris-blue eyes and the hard jawline.

'Nearly there,' he said, driving up the hill to Greenfields.

His emotions were in check again, but Alice was suddenly panicking. Would he turn his van round at the gates of Greenfields and drive away without even thinking about her again? Would he take her indecision as a rejection? And why wasn't she reassuring him now?

'We're here,' Victor said, drawing up at the gates.

Alice didn't move.

'I said, we're here,' he repeated, tapping the back of her hand.

Slowly she climbed out of the van and then turned. He was watching her with a curious expression on his face. One which she tried, but failed, to read.

'Take care of yourself,' Victor said, reversing back into the rough drive.

A moment later he was gone.

It was on his way back to Salford that Victor decided to take a detour. The air was cool when he arrived at Morays cemetery and walked over to Hilly's grave. Slowly, the day was coming to an end.

Deep in thought, Victor looked at Hilly's grave. He should have brought flowers, he thought. Still, he would come again at the weekend. He missed her so sharply that the loss was a pain in his chest, his lips resting for a moment on the earth.

Why couldn't you have lived? he thought. You were so uncomplicated, so gentle. It was almost like loving a child. It was true that he had been a father figure to Hilly. Even as a young man, he had looked after her and loved every moment. She was never difficult, never moody, grateful for every kindness. Undemanding, unsexual, safe.

Victor closed his eyes for an instant and then reopened them in time to see the sun starting to set behind the moors in the distance. The huge black hump of the horizon was shadowed, the light violently brilliant in its last burst of glory. Red sky, red colour. Red for danger, for blood, for life. Red had never been Hilly's colour – but it was Alice's.

The sunset opened its vast red mouth and seemed to swallow the land whole. It was hungry, violent, roaring with life before the last fall of the light.

Chapter Sixty-Four

Alice went back to work at St Ursula's to be greeted with insistent enquiries from the governors. Would she stay? Would she be *kind* enough to stay?

Jilly had been dumbfounded by the news and suddenly became nervous around Alice. Her old friend was important now, one of the upper class in those parts, a woman who wouldn't want to know 'her sort' any more.

It took Alice a while to reassure her, but the questions the governors had raised had gone unanswered and left her in a quandary. What *was* she going to do with her life? Talking to Ray, she had reassured him, told him that the money made no difference to them. He'd been pleased, loving, and then had reached out for her. *And she felt no guilt* . . . The thought unsettled her. Why didn't she feel guilty? She had betrayed him, been unfaithful to the man she was supposed to love – but she felt no shame.

'Miss?'

Alice turned, to see a child looking at her. 'I've got a note for you.'

'Thank you, love,' she said, opening it. Was it a note from Ray, or – her heart hammered – Victor?

We need a new ball cock in the downstairs lavvie.
       Alf

Alice smiled, then burst out laughing. That was what life was all about, the basics. Life wasn't passion, extremes of emotions, it was fundamental – if you wanted to stay sane, safe. With Victor, there was white heat; with Ray, there was warmth. And warmth never burned anyone.

Slowly Alice walked down the corridors which led to the bathrooms on the first floor of St Ursula's. Looking in, she remembered how she and Jilly had washed the children so long ago. Nit combs and fleas had been a nuisance for months, but gradually the parasites had been obliterated. As had the dirt, and gradually violent or negligent parents had learned to fear Alice's power.

Alice tightened a tap to stop it dripping and then went out, pulling the door behind her. The whole school was in desperate need of new paint, new lavatories, new books – new everything. She had the money to buy it all now, to restore St Ursula's. But for several years the council had been talking about closing down the slum schools, and it seemed that St Ursula's days were numbered.

Alice walked on, looking around her. There were still drawings on the walls and pinned to the doors, and notices were still placed on the huge cork board. Next to a faded photograph of Minnie Lomond, was a photograph of the whole school taken two years after Alice arrived. She was in the middle, surrounded by her motley collection of slum kids. Smiling, like an empress.

It was logical to invest in Greenfields, Alice thought. She could put some of her money to good use there and back up Ray's plans ... Thoughtful, she paused by the landing window and looked out. Then some strange and unexpected impulse settled on her. Hurrying for her coat, Alice locked the main doors and left St Ursula's.

It took her a while, but when she finally arrived at her destination Alice stood outside the old building, reading the sign 'NETHERLANDS'. The windows were boarded up, as were the doors. This was the building where she had been so afraid, the building where she had been taught her place in the world. As a no one, a foundling ... Ghosts wandered about the memory with her. The stooped Clare

Lees; Dolly Blake; Evan Thomas, grinning like a jackal under the hunter's moon that night.

The night they caught Alice with Victor.

She shuddered and turned away, walking hurriedly out of the gates towards the viaduct. The main street had changed out of all recognition. There were now electrical shops, cinemas, chemists with bright-coloured advertisements in the window – 'PONDS FACE CREAM', a woman smiling out from a poster. The days of real poverty were beginning to pass, Salford's slums being pulled down or renovated. The old disorder was changing. Soon Alice's memories would become extinct. Before long there would be *no* past for Alice to visit.

But there was a future to make. She walked under the viaduct, a car passing by, a bus flicking on its lights as the night set in. Her work had been her life. The high spirits of her childhood had been driven out of her. She had been made old before her time, and *stayed* old. But suddenly Alice didn't want to be old any more. She wanted to be beautiful, wealthy, in love. In a man's arms. But whose? Victor's or Ray's?

Hailing the next bus, Alice made her way over to Oldham. When she got off she began the long walk to Werneth Heights, the walk she had undertaken all those years before. Only then she had been driven by revenge – this time she was driven by necessity.

The drive was dark, but there were several lights on in the house as she approached and knocked on the door. Remembering suddenly that she had a key, Alice let herself in. The butler had left with Judge Arnold, but the housekeeper and a maid were busy throwing dust sheets over the furniture.

The housekeeper – remembering Alice from her days as nanny – looked at her bitterly.

'We weren't expecting you,' she said, her tone surly. 'There's only some bread and milk in the kitchen.'

Alice could feel the animosity wash over her. 'I'm not hungry.'

'You staying for the night?' the housekeeper asked, her tone brittle. 'Mr Tripps has long gone.'

Alice's face was quizzical. 'Why are you angry with me?'

'You know full well!' the housekeeper replied, folding up a dust sheet and hugging it to her. 'You must have known who you were when you first came here. We thought you were one of us, but you weren't. And you never let on. Well, no one likes people who sneak around.'

'Especially if they end up inheriting the house?' Alice replied shortly, seeing the woman flush.

'I'll be leaving here tonight, as will the others. You want staff, you hire your own.' The woman started to walk away, then turned back. 'Oh, and good luck. You're going to need it. This house is unlucky. But then you know that already, don't you?'

Soon after, they left, the back door closing behind them, a gaggle of figures walking through the side gate and out into the other world. Alone, Alice walked around The Dower House. She had never been inside the old man's rooms and found them as forbidding as he had been. Heavy Victorian furniture crowded the dark walls, a four-poster bed still made up, a cushion with the elaborate initial A resting on the coverlet. Papers lined the window seat, old newspapers, books, torn magazines, and on the bedside table was an old-fashioned starched collar, lying discarded, as though its owner had just taken it off.

Pulling the door closed as she left, Alice walked into Leonard's rooms, and then into her mother's. For an instant she expected to see Catherine lying on the window seat, but it was empty, the curtains undrawn, the hostile night looking in.

Finally Alice moved to the furthest part of the house, where David Lewes had lived with Catherine. *Her parents' home*. The rooms had been left unchanged. But the rich colours had only partially faded and the gilding on the bed and around the mirrors was still brilliant. There was a bedroom, bathroom and dressing room, the latter having obviously belonged to David Lewes. Nervously, Alice stood at the doorway and then walked in. With shaking hands she opened the wardrobe doors then drew out the dinner jackets and black ties her father had once worn. She frowned; puzzled. Hadn't her mother told her that all she had left of David was a handkerchief? Hadn't she known about his things? Or had it been just a manipulative ploy for sympathy? Alice turned back to the clothes. Drawers of scarves, socks, underwear, gloves, were stacked one on top of the other. Each was labelled for a busy man to find his clothes quickly. And then, in the bottom drawer, at the very back, Alice found the photograph.

It was taken a long time ago and was faded. But it showed a handsome man and a beautiful young woman sitting together. The man was dark, the woman fair, her right arm around her husband's shoulder, her left arm holding on to a baby. A baby who was crying in the photograph. A baby who had grown up and was now looking at *herself*, thirty-seven years earlier.

It had been such a long journey, Alice thought, but here it was. *Proof.* Not the proof her mother had publicly exposed, but proof Alice could put in a frame, proof she could look at. *I was somebody's daughter. I was not an orphan, a nobody. I was somebody's child. And no one –* no one – *can ever take that away from me.*

Suddenly inspired, Alice left the room with the photograph in her hand and ran out onto the landing, looking down into the vast empty hall. I'll make a school *here*, she thought. What better place? I can't live here alone, but I can teach here. I can't bring my own children here, but I can bring other people's children. It doesn't have to be as it was. People change, places change.

Elated, she ran down the stairs two at a time. Her future

was set, she knew what she would do. The Dower House would bury its past, as she would; the place would live again and every bad thought and deed done there would be discounted by every achievement. Alice paused at the bottom of the stairs, fired up, her dark eyes determined.

I can do it alone, she decided. I don't *have* to marry Ray. And Victor belonged to Hilly. And *will* belong to someone else who's yet to come. I love him too much, way too much for safety.

Energy spurred her on. She would make The Dower House a force to be reckoned with. She had the space, the money. So what if people talked about her? They had *always* talked about her, a woman who lived outside society, by her own rules. She might be rich now, but she didn't belong with the local gentry, never would. Money could buy her a way in – but they could keep it.

All the money in the world couldn't change who she was. Alice felt a jolt of real power. She didn't have to pretend any more. Money and status had made such freedom possible. In the end she had got what she wanted – but not through revenge, through love. Alice knew that the demons which had driven her parents were in her, but knew she could subdue them.

She was Alice Rimmer. She didn't have to hide, to pretend, to cover up. Her temperament was what she was. She could be excited, enthusiastic, and no one could stop her. People could take her as she was, or leave her alone. She needed no one, and had to ask for nothing from anyone. It was the greatest gift she had ever been given – the gift of being herself.

Oh yes, she thought, there were plans to be made. She would set it all in motion the next day, putting her mother's legacy into good use, clearing the family name.

Downstairs, Alice turned on the lights and then moved into the drawing room. Slowly she went over to the window and looked down at the carpet. Then she glanced out over the dark garden to where her father had run away that night. Moonlight made an entrance suddenly, and looking up, Alice noticed that the moon was full and yellow. *A hunter's moon.*

A shiver ran over her and she drew the curtains hurriedly. Turning on the lamps and closing the door behind her she paced the room, the photograph still clutched in her hand. But the ghosts followed her into the kitchen and watched her as she made some tea. They sat with her, and moved up the stairs with her. They were everywhere, round every corner and behind every door. The house felt huge, bearing down on her, all Alice's energy suddenly dwindling.

Carrying her tea out of the kitchen, Alice hurried back into the drawing room and sat down. But everywhere she looked she saw her mother, or Leonard or the Judge. And then she remembered Robin . . . Distressed, Alice put down her cup and, snatching up her coat, ran out of the front door.

She had been wrong. It was *too* much to do alone. The house was too full of spirits for one person. Badly shaken, Alice ran down the drive and finally reached the huge wrought-iron gates. For once they were closed, the staff having locked them when they left. Pulling at the bolt, Alice struggled to find the bunch of keys in her bag. Her hands were shaking so much that she could hardly separate one key from another.

Then the sound of footsteps on the gravel made her freeze.

'Who's there?'

Silence.

Hurriedly she struggled with the keys. Then there was another sound on the gravel. Alice spun round, dropping the bunch of keys onto the ground.

'Who's there?'

'Me. Victor.'

She tensed at the sound of his voice.

'Open the gates,' he said hurriedly. '*Let me in.*'

Bending down, Alice felt around her feet for the keys. The gravel tore at her fingers and nails before finally her fingers closed around the keys and she stood up.

Hesitating, she looked at the keys in her hand – as he did.

'Open the gate, Alice. Let me in.'

'I can't –'

'You can,' he urged her. '*Let me in.*'

In that instant the hunter's moon came out from behind clouds, its light falling over the two of them. One on one side of the gates, one on the other. The black railings separating them.

'Hurry,' he urged her again, then reached out towards her, his hands through the iron railings.

Her fingers closed over his and tightened their grip. They were suddenly children again, back at Netherlands, clinging to each other through the bars.

'Open the gates, Alice,' he willed her. 'Open them!'

With a dull click the lock finally turned, the heavy gates yawning open as Victor pushed them back. At once their arms went around each other, Victor resting his lips against her cheek.

'We've made it . . . We've come home, Alice. We've finally come home.'